PHANTOM IN THE NIGHT

PHANTOM IN THE NIGHT

Sherrilyn Kenyon
with Dianna Love

POCKET BOOKS

NEW YORK LONDON TORONTO SYDNEY

Pocket Books
A Division of Simon & Schuster, Inc.
1230 Avenue of the Americas
New York, NY 10020

First Pocket Books trade paperback edition June 2008

POCKET and colophon are registered trademarks of Simon & Schuster, Inc.

Designed by Mary Austin Speaker

Manufactured in the United States of America

ISBN-13: 978-0-7394-9657-2

We're dedicating this to our wonderful husbands—
Ken (Sherrilyn's) and Karl (Dianna's)—
who are real heroes, plus they kept us fed.

ACKNOWLEDGMENTS

From Sherrilyn Kenyon

Thank you to Dianna for being such a good sport and always making me smile. I never thought I could cowrite anything, but given that we often share a common brain (LOL) you made it not only easy but a joy. Thank you so much for all the support.

Thank you to Kim, Jacs, Brenda, and Retta for reading all my manuscripts and making great comments. And let's not forget Jack, Carl, Eddie, Aimee, Judy, Soteria, and all the others who make my message bbs a living community where all are welcomed. Thank you, fans, for coming back day after day. You guys rock!

To my husband, for being my shelter in the storm. You are my rock and I'm grateful every day that I said yes when you asked me out to see a movie I couldn't stand. For my kids, who are always my comfort and my greatest source of pride. May God bless and keep you all.

From Dianna Love

I'd like to thank Sherrilyn Kenyon for the opportunity to collaborate and for being a wonderful writing partner who made the experience one I look forward to repeating. I have an even deeper respect for her writing skill after brainstorming and creating this book. On top of all that, you're a great friend.

I also want to thank my husband, Karl, who makes it easy for me to follow my dreams, always there to cheer me on. I have never loved another and am so glad you are in my life. As if that isn't enough, Karl gave us a great comeback for Terri's character. When you find it, you'll chuckle then probably use that same line by the end of the day. Much love and thanks to both of our families and friends, whose support means the world to me.

From both of us

We appreciate Lauren McKenna's support and faith in our ability to cowrite this book. In addition to being a terrific editor, she is a wonderful cheerleader, always ready with a positive word.

Thanks also to Merrilee Heifetz for all the hard work on our behalf.

A big thanks goes to author Mary Buckham, who bounced ideas around and was one of our early readers, plus she enlisted her husband Jim's help when we needed additional Italian history research. Cassondra Murray, a talented writer as well, read and gave us feedback sorely needed from an objective eye. Cassondra's husband, Steve Doyle, provided us with expert advice on Special Force operations and weapons, plus he read the entire story and loved it—confirming our hopes that both male and female readers will enjoy this adventure.

To the RBL Women—thanks for all the support, laughs, and martinis. You are too much fun!

We love our readers and were thrilled to have Hope Williams give us an objective early read. Her feedback was invaluable. You—the readers—are the reason we work so hard to create a book. A huge thanks to all of you who have sent us notes of encouragement, excited to see this first collaboration effort, and who read our books, allowing us to do what we love—write stories. You're the best!

PROLOGUE

A dangerous damn place to run out of dirt.

The grim stench of death in this hand-hewn tunnel strangled every breath Sergeant Nathan Drake sucked in. He hated caves.

Only one way in . . . or out.

He lifted a hand, signaling his teammate, Captain Vic Stoner, who followed fifteen feet behind to hold up. As SOP, Nathan took point leading the way and Stoner covered his back.

This cave had shown more promise than anywhere else they'd searched during the past eleven weeks combing the Chapare jungle in Bolivia. Crates of weapons, both opened and unopened, were stockpiled against handheld missile launchers—enough grenades to turn a small city into shambles. The makings for a terrorist playroom, but not enough to qualify as the Level 5 threat—or biological weapon—Nathan's team had been sent to recon. This cache probably belonged to a bunch of rebels unhappy with South American politics, or a drug runner.

In that case, he was ready to get the hell out of here and return to base. But one thing bothered him.

What miserable son of a bitch had brought female victims here to torture and kill?

Eight skeletons, so far, lay in obscene positions surrounded by dried pools of blood throughout each of the dark, dismal tunnels they'd searched.

Dead ends all.

And they'd found nothing to connect these gruesome killings to the deaths in a tiny village sixty-five kilometers east of here. Man, woman, and child, the entire village had been wiped out without a weapon mark on the bodies. Medical examiners flown in from allied nations concluded the deaths had not been a result of biological warfare, but a deadly virus with no known origin. One that vanished without a residual trace—which sounded like the exact definition of biological warfare.

The unexplained incident had caused unease within national securities of several countries.

And forced this covert op.

Even now he could see the victims they'd found three weeks ago in the village. Gray skin cracked and bleeding on bodies twisted in the throes of agony. Anguished eyes of children staring in hopeless confusion, their skin clawed by tiny fingers.

A constant reminder of why he swore to defend and protect.

And why he was stuck in the back of this freakin' cave.

Nathan swung around to scope their only exit route, everything painted in a greenish cast from his PVS-14 fold-down night-vision monocular.

Stoner held an army-issue M-4 with a Knight Armament suppressor at ready. The short machine gun looked like a toy against the ammo vest wrapping his thickly muscled chest. According to Stoner, three years on oil rigs prior to enlisting had supersized his until-then scrawny body. Right now he was all but invisible, coffee-brown skin contrasting with his pearl-white lady-killer grin when he used it. Nathan and Stoner were so comparable in size, a stranger couldn't tell them apart when they were in covert clothing.

Even when it came to body language.

Stoner's casual stance outright lied. There was nothing relaxed about that man when on a mission.

Nathan lifted his chin in a "ready?" motion.

Stoner cocked his head toward the exit. His "all clear, let's go" signal.

Nathan strode silently past him, watching for any change in the narrow passage he could span with outstretched arms. The dark amplified his senses. As point man, protecting members of his team came above all else. More than a job, he'd found his place in the military, somewhere he could make a difference and still help his mother and brother back home by sending money. He didn't need much to live. Whatever he carried on his back during a mission. His family, both back home and the team he fought beside, was all he valued.

Greed is your enemy, son. Focus your efforts on what

really matters, the people you love. His father had passed down that legacy before he'd died when Nathan was eight. Like his father, he believed in it completely.

His foot bumped something that made a *click* sound.

Shit. Nathan froze, holding his breath. They'd checked for trip wires. Shouldn't have missed this one. Blood roared through his ears. Each excruciating second passed slowly as he waited to be blown to pieces. He'd stand firm. Take the brunt of the explosion if it saved Stoner.

Sweat ran from under his camo hat, down his back . . .

Nothing happened. If he'd triggered a booby trap, he'd be dead right now. Nathan swallowed, took a breath coated with the stink of rotting flesh, then scanned the floor. He hadn't hit a trip wire, just the decaying bones of a narrow foot connected to a leg on his right.

There in the darkness, dried patches of skin clung to a small skeleton slumped in a crumbling pile. So much like the other bodies they'd found in the cave. Serial killer? Small adults, delicate bone structure, partially clothed . . . if at all. Shredded dresses tossed around, some used as rags.

Young women. All with long black hair, like his mother had once worn hers. His line of thought disintegrated when a green laser beam danced on the skeleton's fractured leg.

He glanced up. Stoner met his gaze with the one eye not blocked by the monocular, then lifted two fingers as he pointed at his eyes, indicating they were only here to observe.

Nathan hadn't forgotten his directive. His four-man team had been given specific orders. This was a recon and intelligence gathering mission, nothing more. The goal?

Determine any validity to the reports on terrorist movements in this area.

Under no circumstances were they to engage in a conflict.

Translation: Don't kill anyone. Don't leave any DNA. Complete the assignment without being detected. Get your ass home intact. Ten-four.

He nodded at Stoner and carefully moved toward the weapon cache room between them and the exit point of the cave. When they reached the open space, Stoner stepped forward and let his weapon hang from the dummy cord attached to his vest in order to free his hands. He fished out a camera disguised as a writing pen, complete with a functioning ink cartridge, and began snapping photos of everything.

Now guarding Stoner's back, Nathan studied the hollow space and listened for anyone approaching. Pulaski and Duran were outside watching the entrance, but they'd remain hidden, engaging only if AHBL—all hell breaks loose.

Nathan took in every inch of the room, which was roughly thirty feet in diameter and at least six feet, three inches tall since he could stand upright without hitting his head. One large crate was set off to the side. Ropes attached at two corners had been tossed carelessly across the dirt floor.

A hint of warning tightened the skin along Nathan's neck. With all these weapons stored, where was the patrol? No one would leave this arsenal without a guard.

Not unless they were extremely cocky or terminally stupid.

His gaze strayed to the left, where the least decayed body rested indecently against the wall, a recent kill. Her legs were sprawled wide open, one arm bent at an unnatural angle and enough skin remaining to see how grotesquely she'd been tortured.

Nathan's heart jacked up a notch in anger. The sight sickened him. He gripped his weapon tighter. Were all these bodies nothing more than unlucky women in the wrong place at the wrong time? Prostitutes? Didn't matter. They were someone's sister, wife . . . mother. No woman deserved to be raped, tortured, and murdered. Whoever did this needed to be stomped hard.

"Three tangos approaching cave," came through the earpiece of Nathan's commo headset.

A high-pitched female cry reached his ears before the crunch of boots on gravel echoed against the mouth of the cave.

Stoner wore an identical headset. He was next to Nathan in a flash, camera tucked away and weapon ready. Not a damn thing casual about his stance now.

Nathan signaled Stoner—*You shift to the left side of the tunnel leading toward the dead end, I'll take the right.* They melted into the dark cavity, disappearing from easy view. Every nerve in his body tingled at high-threat alert.

The bastards trudged toward them, stealth obviously an unfamiliar concept. Terse male voices argued in broken Spanish.

Nathan caught enough to know they argued over whose turn it was to be first this time and how they didn't want her to die before they both had a shot. Heart-wrenching feminine sobs were interspersed with pleas for mercy, bathing the room in raw terror as two men entered the weapon storage area.

Nathan tightened his grip. He fought the urge to pound these assholes into next week.

Observe only. Don't engage. His finger feathered across the trigger.

Mangy and dark-skinned, two men emerged from the opening wearing swamp boots and ammo vests. The first wouldn't reach Nathan's shoulder. He sputtered curses between drags on his cigarette and shined the flashlight ahead of his sidekick. The taller one of the two carried a Galil fully automatic rifle pointed at the screaming woman—tango number three—he dragged along by a wad of long black hair. Had to be the leader of this deviant pair, but this one packed enough muscle to make taking him down an event worth charging admittance for.

Small rocks scattered from the woman's kicking feet. She couldn't be twenty yet. Pretty, except for the ugly bruises on her face and arms. Her nose and lip bled. She fought with everything her tiny body could offer up against a gorilla.

Nathan folded his monocular up against his forehead and looked over at Stoner, who had lifted his as well and moved one finger from his weapon in a sign that they were on the same page. Unquestioning trust was something Nathan had only shared with his brother until meeting Stoner.

The woman screamed with enough force to make the dead tremble in fear and yank Nathan's attention back to her. His gut tightened into a knot.

Weapon dropped aside, the head goon had the girl down on the ground, her arms tied above her head to the ropes attached to the crate. Shorty had tossed his cigarette aside and was busy trying to hold her jerking legs.

This had to be done quietly. Nathan released his weapon to hang from the carabiner on his vest, but close enough to use.

"*Hurry up. I will not wait forever!*" Shorty yelled at the leader in corrupted Spanish. He pinned one of her legs with a boot and reached inside his pants, starting this ménage à torture without waiting on his sidekick.

The leader dropped onto his knees between the scratched and bleeding limbs of the struggling woman. He shoved her legs so wide she jerked and screamed in pain. Screeching prayers slashed the silence, pleading for divine help. Her attacker pushed his pants down as far as they would go and grabbed his cock, shaking it at her.

"*You will know a real man,*" he bragged, then released himself to lift a wicked knife from its leather sheath on his belt. "*But first you will beg for me.*"

Nathan moved, silent as a deadly shadow.

The woman wailed so loudly the two men wouldn't have heard an army approach. Hidden from view at their backs, he covered Shorty's mouth and snapped his neck in one move, then lowered the limp body. His need for retribution riding him hard, he reached one hand around the leader's mouth, yanking his head back.

"Whaa—" The tango's knife hand came up out of reflex.

Nathan grabbed his wrist. The horror of what was

about to befall this rapist slithered across his piggish face a second before Nathan shoved the blade deep into the man's lung. Warm liquid squirted over his hand and the air filled with the sharp metallic odor of fresh blood. Hysterical screams of the half-naked woman mixed with the image of decaying carcasses, strewn through the cave like yesterday's garbage, stoked his rage. This bastard didn't deserve to die easy. Nathan twisted the knife, feeling metal grind against ribs.

What was one more grisly image added to his endless stock of nightmares?

A gargled noise spewed from the guy's lungs before he jerked, then stopped struggling, his body fluids expelling with his last breath. Nathan discarded the body, yanked out the knife, and used it to cut the ropes that held the girl down.

His sense of justice was appeased. A small victory, but no other woman would suffer and die for the man's sick lust.

He should go, now, while she was still in shock.

But he couldn't leave her like this, any more than he could let her be raped and killed.

Stoner appeared next to him.

Nathan spoke to the woman in Spanish, hushing her and telling her she was safe. She could go home.

She finally quieted and stared at him as though he were both demon and savior.

"We won't tell anyone about this," he said in Spanish.

Her wild eyes took in everything around her, then shot to his face, which was still covered in camo paint. Her terror-filled gaze fell to his hand dripping with blood. She started shaking her head, whimpering and scooting backward.

"*Go home. Say nothing. Don't go anywhere alone.*" When he extended a hand to help her she backed away and scrambled to her feet. Stoner clicked on the flashlight mounted to his weapon, lighting the way out of the cave.

She needed no more encouragement than that. Nathan followed her outside, but she'd vanished into the thick foliage faster than a rabbit catching sight of a hungry wolf.

When Pulaski and Duran emerged from their hidden positions, Nathan made a cut signal by drawing his hand across his throat, telling the other two what had happened to the tangos. He then motioned silently for everyone to head out and took the lead again. Stoner had plenty of photos and sticking around at this point would be a bad idea. This entire trip had been a bust, except for freeing that woman.

Moonlight spilled down between the trees lighting the way back to camp. Nathan sucked in gulps of fresh air, clearing the residue of death from his lungs, damn glad to be out of that unholy tomb. He set the pace for the next five kilometers. The team hiked as quietly as ghosts until reaching their hidden temporary base.

Second-guessing a decision once he'd made and executed it was just wasted energy. What was done was done. But Nathan had a harder time ignoring that voice deep in his head that accused him of risking the team's safety for one person. He'd have gladly sent them back to camp and dealt with the tangos alone if there had been any way to do so.

As if Stoner and the other two would have listened.

"I'm cool with what went down," Stoner said as soon as they entered the clearing.

Nathan turned to see his three teammates standing there. After all this time, he was still amazed and humbled by Stoner's unquestioning support, but what about the other two? He waited for condemnation, ready to accept his due.

"Yep," Duran said in his rough Texan voice. "Back home, we'd have filleted the bastard, starting with his balls and finishing with his testicles."

Pulaski grimaced. "Uh, D, I hate to tell you this, but those are the same things."

"Not the way we do it, it ain't. See, you have to get the grill—"

"No more grill stories," Stoner and Nathan said simultaneously.

Nathan had never been to Texas, and given all the grisly things Duran claimed they barbecued, he didn't want to. The meals he'd heard about reminded him a little too much of his grandmother's potluck gumbo before she passed away.

Rule number one had been, Never ask Grandma what was in the gumbo. Especially not before you ate it.

Nathan realized they were giving their stamp of approval on what had gone down and not one of them would say a word about the killings once they left. He owed them for the united stand they were taking with him and wished he had it inside him to let them know how much their support meant. But when it came down to speaking his feelings, he was a simple man. "Thanks."

Duran turned to Pulaski and Stoner. "I'm heading out." Which meant he was going to set trip wires and secure his section of the perimeter around their camp. "I say we leave Drake on KP duty." He grinned and strode away.

Pulaski grunted and headed off in an opposite direction.

Stoner didn't move. "What's eating you?"

Nathan raked off the headgear and scratched his grungy head. "It's my job not to put any of you in danger."

"Danger, hell, we volunteered for this." Stoner grinned. "You know, this reminds me of that time in Manila—"

"Let's leave Manila in Manila." His tone was hard with warning, but nightmares should remain in the dark.

Stoner nodded. "Okay, cool, whatever. But if anyone knew all the things we face and what you've had to do sometimes on these operations, you'd get a damn chest full of medals."

Like some shiny pin mattered to him? That wouldn't feed or clothe his family. "Don't want a medal. I want—"

Nathan hesitated. What did he want? His reenlistment papers back? Not even. He wanted to stay in the military, where he'd made a commitment, until his term was up. Except that decision now felt selfish, because his military commitment meant being away from home for another couple of years while his mother needed his help more than ever.

Dammit.

"We'll figure out something." Stoner's quiet brown eyes televised empathy. He'd been standing next to Nathan when the call from New Orleans had come through mere hours before they went wheels up.

Nathan scooped a pile of palm branches up and tossed them aside, cursing himself for the hundredth time. He'd believed his plan had been sound, the best way to help his mother and brother. Finish another tour of duty so he could afford to get his brother into a decent college while Nathan used his GI bill for school. That way, they could both take care of Mom.

He'd been too ambitious, wanting to be more than a grease monkey his whole life. Wanting a future where he could provide for a wife and family and not be forced to live paycheck to paycheck. That life had been good enough for his father . . .

But Nathan had wanted more for the people he loved. His mother deserved security and peace of mind, an easier life. He'd always dreamed of getting Jamie into college.

Right now Nathan would gladly turn wrenches for the rest of his life to be at home for even one day.

If only it were that simple. He'd made a pledge to his squad, was responsible to these men even if they *could* function just fine without him. They were his brothers, too. He'd sworn to watch their backs—the same oath he shared with Jamie.

"Don't know what to tell you that would make any of this better." Stoner hadn't moved, stubborn as a tick on a dog. His calm tone rarely wavered. Nathan envied the fact that he had Freon running through his veins during the worst of situations and wondered how deep it ran . . . surely something could melt his arctic tundra. "Sucks that you didn't find out about your mom being sick until after you re-upped. My aunt had ovarian cancer. She beat that shit. Still living."

Nathan heard him, but his mother was his mother, not someone else's aunt. Big difference. He'd silently promised his father on the day they buried him that he'd take care of her. Now his mom needed him and he wasn't even in the same country.

Gut sick, he kept uncovering camp equipment hidden by the branches they'd cut and piled. How the hell would he make it through the next couple years and not be in New Orleans to help his mom fight for her life?

Stoner cleared his throat, just as tenacious as he was undaunted. "Uh, she won't be alone, Nathan. Your brother—"

"—is the biggest idiot for someone with his IQ." Nathan slung a handful of palm leaves aside. "How can someone that brilliant have so little common sense?"

"Okay, so he's an absentminded professor."

"Absentminded doesn't get you in serious trouble." Nathan raised his hand to stop Stoner from defending his brother further. "You don't understand. Jamie was an introvert in high school, didn't make friends easily, especially with guys who thought he was a smart-ass when my brother aced his classes. So when two assholes came to Jamie to fix a car, he thought they were asking him as a friend. My brother never questioned why the ignition was screwed up, just got excited to prove he was more than an egghead." Nathan lifted the hammocks and set them aside, then started unpacking MREs as he continued.

"Jamie got arrested for aiding and abetting car thieves. Took me and Mom three days to get him out."

"He made a mistake, Nate."

"I know that." Nathan regretted snarling at Stoner the minute the words were out. He wiped sweaty grime from his itchy whiskers, wishing he could as easily clean away a memory that kept him ever vigilant to protect his brother. "Jamie didn't speak for months after we got him out of jail. No one hurt him in there, but he withdrew from everyone. Even ignored me for a while. Once I finally got him to talk again, he was different. Changed. Determined to prove he wasn't a fool. Watching him try so hard to be something he's not has been worse than before. Every time I turn around he's in some get-rich-quick scheme that goes bust. Failure turns him inside out. I keep telling him to just find a decent job and we'll get him into college soon."

"So he'll do what has to be done for your mom."

"Yes . . . no." Nathan shook his head. "That's the problem. I think he's up to something again and keeping it from me."

"Like what?"

"Hell if I know. Just got a gut feeling he's trying to prove he can handle things without me. I don't know. Maybe it's only a new job and he doesn't want to tell me yet until it works out, but Mom can't get better if she has to watch over him, too."

"He may surprise you and step up now that she needs him."

Nathan yanked the go rag loose from around his neck and used it to wipe sweat clinging to his forehead. He shoved the wadded cloth inside the waistband of his pants and faced Stoner.

"Jamie's a decent man, but clueless about the real world.

Hell, if I hadn't had my head up my ass when he called the last time, I'd have found out what was going on with him and come up with a plan for the two of them. Instead, I just got pissed off like an idiot and yelled at Jamie for letting the insurance company tell him some of Mom's treatment wouldn't be covered." Mom had assured Nathan she was fine and tried to sound confident, but he knew she was terrified.

When was he going to learn not to let his temper talk?

"Give yourself a break, man. You got that call in the middle of packing for this op. Not much time to react."

"No excuse for lack of discipline." His father's words echoed in Nathan's mind. He'd expected more of his oldest son. "I'm not a civilian. I know better than to pop off. Should have calmed down and talked to Jamie while I had a chance, before I ended up somewhere I couldn't call him. It's my job to make sure they'll both be okay while I'm gone . . . or if I die."

"Yeah, right." Stoner snorted. "You're either too mean to kill or that damn Ranger coin of yours has voodoo magic. Just don't forget you promised that coin is mine when you do kick the bucket. I swear you've got more lives than a cat, and one of them saved by that chunk of brass alone. Too bad it's against the rules to carry that thing with you. We could use some swamp magic once in a while."

Stoner was trying to help, because he was the ranking officer, and a good man. He hadn't meant to drop a shovel full of guilt on Nathan at the mention of his "challenge" coin. It was the size of a silver dollar, made of brass, and engraved with an Army Ranger logo. And it had a dent where a slug had careened off the thick metal piece, saving Nathan's life once. No monetary value, just a reminder of the promise he'd made to his father.

Most people had photos to carry around. He carried a coin.

"Like I said, it's yours the day I go to meet the devil." Nathan was ready to get off the subject of him and his family. He couldn't do a damn thing about Jamie and Mom until he got back to base and debriefed. A minimum of ten days. "I'll finish unpacking and get the hammocks set."

Stoner shifted his weapon and sighed. "You'll figure out what to do. I've never seen you beat by anything or anyone." He checked his watch, then said, "We've got enough to confirm nothing is going on here but sadism. Make the call for an extraction tomorrow." He marched off into the jungle.

Nathan unpacked their spartan camp before he retrieved the Satellite phone from its hidden spot below a fallen log. He settled back against a tree and booted up the phone, checking for stored text messages. Two from base, one marked as a forwarded message. He grinned. The deal he'd made with his buddy in communications just came in handy. Nathan had won more at the last hand of poker than his friend in Communications could pay, so he'd cut a deal instead—to forward a message from home anytime Nathan got one, no matter where he was on the planet.

He released his weapon to hang against his chest and used one hand to access the message while he scratched his head with the other. His gritty hair stuck out, longer than allowed in the military, but acceptable for those on the army's clandestine intelligence teams, which answered solely to the CO of Special Forces. Not just trained teams, but the most highly trained in the army.

When the text message popped into view, his gut tightened as true, raw fear gripped him:

> Nate—Mom starts chemo this week. She's doing okay, so far. Take care. Laissez les bons temps rouler. J.

Laissez les bons temps rouler. Let the good times roll.

Nathan's face chilled as he read that line again, heart pumping at the true meaning behind his and Jamie's code from childhood.

The day Nathan faced four boys in a gang bent on pulverizing his brother's face, Jamie had started crying about how they wouldn't survive the beating. Nathan had calmly told him to stay out of the way. As the four boys approached, Nathan smiled and said, "Laissez les bons temps rouler." He'd kicked their collective asses and sent them home to Mommy, crying like little girls with shattered teapots. After that, the phrase became a code between him and his brother for when Jamie was seriously in over his head.

Nathan dug out a bootlegged commo encryption unit he'd gotten from a company in Bahrain and plugged the unit into a port on the Satellite phone. The NSA could realistically hear his call, but the probability was remote since this equipment wasn't made in the United States. Nathan dialed Jamie's cell phone and got an answer on the second ring.

"Hello?" His brother's whispered and frightened voice warned him this was going to be bad.

"It's me."

"Nate, I'm in trouble. Bad trouble."

Nathan started to snap at him, but stopped before the rage spilled out. How much money was this going to take to fix? Didn't Jamie realize they needed every penny he'd saved for their mother now?

"What did you do?" Nathan asked in a tight voice. A calm tone was expecting too much.

"Nothing, I swear. I got set up. The Marseaux bunch tied me in with a bust, but I wasn't involved. I swear, I—"

"Jamie!" Not Marseaux, head of New Orlean's premier crime family. Nathan leaned his head back against the tree, kept his free hand on his weapon, and allowed his eyes to close for the first time in two days. "What the hell were you—"

"I went to one of his loan sharks, but I didn't know they were part of Marseaux's network. We needed money. I saw an ad and thought I'd just get a loan until you and I had a chance to figure out something better. I'm sorry, Nate, but you were gone. I was trying to handle this. Wanted to make you and Mom proud."

"What happened?"

"I ended up in the middle of a bust. Marseaux's people were cutting deals and fingering me before I even talked to an attorney."

This could *not* be happening. "Un-fucking-believable. How bad is this?"

"We're in trial right now, because the son of a bitchin' DA got this thing fast-tracked. I got a court-appointed attorney who's about as much good as tits on a boar hog.

He says I can't beat this, that I'm going to be convicted no matter what." Jamie's voice fell apart with the last words. "I only went to get money for Mom."

"Don't blame Mom's cancer. If you'd just use your head once in a while and not trust everyone who offers you quick money you wouldn't get screwed over. I send plenty of money every month for both of you." Nathan jerked upright and pounded the ground next to his leg. "I could have sent more."

"You don't understand, Nate," Jamie shouted. "You're not here. The city condemned this area and we have to move. They're going to bulldoze the houses here. Mom got a little money from the state, but not nearly enough for a decent place. I figured if I got some more cash we could get moved and settled somewhere before she got to feeling so bad. I never know when we'll hear from you, dammit."

Nathan couldn't believe this. He'd been building his savings in case of an emergency back home and would have sent money home before now if not for fear Jamie might squander the whole nest egg in some money scam.

This pretty much counted as an all-out emergency, but he doubted the little chunk of money he had would save Jamie from this legal jam. Each thump of his heart pounded loud as a death knell in his ears, warning of dire consequences ahead for his family. What the hell was he going to do to keep them safe now?

Who would be with his mother while she was going through hell?

"They're gonna put me in prison, Nate. Might be two

years," Jamie whispered. "What am I gonna do? What are we going to do about Mom?"

Nathan covered his eyes with his hand, but that wouldn't block out all the bad scenes running through his mind. His brother would be comatose for the rest of his life *if* Jamie survived prison, which he wouldn't. His mother couldn't face chemo without help. Her family was worthless, had never lifted a finger for her or her kids. And no family on his dad's side.

His pulse pumped furiously with each new worry. Nathan wished for a miracle, but realized he'd have to create one or his mother and Jamie would suffer. One from lack of care and the other from lack of sense.

He bounced his head against the tree, thinking, searching for a better idea than the one that came immediately to mind. But the sickening truth was he had no choice. He accepted what he had to do to protect his family.

It sucked, but then, so did life.

"Listen to me." Nathan took a breath before continuing. Decision made. "If I get you out of going to prison, you have to swear to stay away from anyone who even hints of being a shyster, criminal or otherwise."

"The attorney says I can't beat it, he says—"

"I don't *care* what he says. I'll get you out of this, but you have to swear to use your head and get a real job, no more bullshit deals. Take care of Mom for me. Give me your word."

"I swear I will, you know that. I'd do anything for you and Mom. You really think you can fix this?" Jamie's relief rushed through the lines. "I only have a week before the attorney says the trial will be over. I'll do whatever you say, just tell me what to do, Nate."

Find a way to roll back time so I could have sent you the money before you went to Marseaux's loan shark.

Going there was like losing his temper, neither would solve the mess Jamie was in. "Sit tight until I call you tomorrow. Don't tell a soul—including Mom—you talked to me. Got it?"

"Yeah, but what are you going to do?"

"I'll tell you tomorrow . . ." Nathan rubbed his eyes, sick over what he'd have to do. "I've got to go now, but I *will* keep you out of prison, so you better start holding up your end of the deal *right now.*"

"I will." Jamie was silent a moment, sighed. "Thanks, Nate. Sorry about this. I was just trying to take care of Mom and you know I don't do drugs."

Nathan sighed deeply. "I know, bud. We'll get through this." His brother had never taken so much as an aspirin or a beer since the first time he'd drank and spent a whole day puking his guts out hungover. Nathan ended the call and stared into a star-riddled sky. His father's words echoed in his mind from the day he showed the challenge coin to Nathan after Jamie had been beat up at school.

"I need you to make me a promise, son." His dad's voice had been tight, as if he hated handing this burden to a child.

Nathan had nodded. His dad continued, "A man's word is worth more than all the money on earth. Don't ever break yours."

When Nathan gave him another head nod, his dad held out the coin from his days as a Ranger in the army.

"I want you to have this, but with it comes responsibility. Your brother is never going to be as strong or street-smart as you, so I need your promise that you'll always watch out for him."

"I will, Dad, you know that. Me and Jamie forever." Nathan lifted his hand, palm up, to accept the coin he'd treasured more than anything. That had been a month before his father, an ARCA driver, was killed in a fiery crash. As an eight-year-old, Nathan had never imagined what he would now have to do as a man to keep his word to his father.

To keep his word to his brother.

He shoved up and away from the tree, unplugged the encryption unit and stowed it, then called for the predetermined Friday extraction point. When finished, he laid the phone alongside Stoner's hammock on the ground, still folded. Once Nathan secured his backpack, he removed a green pouch the size of a deck of cards from his belt, which held an emergency locator strobe. He unlaced the back of the pouch and slit the threads on a hidden pocket, withdrawing the challenge coin he always carried.

The mission was over and his team would extract tomorrow.

Nathan stared at the coin once more, then placed it on top of the bedroll, just as he'd promised when he went to face the devil. Stoner would understand the simple message.

As far as anyone was concerned, Nathan was dead.

In two steps, he disappeared into the night.

CHAPTER ONE

New Orleans, Louisiana, two years later

Terri Mitchell studied the naked male lying before her once more. Straight black hair fell loosely around his baby-smooth face. He'd shaved recently. Those chiseled lips were too enticing and perfect, as if shaped by a master sculptor.

How many women had enjoyed this body and those lips? Been pleasured by that captivating mouth?

And why should she care? Terri tamped down on her female interest. She was a professional and shouldn't consider things like this guy's social life or his lean, muscular body, but men didn't come much better packaged than this one. All she'd seen so far was his upper body since the cotton sheet covered his lower half.

Using her pen, she lifted the white cloth to see if there

was anything else she could glean from this inspection beyond the bullet hole in his forehead.

Not really, unless she wanted to add "well endowed" to her notes. Such a waste of one fine-looking male.

Probably not the Fat Tuesday this guy had expected when he got up this morning.

"I like the highlights, the more blonde look. That new?" The radio-announcer-smooth baritone asking that question from behind her belonged to a man she hadn't planned to see again. At least not yet.

Terri yanked her pen away. The sheet fell back into place over the corpse's toned midsection. She swung around to face DEA Special Agent Robert Brady and cursed silently for almost getting caught ogling a body.

"Hello, Brady."

"Nice to see you, Terri. Look good. I like the extra meat on your bones."

"Is that a polite way of saying I'm overweight?" She used to worry about trying to reach a dress size in the single digits. Not anymore. Surviving a nearly fatal attack had put her priorities in order. Stressing over the scale was in her past. If she could just put other things behind her as easily.

Like Brady's smug face.

"I said you looked good. Can't you take a compliment?"

Maybe, if it had come from someone else, but Brady liked his women thin, long-legged, and busty. At five-six she'd never met the long-legged qualification and nothing in her wardrobe had been designed for a slim body. She'd assumed Brady made an allowance when they'd dated because of her chest. Most of the men in her life jumped to the ridiculous assumption large breasts equaled an easy lay. Men had such simple guidelines, she envied them at times . . . almost.

They'd had a few dates, but she'd had enough sense not to sleep with Brady. Terri fixed a smile in place. "Thanks for the compliment."

"What were you doing?" He nodded toward the cold body.

"I'd think it would be obvious—even to you." She winked to soften the dig. "I'm examining a male corpse." Maybe they could keep things pleasant if he didn't bring up the past.

"The hole is in his head, not his dick."

She shoved a droll stare his way. "If I didn't inspect the entire body, I might miss something significant." Especially since she hadn't seen a naked male in so long.

Who knows? Something might have changed.

"You need to get laid." Brady's wrinkled navy suit had lost its polish hours ago. The scruffy, plain-brown hair hadn't changed, still looking both sexy and as if he'd just gotten out of bed and finger brushed the thick locks. How unfair. Men not only got away with bed head but turned it into a vogue style.

At a loss for a stinging comeback, she just arched an eyebrow.

"What?" he snapped.

She let out a tired breath and raked him with a peeved glare. "Why is getting laid a man's answer to everything?"

Brady shrugged. "Maybe because once we get laid, most of our problems are solved." He broke out a megawatt smile intended to wear down her resistance.

Which should have been easy since she'd never been on the first page of anyone's little black book.

Terri wasn't in the market for marriage, but neither was she willing to climb into bed with a man she had no real feelings for, which meant his original primitive assessment of her mood was probably correct.

Change the subject now, before . . .

"Why didn't you return my calls?" His face lost all joking appeal, ruining any chance of avoiding this conversation.

Might as well get this over with. "I did return your first call and left a voicemail I'd be out of pocket for a while."

"A *while?*" He stood away from the doorjamb, rising to his imposing stature. "Most people would take 'a while' to mean a few weeks, not three months." A six-foot male leaning toward her in an intimidating posture would have rattled her right after the attack, but not now.

After leaving the hospital—and the DEA—she'd spent endless hours with a personal trainer to even the field with dangerous men. She didn't want to ever feel weak or helpless again.

"I had to do a major rehab—" Terri started.

"I know that, but why did you hide from me?"

"Hide?" Was he insane, insensitive, or just plain unobservant? She growled under her breath and slapped her clipboard down on the body, then winced over her lack of respect for the dead.

What was it about sexy men that undermined her confidence?

"There are very few rehab facilities in New Orleans since Katrina. Or haven't you noticed?"

"That's not the real reason you cut out. The agency would have—"

"What?" She strangled the pen in her fist, then crossed her arms to hide her hands. "The DEA turned its back on me and left me out to hang."

"Not exactly. *You* made the final decision."

"Oh, sure. I resigned. You're right." She clicked the pen head up and down, then stopped. The last thing she wanted to do was televise a slim hold on her control. "They suspended me and started an investigation while I was hooked up to tubes in a hospital. Excuse me if I'm just a little . . . irritable."

Brady paced two steps away, hands in his pockets, then paused and met her gaze with a shielded one. "What did you expect them to do?"

"I expected them to—" Her throat clogged. Pain and humiliation wrapped around the memory that shadowed her thoughts daily. "I expected them to believe me and to back me up. Not to blame me for Conroy's death or suspect me of working with Marseaux." Damn them all. Who could possibly think she'd kill her partner and join ranks with that vermin Marseaux?

"The DEA has not taken any action against you."

"Yet."

"True, but in two weeks they'll make a final determination and close the case."

"Or charge me with a crime." She raced the clock to prove her innocence and find Conroy's killer. DEA Internal Affairs was racing just as hard to charge and convict her.

"Stay clear of any trouble and you should be fine."

Terri let a humorless chuckle escape. Brady should just say it straight: Don't get caught associating with any felons.

Easy for him to say. She needed contacts, to groom new informants, and that meant consorting with felons. No easy task with word out that her last snitch had died after she and her partner, Conroy, had been ambushed. Her best contact on the Marseaux case had been found murdered the next day.

The minute she'd awakened after surgery, Terri had quickly realized the questions being put to her were DEA interrogation level, not just for information. She'd put her faith in them and they'd screwed her.

Never again. While going through rehab she'd been recruited by BAD—the Bureau of American Defense— and now worked for the multijurisdictional covert agency that protected American citizens wherever they might be found. The DEA didn't even know BAD existed. Another reason she'd signed on.

Two weeks. Terri swatted an errant curl off her forehead. She'd be lucky to find a felon willing to talk to her again.

"Save your advice. I didn't get into trouble before." Terri cringed at her shrewish voice. She owed the DEA nothing, but she did owe Brady for making a clean shot at the man who had tried to carve her a new body with a twelve-inch butcher knife. Reaching inside herself for the calm she'd been taught in self-defense training, she took a deep breath. "The agency didn't want me back, and even if they had I'd have been stuck at a desk job. Might as well post a bulletin stating I'm not trustworthy in the field."

More importantly, she couldn't clear her name or find out who had set her and Conroy up while sitting at a desk, answering phones. Signing on with BAD gave her a fighting chance.

Brady had the decency to look uncomfortable. His gaze wandered around the room before he muttered, "Neither here nor there at this point." Then he focused on her again. "So you got plans for Fat Tuesday? Want to hook up for a drink later?"

She hadn't been asked out in a while, so on one level that was flattering, but not a path she wanted to travel again. Especially not with him. "Not right now. I'm pretty busy." *Proving my innocence and convicting a vicious killer— you know, the usual stuff that might preoccupy a woman facing prison time.*

His eyebrows tilted together at the lie, seeing the truth behind her words, but he didn't press the issue. "Still haven't figured out what you want, huh?"

She tensed at his dig. Three glasses of wine after a long day four months ago and she'd blabbed to him some of her most personal thoughts. But that wasn't enough humiliation for her. Oh no, she had to finish with telling him she didn't know what she wanted out of life.

He'd used that as an invitation to help her figure it out.

Talk about having a blonde moment. She shook it off. "Well, sugar, half of figuring out what you want in life is by figuring out what you don't. Let's just stick to business, okay? What are you doing down here? This isn't your usual area." Terri picked up her clipboard.

"I'm on a case." He glanced to the decedent. "What's your interest in this body?"

She relaxed. Brady had come in because of the male victim and not just to see her. Maybe they could keep this professional after all. "John Doe was found at noon today in the area I've been investigating."

Brady's eyes widened a bit. "What are you working on?"

"I can't discuss that with you any more than you can discuss your case with me."

Curiosity burned deep in his eyes. "So where you been? Who you working for?"

She considered her answer and decided best to stick with the cover she'd been given by BAD. "I'm consulting with the New Orleans Police Department."

"Ah . . . I heard about that."

Terri didn't take the bait to explain. She stonewalled, forcing him to carry the conversation if he wanted to continue.

He cleared his throat. "Got a buddy in the NOPD who says there's a rumor you're with some private agency. Who?"

She rolled her eyes at him. "And I slice open chickens at midnight to sacrifice to the great gods of Santería. I'm just a consultant, Brady. No real news there." Confidence returned, she served that up in a bored tone. "Anything you can tell me about this body?"

Brady's gaze danced from her to the body and back. He was clearly buying time to decide what—if anything—he should share. She doubted he'd give up anything of use.

"Guy's name is Nathan Drake. He was running drugs and tried to double-cross the wrong family."

Every alarm in her body rang out. Why would he share that when the concept alone went against his very nature? "How do you know this?"

"He was our snitch inside an organized crime family. Drake got greedy and tried to work one angle too many. Got what he deserved." Brady pinned a gimlet stare on Terri. "That's why you can't trust these guys."

Her face heated at his unexpected censure. She'd paid the price for trusting a snitch—a felon—who'd double-crossed her. She didn't need Brady to remind her, but criticizing him would stymie this unexpected flow of information.

Terri suffered in silence and hedged for more. "Thanks for the name. I'll pull this guy's rap sheet when I get back to headquarters."

"Save you some time. He doesn't have a rap sheet."

Now that surprised her. "You sure?"

"Yeah. His brother, Jamie, is doing hard time for running drugs, supposed to get out in a month. We found Nathan when he buried his mother a few weeks back and someone in our unit mistook him for Jamie."

"They look that much alike?"

Brady licked his lips, then said, "Pretty close. We

dug around, found out Jamie was still in prison and that Nathan was listed as MIA from the army two years ago . . . the same time his brother got put away. Didn't take much to figure out he'd gone AWOL to come home and take care of his sick mother."

That made sense. It also made her ache for the poor man on the gurney. Shame to do something so noble and then end up like this. "So what did Nathan do for you?"

Brady shrugged, his gaze moving around the room as if he was contemplating how much more he'd share.

Or was he shading the truth?

He paced two steps again as he spoke. "Nathan had special training in the military. We approached him and said we wouldn't tell the army about finding him if he'd go undercover and help us nail the head of the family. He agreed, got a job in a shipping company, a front for moving contraband."

In other words, Brady caught the poor sucker at a real low moment and coerced him into working for the DEA.

Terri tried to think professionally and keep her emotions locked away, but this guy had basically died because he got blackmailed into helping the Feds. "You screwed him."

"Not really." Brady broke eye contact as he spoke, a sign he was hiding something. "We had good intel. Nathan was dealing drugs, just not at the level his brother Jamie had. We didn't ask him to do anything he wasn't already into."

Terri accepted the information, with a healthy dose of suspicion. She'd worked with Brady long enough to know he was either holding back or tweaking the truth.

He crossed his arms. "We gave Nathan a file on the major players in the family we were after and asked if he thought he could get inside."

"Like he had a choice?"

"Everyone has a choice, Terri." His tone carried more weight than the topic they discussed. He wasn't over her subtle rejection, nor had he found it subtle.

She broke eye contact this time. "Whatever."

Surprisingly, Brady kept talking. "Nathan said he knew the family from what his brother had told him. Said he'd go in if we would get his brother out of prison early and clear his military record. I agreed. *If* he'd gotten us what we needed by this Friday, I'd have had his brother out by this weekend, barring any discipline issues. So *he* screwed himself."

She frowned. "How long has his brother been in the pen?"

"'Bout two years."

"Then why the rush to get him out a couple weeks early?"

Brady's gaze flattened, uncaring. "Maybe because their mother was so close to dying. Or maybe he just wanted something in his wasted life to look noble. Who knows?"

Terri considered that. She also considered another possibility. Like maybe this body had nothing to do with her investigation at the docks. Just a coincidental matter of the body being in the same proximity at the wrong time.

She ran Brady's words through her mind again. "Could you really get his brother out or were you just bluffing?" Just how straight had Brady played this game with Drake?

"Jamie is due out in a month. Warden claims he's a model prisoner. Wouldn't have been hard to cut a deal to spring him early so long as the warden didn't buck us. But this guy Drake turned out to be a dead end—no pun intended—in our investigation." Brady grinned. For once, he didn't look attractive or sexy, just annoying and arrogant.

"You're so hilarious." Terri refrained from shaking her head and calling Brady a jackass. The effort would be wasted on him, because he was after all a jackass. She turned to the deceased. "I need to get back to work—"

"You're done. He's part of our investigation." Brady had put just a little too much emphasis on "our." "Nothing here for the New Orleans PD. This stiff belongs to us. If they have any questions tell them to contact me, but hands off as of now. I'll have Drake picked up tomorrow."

Terri stood up to face Brady. What was so important that he'd make an issue out of one drug mule's body? She had a job to do. If she could determine this didn't fit with her investigation then she'd let Brady have his way.

How much more would he share? "What drug family was connected to the shipping company Drake worked for?"

Brady's chest moved slowly with several breaths, delaying again . . . and piquing her interest. "The Marseaux group."

Terri nodded. "Okay, that clears up his identity and simplifies my list of things to check. I've got plenty on my plate without getting involved with the DEA." She snapped the clipboard to her chest and smiled, offering a sign of her appreciation. Brady's "insider" buddy in the New Orleans PD had no way of knowing BAD had sent her undercover to find out if the Marseaux family was supplying weapons to a terrorist organization.

On the other hand, BAD didn't know she'd jumped at the chance to remain in the field because she had her own mission—to ferret out who had set her and Conroy up for an ambush.

She was flying solo and planned to keep it that way.

Any connection to the Marseaux family was priority one.

Nathan Drake's cold body just became a hot topic.

Warden McLaughlin hung up his phone, not believing how bad some people's luck ran. Given what he did for a living, he was certainly no bleeding heart, but he'd wanted to do more than babysit convicts when he'd decided on a career in the penal system. The more inmates he could rehabilitate for release, the better for everyone, since a chunk of the prison population was going to be released to live among the innocent at some point. Turning these prisoners around was the only hope society had.

The inmate leaving today was a suitable candidate to integrate back into society with little problem.

Until now. Damn.

Mattered not. At this point McLaughlin couldn't change what he'd worked so hard to put into motion for the guy. Particularly since he honestly believed this con wouldn't return or be a threat to anyone else.

At least that's what he'd thought all the way up until that phone call. Now . . .

Yeah, Jamie Drake would probably be back, and for a much longer stay next time.

His desk intercom buzzed. He pushed the button. "Yes?"

"Drake is ready to be released, sir."

McLaughlin let out a tired sigh of resignation. "Be right there." Stealing himself for what he had to tell this unlucky bastard, he got up and left his office to set the con free.

When he reached Drake, the guards had the beefy guy in cuffs and leg chains. A final reminder of where Drake had been for two years, but one that would only add insult to the news he had to give him.

Life was bad enough for Drake and would only get worse in a few minutes. Humiliating him further right now was just plain dangerous. McLaughlin jerked his chin toward the officer beside the con. "Remove the cuff and chains."

The officer blinked in question at the unorthodox order, then did as instructed. McLaughlin studied his soon-to-be ex-con for any sign of appreciation and found none in Drake's granite expression.

Then again, any other reaction would have surprised him.

"I'll walk out to the road with you." McLaughlin turned to where another of his guards opened the door for him.

"Why?" There was no mistaking the suspicion in Drake's voice, or the menace attached that warned anyone against trying to prevent him from leaving. He'd done his time and knew they had to let him go.

McLaughlin didn't want to stop him any more than he

wanted to be the bearer of such bad news, but some days it just plain sucked to be the head honcho. "Want to talk for a minute."

"Soon as my brother shows, I'm done with this place"—he turned a cold, dead glare on McLaughlin— "and with you."

In that moment, hearing those chilling words, McLaughlin was reminded of how it had taken five hefty guards to pull Drake off another inmate who had attacked him.

And the guards hadn't come away unscathed.

McLaughlin nodded in the direction of an armed guard, who understood the signal meant he should follow the warden to the street.

When Drake accepted his bag of meager belongings, the paper sack included some cash and a change of clothes McLaughlin had slipped into storage for the man. A rare sign of weakness and respect that no other prisoner had earned from him in all the years he'd been a warden.

Drake dipped his head down and stepped through the open doorway to the outside.

McLaughlin fell into step behind the con who had been an exemplary inmate. Drake had never raised a hand to anyone who hadn't attacked him first. Unfortunately that one time last year when he'd defended himself had cost Drake an eleven-inch ragged scar across his chest and another three months tacked on to his time.

But the inmate who had tried to kill Drake with a chair was still in the hospital.

Drake never slowed his pace as he strode between towering chain-link fences toward the barbwire-topped gate.

Two buddies of the man he'd put in the hospital called out obscenities Drake seemed to ignore until one of them yelled, "Too bad your mother died before I got out. Would have liked to have given that bitch a hard ride."

Storm clouds rumbled overhead, drowning out the rest of his taunt.

Drake never slowed his step nor turned to face the jeering pair when he sent them a middle-finger salute.

That was what worried McLaughlin. This guy hadn't said a word to a soul since hearing his mother had died. The bird he'd just shot was the most emotion McLaughlin had seen in two years.

When Drake passed through the gate, his shoulders dropped a tiny notch, just enough to make McLaughlin think this cold son of a bitch at least felt relief at being free again.

"I got some news," McLaughlin started.

Chilling gray-blue eyes turned on him. A gusty wind blew strands of Drake's black hair loose from the severe ponytail he wore. "What?"

That one word carried more threat than an entire band of armed vigilantes. McLaughlin had faced a lot of seriously whacked-out criminals in his life, but Drake's unrelenting control and lifeless gray eyes raised the fine hairs along his arms when their gazes locked.

Might as well stop procrastinating.

He took a step back—for safety's sake—before he spoke again. "Just got a call. Your brother won't be picking you up."

Drake's eyelids lowered a fraction, enough to ratchet

up his death-to-anyone-who-gives-me-bad-news look. "What'd he do now?"

McLaughlin glanced away. "My friend Percy Philips called. By the way, Percy will be your parole officer. His information is in your bag. Make sure you contact him no later than the end of the week. He's got a line on a mechanic's job for you." McLaughlin hoped the idea of having a job would soften the news he was hesitating to deliver. He'd asked Percy to keep Drake's release quiet to give the guy a break before he faced society.

"Didn't ask for your help."

"True, but you could use it, and I owe you for fixing my Roadrunner after everyone told me to get a new engine. That car is worth a hell of a lot more now that the original parts work."

"Back to my brother."

McLaughlin sighed. He couldn't delay the inevitable any longer. "Percy talked to a buddy of his in the New Orleans Police Department . . ."

Drake visibly relaxed and expelled a tense breath. "I'll spring Nathan from jail soon as I get home." He turned to look down the only road that led to civilization in this part of Louisiana. "How far to New Orleans?"

"About fifty miles. But your brother isn't in jail, Jamie. He's . . . dead."

❧

Nathan Drake inhaled, taking that blow hard as a steel bar to his solar plexus. No. His brother couldn't be dead. Not after he'd taken Jamie's place at the trial, spent two years in this hellhole, convinced everyone from attorneys to jurors to this warden he was Jamie for one reason.

To protect his brother.

Jamie dead. Nathan couldn't fit those two words together. He swung around, hatred boiling over at everything in his path.

A rifle cocked behind the warden.

McLaughlin lifted his hand, a silent order for the guard to stand down.

"How . . ." Nathan cleared his throat after that first ragged word. "How did he die?"

"Not real sure—"

That tiny sliver of emotion Nathan had shown dissolved behind a mask of fury that had backed dangerous inmates away. "Don't. Lie. To. Me."

McLaughlin sighed. "Percy says the police told him your brother had been found shot at the docks. They believe the shooting was drug related. They think . . ." He hesitated, shielding something. "Your brother was running drugs."

Lying bastards, all of them. Jamie never touched anything harder than aspirin. Drugs. One man controlled seventy percent of the drugs through New Orleans: Marseaux, the same prick who had forced Nathan into the only choice he could make two years ago—to give up everything to take Jamie's place in a cell.

"Look, Drake, I know this is bad, especially since you two are . . . were twins. Got a pair of twin grandkids, so I understand how close you had to be, but don't blow this opportunity. You can't change the past. I know you got a raw deal with the extra months, but the attorney for the guy who jumped you was connected. I did everything I could to get you out in time to bury your mother or you wouldn't be leaving a month earlier than you should. Unfortunately, no one moves fast in the government or you'd have made her funeral. I know it doesn't feel like much right now, but you're a free man again, so don't screw up. Don't want to see you back here before the paperwork is filed."

Lightning popped and fingered across the sky. McLaughlin tilted his head back to size up the swollen rain clouds. "Looks like a wet night for Fat Tuesday."

Fuck the weather. Nathan swung away and started walking in the direction of the bus station. He paused, but didn't turn around. McLaughlin had given him a fair shake. Had tried to get him out early. Nathan hated everyone in law enforcement for not taking Marseaux down, but he owed the warden something for at least trying to spring him in time to see his mother before she died. "Thanks."

"Want the name of the guy who has the job for you?"

"No."

"Then bury your brother and stay out of trouble," McLaughlin warned.

"Might do one of those. Either way, you won't see me here again. Give you my word on that."

Someone would pay for killing Jamie.

He gave his word on that, too.

❧

Terri wrinkled her nose at the stuffy smell of over forty people working too close for her personal taste. She slugged down another cup of coffee, or the closest equivalent they served in this satellite precinct not far from the Broad Street police headquarters. New Orleans still struggled to recover from Katrina and the criminal element had quadrupled the need for law enforcement. This precinct had been formed primarily to handle the overflow of murders and drug trafficking.

Lifting the strap of her handbag to her shoulder, she headed for her car. A shooting pain in her right thigh sucked the air from her lungs. Her leg was letting her know she'd been on her feet for too many hours in the past few days. Unfortunately, that wasn't going to change.

"Hey, Mitchell!" Sammy lifted off his seat from across the room at his desk. The rookie officer designated as her assistant on the Marseaux investigation waved a piece of paper and yelled again. Noise from overlapping conversation washed away his words.

She changed directions, careful to keep her stride smooth. Walking without a limp wouldn't be quite so difficult if she didn't have to navigate around crowded desks and people clustered in open space. And if she hadn't worn a skirt suit . . . but sometimes a woman in a skirt still caused men to drop their guard. She'd use any weapon to get what she wanted—the bastard who had set up her and Conroy.

". . . another missing blonde. Starting to make me wonder if they're just lost," one detective joked as she passed.

Terri slowed enough to make eye contact and narrow her eyes to send a "you're a jerk" message. The detective's gaze sobered, but he shot her a look that said he pegged her as another one from the brainless blonde gene pool. Men.

Sammy waited, reclined in his desk chair. Tawny-brown hair in the latest short style, a Colgate grin on his clean-shaven face, and a pleasant personality.

"What you got, Sammy?"

"Address on Nathan Drake and a little background."

"Cool beans." She took the paper he offered, which had a few notes neatly written in block letters, and started to walk away.

"By the way, the body's gone."

Terri swung back to face him. "What?"

"DEA staff was supposed to pick it up this afternoon for their coroner, but when they got to the morgue the drawer was empty. Everybody's freaking out. Tony runs the graveyard shift. Said he's been getting an acid enema over it from the DEA for the last hour."

She'd seen the body late yesterday at the morgue, less than twenty-four hours ago. Nathan Drake had been stone-cold dead so he sure as heck hadn't walked out, or . . .

No, she castigated herself at entertaining for an instant the idea that he'd gotten up on his own. This wasn't an Anne Rice novel. It might be New Orleans, but dead people didn't walk around here.

So who had wanted the body? And why was this body so important to the DEA?

"What about security cameras outside, Sammy?"

"Not a thing on any of them. There was one skip in time for about four seconds last night, but they have three cameras covering the entrance since that guy went postal on them a couple months ago. Nobody could make it past all three undetected with only four seconds to do it . . . unless he was a ghost." Sammy grinned again and waggled his eyebrows. "Of course, this *isss* Nawhlinss, home to ghouls and vampires."

"Yeah, right. Let's stick to reality. I doubt a ghost stole the corpse. Thanks for the address and the heads-up about the body." She strolled away, working hard not to grimace with each step. By the time she'd reached her Mini Cooper, Terri had changed her mind about going home for different clothes. If Brady and the rest of the DEA were tied up at the morgue searching for a body, this was her best chance to snoop through Drake's house.

She started to punch the directions into her GPS, then blinked at the address. The Drake house was close to hers in the French Quarter.

Except the Drake house was on Rampart Street—not the safest area.

Terri rolled her windows down and pulled out of the parking lot filled with unmarked sedans and squad cars.

Cool February air infused with the rich smells from neighboring restaurants fanned her skin and hair. Cajun cooking might have become a household term in most of the country, but those native to Louisiana knew the cuisine of this state was more than gumbo and boiled crawfish. She was happy to see the businesses coming back and the city rebuilding, but the continuous rows of broken and boarded-up windows declared there was still much to do before the city returned to its former glory.

When she passed her house, the one she shared with her grandmother, Terri mentally checkmarked a note for her to spend a few hours at home during the day soon. She worked nights by choice and her grandmother was self-sufficient, but that didn't stop Terri from worrying over her only real family.

When she reached her destination, Terri continued on past the Drake house to park down the street along the curb. She cut the lights and studied the neighborhood. Just a quiet Wednesday night. Probably more than a few nursing hangovers from a rowdy Fat Tuesday. She unhooked her earrings and removed her watch, then opened the console. Dumping the jewelry inside, she withdrew her handy pack of easy-entry tools for breaking and entering, which fit in the pocket of her small shoulder bag.

The same place she kept her SIG P229 9 mm. Sure as hell didn't have a spot beneath this black suit.

She tugged on the neckline of her aqua knit top, which fell back into a low scoop. Screw it. Time was flying by. One glance at the side mirror confirmed her lipstick was gone and makeup faded. Good. Most people would dismiss her as an office worker or retail salesgirl at the end of a long day. She snagged a pair of plastic gloves from the box of them she kept on the backseat for unexpected crime scene stops.

Jeans and a pullover would have been nice for this B&E, but a risky waste of time with Brady so hot to find Drake's body. He might show up any minute just to see if he could find a lead here on what had happened to the deceased.

At least that's where she'd start if she were in his shoes.

Terri exchanged the short pumps she'd worn all day for sneakers stored on the floorboard of the backseat. The ability to run always improved one's chance of not getting caught . . . or cut into pieces.

She wasn't much for running and didn't want to strain her bad leg, but it never hurt to be prepared for any possibility. She flipped the strap of her purse over her head and shoulder, securing it across her body. Been a while since she'd used her B&E tools. Now that she worked for BAD, she could bend rules when necessary without any sense of guilt. Only fair.

The DEA hadn't minded twisting the rules against her. She'd been a fool to trust them just because they were law enforcement.

But she wasn't cutting BAD any slack, either. From the agents she'd met so far, none seemed to have come up through any normal government channels.

In fact, most of them set off her felon detector big-time.

Who was she to judge? She could be facing prison soon.

Terri locked the car and kept to the shadows created by a full moon, then hiked along the sidewalk past a couple houses until she reached the one next door to the Drakes.

Music floated from the neighbor's courtyard, mingling with the aroma of barbeque filling the air. Terri's mouth watered. The food in the courtyard smelled better than anything she'd ever cooked in her grandma's kitchen.

A door squeaked open across the street right before an old man with a heavy gray jacket emerged with his little fluffy mutt on a leash.

Once he reached the street and turned the opposite way from her destination, Terri hurried to the broken concrete walkway of the Drake house.

The well-maintained blue wood exterior snubbed the rougher exteriors of the houses on each side. No obvious Katrina damage to the Drake home. Black shutters were drawn tight over the windows, no slats missing. Like all the other houses on the street, this one was narrow with white gingerbread latticework around the eaves. The quaint dwelling strangely reminded her of something out of an old fairy tale. Everything appeared tidy, except for some dirt and debris piled across the narrow strip of overgrown lawn.

She paused at the locked wooden gate on the side of the house that prevented strangers from pulling into the drive. A simple, cheap padlock held the chain hooked through the rickety wood structure in place. She pushed the gate ever so slightly and peeked through.

No nosy dog came charging up from the small courtyard.

Nathan Drake had probably tended the house while his mother lived here, but not in the past couple weeks, according to the overgrown patches of grass. The only information Terri had found in addition to Sammy's notes was an obituary notice that Lydia Drake had succumbed to cancer. Very minimal obit details.

She indulged a pang of sympathy for the guy's loss, but nothing excused working for a drug dealer. And his brother was in prison. What a disappointment for their mother.

At least they'd had their mother longer than Terri had been with hers. She'd gone to bed one night at a girlfriend's house in north Louisiana, thinking life at fifteen sucked just because she couldn't get a driver's permit yet, and woke up to a real nightmare. Her mother had been shot during the night and died before Terri reached the hospital.

A dog howled way off in the distance, waking up her common sense. She had to be quick about this or Brady might catch her. Hell, from the look of this neighborhood, she risked being mugged if she dallied any longer. With her gloves slipped on, Terri moved to the lifeless front porch shrouded in deep shadows and tried the doorknob as a standard move.

The door opened.

Hair raised along her arms. *Enter or not?*

Glancing around to assure no one was near, she unlatched her purse and slipped her hand inside to touch her 9 mm. She shook off her trepidation and entered, but prepared. The house was dark and quiet. Empty feeling.

Once inside she used a tiny LED flashlight on her key ring to scan the contents. She'd entered through the small living room and headed toward the kitchen, which smelled clean. The counters were spotless, but drawers stuck out half opened. A note had been taped to the refrigerator that hummed with life.

Terri bent at the knees, gritting her teeth over the sharp twist of pain that screamed from her right thigh. She held the light up close to read the note penned in a neat script. Below yesterday's date, written in marker were the words, "If I don't make it by tomorrow A.M., Laissez les bons temps rouler."

The body had been found around noon yesterday. So what did Nathan Drake miss doing, or whom did he miss meeting?

Chill bumps rippled over her skin. Had he known he might not come home?

If so, who had he left the note for? Who else had keys to this house?

A sharp pain jabbed down the inside of her leg. She straightened up and stretched the muscle, easing the ache.

Terri headed from the kitchen up the hallway to the living room, where more drawers on end tables had been left pulled out.

Didn't look as though Brady had been through the place. The DEA was usually a tad bit neater in their covert searches. Which begged the question, "Why not?"

She moved three more steps and paused when she reached a bedroom. Frilly lace drapes hung quietly above a chest with glass figurines on doilies. A bottle of White Shoulders cologne shared space with the figurines. Soft light beamed from a night-light low on the wall, an incongruous glow of life in a house with no living occupants, based on Sammy's notes. The crocheted coverlet draped over a pristine bed indicated a woman's room. Nathan's mother, Lydia Drake?

Not a drawer open. In fact, nothing seemed disturbed.

Terri moved away to the next door, wanting to search the only other bedroom in the small house. A glance in the room told her someone had been staying in there and the simple decoration indicated a man's taste.

Nathan's room?

Moonlight sliced through the slats of the shutters on windows. She turned off her key chain flashlight and tiptoed in. When her eyes adjusted, the first thing she noticed was a drawer open on a small table where papers had been disturbed and piled on top of the desk.

Terri reached for the papers.

Out of the darkness, someone with large hands grabbed her from behind.

One thought registered. *Shit.*

CHAPTER TWO

The intruder had underestimated the power needed to hold her, but he'd shifted her purse to her back out of easy reach.

Terri made a two-punch move. *Right. Left.* Arms now free, she swung around fast, guessing at the position of his head. Her whole body jarred when her elbow smacked his jaw.

His head snapped back with a nasty cracking sound. He cursed, stumbled backward, but quickly caught his balance and blocked her exit.

Crap. This one wasn't going down easy. And she couldn't reach for her weapon without lowering her defense.

She couldn't make out his face in the dark, but had no problem discerning his size. Moonlight threw shadows past his massive silhouette.

Options ran through her mind. She'd taken her instructor down and he wasn't exactly a weakling at over two hundred pounds. Not this big, though.

The man shook his head and stood very still, watching her.

Blood pumped furiously through her chest. She licked her lips, hoping the adrenaline charge would give her enough of an edge to beat him.

No matter what, she would make him pay for anything he got.

"You're a surprising little thing."

The disbelief in his muttered words stroked her ego until she picked up the underlying anger.

"No, I'm a *dangerous* little thing." She positioned her feet and feinted to his right. Her bluff worked to draw him out of position. She gritted her teeth against the inevitable pain, took a step, and threw her weight onto her injured leg.

Then shoved her left knee up hard. Big mistake.

The bastard blocked his groin with both hands faster than she'd ever seen a man move.

Terri lost her balance, hopping to stay off her right leg, but pain knifed up her side.

She sucked in her breath. The white-hot burning in her thigh caused her to hesitate to attack again.

And cost her what little edge she'd just gained.

Quick as a whip, he caught her by one arm and spun her back against his chest. His arms wrapped her like giant manacles, immobilizing her.

Shit!

Terri struggled but knew when she'd been beat. This was the downside of refusing to work with a partner again.

"What do you want?" she demanded and damn if she

didn't sound mad enough to back up the fury in her tone. Her pulse kicked into hyperspeed. She struggled. Panic would not help her, but the fear of being a victim again after the knife attack hid just beneath the surface under a thin veneer of confidence.

He said nothing. His chest expanded with each breath, but she hadn't been a real challenge for this guy. No one with his lightning reflexes would be winded. In fact, he'd contained her without roughing her up, which took effort.

Hope blossomed in her chest. He might not kill her.

Maybe he was just a thief.

"You find anything good here?" she asked, trying to prod him to confirm his presence.

Still no reply. Great impression of a statue.

She had to calm down and think. Calm equaled control. Her handbag was still intact and had moved back to her hip, but still out of reach while he held her. She glanced around for a weapon or something she could use as one.

The papers and open drawer snagged her gaze. Why go through the drawers of this house? What did people hide of value in drawers?

Jewelry, cash, checkbooks, credit cards . . .

The possibility of him being a thief was beginning to sound pretty plausible. Maybe he read obits, knew how to locate the houses and hit the ones that looked like easy pickings. She wanted to slap her head for not taking the unlocked door more seriously.

"Guess you've combed this place pretty good." She tried to turn her head. Not going to happen until he gave up this intimidation routine.

She knew the stay silent tactic. Let the other person babble. No problem. She'd play along and talk if that gave her any chance of weaseling her way out of this.

Terri took a breath, feeling back on her game, even if she was in a compromised position. Her best bet would be to convince him she'd also come here for a heist.

"Hey, buddy, I had no idea we were casing the same house. My bad. If you'll let me go, I'll stay off your turf." She tried to flex her arms, but she'd have an easier time flexing against a tree limb. This guy must spend his days as a gym rat.

A lock of her wavy hair tumbled into her eyes. She huffed the curl back and waited for him to make a move. Preferably, not an aggressive one.

"What are you doing here?" The softly spoken words were delivered in a voice as chilling as a block of ice.

She would not let him intimidate her. Her palms were slick, but everyone got sweaty palms, even undercover agents. She'd dealt with dangerous perps back when she was with the DEA.

"Same as you, just looking for something to pawn." Terri prayed she was right. He didn't act like someone on crack so maybe he'd just been sifting through the house for loose cash, credit cards, and jewelry. A smart thief wouldn't want to add assault to the charges if he ever got caught.

An encouraging thought . . . if he was sharp.

"Right." He made a sound that was a cross between a scoff and a grunt.

What? He didn't think she was capable of B&E, just got lucky with the door being open. If he only knew. She could pick a lock faster than he could sneeze. Just ask the judge who sentenced her to a year in juvie when she was sixteen.

"Hey, I can get into anything." She scoffed right back. "And had I broken in first I wouldn't have left the door unlocked. So what are you after? Jewelry?" Play along and keep him talking even if he did act as though he was being charged by the word to speak. He'd lower his guard at some point.

"Nothing here to pawn," he said.

Just as she'd thought. A thief. He hadn't tried to peel her clothes off. If she acted cool and casual about all this, she might just walk away unscathed.

Unfortunately, she'd never been cool in her life so friendly was the best to expect from her acting repertoire.

"What do you want?" His blunt question made her jump.

She clenched her fingers to keep from snapping at him. "Nothing, really. Just making a quick hit and moving on. I've already told you this place is all yours. You're right, there's not a thing I can make a dime on."

"You left a desk job in a suit and put on sneakers to hit a house you hadn't even cased properly?"

The teasing curl of his voice insulted her, but she was beginning to feel better about getting out of this little mess she didn't want Brady or anyone in the NOPD to find out about. If this guy had been a serious whacko he probably would have hurt her by now or said something creepy.

"Okay, I admit I suck at B and E." Not really, but he might take pity on a novice. "And, yes, it's obvious I haven't been cracking houses long. I may just give it up after tonight. I'm embarrassed enough. Can I go . . . please?" She smiled, working the whole blonde act to the hilt.

"Not yet. You owe me for stepping on my turf."

Terri stopped smiling and held her breath, assessing what he meant. Her throat tightened at the first images that popped into her mind. How was she ever going to trust her instincts around a perp again if she'd pegged this guy so wrong from the start?

"Wh-what else do you want?" She ground her teeth at her jittery words and swallowed against the lump of fear crawling up her throat. Her heart thumped so hard he had to feel the pounding beneath his forearm, still wrapped across her chest.

"Take it easy. I. Don't. Hurt. Women."

Terri would have dismissed his words outright if not for the profound tone of insult behind them. The pressure of his grip eased as if he wanted to prove his words by lessening the sense of threat.

Or was she just trying to convince herself she could handle this? In fairness, he hadn't flexed a muscle, hadn't made a forward move of any sort on her.

He hadn't forced himself on her. She felt a little better, but not enough to give him any more leeway than she had already.

What was with this silent treatment?

"Okay, so what *do* you want?" she snapped.

He shifted.

She tensed when he leaned closer until his warm breath feathered against her skin. Scream for help and risk a backlash or hold still and be patient?

While her brain churned with the frantic debate, he inhaled deeply. Then he breathed the air back out slowly as he whispered against her skin.

"You smell good. Damn good."

That was it?

Smelling her should freak her out and did on some level. But for some reason his words filled her with a deep sadness. He hadn't put a hand on her except to stop her from fighting him. If she allowed him this concession, would he let her go?

"I doubt you'll find me appealing." She'd first try to deter him from wanting more. "I've been up for close to twenty hours and have a hard time believing those deodorant commercials are true. I'm sure you could find a better female to sniff, maybe one with a more expensive perfume than eau de bath soap."

He inhaled again, slowly, as if he savored the breath, and whispered, "No, you smell natural and real. You smell the way a woman should. Nice." His husky voice added to the simple action of breathing in her scent had a strangely erotic appeal, spun her nerves into a frenzied tangle. He nuzzled her hair and she went perfectly still. The movement brought them close. Rogue hormones started setting up camp.

And if that wasn't a stupid reaction to a stranger who held her captive she didn't know what was.

Brady was right. She needed to get laid if a thief could raise a sliver of sexual interest in her. Bad as it sounded in her mind right now, she was sort of turned on. Had the attack three months ago distorted her emotions to the point she needed to be in danger to feel excited? With all the emotional baggage she already toted around after that night, she hoped not.

Nightmares of knives, screaming, and blood.

She'd been so sure she would die that night.

Buried terror of fighting a man armed with a razor-sharp blade who outweighed her by a hundred-plus pounds burst alive in her mind. She shut her eyes against the images and the sound of her voice screaming when he stabbed her leg, yanking the knife and ripping flesh.

"You're trembling." The perp holding her cursed something in Cajun and physically withdrew from her without releasing his hold.

Damn him for unleashing the vulnerability she'd chained down so she could face the world again and function like a normal woman.

"I *won't* hurt you," he repeated, irritated.

She couldn't hear anything but the pounding in her ears.

Her chest rose and fell faster with each breath. His assurance meant nothing to her. The last criminal she'd believed had led her into a deadly ambush.

"I'm going to let you go. Get the hell out of here and don't come back." All joking was gone from his voice. He sounded as cold and heartless as he had when he'd first spoken.

She started to say she'd be happy to vacate the premises, but his arms released her so quickly she just stood there for a second, regaining her bearings.

Terri snatched at her purse and wrenched out her

weapon. She spun around to the door, carefully checking the hallway.

Empty in both directions.

No time to waste when she'd been given a break. She hurried back through the house, more than happy to get the hell out.

On her way through the kitchen, she glanced at the refrigerator out of reflex to check the note once more.

The pale yellow paper was gone.

"What the . . . ?"

Why would a thief take that note?

"Leave now and don't come back." The words were whispered eerily from the hallway behind her like an unearthly warning.

She ran to the front door and scooted outside, down the porch, and across the street before reminding herself to breathe.

Who was that guy?

She had no idea, but one thing was clear. He sure as hell wasn't a thief.

❧

From inside his mother's house, Nathan watched the woman flee across the front lawn to the other side of the street. Moonlight shimmered along her shapely form.

Breaking and entering. Right. In that getup?

She was some level of law enforcement. He'd bet Federal, if not for her quick game to pretend at being a perp.

He'd have expected less creativity and more posturing from a Fed.

And to have a partner.

What the hell was she doing out here alone, breaking and entering in this neighborhood? Didn't she realize how reckless that was?

Nathan cast another look at her before she vanished into the shadows. She smelled like a spring day when flowers start to bloom. Like nothing he'd breathed in for the past two years.

Like something he'd wanted to feel next to him in a bed at night. His body stirred to life again, hard and wanting, just pissing him off more.

First woman he'd encountered on the outside and she thought he was going to rape her. Not bad enough he was an ex-con and deserter, now he'd sunk to true scum-of-the-earth level.

Great, just great. The only thing to make him a worse asshole would be to kick a puppy.

Nathan scowled at her and himself. He had no time for women right now. Getting hot and bothered over one connected to law enforcement proved he didn't have a discerning ounce of blood in his loins.

He lifted the yellow note he'd snatched off the refrigerator.

She'd read the note on her way in. He'd dismissed her interest in it as her just nosing around, but she'd paused to look for the slip of paper again on her way out. Why would she care about Jamie's note?

The one he'd left for Nathan yesterday when he was still alive. Twenty-four hours earlier and he could have saved Jamie.

A rush of anger cleared the lusty fog. Nathan needed information and bet the skirt that just left knew something.

CHAPTER THREE

"What's the holdup?"

Duff maintained his calm, but answering this puffed-up lobbyist strained his patience. "New Orleans customs is sitting on a stack of shipping containers. I was told the package would be accessible by now, out of customs, so the holdup's not on my end."

"Look, mate, we have a great opportunity here, both of us. One that might not ever come again. I need everything in place in a few days. This next Tuesday is not a soft date. Not like I can just reschedule this."

Few people understood the importance of timing as much as Duff, certainly not this groomed and spoiled Aussie who made his living pulling the strings on powerful men. Parker's only concern was leveraging a vote in the Senate for his client Zolono Pharmaceuticals, one of the largest in the world . . . that wanted to be *the* largest. Small potatoes compared to what Duff had to handle.

"I'm well aware of your schedule." Duff paused before dropping his next little bomb. "It's why we'll have to go to the backup . . . plan B." Duff glanced at the monitor on the desk next to where he stood. The live feed from Parker's D.C. office shared more than a videophone call would where the person on the other end of the line would know they were being observed.

Parker had been pacing since the minute he'd answered Duff's call. Now he stopped at his window with arms crossed. Bluetooth hooked to his ear, he gazed out over a distant view of the Mall that stretched from the Washington Monument to Capitol Hill. Duff knew the view well. He'd checked out the entire office when he'd inserted the hidden camera feed. Parker wouldn't be enjoying his plush lifestyle much longer if he didn't swing the pharmaceutical deal. For that, he needed Duff, because Parker's only weapon was charm.

Duff checked his watch. Time waited on no one. "I need to make a move."

"I never wanted any part of plan B. We discussed that. Marseaux will go crazy if you touch his shipment."

"Marseaux assured everyone he'd have that container available by now, that he could get his drug shipment past customs without a hitch. *He* dropped the ball, so what can he say?" Not really Marseaux's fault, but the drug lord owed favors and his loss in this would balance out another debt.

"You have a point, but it's not like he knows the real reason behind the drug shipment, right?" A little note of insecurity crept into Parker's normally confident voice.

"He knows as much as he needs to. Your call. Say the word and I'll contact one of my people to get the ball rolling." As if Parker had a choice? Duff fingered his cell phone, wishing he had *his* Bluetooth, but the *fratelli* didn't allow those in meetings.

Duff glanced across the elegant hotel room where his superior, Fra Bacchus, sat in a crimson leather chair, patiently waiting for him to finish the call.

And watching his every move.

"Once the New Orleans PD gets involved, you'll have Marseaux on your doorstep," Parker reminded him.

"I can handle Marseaux." Duff checked the monitor.

Parker drove fidgety fingers through his hair and paced the length of his sprawling office. Up until two years ago, he'd been the envy of every lobbyist on Capitol Hill, the man with the power, until one big deal fell apart after another. His golden touch had tarnished to cheap brass and would quickly turn into shit if he didn't give Zolono Pharmaceuticals the votes they needed to approve a bid to take over a struggling midsize firm—a monopoly venture, no matter how he colored the proposal.

Duff frowned when Parker picked up a file on his desk, his face relaxing with a forced calm before he spoke. "By the way, Duff, *my* contacts in New Orleans said the NOPD has a consultant working with them, prior DEA. A sheila is focusing on high-profile drug operations in the city, specifically Marseaux."

"She won't be a problem. If she is, I'll deal with her." Duff fingered the focus on the monitor, enlarging the screen until he could see the file in Parker's hand. Mitchell, Terri. He heaved a deep breath, maintaining his control. Had to. He lived under a microscope.

"But, what if she—"

"Don't. Worry." Duff had given this clown more leeway than he deserved. "What if the world ended tomorrow? What if you got laid? 'What ifs' bore me. Let me do my job. I'll get the product in place as promised. We still have plenty of time to hand the serum to my people. But we can't release any of it until I know for sure we have all the antidote and that the serum *will* indeed work. You just have to assure me payment is ready for the next step."

"Payment will be as agreed." Parker dropped the file on his desk and pinched his brow. "I guess we go to plan B and hope the fallout from Marseaux can be managed. I just . . . we need to limit the deaths, even if it is for a good reason."

"Having an attack of conscience? I didn't think that happened in your line of work."

"Regardless of what you think, lobbyists play an important role. If I get the votes Zolono needs, they'll be able to acquire a potential vaccine against breast cancer from a struggling company without the resources to make it a reality. They could change the future of women in this world."

"Hot damn, you are good. I like how you slide right past how this Senate vote and hostile takeover will catapult Zolono into an international entity that can outpace any competition once the vaccine is turned into a household name. Your CEO buddy kills thousands to save millions. Cherry deal."

No comment.

Duff glanced at the monitor where Parker was gritting his teeth and shaking his fist at an invisible adversary. Some people just can't take pressure. "Don't get your backside up.

We'll move ahead as planned and Zolono's CEO will never know his role in all this."

One flick of a control and the camera zoomed in tight on Parker's face. Sweat beaded across his creased forehead. But the little prick stretched his neck, an obvious stab at relaxing, and managed to sound like he had the world by the balls when he spoke.

"I should hope so, since you came highly recommended for a discreet operation. And, I don't want Marseaux coming to D.C."

Discreet. Hell of a way to describe a covert operation for mass execution. "Anton Marseaux is a businessman. He won't like what happens, but he'll understand. He has no knowledge of you, so no worries—right, mate?" he mimicked. "I'll have your product in place by this weekend, in time for Tuesday. Have your next installment ready."

"That's cutting it close, but this weekend should work. I've got a meeting with the client on Friday. I'll have the funds ready to wire after that."

"One more thing, Parker. Don't contact people to check up on me. It just pisses me off. Not a smart move on your part." Duff cut a look at the monitor in time to see Parker yank on the collar of his pale blue silk shirt. Baggy eyes had turned his thirty-two-year-old face into a man closing in on middle age.

"Fine. Just keep me informed."

Parker hung up, then swiped his desk clean of files and pens. Temper, temper. Duff punched a button, ending the transmission.

He closed his cell phone and turned to Fra Bacchus.

His short but dangerous superior sat in a reclined position, as at home on the top floor of New Orlean's finest five-star hotel, as an eagle perched in its nest above the world. Gray hairs invaded the short brown hair on his head. One eye drooped slightly, giving him a perpetual look of not quite getting what someone said, which was far from the truth with this genius.

"Parker's snooping in New Orleans," Duff informed him.

"He will find nothing more than any average person who noses around, because he is, after all, only average." Narrow fingers on one hand tapped against the Fra's robe-covered knees. Hands Duff had been on the punishing end of until he'd proven himself a top general for the cause. He suppressed a shudder at how strong and invasive those fingers could be.

"Of course, Your Exalted." Duff crossed the room to refill the Fra's wineglass. "I may have to . . . remove the Mitchell woman."

The Fra stopped tapping his knee. Duff held his breath. Had that been transparent?

"I'll let you know if that is necessary."

Duff nodded and allowed his lungs to release a tense breath. No unnecessary deaths. Committing one was a serious infraction the Fratelli took painful measures to prevent.

"Is everything in place?"

"Yes, Your Exalted. I have forwarded the tip on the drugs to a snitch in New Orleans who is probably already counting his wad of cash from an NOPD detective." In a few hours, law enforcement would be crawling all over stacks of metal containers in the shipyard, searching for drugs they would locate in the one next to where the Drake body had been found.

That would draw the attention of the Mitchell bitch.

Good. Duff smiled to himself. He liked blondes.

His favorite shade of fear.

"Very well. You may go, Duff."

When Duff reached the door, the Fra called to him.

"Yes, sir?"

"Please don't disappoint me, Duff. You know how I hate that."

Duff caught himself before he cursed. The Fra always used those specific words right before he'd commence with the "punishment proceedings," as they were called. Duff's palms sweated with memories of being tied spread-eagle against a wall.

"No, sir, I won't disappoint you." *I'd slit my own throat first.*

❧

Nathan finished closing drawers in the house. Jamie wouldn't have left him a note anywhere this obvious, but he couldn't risk not checking. His throat muscles clenched to the point he couldn't breathe. First Mom, now Jamie. He'd let everyone down.

He should have taken the beating in prison so he would have gotten out two months ago.

Had he done that, Jamie would be alive now.

Dammit. He should have done a lot of things, but

second-guessing decisions had never been of any use. He could accept his mom's death to some degree, but not Jamie's. Someone was going to pay for getting his brother involved with the Marseaux family again. Nathan knew that bastard had drawn Jamie in somehow. His brother's note on the refrigerator had said "If I don't make it by tomorrow A.M., ..." Jamie knew he was supposed to be at the prison in the P.M. and they'd used that same code of initials— A.M.—for Marseaux during the trial. Nathan wouldn't fault Jamie, because someone had duped his brother. As clueless as Jamie could be, he wasn't *that* stupid. Someone caught Jamie when he was vulnerable and hurting after their mother had died.

Nathan winced from anguish tearing through him again at the thought of his brother not being here to greet him. At the thought of his brother lying dead on the ground like disposable trash . . .

His grief turned to rage. The bastard who shot Jamie had made a dangerous mistake and he would pay for it tenfold. In blood and with his flesh.

Nathan stared around the room where moonlight spilled in. Where was Jamie's personal hiding place in this house? When they'd played as kids, Nathan had found Jamie's secret stash of possessions when he picked the same spot for concealing his personal booty. After that, they just shared any hiding place since one would never take anything from the other.

Knowing his brother, Jamie's new spot would be well concealed.

Nathan checked his watch. Twenty minutes after

eleven—he was out of time. He had a half-hour drive to make and didn't want to be late.

After locking the front and then back door, he went to the garage, where two vehicles sat side by side. A six-year-old Chevy Lumina that had once been a shiny cinnamon red had lost its polish. Now it looked more like a well-savored Tic Tac.

The second car was hidden beneath an all-weather beige chamois cover. And the instant he saw the shape, he knew what it was, even though his mind denied the possibility. His breath caught as anticipation filled him.

Nathan approached the cover reverently so that he could touch it again. His fingers sank into the supple chamois, which was like touching the finest velvet. Only a woman's skin was softer, but not by much.

Soft as the skin of the B&E artist he'd just touched . . . and wouldn't again, unfortunately. *Forget the woman.* Nathan traded the frustrating thought for an endearing one.

He couldn't believe his brother had kept this . . .

A '72 AMC Javelin. Even though his father had told him to never covet a possession, this car was everything to Nathan. Sliding the cover back, pleasure filled the empty pockets of his battered soul as he saw the gleaming black paint. Even in the dim light, his baby shined and beckoned him like a lover. There wasn't a piece of this car that he hadn't held in his hand at some point.

Not a single part he hadn't cradled when he'd done his frame-off restoration.

His breathing ragged, he finished removing the cover

to expose the gleaming blower that jutted out from the hood almost a foot high. Unlike the side pipes, which he'd ordered in matte black, this was the only part of the car that stood out against the stark black. And when he held the throttle open, this machine rumbled like thunder. It was so deep in sound that he could feel it all the way to his bones.

That sound of power, that unique feel of raw, unbridled potential . . .

With perfect, clean lines and a chassis built for speed, this was the car his father had bought as a teen but never had the money or time to restore.

Nathan had told Jamie to sell this for the money it would bring.

Thank God for once his brother hadn't listened to him, and the fact that Jamie hadn't brought a sting to his eyes. His brother had known what the car meant to him and he'd saved this one piece of Nathan's former life for him.

His gaze blurring, Nathan glanced around the unfamiliar garage until he found a tall cabinet next to a workbench. Without a doubt in his mind, he strode over and wiped his hand over the top left edge until his fingers bumped a key on a leather ring.

He and Jamie had always left the car keys where they could find them easily. Searching thin drawers on the tool chest, he located a stash of wire ties long enough to work as handcuffs. Four folded shop rags sat in a stack at the end of the workbench. He grabbed the stack. On the way back to the Javelin, Nathan opened the Chevy doors and stuck his head in to retrieve the garage door opener.

White Shoulders cologne danced through his nostrils.

His mother's favorite. He and Jamie had never failed to buy that for her birthday after their dad had died. Unimaginable pain and guilt speared him as he remembered the past. He longed to see her pretty face full of life one more time. To hear her tinkling laughter.

To tell her he loved her and was sorry he'd failed to keep Jamie safe. Two years of hell in prison was nothing compared to coming home to an empty house and knowing all that truly mattered to him was gone. He'd given up his freedom, his career.

Jamie had given up his life.

Rage punched its way past the hurt and pain to remind Nathan why he was here and what he had to do.

He swallowed the lump in his throat and snatched the plastic garage door opener from the visor. Paybacks were hell and, in this, he was the devil out to collect that bill.

He shoved the car door shut and climbed into the Javelin.

One turn of the key and his baby fired up without hesitation. Jamie wasn't a half-bad mechanic in his own right. He'd kept the battery charged and the engine tuned. Throaty mufflers rumbled as low and predatory as a black jaguar stalking its mate, owning the night and anything in its path. The vibration in the seat made his heartbeat race.

He pressed the small black box and the garage door raised.

The engine revved softly. His pulse vibrated with the feel of freedom and the power now his to control. He shifted the car into gear and drove slowly out to the street, closing the garage door behind him. When he reached the next block, the engine was warm, oil flowing through the valves, and the road was clear.

Nathan stomped the accelerator and dumped the clutch, laying a strip of rubber for fifty feet as this bitch screamed with power. Adolescent, but he didn't give a damn right now. He needed to hear this car purr and roar.

Nathan shouted, drunk with exhilaration. He was finally in control again. His life was his own. No guards or anyone else telling him what to do and when to do it. No one shouting orders or insults.

Time to ruin a few people's lives, the way they'd ruined his and Jamie's.

He navigated the streets of New Orleans with ease, then parked his car down a deserted street connecting a maze of alleys in the Warehouse District. After locking the car, he shuffled between buildings squeezed so close together a rat would get claustrophobia. Two blocks over he emerged next to a Dumpster that reeked of rotting food. Best place to wait since the smell alone would drive others away.

Decaying food was nothing compared to the things he'd experienced in the army or in prison. Few odors would ever match the one of that cave in South America.

Not a memory he wanted to relive, but one that had come back to life with the news reporting how a settlement in India was wiped out mysteriously this week. Those deaths were too similar to the ones in the South American village two years ago.

Same pattern of dying, right down to the grotesque bodies.

Nothing on the news about biological warfare, but he'd had plenty of time to think about those South Americans killed by an unknown virus that had not shown up anywhere else. Until now, and, from what the news reported, ten months ago when an entire village in the Congo had died of a mysterious virus.

Too many coincidences. Intelligence agencies and the military had to be thinking biological warfare. They should . . .

Nathan caught himself. He had to stop trying to solve the world's problems. Didn't he have enough of his own to keep him busy? He had maybe five days—if he was lucky—before he'd be faced with disappearing permanently.

The low putter of a big engine with custom pipes approached. Nathan tucked deeper into the crevice created between the Dumpster and the wall, and waited.

A Hummer rolled into place, right where it had parked earlier today. Some vermin were creatures of habit, Bennie Larriot being one. Same place he'd been for five years. Just a new set of wheels. True to form, neither Bennie nor his driver had been packing earlier. Being an attorney—one of Marseaux's—Bennie took no chances with being caught with a weapon in the car.

Nathan had no doubt a weapon was hidden in the car any more than he doubted the possibility of easily finding it.

Narrowing his eyes, Nathan steeled himself for the coming fight. He had the wire ties and a shop rag tucked inside the waistband at the small of his back, ready.

The driver got out, scanned the tight area, and dismissed

any threat as nonchalantly as he had before. No bodyguard would be better than a lazy one. The driver stalked around to open the passenger door.

Nathan made his move the minute the driver turned his back to him. Launching himself from the shadows, he slammed the bodyguard against his head to daze him and kicked the back of his knees, taking down two hundred fifty-plus pounds in less than three seconds. The guard's head bounced against the ground, finishing him off.

The shocked expression on Bennie's face lasted the same three seconds before he produced a switchblade.

Nathan was faster. He wrenched Bennie's arm up and back. When the pig opened his mouth to scream, Nathan shoved the shop rag into the gaping hole, then hit Bennie upside his head hard enough to knock him out. He loaded Bennie into the backseat, where he wire-tied his hands and feet, then lifted the keys off the unconscious driver and drove the Hummer away.

Nathan planned to find out how Jamie had become entangled in Marseaux's plans. Who had drawn his brother into this bunch? The NOPD and DEA had never been able to nail Marseaux. If Nathan uncovered anything that would help put the drug lord away, he'd send the evidence to someone.

That is, if there was anything left of Marseaux to arrest once Nathan was through with him.

He wended his way through the streets, where the midnight crowds could fulfill their fantasies with easy sex and euphoric drugs. He parked the Hummer next to Le Morte Noir—the Black Death—the name he and Jamie had jokingly dubbed the Javelin after a late-night cruise for frog hunting.

Pushing the memory aside along with the bitterness that followed, he unloaded Bennie, then drove the Hummer a mile away to what was left of the Ninth Ward, where he'd grown up.

Local chop shop owners wouldn't believe their luck when their street scouts found this sitting duck out in the open. They'd have this baby fully dismantled in twenty-four hours . . . or less.

Nathan hiked back to his car and fired up the Javelin. He drove a circuitous route until he reached his carefully thought-out lair. The last place anyone would look. He parked behind the silenced printing company abandoned in Katrina's wake.

After his father died, his mother had worked here to put food in their mouths and clothes on their backs. Jamie and he had run amok in this same parking lot after school, waiting for their mother to come off shift so they could go home and eat watered-down soup.

He managed to get Bennie out of the car, grunting under the titanic weight. So what if he banged the bastard's head a few times? The least of Bennie's worries after tonight would be a painful headache.

It took several minutes to get Bennie inside the trashed cement-block building and lug him to the proper room, which he'd already set up in expectation of the next couple of hours. Hanging the bastard by his wrists wasn't quite so simple, but a half hour of sweat had Bennie right where Nathan wanted.

The pig could hang there, drooling, a minute while Nathan finished the last details of his surprise. He grabbed a screwdriver to remove set pins on the miniature stage floor beneath Bennie. The whole contraption was only five feet across. Plenty of room for an entertaining show.

Manic scratching and chattering from rats looking for a meal and freedom disrupted the peace. Given the number of rats who used to call his house their home, the sound was almost comforting to Nathan.

He patrolled the exterior once, assuring himself no one was near. The owners had built this far outside the city's center to save money. Nathan appreciated their planning now. He returned to the corner he'd cleaned up for this exercise and sat on a ragged bar stool.

After Bennie, the next on his list was Thibadeaux "Fin-Man" Finney, an equal-opportunity snitch with ties to any organized crime family that paid his price. He managed to stay alive by keeping a goon squad of bodyguards supplied with drugs. He thought they could keep him safe.

But there was nothing and no one who could keep the devil at bay once it was time to give him his due. FinMan had a few more hours of peace.

Then the devil would be beating down his door.

For now, Bennie had napped long enough.

Nathan lifted a pitcher of cold water sitting at his feet and splashed him in the face. Bennie came to, spitting and coughing, slinging wet hair from his eyes. Water dripped from his chin onto the plywood board thirty inches below his dangling feet. Chicken wire with small holes surrounded Bennie in a circle five feet in diameter, six feet off the floor.

Bennie still wore his boxer shorts just because Nathan didn't want any more information on that flaccid body than he already had. Especially with a barrel gut on Bennie that hung out like biscuit dough from a half-popped can.

"What the hell is this? What do you want?" Bennie shouted curses and demands without relief. He twisted back and forth, causing the ropes tied to his wrists to cut his skin.

The only light in the room shined on Bennie, right into his eyes. Nathan kept the hood of his sweatshirt jacket on and moved close, but not close enough for Bennie to get a glimpse of someone from his past just yet.

Nathan curled his lips into a smile of contempt, ready to get down to business. "Bennie!" He waited for Bennie to shut up, then said, "Heard about all the homeless boys you've taken in. Real benefactor, aren't you? Bet they didn't think so after you raped them. I tried to copy the way you tied them up when you left those kids alone. Did I get it right?"

"Fuck you, asshole. You're a dead man," Bennie warned, but his voice quivered when he delivered that boast. He squinted into the light.

"What do you know about Nathan Drake?"

Sweat poured down Bennie's face. "Stone-cold dead. You working with that DEA bitch? I had nothing to do with Drake."

Could the attractive B&E poser who broke into his mom's house be DEA? "What DEA bitch?"

"Gimme a break. Like you don't know. Everybody knows her. She's been busting everyone's balls about Drake.

What? She wag her hot butt at you? Huh? You get any of that? If not, you lose. I heard she'll swap that ass for any amount of information." His nostrils flared as he fought even harder against his bindings. "I'm gonna kill that whore and you, too, if you don't let me go."

This piece of shit deserved some serious lead therapy—if only Nathan had a gun.

Bennie's lucky day.

Nathan had never enjoyed shooting a man, but that feeling might pass once he faced Jamie's murderer. He reached up and pushed the hood off his head and leaned forward to let the light catch his face.

Bennie gawked. His beady eyes rounded to the size of black dimes. "You ain't dead," he whispered. "Men at the docks that found you said you had a hole in your head. Deader than a doornail."

Frantic clawing broke through the red haze of anger Nathan barely kept tethered. Bennie's gaze shot straight down to the origin of the sound—the plywood floor beneath his feet.

A thin piece of wood that was a removable false bottom to the enclosure.

"W-w-what's that?" Bennie stuttered, not quite as cocky.

He'd find out soon enough. "Who sent the shooter? Who wanted me dead?"

Bennie trembled. His gut heaved with panicked breaths. "I-I don't know."

"I think you know something." Nathan reached down and stuck his fingers into the holes he'd cut for a handgrip and slid the board out of the way.

Bennie's eyes bulged and sprung tears.

Two years ago, Jamie had researched everyone he could on Marseaux's payroll while Nathan took his place during the trial. What Jamie had lacked in street sense he'd made up for with amazing research and computer skills that led to an interesting tidbit on this warthog.

Bennie feared rats more than death.

The floor of the enclosure moved with wall-to-wall street rats, hungry and vicious rodents. With the lid out of the way, they started biting at each other and crawling all over one another, leaping.

"Get me outta here." Bennie swung back and forth, kicking his feet.

Bad idea. That excited the rats even more.

"Not until we finish chatting, Bennie. I've got plenty of cheese and nowhere to go until you tell me what I want to know." Nathan swung the cheese down to where Bennie's legs dangled.

One of the smaller rats leapt up to brush Bennie's right foot. He screamed like a little girl and jerked his legs higher, an impressive sight given the girth of his Michelin-style belly. "Marseaux . . . had to be him."

Nathan waited for more, but Bennie denied him. He teased the rats with the cheese, stirring them into a bloodthirsty rage before he jerked it up and hooked the string to the front of Bennie's shorts.

His captive wailed, jerking his feet up.

"Scream all you want, Bennie. No one will hear you out here."

"I-I told you. Help me!"

"Help *you*? Like you *helped* those poor homeless boys just wanting a place to sleep and eat?" Nathan shook with the need to make this pedophile pay for hurting defenseless children.

Death wouldn't clear his tab, but a dose of terror would be a fair down payment.

When Bennie couldn't hold his feet up any longer, a rat jumped straight up, claws digging into the pudgy big toe. "That's all I, ahhh—" he cried out, eyes and nose running.

Three more rats jumped, two catching hold. Blood trickled down his foot.

Bennie screamed.

While Doughy exercised his lungs and struggled to walk on air, Nathan considered his next options once he was finished here. He fished a business card from the chest pocket of Bennie's jacket and moved the black type under the light.

TERRI MITCHELL, LAW ENFORCEMENT CONSULTANT. Nothing about the DEA, but undercover operatives didn't advertise. The card had a photo—didn't do her justice—and a cell number.

Plenty of information for Nathan to go on to find out what his little B&E babe knew about Jamie's death.

Nathan put the card away. Bennie was blabbering something about the dead bodies walking around. "Where did these guys see my body? What shipyard?"

CHAPTER FOUR

"I'm on the way in, Sammy. What's the status on the container at the docks?" Terri flipped open a notepad as she drove to headquarters. With commuters headed for home clogging the roads downtown, she could have walked from her grandmother's house to the police station faster.

"NOPD and DEA argued over jurisdiction and right of evidence possession, but we won the battle for once. Captain Philborn ordered a tractor trailer to pick up the container. It's on the way to our secured yard right now. I got a note here for you somewhere." The sound of paper ruffling and low muttering followed.

"I'm not surprised the captain got his way. He's pretty persuasive." Terri swerved into a faster lane.

"Nice to see us get a break once in a while, but only fair since the tip came from a contact that belongs to one of our guys. Damn, where is that message?" More fumbling noises.

"Clearly belongs to the NOPD," Terri agreed, not the least bit guilty about her role in all this.

After Sammy called this morning to alert her about the drug bust at the docks, she'd phoned the head of the BAD agency, Joe Q. Public—yes, that really was his name and anyone who teased him for it regretted the error shortly thereafter—for some assistance. Joe had a friend in the DEA who owed him a favor so the pissing contest was shut down quickly. She'd had just enough time to get Grandma to a doctor's appointment and back, grab a late lunch, and change into her just-the-facts charcoal gray suit. One with pants instead of a skirt this time.

Joe hadn't jockeyed the container out of the DEA's hands just to give the NOPD first shot. He wanted the contents examined by a BAD representative first, and she intended to be the one he sent in. She needed first crack at it to see what else might be inside besides the drugs.

Could this be the shipment Conroy had been trying to tell her about the night they were ambushed? The one with something more than a shipment of cocaine, something deadly? If Conroy had lived, Terri would have met the woman who told him a bizarre conspiracy story that involved secret material being transported with one of Marseaux's drug shipments.

One thing bugged Terri. Why had the snitch waited so long to make the call to tip NOPD about the drugs? Why now?

"Here it is." Sammy triumphantly read off Brady's name and phone number.

"Anyone else call?" She'd deal with Brady in due time.

Maybe he wanted to talk about the body . . . or drinks. She hoped not.

"Someone called here asking about you this morning."

"Yeah? Who?"

"Didn't say. The call was routed to me. This guy wanted to know if you were with the NOPD. I told him you consulted. Then he asked what kind of consulting work you did. I told him I couldn't share that type of information."

"Good. Probably someone I interviewed about that body from the docks, which reminds me—did the DEA find the body?" She tapped her brakes and grumbled at the sluggish movement. Terri hated the traffic but loved the city. Good thing, since she wouldn't move away from Grandma, who had lived in the French Quarter since long before it became chic to own a condo there.

"Nope, nothing yet on the stiff. And that guy who called asking about you, I don't think he was someone you interviewed."

"Why not?" She lifted her cup of coffee and took a sip.

"He asked if you consulted on B and Es."

Terri spewed coffee on the steering wheel and cursed. Good thing she'd only taken a sip. She stuck the cup back in the console cup holder and grabbed a napkin, wiping her pants leg.

"You okay?"

No. She swiped her hands and steering wheel, then growled over the spots on her clothes. "Yeah, I'm fine. Someone cut me off and I spilled coffee. That guy sounds like some lunatic. Just ignore it. I'll be there in a few minutes."

She hung up and brushed her palm across her forehead and the top of her hair. How had that perp found her? And who was this character? Why would he track her down at the police station?

He wasn't behaving like a common thief. He was starting to sound like a stalker.

Or someone from another agency.

And he was really starting to tick her off.

She parked the car outside in the lot reserved for everyone working in the temporary precinct and moved as quickly toward the two-story building as her leg would allow her. Her leg muscles seized up when she sat for more than fifteen minutes and hurt like a son of a gun when she stretched them.

Once she reached her desk, Terri eased down onto the chair, grimacing when she hit that one point in bending that turned her stomach with the sharp ache.

Her phone rang before she had her hands free. If this was that thief from the Drake house, she'd ...

What?

She didn't know, but the minute she did he'd get an earful. Snatching up the receiver, she answered briskly: "Terri Mitchell."

"This is Sammy."

She stretched her neck to see around people between her and Sammy's desk, where he grinned and flapped his hand in a wave. "What do you need, sweetie?"

"You got a visitor on the way up."

"Who?" But she knew the answer before Sammy said, "Josie Silversteen from the DEA's office."

The woman was already leaving the elevator, snapping toward Terri with determined steps. Five-eight even without the slut shoes she strode forward on, Josie's navy-and-red-striped business suit fit her perfectly shaped body. She had the look of a corporate viper with an ax to grind.

She paused at Terri's desk and gave her a withering stare. "Want to tell me what happened to that Drake body?" Long brunette hair swept across her shoulders when she leaned her head down and made a show of wiping off the wooden chair situated for visitors.

Terri blinked a minute, trying to get her bearings. What was Satan's spawn doing here? What would make the Queen Viper come down from on high to visit the little people?

Josie snapped her fingers in the air as she sat down in the chair, somehow without splitting the overly tight skirt. "Mitchell, you here or what?"

Terri blinked twice and quelled the look she really wanted to give Josie. "I'm here."

Josie let out that irritating noise Terri hated. The one that sounded like a gruff spurt of steam escaping a teapot. "Do I gotta repeat myself?" she said in a Jersey snark. "What's the matter? Can't you follow along or what? Here, I'll use small words so that you won't get lost again, *capisce?*"

Terri curled her lip at the sarcastic terror who had given one hundred and ten percent to making every day of Terri's life at the DEA miserable. Josie had even campaigned for her position from the first day Terri spent in the hospital after the attack.

And got her job, damn them all.

Silversteen could put on that phoney street slang, but she was from old money in New Jersey. Why couldn't she have stayed in the lap of luxury and not been a sandspur in Terri's hide?

"Okay, real slow this time, Mitchell—"

Terri glared at her. "This isn't the morgue. What? You get lost or something?" She mimicked Josie's accent. "If you got stiffed on a body, that's your problem, not mine. No pun intended." Terri tapped her fingers on the desktop, ready to end the unscheduled meeting.

"Very funny, Mitchell. That Drake killing is *our*"—Josie tapped a maroon fingernail against her chest—"jurisdiction. Did one of these NOPD boys pull a fast one?"

"Why would they?" Terri slapped her hand down on a stack of reports and leaned forward. "Look, I'm busy and not interested in your missing body. Why don't you call Dolly Parton, Jane Fonda, and Lily Tomlin to put together a search party for the hospital bathrooms and stop wasting my time?"

Josie studied her perfect manicure. "You're the last one to see the body. In fact, Brady said you were giving the corpse hot looks. Never been into necrophilia myself, but I guess it's hard for a gimp to get laid."

Terri's face flamed with embarrassment. Beautiful, wealthy, and not half bad at her job, Josie went right for the buttons that destroyed feminine confidence in other women and never missed an opportunity to exploit a weak spot. Terri clutched the edge of her desk to keep her fingers busy so she wouldn't use anything around her as a weapon.

"Oh, sorry," Josie cooed in a phony tone and splayed her hand above her immense bust. How did a woman stay that skinny with boobs the size of cantaloupes? "My bad for mentioning your leg. So how's the rehab going? I'm surprised you'd come back around an investigation after, well, you know . . . *the* screwup."

"I didn't screw up."

"Tell that to Conroy's widow."

Now that burned on a level so deep it was all Terri could do not to reach out and start ripping out Josie's brunette mane. Her knuckles turned white from the pressure of keeping them in place. "If that's all you came to talk about, you know where the exit is. Or should I reacquaint you with the street, butt first?"

Josie lifted her delicate brows and cocked her head slightly in a look that let Terri know she didn't take her as any kind of serious threat. Big mistake there. Terri could have had her skinny ass down in less time than it'd take to dump a cup of coffee. "No, that's not all. Talking to me right now would be in your best interest."

"Why?"

"In case you've forgotten—I know, a problem for blondes—you're still under investigation. Refusing to work with the DEA could be considered a hostile attitude."

Terri's street fighter genes simmered, wanting to burst out of her skin and show this viper exactly how hostile she really was. "I haven't forgotten and I haven't been hostile." Yet. "So get back to your point in this visit."

"That is my point," Josie purred. "I'm now heading the investigation on you and Conroy."

"What do you mean, Conroy? He's dead, for crying out loud."

"This investigation has moved in another direction that I'm not at liberty to discuss. We know someone was sharing DEA information with Marseaux. Right now, all evidence points at one of you two. So if it's Conroy, poor Sally won't get any benefits." Josie's lips pooched in a fake expression of concern. "However, if it's *you* . . ." She smiled, genuinely excited. "You'll have all the benefits allowed any other Federal prisoner. Now, you want to play nice or push me to hunt answers elsewhere?"

Stunned at the audacity of that threat, Terri couldn't believe the length Josie would go to bury her. Bad enough that she and Conroy were both suspected of working with Marseaux, but to deny his widow benefits would be the final insult.

Sally had serious back and kidney problems. The one plus for Conroy's widow was that Josie would use the full force of the law to nail Terri first.

Much as she'd like to blow off this pain in her butt, Terri had to play smart to win. That meant keeping Josie close while she searched for a way to clear her and Conroy's names.

"Why are you clueing me in on the investigation?" Terri asked.

Josie's eyebrows shifted in amused surprise. "Good question. You do have a brain, after all. I know you think I'm out to get you, but everything is not always about you. I'm going to find the leak in the agency *and* the missing Drake body. If you want a fair shake on this investigation, then don't work against me."

"I'm not so naïve as to think your wanting to work together has anything to do with getting a fair shake and everything to do with how many rungs you can hike up the DEA ladder in that streetwalker skirt. What do you want to know?" She'd asked that with the same enthusiasm of answering phone solicitations.

Josie came as close to frowning as Terri had ever seen but managed to stop before she creased her perfect brow. "You know anything about a guy called FinMan?"

Yes, but Terri didn't want to share much more with Josie since FinMan was one of Marseaux's street weasels. "I've heard his name mentioned around here."

"He's a contact I've been grooming. Sells to everyone, but mostly drug runners. Called me this morning pretty shook-up, which is saying a lot for a man in his profession. Said he had a visitor around two a.m. who strung him up by his ankles to make him talk."

"Doesn't sound so bad to me." Terri smiled to herself over this creep getting a taste of his own treatment. She'd heard more than she cared to recall about FinMan's kinky side and how bad he'd hurt several hookers. He deserved to be strung up naked, and worse.

"It might if you were male, hanging upside down naked and got nervous, then whizzed all over yourself. Gravity is not your friend at that point."

"Eww. Save those tidbits for when you're in the men's room . . . updating your contact information."

Josie leaned back and offered her a droll gaze. "You know, Mitchell, you weren't this clever when you were at the agency."

"No?" Terri mirrored her movements, placing her own hands on each arm of the rickety chair. "I thought it was pretty hilarious every time I outshot you on the pistol range and closed more cases than anyone else in my department. Now that I don't have to deal with backstabbing coworkers, my sense of humor has only gotten better." Probably not smart to poke at a cobra, but Josie would suspect Terri if she turned all girlfriend nice.

"You nailed a lot of paper targets, but missed the mark big-time on your last mission." Josie crossed her legs and leaned forward, propping her arms across her knee. Her voice dropped a notch. "It's one thing to kill a practice target and another to eliminate a threat. I wouldn't have let someone take my partner down from behind."

Muscles squeezed tight around Terri's heart every time she was reminded of Conroy's death and that night. She wished she could remember all the details, but she'd been knocked out from behind and came to with a knife-wielding madman hunched over her. She had to live with her mistakes and those nightmares, but she didn't have to put up with Josie's garbage anymore.

"Whatever. I've told you what I know. If you've got nothing else to discuss, Silversteen, I'm done."

"Much as I'd like to spend my investigative time on someone better qualified than you, I can put a case ahead of any personal differences. Even if it means wading through all your crap to find the missing body and close this investigation. But if you can't put the job first or want me to come to my own conclusions, just say so."

Terri drummed the tip of her pen on a stack of reports.

Just find out what she wanted and move on. "Okay, I've heard FinMan mentioned around here and that he has a couple full-time bodyguards. How does he figure into the missing body?"

"More than a couple bodyguards, and this phantom guy took them all out, except one that was out of town, without being seen or touched, and got to FinMan."

Terri paused her hand. "What do you mean, 'phantom guy'?"

"That's what I'm trying to tell you, blondie. He said the dead guy at the morgue had come after him. Strung him up and threatened to cut off just enough of his nuts to make him bleed very slowly and never get hard again."

The dead guy was alive? No, not even possible. "I can see how that probably freaked out FinMan, though I doubt any of the local prostitutes would have taken up a collection for an implant. Who'd he think the guy was?"

Josie huffed. "You really are slow. One more time, Fin-Man said it was the dead guy."

Terri pulled her arm back. "That's impossible. What did Brady say?"

"Screw Brady. He's working for a different department and doesn't share, so why should I? My boss wants this body found pronto. I plan to kill two birds with one shot since most of the places I'm going for background on you and Conroy might know something about the body. So if you hear a word on that corpse, you need to call me first. Got that? In fact, a word to the wise, don't go getting chummy with Brady again."

Terri had no interest in being chummy with anyone,

particularly Brady, but where did this twit get off telling her who she could talk to or not?

"Are you threatening me?" Terri slowly rose from her chair. She was a vision of calm even though she wanted to flatten this witch into a furry brown doormat.

"No, don't confuse that statement with something as simple as a threat." Josie stood and glared down her narrow nose at Terri. "You share anything I've told you with Brady and I *promise* you I'll come looking for you. You're fair game now that you aren't a Fed anymore, and you're at the top of my investigation list. Use your head for once. Don't get in my way."

"Don't worry, just as long as you stay out of *my* way," Terri snarled right back.

"Oooohhh, I'm worried. You gonna kick my butt with your one good leg?"

No, but I might gouge out your eyes and play marbles with them. "Good luck finding Drake's body. At least he won't have a problem getting hard for you." Terri tried to catch those last words before they escaped, but as usual her temper had raced ahead of her brain.

Conroy had been one of the few male agents who failed to hit on Josie during her first year. That he was happily married meant nothing to her. Josie had caught him in a black mood, drinking alone at a local watering hole while his wife was out of town. She pulled out all the stops to get him in the sack. He'd said no. When she called him a limp dick, he smiled and told her he only had a problem getting it up around a slut.

Josie lifted her purse, her face a blank mask of calm.

"Enjoy your freedom while it lasts, Mitchell. *Tic-toc.*" She strolled from the offices with the regal bearing of a queen.

Terri made a childish face at Josie's back.

The room quieted near her. She glanced around and caught a couple gazes straying her way, so she glared them into submission, then plopped back down in the chair.

Dammit! Whoever had decided to put all of them in a common room should be cursed with a plague on their privates.

The phone rang again.

She snatched it up. "*What?*"

"Damn, Terri, don't bite my head off."

She relaxed at the smooth Latino accent. His was the only voice that could have soothed her fury. "Sorry, Carlos. What have you got?"

"Plenty of fine wine and silk sheets with a high thread count."

Terri smiled. Carlos Delgado had been the first agent she'd met at BAD when Joe's partner, Tee, showed Terri around. Carlos had a half smile that meant anything from he couldn't take you seriously to he'd like to strip you naked. As a woman, she'd immediately read the latter into his expression, which had drawn a sigh from her but nothing more. She knew better than to get involved with a teammate, even if he did put a Latin god to shame.

"You do brighten my day, Carlos."

"Anything to be of *service* to you. And I mean that in every sense of the word."

Terri chuckled, forgetting her anger for the moment. "What's up?"

"It's obviously going to take a lot more work to get dinner with you, but I'm a patient man. Back to business. The container is in the yard. Joe tied up Philborn with paperwork for two hours—starting now—before the crime lab can dust for prints or remove any evidence. We need someone inside to do a survey and take photos of everything, not just the drugs."

"I'll head over there now."

"Wait for me to pick you up. I'd be there already if not for the damn traffic crossing Lake Ponchatrain."

"I don't need anyone to go with me. If I go now that's at least an extra half hour."

"Joe and Tee agreed to let you work solo . . . to a degree. Everyone has backup at some time, Terri."

"Even you?"

"I do if I think I need it."

"Then give me the same latitude." Terri lowered her voice and turned away from big ears. "Admit it, Carlos. You wouldn't stop another agent from going to the container alone with this short window of time. Don't treat me like I'm not capable of doing my job."

Carlos grumbled something in Spanish under his breath that she had a feeling translated into how difficult women annoyed him. "Don't make me regret it."

"I won't." Nice to win one small battle. "Give me the address and I'm out of here." Terri scribbled the address on a small notepad.

"One more thing. We're getting some strange intel connected to Marseaux. Keep your ear tuned for anything odd to do with the Drake body."

How could one corpse be so popular?

"What do you mean?" She kept her voice down and turned around, eyes scanning the room for anyone who might be listening to her conversation.

"Hooknose Rodaine landed in the hospital with a concussion and cracked ribs."

That didn't surprise her. "He must have snitched on the wrong person. Why the concern?"

"I couldn't care less if he floated up the Mississippi ass first since he's not one of my contacts. He's tight with the Marseaux bunch, but that's not the weird part. Johnny Boy on the south side ended up in the hospital, too, with a broken arm and crushed kneecap. His story matches Rodaine and those two hate each other."

"What story?"

"They both claim a ghost tried to kill them."

Terri went still. "What kind of ghost?"

"They say it's Drake's spirit come back from the grave. And get this—they claim the ghost rides around in some souped-up ride. No one has seen the car, but they say you can tell he's near by the sound of his mufflers. See what you can dig up on this Drake character. I'm thinking Drake was more than a mule."

Tiny bumps pebbled her skin. She rubbed them, feeling a chill wash over her. What was going on? "That makes three."

"Three? Are you serious? Who else was attacked?"

"FinMan, everybody's favorite information peddler."

"I know him. Works for the highest dollar of the day and has a bunch of slabs of beef he calls bodyguards."

She nodded. "That's him. I heard from a DEA agent FinMan claims he was strung upside down by his ankles, naked, and threatened with no future as a porn star if he didn't talk."

"Really?" Carlos chuckled.

"He claims it was the dead guy, too. What do you think is going on?"

"Probably somebody who either is a good makeup artist or has one and wants to screw with these guys."

"Maybe, but it doesn't make sense." What was the thread that tied all these people together?

"Yeah. What does this guy want? No one will tell what they said to Drake or whoever it was who jacked them up. They all swear they gave up nothing. Better to suffer in silence than have Marseaux think they caved and squealed anything about him."

No kidding. Marseaux would do a lot more than just threaten. "FinMan was strung up prior to the drug bust so you have to wonder if he panicked, spilled the beans, and is behind the leak on that."

Terri glanced at her watch. Was Carlos keeping her on the phone until he arrived?

Probably so.

"Thanks for the call, Carlos. It did a world of good for my feminine ego. I gotta go."

"You know, I could stroke so much more than just your ego."

"I'll keep that in mind." Terri laughed, ignoring the offer.

She hung up and hurried down to the garage and

moved the large canvas tote bag with all her investigation paraphernalia to the front seat before driving over to the lot. The sun disappeared too soon on winter days, leaving the world dark and gloomy beneath a canopy of clouds.

New Orleans always looked spooky this time of year. Yet she couldn't imagine living anywhere else. She really loved this city, which was more than just a home. This place was part of her.

Once Terri reached the lot, she showed her ID and was heartened to learn she'd been given access. Joe was brutally efficient.

She signed in, accepted a key for the lock, and drove past a set of storage buildings that had been donated to the city with this chunk of land. Slick cars, fast boats, and other illegally purchased confiscations covered two-thirds of the landscape.

The white container sat perched on a small rise, the metal box looking as out of place as a lost white elephant amidst all the sleek vehicles from drug hauls.

Terri parked in the gravel area. She grabbed her tote bag and a honkin' big battery-operated lamp that would light a ten-foot radius. When gravel changed to soft dirt, she chose her steps carefully to keep from aggravating her thigh.

Who decided the container had to be uphill? She shivered against the wintry breeze sliding across the ground and swirling in open spaces. Should have brought her wool overjacket, but she'd been in too big of a hurry to get here. Besides, it shouldn't take long to determine if there was anything she could learn from the drug shipment that would have a bearing on her covert investigation for BAD.

When she reached the container the lock hung slightly open on the door. Hadn't the security detail delivering this box made sure the lock was set? Just because it was inside a secured lot didn't mean they could leave the container so easily accessible.

The left door creaked when she whipped it open and shoved her head inside. A light shining in the rear area flashed up to blind her.

Footsteps pounding toward her from behind registered.

She froze. Time blurred and slowed in her mind, but everything happened in milliseconds as she reached for the 9 mm in her tote.

Hard fingers clasped her arm first and yanked her back from the container.

A bullet pinged off the door where her head had been before she'd been wrenched backwards.

Terri stumbled, losing her balance when her foot caught on a rut of clumped grass and roots. The tote fell from her shoulder. On her way to the ground, she saw a black silhouette against the bright white container right before her head hit a hard edge. Sharp heat stung her scalp.

Stars swam in a black sea behind her eyelids.

⊷

Nathan grimaced when he heard the woman hit the ground with a solid *whump*. A soft groan of pain slipped from her lips. Dammit. He'd barely reached her when she'd pulled the door open. She'd left him with no option except to yank her away before the perp in the container took a shot and her head exploded into tiny pieces of skull bone and brain matter.

All he could do for her right now was stand between her and the threat that would surely come looking to finish the job.

The single overhead halogen on a tall pole at one end of the gravel parking lot sent a mere hint of light to this area. Nathan couldn't see her face, but hoped the worst she'd end up with was a bump on her head.

He plastered his body against the closed door on the right, waiting for the shooter to come out. The tip of a gun peeked into the opening, then a shadow slashed across the open door.

Nathan latched onto the arm and jerked the body fully outside. The shooter swung around fluidly, hitting Nathan with a bone-jarring kick to his side. Nathan sucked in a sharp breath and returned the favor with a kick of his own and two quick hand jabs to the arm he was pretty sure still held a gun. When metal hit a nearby car, he had a microsecond for a quick assessment of his opponent.

Fast, skilled, and deadly. Professional. This was no thug or goon. This was someone who made a living hurting people.

The air whooshed with flying hands and feet. Nathan blocked one blow, catching others against his face, chest, and arms every time he made a wrong move.

With so little light, he fought blind, but didn't think the other guy had any night-vision gear so neither had an advantage.

Nathan dove forward on the attack, slamming solid hits and kicks with blinding speed whenever the dim light shed a small amount of aid.

Grunts of exertion and the thud of one blow after another filled the night air. Nathan had endurance, but this guy had speed, which Nathan had lost in prison with the lack of any training beyond weight lifting.

His best offense was to attack more aggressively and hope for a break. He got in one really solid lick that sent the guy stumbling backwards, but the son of a bitch hit the ground, rolled, and scrambled away in the darkness.

Nathan waited, trying hard to catch his breath. Where was that bastard? Had he left or was he hunkered down, waiting?

A moan behind him drew his attention. He backed up, keeping an eye out for any movement. When he reached the Mitchell woman, he knelt down and lifted her upper body into his arms so he could feel the back of her head. A lump, just as he'd thought, hopefully not bad enough to be a concussion.

Her head lolled against him and her hand came up to his chest. She grumbled incoherently. He stilled with the strange feeling her simple contact stirred within him. He hadn't been touched by a female in a long time. Her hands gripped his shirt as if she needed to anchor herself or reached for comfort.

Nathan instinctively drew her closer to his chest, an ingrained need to protect her.

Something scuffed the ground not far away.

His attention snapped back into gear.

He scooped her into his arms and slipped inside the container. With only his hands as weapons, he had no way to neutralize a threat with a gun and he'd bet his attacker had located his weapon by now.

But a professional wouldn't make the mistake of coming inside this container without knowing if Nathan was armed or not. He wouldn't leave, either, if what he'd come for was still inside here. At least, not if there was hope of retrieving it.

As soon as Nathan determined that the woman was okay, he wanted to survey the contents and see if anything was disturbed.

He shifted the supple body in his arms, ignoring the desire to feel her hands on him again, but with purpose.

Don't go there.

This hadn't been his plan when he'd followed the container from the docks to this yard.

After a short time of hanging upside down and naked, FinMan had given Nathan the scoop on Marseaux's latest drug shipment sitting at the docks. Nathan had reached the container yard in time to see police swarming around one in particular. The NOPD had guarded this container until a tractor trailer showed up, then transported it to this holding facility. He'd cased this place for two hours, waiting on nightfall.

Just when twilight had faded and the only light to flicker on had been the single pole light in the parking lot, he'd started to clip the fence wires and enter.

That's when he saw the other intruder scuttle from point to point across the uneven terrain. He'd held back and waited in hope of following the guy.

A decent plan until Terri Mitchell showed up. Nathan recognized her the minute she'd stepped from her car and started up the hill. She had the sexiest walk he'd seen on a female since he couldn't remember when, one he wouldn't soon forget. Unfortunately.

He wouldn't forget her scent, either, or her soft skin.

Or a mouth that begged to be kissed. He could steal one, but that just didn't seem right, even if she was a cop.

She stirred against him. Her sweet body invited thoughts he hadn't entertained in years, literally. Like how much he missed spending the night in a soft bed with a woman he could devote hours to pleasuring. But a woman like her would probably want more than a hot roll between cool sheets.

More than a man as cold and dead inside as he was.

The Mitchell woman stirred with a start, panting.

He considered putting her down, but wasn't sure what she'd do once she came to in the dark. There wasn't much room to move around in this space if she panicked. He knew the minute she was conscious by how fast she stiffened in his arms.

"Put me down." Her order had a ring of unease to it.

Nathan lowered her feetfirst, steadying her until she jerked away out of his grasp. Her shoes scuffed against the wood floor of the container, backing away from him.

He spoke to her softly. "Stop, before you fall again."

"Who are you? What do you want in here?"

"Keep your voice down. And before you go all badass cop on me, I'm the one who saved your life outside."

"How do I know that?"

Was she serious? "Let's use some logic. You stuck your head in here. Someone tried to use it for target practice, but I yanked you away before you ended up headless. If I was the shooter, you'd be dead now and we wouldn't be having this conversation."

"You're *that* guy," she whispered, surprised. "The one in the house. Nathan Drake's house."

CHAPTER FIVE

"Shh." As soon as he spoke, Nathan wondered why he'd bothered. He doubted that would keep this Mitchell woman from talking, not now that she'd realized he was the one she'd met while breaking into his mother's house.

He wasn't saying another word. Hell, he'd just said more than he had in the past two years.

"What's your tie to Nathan Drake? Do you know where his body is?"

"Keep talking and the shooter will catch us with our guard down," Nathan whispered. He shouldn't have to tell her that. Wasn't she in law enforcement?

The container fell so silent he thought she'd stopped breathing.

She shuffled back another step until her foot bumped something he guessed was the wall.

"Be still." He couldn't see her but all noise ceased until

he caught the sound of her short breaths. She was rattled and barking at her wasn't helping. *Way to go, Drake.* Had he forgotten how to be civil to a woman? To be honest, yes. He hadn't shared a social conversation with anyone in so long he'd obviously forgotten how to converse without making it sound like a threat.

"I'm not going to hurt you," he said quietly. He'd never harmed a woman in his life and didn't care for feeling like a threat to one now.

"Okay." She kept her voice just as soft.

"I'm moving closer to talk. Don't panic."

"Okay."

One-word answers. She was still afraid of him, but he didn't have all night to soothe her. She didn't make a sound as he moved forward again, slowly. He lifted the hood of his sweatshirt jacket back over his head, then stretched his hand out high above where her head should be so he would touch the wall before he bumped into her. When his fingertips bumped a hard surface, he stopped and leaned down.

"What do you want?" she asked.

"For you to calm down."

"Why are you angry?"

"You don't have enough time to hear the list. I'm going to take a look at the contents of this container and see if I can determine if he got what he came for. You could help."

No response. He hadn't slept in almost two days of being on the move, but his time was limited. Once word got around that the Drake ex-con was on the streets and not checking in with a parole officer, his time would be up. He'd have to go to ground. He wouldn't gain any real time by physically checking in with his parole officer, and couldn't risk picking up a tail sent by the law or Marseaux's people.

Which meant he had to move this along faster.

Nathan checked his anger and worked on sounding patient while he explained, "The guy who tried to kill you will be back if he didn't get what he came for."

"So look at the contents." She sounded less nervous and maybe even annoyed herself.

"Not without you. I can't protect you if you're between me and him or out of my reach."

"I don't need your protection." Annoyed and cocky this time.

"You got a gun?" He knew the answer. If she'd had one, she'd be pointing it at him right now.

Silence.

"Neither do I," he told her. "I'm going to take your arm so I'll know where you are while I'm moving around."

"No."

He clenched his fingers. Patience. At least she was talking, even if she still acted like he was going to drag her off by her hair.

"What if you hold my arm?" he asked, searching for a way to get her to cooperate.

No reply.

Her lack of faith in a man who had just saved her life wore on him. After two years of defending his personal space and refusing to be touched, even if it was a simple handshake from another inmate, Nathan felt an odd urge for this woman to give him that one concession.

To acknowledge that he deserved to be accepted as a decent man and not feared.

"Please, take my arm," he urged gently and waited, one second, two, three . . .

A delicate hand bumped his arm, jerked back, then the fingers returned to slide down his arm to wrap around his wrist and flame his skin everywhere she touched.

He hadn't realized until that moment how much he'd missed the connection to another person. To a woman.

If he was still alive when this was all over, he might try to find a woman he could spend a night with. One who would understand that he wasn't worth investing any serious energy in, someone who would expect nothing from an emotionally bankrupt man.

Add fifty bucks and that would be a hooker, Einstein.

Nathan jerked his mind back on track and reached into his pants pocket. He removed a tiny LED light and squeezed it on, scanning the interior of the container. The only area disturbed were boxes in the back section to the side of a generator framed inside four-inch steel tubing. One section of the tube frame had been cut open, leaving jagged edges. They'd used an acetylene torch. A cardboard box had been ripped open.

He moved around cautiously so he didn't break the fragile contact she allowed. Shining the beam of light ahead of them, he led her down the middle and kept an eye on the door. When they reached the area where the package had been opened, he looked closer.

Two teak carpenter tools—a hand plane and an L square—were lying beside a crate. Fancy carved stuff that no real carpenter would use.

She released his arm and leaned past him to look, but said nothing.

"Does this make any sense to you?" he asked.

She glanced up and squinted at him, but he kept his face shielded. The tiny light caught the soft curve of her lips. Pretty mouth.

"Uh, no, I have no idea why he was searching here," she mumbled.

Liar, but Nathan wouldn't risk losing what ground he'd gained with her by saying so. The guy outside probably hadn't gotten what he came in for because that was the only box open. If he'd been finished, he wouldn't have missed that shot.

He'd have been heading out, weapon ready.

The Mitchell woman stood upright without speaking a word.

"Do you have a radio?" Nathan asked her.

"No."

"Aren't you with the NOPD?" He shined the light up to illuminate her face, but not straight into her eyes.

"Not directly."

"Where's your purse? Didn't you bring any mode of communication?"

"My purse is in the car. I didn't think I'd need it to inspect a metal box," she snapped and brushed hair from her eyes, though the mass of blonde curls teasing her shoulders seemed oblivious to any kind of coaching.

He liked the rebellious hairstyle, and the spark of backbone she showed him in spite of the situation. She appealed to him in a saucy way. That he was turned on by a woman in law enforcement who didn't like him said a lot about how long he'd been celibate.

"So what are we going to do?" She had crossed her arms and if he could see her feet he'd bet she was tapping a toe. "My cell phone is in the tote I dropped when you knocked me backwards."

What? "I did *not* knock you backwards. I pulled you out of the line of fire."

"Whatever."

Did she not understand what he'd done? "I'm going out to get the tote bag—"

"Like hell you are," she sputtered.

"Yes I am, unless you want to spend all night in here with me." Had he really said that in a any-chance-you-might tone? *Loser.*

Silence.

Nathan sighed. *Yep, loser.* He didn't have much ego left at this point, being an ex-con and all the amenities attached to that title, so who cared? And what had he thought? That she'd vote to spend a night with a man she probably rated along the lines of low-life sex offender?

He shook his head to clear those ideas and to focus on what was important. "From the way this stuff is stacked, doesn't look like anything is missing. Which means the guy outside might try to come back in here and look some more. I don't have a weapon so I have no way to fight back against a nine millimeter. I'm going back to the door." He started forward, slowly, waiting to see if she'd follow.

She grabbed his arm.

His heart did an extra thump. Nathan smiled over the

gesture, small, but something that made him feel less like an ex-con and more like a man.

At the door, she tugged on his arm. When he turned to her, he leaned close to listen. She had the most feminine smell, soft and fresh.

She whispered, "Don't go out there. He might shoot you."

She's worried about me? Really? "He won't." Nathan took her comment as a positive sign and leaned a little closer to where her lips had whispered, zeroing in on her mouth. He'd like to find out if her lips were as supple as they looked.

"You don't know that," she countered.

Her warm breath tickled his nose. He knew exactly where her lips were.

Tempting, oh so tempting.

"I do know he won't shoot me," Nathan assured her. "The minute I throw your bag inside, call for backup."

Her hand touched his shoulder this time, holding him captive. He soaked in her scent, wanting to taste her more than he'd wanted to taste anything in the last two years.

"They'll arrest you if I call anyone," she said in a husky tone that sounded sexy, and inviting. Or was he just hoping so?

"They'll never see me."

She said nothing, but he felt her lean toward him just a sliver, enough to ramp up his pulse.

"Who are you?" She licked her lips. "I—I want to know how to find you." Her fingers tightened, gripping his shoulder.

He hadn't kissed a woman in over two years. He'd likely

never get another chance to kiss one this nice anytime soon, maybe not at all once he went on the run. He leaned another millimeter closer and . . . what the hell?

Nathan drew her into his arms and kissed her with a mix of tenderness and need. She kissed him back for all of ten seconds then pushed away.

"What are you doing?" she asked in a terse voice that washed over him as briskly as a cold shower.

"Nothing." He released her and lifted up, feeling caught with his hand in the cookie jar.

The brittle silence that followed did nothing to change that sensation.

Disgusted with himself over the momentary lapse in judgment, better known as gross stupidity, he focused on his next move.

Get her tote so she can call in backup and run off the guy who had already taken a shot at her once tonight.

"Wait here." Nathan dropped down on his knees and eased out of the container. He slithered across stubby patches of grass and dirt to the area where she'd fallen. Using one hand to feel for the bag and keeping the other beneath him to shove up if he had to, he searched the ground, listening for any vibration of movement. His fingers touched a stuffed bag. He grabbed the material, found the top, careful not to dump it, then slithered back to the container door and shoved the bag inside.

That hadn't been the way he'd envisioned his first encounter with a woman when he got out of prison. Stupid to kiss her in the first place. He was lucky she hadn't screamed bloody murder.

He'd find a spot where he could watch until backup arrived. He shouldn't care. She was a cop, after all, and not the least bit defenseless at the moment, but still a woman. One who probably had her weapon trained on him at this minute.

Damn if he didn't like her spunk, though.

When he turned to worm his way back up the incline, he heard, "Thank you, mystery man," whispered behind him.

Nathan blinked in surprise, then grinned.

"Mystery man" was a step up from criminal.

He'd covered twenty yards when floodlights flashed on at the entrance. The electric gate rolled shut. Men scrambled into a squad car, then spun the wheels, getting turned around and up the incline to the gravel parking lot.

Once the two officers reached the container, Nathan drifted back slowly, then circled around to where her car was parked and opened the door . . . she'd left it unlocked. Did she think her car was safe just because it was inside a police facility?

She probably wouldn't do that again after tonight

Nathan found her purse and, yes siree, her driver's license. He committed the information to memory and put everything back within less than a minute. After another check on the excitement surrounding the container, he made his way to where he'd entered the compound. Once outside the fence, he hustled to the Javelin and drove just short of the electric gate, parking on the opposite side of the street at a rental business. He kept the engine running slowly. The muffler rumbled low.

Another squad car arrived and punched a code to open the gate.

Plenty of protection around the sexy law enforcement consultant and enough to keep her busy for a while.

Nathan had a couple of people to visit, but he wasn't through with Terri Mitchell. Interesting that she lived in the same zip code as his mother's house.

He drove off the lot and idled slowly down the street until he was far enough to open up the Javelin and let it roar. Who'd been inside the container?

What was the intruder after?

Bet this Mitchell woman had an idea. All he had to do to get her to talk was catch her with her guard down.

And without her gun.

⬧

Terri walked into the house and closed the door quietly. Rambling sounds from the television in her grandmother's room carried into the kitchen.

That worked for Terri. She wasn't ready to chat.

She carried her purse and tote bag down the hallway, tiptoeing past her grandmother's room. When she reached her bedroom, Terri dropped everything in her hands on the floor. She stood there a minute, not believing how the evening had played out. The laugh that escaped her came out in a disgusted sound.

No one would have believed her even if she'd tried to tell the truth. Still, it might have sounded better than the lame story she'd made up on the cuff once the officers from the gate showed up.

They'd wanted details, a description of the assailant.

Terri combed her fingers through her tangled locks and shook her head. Description? All she had was the man who'd saved her. He'd been six-three or -four, short-tempered, dangerous, a professional operative of some sort, deep, sensuous voice, great kisser . . .

Not what she'd expected when she jumped at the chance to inspect the container. Not what BAD expected, either.

Joe would not be happy, but Carlos would be much less forgiving. He'd never bend again.

Glad to be home and safe, Terri rubbed her aching forehead and started peeling off clothes, which she tossed on a chair. Grandma would understand if she didn't watch an hour of television with her tonight. A hot bath and a glass of wine cured many ills when all else failed.

Her cell phone vibrated, humming against the contents of her purse. *What now?* She dug it out, fumbled it, dropped the thing yet again, and groaned over the unknown caller ID. "Mitchell."

"What went wrong?" Not the lighthearted Carlos she'd bantered with earlier.

"I walked in on someone already going through the contents in the container and not one on our team or the NOPD's."

"Any idea who?"

"No. He was working entirely in the dark except for using a pin light . . . and a gun." She hunched her shoulders, waiting for Carlos to go ballistic over her refusal to take a partner.

He didn't. Instead he asked, "How did you get out of that?"

"I did, that's all that matters."

"No, it isn't, Mitchell."

He was all business now, calling her "Mitchell" instead of "Terri." She debated how much to tell Carlos for as long as it took to sigh.

"I did have help," she admitted.

"I figured so."

That cut her deep. "Why? You think I can't do this job?"

"Don't get girlie on me, Mitchell. You want to be treated like the rest of the team? Then you get the same heat the rest of us would for going in without a partner. Your choice. Shit happens and even the best operative gets caught with his pants down from time to time."

Her face seared with embarrassment. He'd given her exactly what she'd asked for and she'd blown the mission. So she had to buck up and accept responsibility.

"You're right. Sorry. Yes, I had help and, yes, I needed help or I might have been injured."

Or killed.

"Okay. Now you understand what having backup means and why it's necessary."

She still didn't want a partner, but Carlos had settled down so now wasn't the time to argue that point further.

"Give me the rundown on what happened and what intel you did get," Carlos said.

She told him what had happened, sticking to the facts except for her ridiculous reaction to her mystery man . . . and that kiss. In those last moments, she'd been touched by his determination to protect her from a man with a weapon. His power had surrounded her, but not in a threatening way. She'd sensed he wanted something from her, yet felt mesmerized. Call her crazy, but she'd *wanted* him to kiss her. That and temporary insanity were the only excuses available.

Not intel she needed to share with anyone from BAD.

Carlos's voice was deep and more relaxed now. "Tell me again about the contents."

"There was a generator inside a steel frame. The snort was hidden inside the steel tubing. Couple boxes of trinket-type things and a box of building tools, ornate ones like something you'd display rather than use."

"Look like anything was missing?"

"Not that I could see. He didn't leave with a box in his hands, so if he got anything it was small enough to carry on his person." She hadn't technically seen the intruder leave, but felt like her mystery man would have mentioned that.

"What about this help you had?"

"I have no idea who the second guy was or why he was there. He fought the first guy, gave me my tote bag, and left." That was a little thin on details, but close enough to be truthful.

"He doesn't identify himself, helps you, then leaves? That makes no sense."

Tell her about it. "Hey, I'm as mystified as you are."

"Meet me tomorrow so we can go over this in person."

Why did that make her cringe like a kid being told to see the principal after school? "Name the place and time."

Carlos gave her the meet location. Terri hung up the phone, still wondering about the container's contents. Why had the intruder been searching the other boxes when the drugs had been packed in the steel frame around the generator?

NOPD had used a torch to cut open one section of the frame at the docks, that was pretty obvious tonight.

If the intruder had come for the drugs, wouldn't he have known where they were hidden?

Terri finished undressing, cranked up the shower controls to boiling, and climbed in. Wine and bubbles would have to wait for another night. Steamy water gushed over her battered body, draining away the last few stubborn kinks of stress.

She stepped from the shower, snagging a towel from the vanity to twist her wet hair into a turban, then grimaced when she touched the lump on her head. No complaints. The goose egg knot was better than having her brains scattered from a bullet, thanks to . . . *him*. Who was he? What was he?

Questions for tomorrow she'd be better able to answer with rest.

Terri wrapped a second towel around her body, tucking the corners in at her breasts while she listened with half an ear to the sounds of the house. Grandma's television chattered on down the hallway, but Terri's bed crooned, tempting her to lie down for just a few minutes, then she'd get dressed and go visit Grandma.

She fell across the spread facedown. Her eyelids drifted shut. She yawned and stretched. The towel covering her fell loose with the movement.

A hand slipped across her mouth at the same instant a body settled over the top of hers.

CHAPTER SIX

"Don't panic." He whispered close to Terri's ear, just in time to avert an all-out anxiety attack.

It was him again.

She slapped the bed next to her head.

"I'll uncover your mouth if you promise not to scream."

Scream? No. Snarl? Yes.

But she gave him a thumbs-up signal, determined not to upset her grandmother, who hopefully wouldn't hear something and check on her. As bad a position as she was in, Terri believed this guy would not hurt her. He was doing a great job of royally pissing her off, though.

When he removed his hand she whispered, "What is it with you?"

"We need to talk."

"Ever consider knocking on a door?" She kept her voice just as low as his.

"Not a wise idea for me."

"Why? Because then I'd know what your face looked like?"

"That's one reason."

She really wanted to see his face. See who was stalking her, making her insides jump. "How did you find where I lived?"

"You should lock your car. Checked your driver's license."

"The only place you could have done that was—"

"—at the yard where the container was, while you were busy explaining to the boys in blue what happened," he finished.

How had he managed to do that without being seen? She was beginning to realize just how well trained this guy was. But trained by whom? An intelligence agency? The military?

"What kind of consulting do you do?" His tone hardened like cured concrete.

She really was not up for this. Did he think he could just waltz in here and interrogate her? While she was only wearing a towel?

"You want to talk? I'll start. Why were you in the Drake house the other night?"

"What do you know about the Drakes?" he countered.

Terri considered head butting him, but she already had one lump on the back of her skull. She lifted a hand to rub the spot. Her turban came loose so she shoved the towel over the top of her head to the bed.

"How's your head?" His warm breath raked the hyperactive nerves along her neck and shoulders.

"Fine."

"Sorry. I had no better choice at the moment."

And he'd saved her life by jerking her away. "I don't mind a few bruises, considering the alternative. Thank you, by the way."

"You're welcome."

He held her in place, but kept his weight levied just close enough so he wasn't smothering her or trying to intimidate her. She'd felt enough earlier, and with this contact now, to know this guy was ripped, dangerously so, but at the moment he seemed concerned for her comfort, protective. Even more disturbing was how she felt—totally at ease with his body hovering over hers.

Her breathing hitched, excited.

Good grief. Brady was right when he'd joked she needed to get laid. But not with a man she couldn't even identify visually. A man she should fear, but didn't.

She had good survival instincts and didn't doubt them now. This guy had never threatened her. He always made sure she understood his intent. He seemed to be watching out for her. Like a masked guardian angel.

Regardless, she had to wrangle control back from him.

"If you want to talk, you're going to have to share. This isn't going to be much of a conversation if you answer my questions with more questions." She couldn't believe she was becoming Christine to his Phantom of the Opera-like appearances. Hell, she didn't even like the movie. And yet he was so intriguing in the strangest way and there was something almost erotic about being pinned to a bed by an unseen man who was fully clothed. How could that be?

She realized why. He hadn't put a move on her, no come-on line, no pretense. The only mystique was his hidden identity, a significant one, but no flirting games.

"Here's the deal . . . I'll share if you will."

Her ears perked up at that. She'd worked the street for the last couple of weeks trying to build contacts, find someone to cultivate as an informant, but her last snitch had died an ugly death. No one wanted to talk to her. This mystery guy knew things or he wouldn't have been at the Drake house or the container.

Tonight had been a bust. If she didn't produce information soon, her value with BAD would drop to zilch. She had to keep that job, needed their resources. Maybe if she walked away from this encounter with something worthwhile to take into the meeting with Carlos tomorrow she'd redeem herself a little.

"What's it going to be?" he asked.

Did he have any other tone than surly?

"I'm game." Terri cringed over the breathless answer and shifted, then stilled. Her bottom felt exposed. The towel was basically just covering her back. How did she always end up in a compromising position with this guy? She moved her hand around, but her wrist bumped into his.

She felt a tug on the towel, then the edge moved over her bottom. Did he read minds? She had to ignore the situation and find a tie to this case.

"Did you work with Nathan?"

"No. What do you know about the Drakes?" he asked.

What? Did he really think that was sharing?

But one of them had to make a move. Since he wasn't willing, he'd better recognize a sincere gesture and share in return. "Here's all I know. Nathan Drake's mother died of cancer recently. Jamie Drake is in prison for running drugs and Nathan got capped at the docks the other night. When I last saw him he had a hole in his forehead, so cause of death should be a no-brainer. What about you? How do you know the family?"

He didn't say a word. His chest moved against her back with several labored breaths. That wasn't a tough question. Why the hesitation?

Short on patience, she started to read him the riot act when he said, "It's personal."

Terri paused at the ragged sound of his voice. "Did you know Nathan well?"

"Better than most." He shifted an arm closer to her side, but didn't touch her.

Terri held her breath, waiting to see if he moved again. He didn't. She sighed at the heated direction of her thoughts and concentrated on shifting puzzle pieces around in her mind, trying to fit something together. Nothing. She fished for more.

"There's a phantom or ghost of Nathan Drake going around harassing people. Know anything about that?"

He snorted. "Harassing people?"

"Actually, he's been pressuring snitches and some of Anton Marseaux's muscle. Are *you* pretending to be him?" She tried to turn quickly to get a look, but he was faster and lowered his body to stop her.

"No." Nathan gritted his teeth when she moved. He'd

kept his lower torso off her for more reasons than not wanting to place too much weight on her. He was hard as a rock staring down at this practically naked woman, damp from a shower and with only a slip of material separating them.

She stilled the minute their bodies touched.

He sighed, wondering how he'd gotten himself into this predicament. "Don't turn over and I won't press against you, okay?"

She nodded, but remained silent.

Nathan bit down on a curse over the position they were both in. He hadn't wanted to frighten her or make her uncomfortable, but he had to talk to her when she wouldn't fight him. He lifted his lower half off her again.

"Do you know Jamie Drake?" she asked.

He flinched at Jamie mentioned in present tense. "Yes."

"What's the connection between you and him?"

"Might say we're close as brothers." He probably knew more about Marseaux than she did, which meant he should warn her off this case and get the hell out of here while he had a smidgeon of sanity left. "I came here to do more than talk about the Drakes. You've got to back away from this case. You're in danger after tonight."

"I can't back away."

"'Course you can. Take another assignment." He wanted to shake some sense into her.

"Can you back away from whatever you're after?"

Not a chance. "No, but I have . . . strong reasons for continuing."

"I have my own reasons, too."

"Enough that you're willing to die for them?"

She didn't answer at first, then asked, "Are you?"

"Yes."

She took a deep breath before she spoke again. "I don't plan on getting killed, but I accepted the risk when I signed on to this line of work."

He wanted to laugh at her naïveté—those words were so much easier said than done. "You don't know what you're dealing with." What she could be facing.

Nathan wasn't even sure. The further he got into this, the bigger and deadlier the tangle. "That guy in the container tonight was a pro, not a drug mule or thug. I don't know what he was after, but someone hired a highly trained operative for a specific purpose. You got lucky tonight. *Real* lucky. If you get in his way again, he won't miss."

"Why do you care what I do?"

"I don't want to see you get hurt." That came as no surprise since he didn't want to see any woman hurt, but what did catch him off guard was how much he wanted her out of this and safe. "This is my fight, not yours."

"What makes you think you can claim my case as yours?" She muttered something under her breath about arrogant buttheads making asinine assumptions. He couldn't catch the rest.

Nathan kept trying to ignore the sweep of her neck where damp curls lingered and the delicate curve of her shoulders. They were perfect. Smooth as satin and shapely. She was not some stick woman.

This one wouldn't break if she had robust sex with a man.

And he wouldn't last much longer if he kept thinking of sex while hovering so close to a body this tempting.

"Well?" she groused, impatiently waiting for him to answer.

He had to backtrack mentally to remember her last question about why he thought her case belonged to him.

"How long have you been on this case?" he asked.

"A month."

"What's your objective?"

"I can't share those details with you."

"Let me guess. You're trying to nail Marseaux." He had a feeling she was up to much more than that but she wasn't going to tell him.

"Maybe."

He admired her stubborn tenacity in light of the position he had her in. "In my case, this situation goes back to a long time ago, long before you got involved. Long before you probably heard his name the first time. I *will* find Marseaux and make him pay for what he's done. You'll just get in the way if you don't back down and stay away."

You'll just get in the way? Terri gripped the sheets as bitter memories tore through her. Why hadn't he added "little missy" to the end of that condescending comment?

Aching pain bit her hard as she remembered her poor mother, who'd paid the ultimate price for being in the way . . .

This asshole couldn't have made her any madder had he tried. She didn't have to play nice with this guy and she wasn't about to. "I'm done with talking to you until you're ready to talk to me face-to-face. In the meantime, get off me and stay away from me."

"You'll be taking a huge risk to stay on this case and I may not be around to protect you the next time."

Like she needed his help? "I might ensure you *aren't* around next time by shooting you now if you don't get off me this minute." She kicked her feet a couple times. One day, she would get him back and be the one on top.

"You don't want to shoot me."

She heard the smile in his voice. Hadn't helped himself then at all.

"Oh, yes I do," she said from between gritted teeth.

"You'd regret it."

"Why?"

"Because." His body lowered closer. "I couldn't do this."

She held her breath, wondering what he couldn't do.

He didn't move another muscle for a moment and the anticipation threatened to kill her. What was he waiting on?

Her. He waited to see if he'd frightened her. More curious than anything, Terri stayed perfectly still.

Then he kissed her shoulder and ran his lips along her skin, exploding heat missiles everywhere he touched her. A woman in her right mind would demand that he stop, right now, and leave, but she hadn't been in her right mind since the first time they'd met.

He moved to her neck and she couldn't will herself to do anything but lie there, indulging in this moment of pure pleasure.

If anyone from BAD found out about this she'd be toast.

His fingers brushed across her shoulders and she shivered. Heat coiled, twisted and churned low, wanting this man to do so much more than caress her neck.

He was truly a thief, stealing kisses in the dark and making her ache to feel him inside her. She hadn't been with a man for . . . too long to recall.

A deep inhale of breath shuddered its way out of her lungs. Just when a lick of common sense was about to return so she could find the power to make him leave, he whispered in her ear, "You're so beautiful."

In that case, she could suffer through another couple seconds.

He nuzzled her hair, kissed the bump on her head, then said, "Sorry."

Manners were nice. He apologized for being so forward.

His body lifted off her.

Terri started to rise and turn, but the towel around her jerked loose and floated down over her bottom.

"Hey!" she yelped. Terri grabbed for the terry cloth material. "What are you doing?"

"Ensuring you don't move until I'm gone. Back off this case before you get hurt."

Nathan withdrew from the room into the dark hallway and lifted the hood over his head as he slipped down the hall. He was out of the house before she could have gotten off the bed and pulled the towel around her.

As if he wasn't hard enough from lying over her, he'd jerked the towel harder than he'd intended and exposed her entire backside.

Staying another minute after that would have killed him.

She'd let him kiss her skin. He didn't know what had possessed him to take that liberty. She should have cursed him and threatened to use her gun on him again, not . . . purr.

He was on the road to losing his mind and wanting her would drive him mad that much quicker.

Nathan hugged the shadows until he passed another house. He moved to the sidewalk and casually strolled along, hands in pockets. The oversize hood kept his face as shrouded as the Grim Reaper's.

At the first cross street, a disturbance on his left drew his attention. Some thug was talking to a little old woman and she didn't look happy. She backed up a step.

Not just a thug, a mugger.

Nathan quietly moved in her direction.

❧

A steady tapping disturbed Fra Bacchus from a most enjoyable nap where a female *discipul* had been serving him in a reverent position . . . upon her knees. He straightened up from where he'd fallen asleep, slumped over in his chair again.

Tap, tap, tap.

Who dared to interrupt his evening repast with his favorite glass of merlot? He missed the days of using a leather whip on those who crossed a *fra*.

Now he only used one for pleasure.

"What is it?" he snapped, brushing his fine hair into place with his hands.

The door opened a fraction. "Fra Bacchus?" Linette inquired in a voice created by angels.

"Yes, child." He smiled to himself over the reference. A twenty-six-year-old woman whose best assets filled a double-D cup bra was no child.

"Consul Vestavia says it's important he meet with you." Her face was an Italian masterpiece of dark brown eyes, thick lashes, and full lips, the smooth canvas framed by long black hair. A descendant of Roman bloodlines that ran all the way back to Constantine, she'd been trained from day one to serve a higher purpose with the Fratelli de il Sovrano—Brotherhood of the Sovereign, the rulers. Only the purest were chosen to serve his rank.

Bacchus had taken over her training when she'd been brought covertly to him at eighteen. She'd served him and the order well once he'd brought her to heel.

"Have him wait ten minutes, then bring him in," Bacchus said in an understanding tone. He was anything but at the moment.

He'd just finished removing everything of significance from his desk when Linette tapped again and opened the door. He smiled at her and nodded his approval to allow his visitor entrance.

Consul Vestavia entered with the arrogant swagger that had rubbed Fra Bacchus wrong from their first meeting. That this man had reached the level of consul showed the lack of intuitive ability of the other eleven *fratelli* ruling the North and South America province. Vestavia had proven himself worthy time and again—to others—but Bacchus didn't trust the man.

Maybe it was the rebellious look of scraggly hair, thick beard, black jeans, leather jacket, and gray T-shirt. A bad motorcycle hoodlum cliché. His tinted wire-rimmed glasses didn't fit, either. Everything raised red flags to Bacchus, but to declare as much to the other eleven Fras would be akin to questioning their ability to rule.

Which he did question, but silently.

Vestavia eyed the room, probably searching for a camera.

He'd never find it. The consul insulted Bacchus by thinking his surveillance equipment would be so easy to locate.

"Thanks for the audience, Fra Bacchus. Good to see you." Vestavia sat down in the leather chair facing the desk.

"And you." Bacchus leaned back and crossed one arm over the other, sliding his hands inside the wide sleeves of his robe. When in his private quarters, he preferred the ceremonial clothing to the constricting suits. Particularly the easy access allowed by the lap of his robe whenever Linette was close enough to make him hard and he had to shield himself from others also in the area.

Vestavia eyed the half-empty bottle of wine and the drained glass. His eyes crinkled. "You appear healthy as an ox. Must be true what the doctors say about red wine being good for your heart."

"Quite true. In fact, it has been used medicinally for many years," Bacchus said. *If I thought it would cure you of being alive I'd give you a case.* "I am pressed for time, so . . . ?"

"I hate to bring up a distasteful matter, but I believe you

have a discipul breaking rules and taking unnecessary lives."

"I would know if any discipul did not adhere to the rules. I would know if unnecessary lives were being taken. There have been no random deaths." Bacchus belted his anger under control, for now.

Vestavia smiled, a false expression his eyes failed to support. "You know, I'd be careful not to make the same mistake the Fratelli di Illuminati made when they committed the sin of pride."

Bacchus gripped his forearms like necks needing to be wrung, his nails biting into his skin until he relaxed. "I would warn *you*"—he said in slow measured words—"to take care how you speak to me as I am a sixth-generation Fratelli de il Sovrano, a truly illuminated one, and you are merely a consul. Those who have tread too closely to the light in the past have been burned."

Vestavia stared at him with those empty eyes. The *fratelli* had erred when they voted to make this man a consul, only one step in power away from becoming a *fra*. But a ruling position around the table of twelve only came available after a death. All the *fratelli* had a trusted general, just as Bacchus had Duff. Bacchus had convinced three other *fratelli* to vote against Vestavia, but in the end the majority had persevered.

"I'm just pointing out a few potential problems the order might frown on," Vestavia said.

"Since you brought up the topic of unnecessary deaths, Marseaux is not pleased. Finding a body around the container was sloppy." He tilted his head and let the unspoken accusation fall between them.

That stirred a reaction in Vestavia, who stiffened in his seat, then relaxed just as quickly. "You're joking, right? I figured *you* ordered that one. Killing Drake fits into the plan, like all those deaths of innocent villagers in India this week. You know, part of the master plan." He delivered his counterpoint with the precision of a surgeon quickly cutting to the nerve center.

"Don't overstep your position, consul. You are not worthy of being privy to the master plan and you should well know it. I would remind you the penance for the sin of defiance is severe and painful." Bacchus smiled at the possibility of seeing Vestavia reprimanded. Even better if Bacchus were awarded the honor of inflicting the punishment.

"Hey, chill out. I'm not defying anyone. I'm one of the *fratelli*'s most faithful followers and humbly beg your pardon for any misunderstanding."

The lilt in his words raised hairs of suspicion along Bacchus's arms again. "Apology accepted and duly noted." Only because he would not give Vestavia the satisfaction of knowing he'd really annoyed him.

"Brady is becoming a problem," Vestavia said, changing the subject. "So is the Mitchell woman consulting with the NOPD. She used to work with Brady at the DEA. I think she's with another agency. We should find out which one."

"I am keeping tabs on Marseaux, the DEA, and the NOPD. Neither Brady nor Mitchell will interfere with our current plans." Bacchus would not share a thing with Vestavia about the current plan with the vials unless the *fratelli* pressed to include him. A curse on Fra Diablo, head elder of their twelve, who supported Vestavia and led the vote to approve his consul position.

"How can you be sure those two won't interfere?"

Bacchus really wanted to order Vestavia shackled for his rude impertinence. "The means don't concern you." He lifted his wrist into view and glanced at his watch. "Unfortunately, I must prepare for another meeting. Go in peace."

Vestavia stood and walked to the door. He opened it and paused to look over his shoulder at Bacchus. "I'll be back." The door closed silently behind him.

Bacchus shook with fury. No member of the Fratelli de il Sovrano questioned a *fra* except an equal, particularly not lippy consuls. Once Vestavia became expendable, Bacchus would make arrangements to remove the man since a *fra* was the only one who could execute a "necessary death" order.

He lifted his cell phone and sent a text message to Duff:

Find out what agency the Mitchell woman is working with. Maybe she's still with the DEA and the consulting is just a scam.

He received an immediate "As you wish" reply.

⁓

Terri wrenched the towel up so that she could cover herself and rolled off the bed. She ran to the door, knowing it was a waste of time but checking the hallway all the same.

He was gone. Again. No name, no idea who he was nor where he'd come from.

She'd met him while breaking into the same house, had kissed him in a dark container inside a police yard and all but turned to him while he'd straddled her towel-covered body.

More damning than all of that? She sort of liked this guy. She didn't want to, but there it was in black and white.

And she was sure beyond a doubt he was the phantom interrogator terrorizing Marseaux's contacts.

Could any woman be more stupid when it came to men?

The television still played in Grandma's room. Terri pulled on a pair of warm-up pants and dug around until finding an oversize green T-shirt she only wore inside the house, which declared in bold white text: IF YOUR GUN IS BIG ENOUGH, I'LL SURRENDER WILLINGLY.

She toweled her hair dry and walked down the hall to Grandma's room. Good thing Grandma hadn't heard a noise from Terri's room while she'd had a visitor. The poor thing would have had a heart attack had she found an unknown man in her house. Not that Grandma would have seen this guy since she was blind, but that would have just scared her worse.

Terri tapped on the door, listened, and only heard the television. Had Grandma fallen asleep sitting up again? Terri opened the door.

No Grandma. Terri's heart jumped. She glanced around, panicked at her first thoughts before she caught her breath.

Grandma had a bad habit of walking around at night.

Okay, she was worried about her grandmother, but annoyed, as well.

Where could Grandma have gone *this* time? Terri ran to the kitchen where she left a pair of sneakers to slip on for taking out the garbage. She grabbed a flashlight and rushed outside. The last time she'd discovered her missing, Terri had spent four hours walking the neighborhoods only to come home and find Grandma sitting in front of the television, complaining that people sounded stupid on reality shows.

Grandma might not be so critical if she could do more than listen. She was self-sufficient for a blind woman, but that didn't include being able to defend herself against a threat. Which is why Terri wished to God Grandma would stay inside after dark.

What is dark to me? Grandma always countered. *I like the night, it's peaceful.*

It's dangerous as hell, too. Terri didn't want to limit her grandmother's mobility, but neither did she want to lose the only family she had. Bad things happened at night. People died violent deaths, sometimes by accident.

A painful lesson both of them knew all too well.

At the street, Terri looked both ways and did a double take when she glanced down to her left.

There came Grandma, and a tall man dressed in black pants and a gray sweatshirt with a hood that shielded his face.

Terri cursed silently over leaving her gun inside the house. She gripped the flashlight like a weapon and headed straight for her grandmother.

When she got within thirty feet, Terri said, "It's me, Grandma. Are you all right?"

"I'm fine, dear. Just taking a walk." She said that like there was no danger in the world for a seventy-year-old woman out walking the streets alone.

Terri kept her eyes on the man, sizing him up as she moved forward slowly. Would he continue walking and close the distance between them or did he have sense enough to back off? If he lacked it, she'd make him regret the mistake once she was between him and her grandmother.

Her grandmother kept coming toward her in an excruciatingly slow gait. "Some guy tried to mug me over on Ursulines."

That sent Terri's already furiously pumping pulse into overdrive. She lifted her gaze to the man who now slowed his steps, allowing a gap to grow between him and her grandmother.

"I'll deal with this guy, Grandma. Just go on into the house. Your shows are on."

Her grandmother stopped, just quit walking right between Terri and the threat. She wanted to scream.

"Him? He's not the mugger. He ran the mugger off. Well, I'm not sure he ran him off, he might have knocked him out. I just heard some bumping and cursing, then it got quiet."

Terri blinked, then glanced from her grandma to the guy, who took another quicker step back, then another.

"We make a good pair," Grandma said. "I'm blind and he's not." She laughed and walked forward again. "I got tired of hearing all that bad news about India. Shame about all those people, but I guess you're right about walking around at night. It's all the same to me, dark no matter what time it is. I just think it's quieter and less car fumes . . ." She kept chattering away as the man drifted farther back until he disappeared in the dark.

When Grandma got close enough, Terri took her arm and guided her toward the house.

". . . but that Drake boy has always been nice to me."

"What did you say?" Terri stumbled, then recovered and stopped.

Grandma lifted her sunshade-shielded eyes that were milky orbs beneath the dark lenses and cocked her head. "I said the neighborhood used to be safer back when Lydia was alive. Her boy has always been nice to me."

"You knew Lydia Drake?" Terri's hands shook. She glanced over her shoulder at the empty sidewalk.

"A little. I met her when I was out walking and dropped my cane on the sidewalk. Lydia picked it up and asked where I lived, then said she was going back the same way. I talked to her a few times over the years when I walked down her street, that's all. I could tell she was sick, so thin I could feel her bones when she'd let me hold her arm. One of the neighbors took me to the funeral while you were still doing rehab."

Terri looked back into the darkness where the man had vanished. "So you think that was her son?"

"It's her son. After he knocked that guy over the head—and I'm pretty sure he knocked him out—he asked me what street I lived on and when I told him he said he'd take me home. That's all he said, but I heard him talking to Lydia sometimes when I was walking past her house. I recognized his voice tonight, but he sounded sadder this time. I told him I was sorry to hear about his momma. He didn't say much after that, just 'thanks,' so I didn't say much to him. Some people can't talk about a death."

Had he just said that to appease her grandmother or should Terri believe her grandmother had heard the voice of a dead man now flesh and blood? The only possibility was for that man to be Jamie Drake, the brother who shouldn't be released from prison for another month. No way Brady would do the dead guy a favor and still get his brother out early after Nathan Drake had failed to produce for the DEA.

"What else do you recall about him?" Terri asked.

"That's pretty much it. Nice folks. I didn't know Lydia well, but I miss her." Grandma sniffled. "She was a kind lady."

Terri let it go rather than make her feel sad. "I'm sorry about your friend. I have to meet someone for lunch tomorrow, but I'll try to come home early so we can have a meal together."

"I'm gone tomorrow. Myrtle and Jackie are picking me up. Did you forget I was going to Chicago with them?"

"Tomorrow, really?" Terri did a mental calendar check and, yes, Thursday was Grandma's trip with her two friends. "Guess it did slip my mind."

"You need to take a break, stop working so hard." Grandma stepped away from Terri at the kitchen door, back on familiar territory. "I'm packing tonight. I'm walking in the morning, like always. So don't send the hounds out on me if I'm gone when you get up."

"I won't." Terri smiled over the cranky tone she forgave without thought. This woman had sprung her from juvie and raised her after the death of her mother. Grandma had shown her more love than any child could imagine.

Inside the house, Terri checked the locks and headed for her bed, more confused than ever.

Could Grandma be right about the Drake boy? Could it be coincidence, or was he also her mystery man? If Terri believed that, then she'd been protected and kissed by a phantom. A ghost. Or an escaped prisoner, but she'd have heard about that if Jamie Drake had escaped. She'd do some checking tomorrow.

That man felt too real to be nothing but a figment or a spirit bound to the human plane. And if he were solid, it begged an even more important question.

Would a phantom leave fingerprints?

CHAPTER SEVEN

Sunlight shafted between the slit in the curtains.

Nathan came awake immediately, just as he had for the past two years, alert for any threat. No threat. One more morning he hadn't died in his sleep, but he felt no more rested than when he'd been locked in a cage at night. He might never rest easy again after living on cat-naps for two years.

He rolled over in Jamie's bed and propped his head with his hand. Staying here was risky, but he'd set up an alarm system in case someone tried to enter unannounced.

Like maybe a sexy burglar in a business suit with a head of wild blonde curls? And a set of curves his hands itched to mold around. She had a body of pure sex wrapped in silky skin.

He could have spent hours working his way down her smooth back last night, fingering her legs gently apart to touch . . .

Shit. What was he? Some kind of masochist?

Nathan cursed lividly. He was as hard as the headboard and damn tired of relieving that ache on his own.

How about using his brain for something other than fantasizing over a woman he'd never see undressed again. He studied the room for only the hundredth time, yanking his thoughts back to his immediate problem.

Jamie always left him notes, had since grade school. Where would he have hidden information?

Why had his brother gone to work for Marseaux? What could have possibly driven him to do that? Had Jamie known he'd taken a job in a shipping company that was a front for one of the drug lord's operations? In the last letter Nathan received in prison, Jamie said he was doing okay at the garage working on cars and helping out with the books. The kid was a whiz.

The kid. Nathan smiled.

Jamie used to grump at Nathan that he was only two minutes younger, but Nathan came out of the womb an old man. And Jamie came out with a load of brains and too naïve to survive on his own. Had to be the genius intelligence at fault for Jamie's inability to size up a threat in advance or know when he was being played.

Jamie had always been too busy figuring out some mathematical equation or working on an intricate puzzle to see the world around him. Once Nathan explained cars, Jamie came up with a simple way to improve performance. That's when Nathan had made up his mind Jamie was going to college. The world needed someone with his gift, and a genuinely good person.

But naïve to a frightening degree.

Jamie had been oblivious to his appeal to females until Nathan clued him in.

And given him the talk on women their dad should have.

He'd been there the first time a woman had broken Jamie's heart. That was Jamie, all heart, and willing to do anything for anyone, starting with his mom and brother.

Nathan realized he was squeezing the life out of a harmless pillow. He released the wad of foam. The world was never going to be the same again without his mother and brother.

He wanted revenge to a degree he couldn't explain, especially not to Terri Mitchell. Nathan would not rest until justice was served. He'd rarely killed outside of his orders and only when the situation called for extreme measures, but he had no problem playing judge and jury when no one else would . . . or could.

Trying to predict the future was futile. He'd make decisions as he faced choices. The army had taught him to execute a directive with calm, cool rationale.

To terminate his target when the time came with the same detachment.

Now his first decision was what to do about Terri. He sat upright and shoved the sheets away. Hold it. When had she become "Terri" to him?

About the time he'd kissed her?

Yeah, that would be the moment. That was one itch he needed to ignore.

Speaking of an itch, he scratched his head and the burr

on his cheek. He hadn't shaved since getting out of prison, but today was the day.

He sighed over the simple pleasure of a hot shower, alone. A small joy and one he'd never take for granted again after being caged with predators for two years. Guilt came knocking mentally at the reminder of being out early and that the warden had helped him. He slapped the water faucets off and toweled dry. The warden had bet on a bad horse. Nathan had made it clear he wanted no one's help.

Dressed in a clean pair of jeans and black T-shirt, he rambled back to the bedroom, considering if he could at least buy time by calling the parole officer. Couldn't hurt at this point.

Nathan lifted the cordless phone and dialed the New Orleans number the warden had stuck in his paper bag.

"Percy Philips is out of the office. Please leave a message . . . *beep*."

"Jamie Drake checking in." Like that was going to cut it with a parole officer? "McLaughlin said to check in by tomorrow, but I, uh . . . stepped in a pothole and sprang my ankle. Swelled up like a mother. Not like I can afford a doctor. Going to be tough to make it across town to your office without crutches. I don't have a number to leave. I'll call back."

He returned the phone to its cradle. Philips would probably still send the dogs out after him when Nathan didn't show tomorrow, but maybe he'd wait until Monday to do it.

Nathan was headed to the garage when someone

knocked on the door. Every nerve in his body went tight even as he acknowledged that most threats didn't knock on the front door.

They kicked it in.

Sliding the curtain aside a tiny fraction to peer at the porch, he would have cursed if not for the possibility his visitor might hear him. The tiny gray-haired woman leaning on a metal cane was Terri's grandmother.

She tapped again, waited a minute, then shrugged and tottered down the steps and out the walkway. At the sidewalk, she turned in the direction of her home, paused, and glanced back with a smile.

Terri's grandmother waved, then walked away.

He couldn't stay here at night anymore. Not now that Terri Mitchell's grandmother had recognized his voice. He'd been tempted to ask her about his mother when she'd said, "You're the Drake boy. I'm sorry about Lydia. I miss her. She was a dear woman." Those words had almost broken him, had reminded him that he'd never see his sweet mother again.

He forced that thought aside and focused on the most important part of the impromptu meeting. If Terri's grandmother knew his mom, then Terri might know more about his brother than she was letting on.

Nathan had gleaned new information last night after leaving Terri, like the rumor that Jamie had been talking to law enforcement.

For all Nathan knew, she might have been involved with a bust where Jamie got caught in the cross fire. For her sake, he hoped she had nothing to do with Jamie's death.

If she had, it would take more than a towel and a nicely shaped ass to divert him from what he'd do to her.

And this time, she wouldn't enjoy his next visit.

❦

Terri drifted in and out of a restless sleep, running from strangers, then running to a man she could never see clearly enough to identify, but somehow knew it was *him*. Every time she got close, the shadows would swallow his head or he'd turn away.

Darkness surrounded her. She lay facedown on a puffy cloud. Sensuous male lips teased her neck, then moved erotically down her back and over her bottom. No towel interfered. She floated in the mist. His hands cupped her waist, then slid up her sides, gently massaging. She burned for more. His fingers touched both breasts at the same moment. Her breath caught at the exquisite torture.

His fingers caressed her flesh slowly, then brushed across her nipples, which hardened into sensitive buds. One hand drifted low, barely touching her abdomen, sliding between her legs. He teased the delicate folds.

She shuddered.

The roaming fingers moved away from her. She curled into herself, twisted into a knot of painful need.

Aching to have him back, she moaned.

He turned her over and whispered to keep her eyes shut. If she saw him, he'd vanish and that was the last thing she wanted. So she complied. He kissed her, sweetly at first, then urgently, pushing her for more.

His fingers caressed her face, her neck, breasts, everywhere except the center of her need. She ran her hands through his hair, surprised to find it long and silky. Finally, his hand moved down, stroking between her legs where her body screamed to be touched.

She arched, cried out, begged him not to stop.

The wind swirled, spinning her cloud 'round and 'round as he slowed his rhythm, then moved her closer to the edge. His hands drove her wild with an expertise no mortal man could possess.

She hovered, teetering so close to release, ready to take the leap when he was suddenly gone. She peeked, but it was too late. His face was nothing more than smoke.

He faded away, muscular arms outstretched, reaching for her.

No! Don't go. Her whispered cry vanished in the wind. She'd reached for him, too, but he'd disappeared into a black void.

Terri came awake with a start, breathing hard and frustrated as hell after the vivid dream. Her skin quivered. She still felt his invisible touch on her skin like a ghost lover. Heat banked beneath the sheets.

She brushed a swatch of hair from her eyes. If he was half as good as that dream, making love with that man would be unbelievable.

Then again, that's why it was called a dream—not real.

And just thinking about climbing in the sack with a faceless stranger was grounds for BAD to reevaluate her mental health.

Her gaze tracked to the digital numbers on her alarm

clock, the only thing she could see in the dark room. The lusty fog cleared slowly.

Almost eleven in the morning, but still early for her. Blackout shades and heavy drapes kept the room pitch-black so she could sleep past noon when she needed to. Not this morning. She had an hour for a cold shower before she had to meet Carlos.

Grandma would be gone already with her buddies.

Terri froze. She expected the house to be quiet, but her skin shivered with the feeling that someone was in the room.

"Don't panic."

She should be used to hearing *his* deep-timbered voice in the dark by now, but she still jumped. "What the hell are you doing here again?"

She squinted in the dark to where a tiny puff of light curved around a shape that could be a head next to the window. Had she said or done anything embarrassing while she'd been asleep?

Like that was more important than having a stranger pop in without an invitation? An agency psychiatrist would fill up two legal pads with notes on that. She was getting damn tired of this guy showing up anytime he pleased and not even letting her see his face.

"I have a question." His smooth voice slid across her irritation, rounding off the sharp corners, but not enough to get him out of trouble.

"Tell you what. I'll give you my cell phone number so you can just call me the next time you have one, and save you all the effort of breaking and entering. Free up a lot of your day."

She heard a sound in the darkness that might be a laugh.

Or maybe a growl.

There was one way to be sure. She inched her hand toward the lamp.

"Don't."

Terri snatched her hand back, fisting it. "Why not? What have you got to hide?"

Silence answered her, then a sigh before he spoke. "That's not what I came to talk to you about."

She wished he could see the peeved glare she sent him through narrowed eyes. "Ever notice how these are one-sided conversations? And no offense, but I'm not in the mood since I'm not a morning person. I don't even want to hear the sound of a human voice before noon and definitely not before I've had my coffee. So why don't you make an appointment for when I'm awake and in a better mood?"

As usual, he ignored her less-than-friendly words. "Did you know Lydia Drake and her son?"

Was he serious? "No. Are we done? I've got to get a shower and make a meeting."

"How does your grandmother know him?"

Terri leaned back against the headrest. "That *was* you last night. I knew it. Grandma said she recognized your voice, that you were Lydia Drake's son, Nathan. Grandma is never wrong about voices." She waited for him to dispute that.

Then again, if he was Nathan Drake, he'd know whether or not Nathan knew her grandmother and his mother . . .

If he was Nathan Drake, then whose body had been at the morgue?

A person could get dizzy trying to follow all that first thing in the morning.

"I'm related," he said finally. "The boys in our family all sound alike."

That made more sense than anything else. A male cousin maybe, new player in the mix no one had thought about. She'd put Sammy on researching the Drake family. "So you aren't Nathan?"

"Who I am doesn't matter."

She made a face at him since he couldn't see her in the dark. Or could he? He'd seen her reaching for the lamp.

"I think you're working for a spook agency," she said. "Which one?"

"Who do you work for?"

Touché. "I really can't play twenty questions with you this morning." She swung her legs around to the side of the bed, preparing to grab her robe and head for the shower.

"I want to know what happened on Fat Tuesday."

She paused. "The night of the Drake shooting?"

"Yes. I want to find out who killed him."

"Sorry to put it this way, but I've got bigger problems than hunting down whoever killed a drug mule."

"He wasn't running drugs."

The threat to anyone who disputed his words was clear. Terri's arms rippled with a chill.

"Okay, let's say we agree on that point," she offered cautiously. "Why would someone kill him execution style?"

"That's the question, isn't it? Marseaux is part of the answer, but I don't know if he's the only one involved."

"Why do you say that?"

"Because Nathan Drake would not have gone to work for Marseaux unless he was pushed into a corner."

She started to argue in defense of the DEA based on what Brady had told her, but she didn't know this guy or how he was associated with Marseaux. "So you think Marseaux killed him?" That's what everyone at NOPD thought and she'd bet that was the DEA's conclusion.

"No, I don't." His voice had moved to the other side of the room near the door to the hallway.

Terri frowned. "Why not? That seems to be a logical conclusion."

"Did anyone find Marseaux's calling card?"

"The outline?" The drug lord's normal MO was to have his hit man spray a crime scene–type outline around the body because he mocked law enforcement.

"Exactly."

"No, but the body was—" She hesitated. Where did she draw the line with this guy and her investigation?

"—found at the docks? I know that. If you want my help, you have to share."

She considered what to tell him and chose enough to prove she'd share, but nothing critical. "Right. The initial review by the coroner was that Drake had been killed somewhere else and then his body was dropped at the docks."

"Another thing Marseaux doesn't do. If he wants to make a statement, he has the victims hit at specific settings to let others know they're not safe from his reach. He wouldn't move one unless he intended to keep the death a secret."

The fact that he was correct should scare her more than all the other weirdness about him. "How do you know so much about Marseaux?"

"I've had time and access to better resources than you have available. I know how he operates and who he's connected to."

"Then let's help each other." She needed an informant.

But could she really trust another informant? She shivered at the memory of what happened last time, but informants were a necessary evil. She didn't have much choice at the moment if she was going to find Conroy's killer and fulfill her obligation to BAD. They suspected Marseaux of moving funds tied to terrorist activity, but needed solid evidence to move on those suspicions.

"How can *you* help me?"

She ignored the humor underlining his question. "You want to know about the murder. I have access to whatever information the NOPD has and I have a good friend in the DEA. I'll share what I find out on the Drake death if you'll help with Marseaux."

"You should leave this case alone."

"We've already had this discussion and you lost it. So do we have a deal?" she asked.

He muttered something that rang of irritation. "I'll let you know. I'm leaving. If you get up before I close the door, I'll lock you in the room."

"You can't do that."

"You sure about that?"

She had no answer.

He hesitated. "One more question?"

"What?" she snapped. If he wanted a sweeter tone he should have shown up with coffee.

"What were you dreaming about when you woke up?"

Her face was on fire. She jerked the sheets up over her gown in a purely feminine reaction.

The door opened and closed so fast she was stunned for a second, then jumped up and ran to open it. The door gave about two inches, then stopped. She could see a string between the door and an umbrella that was crossways of the opening.

Terri yanked once more out of frustration, then returned to her bed to flip on the lamp, which did not turn on. No surprise there. This guy took no chances with exposing his face. She felt for the nightstand and knocked something that bounced on the floor she had a sick feeling was her cell phone. When she found the drawer and opened it, she removed the flashlight she always kept there.

Her cell phone was on the floor with another chip in the plastic. She shined the light on the nightstand, where she found the bulb he'd unscrewed from the lamp and a pair of scissors he'd thoughtfully left behind.

Bastard.

She should be stomping mad, but their relationship— if you could call it that—was so bizarre she just sighed, cut the string to open the door, and headed for the shower.

"I see no reason for concern just yet," Fra Bacchus argued again, tired of this phone conversation. He leaned an elbow against his desk, supporting his head with that hand. "We will retrieve the vials this week."

"I'm hearing conflicting reports from your area." Fra Diablo spoke with the authority allowed the superior *fra* of the twelve reigning *fratelli* of North and South America.

"Since I'm the only person who should be reporting from this area, I feel it only fair I'm given the source of this conflicting information."

Fra Diablo paused for a few seconds. "Just remember that you will be held accountable for everything in your area. That includes the actions of any *discipuls*."

Bacchus didn't care one bit for Fra Diablo's sharp tone nor the insinuated threat. "I never forget my responsibilities nor has my loyalty to the *fratelli* ever wavered." He lowered his tone. "So I would humbly remind you of our oath to each other, which includes uncompromising support. Do I have it or not?"

"Of course you do. I am only saying to make sure your *discipuls* do not disappoint you . . . or me. Hold on." He spoke muffled words away from the receiver, then said, "I have another call waiting I have to take. We'll speak more later."

"Go in peace." Bacchus hung up the phone and slapped the desk. Once this operation was completed, successfully, he intended to call a meeting to discuss Vestavia. Bacchus would bet serious money that disrespectful miscreant was behind this dissention.

A tap at the door reminded him he had a meeting. "Come in, child."

Linette opened the door and announced, "Your general is here." She stepped aside to allow Duff to enter his chamber.

Here was a soldier completely faithful to the *fratelli*. Bacchus was tempted to put Duff on Vestavia's tail, but not even a *fra* could be absolved of authorizing a *fratelli* soldier to commit surveillance on a high-ranking member.

Not without proof.

"I haven't found the Drake body and Brady is turning into a bigger pain in the ass by the minute." Duff dropped into the chair facing Bacchus, but his gaze wandered away.

Bacchus should reprimand Duff for his language, but he allowed this general more latitude since his passion for their cause fueled the crude words. "No one could have anticipated the body being stolen."

Duff brightened at the reprieve. "Not even Brady. He's still hunting for the body, too. I don't think he knows whose bullet is in the corpse's, another point in our favor."

"Let's hope he doesn't. Keep an eye on Brady, even if it means having to work alongside the cur."

The disgusted sound that came from Duff's throat would have appalled the other *fratelli*. Bacchus shared his sentiment about the irritating DEA agent. "We all have the occasional undesirable work. Do whatever it takes to stay on top of him and Marseaux. Some may disagree, but I believe Brady is a danger to our order and the master plan."

"I won't let you down." Duff shuffled uncomfortably in the leather chair. "Need to ask you about something else."

"What?"

"That Mitchell woman, who *should* have died three

months ago, is getting in the way. She's the reason the NOPD put four men guarding the container after I was there. Four men they can't afford with short staff. I figure they'll cut back to one soon, but if Mitchell interferes again I may have to . . . deal with her."

Bacchus quelled his first reaction, which was disgust. Duff harbored a sickness when it came to women, blondes in particular. Females as a rule needed guidance and discipline to reach Linette's level of expertise in serving, but this general of the Fratelli de il Sovrano took the punitive action a step too far.

If any of the other eleven *fratelli* caught wind . . . Bacchus wouldn't be able to protect him, but Duff hid the evidence well. "Tell me you have not committed the sin of indulging the flesh."

"Of course not. I gave you my word not to touch any woman while on this operation, and I haven't."

Bacchus admired the way Duff's gaze never wavered during the blatant lie, but this was not the time to chastise him. He was the only general Bacchus could depend upon to protect him and the order. Fed by a steady diet of unrest across the continents, the Fratelli de il Sovrano had risen fierce and strong as a newborn phoenix to silently become the multinational fist needed to rule. Young visionaries were drafted into the order, but those whelps required the experience of the equally brilliant *fratelli* for guidance.

As one of the twelve ruling this continent, Bacchus possessed the ability to employ a certain amount of autonomy on decisions such as now with handling the Mitchell woman.

Allowing Duff to deal with her might be in everyone's best interest. Bacchus needed his general's undivided attention. Worded carefully, Bacchus could insinuate permission for Duff to indulge his nasty pleasure without specifically endorsing the action.

"It is *your* responsibility to complete this assignment without drawing attention to yourself or the order," Bacchus instructed carefully. "Remember the rules when executing each step of our plan. You have the authority to handle the Mitchell woman if she steps in the way again. Use your best judgment."

Bacchus mentally patted himself on the back for that brilliant piece of direction, which could be construed several ways. He hadn't specifically reminded Duff of the first rule, no unnecessary deaths. He'd leave the choice up to Duff when the time came to deal with the Mitchell woman.

Duff frowned for a moment, then his face brightened. "Don't worry. I know exactly what to do with Mitchell."

⤎

Terri picked up her pace to reach the Acme Oyster House and silently cursed over the ache in her thigh.

But she'd rather do jumping jacks on her bad leg than face Carlos Delgado, the BAD agent Joe had put in charge of this op. Silly to be worried. She hadn't really done anything wrong, but with every step closer to facing him, her conscience taunted her that she'd screwed up last night. Which wasn't a fair judgment at all.

How could she be blamed for this Drake phantom catching her in a towel?

A phantom who drove her pulse out of sight with one kiss.

No harm, no foul. Right?

He shouldn't have done that.

Okay, she shouldn't have allowed him to. Admit the truth. Deep in her psyche she'd justified letting him kiss her with the simple reason that no one would know.

Under the bright glare of daylight she suffered an attack of guilt at every stray glance her way, as if the world knew she'd made a mistake.

Get a grip or Carlos would see through any professional façade she erected for this discussion. She only had to explain in professional terms how she'd escaped a shooter and describe what she'd found in the shipping container.

The key would be not letting eagle-eyed Carlos see how her mystery man had breached her emotional defense.

Terri reached the glass entrance door as it magically swung into the restaurant, followed by a cheerful woman in a black T-shirt and black jeans who greeted her. She pointed out the table where a male guest waited for a Ms. Mitchell.

Terri didn't need directions. All she had to do was search for a chair in a corner facing the entire room. Carlos had serious paranoia issues, but it was warranted from what she'd gleaned around BAD. Rumor was some very dangerous people might want to see him dead.

She gritted her teeth to walk without any limp and headed for the table.

Carlos slouched in the chair with a confidence reserved

for a man who had no doubt about his prowess with women. He sat upright as she approached. Terri wished he'd remained at ease.

The planes in his face sharpened with the dark gaze beneath a lock of black hair cut at sharp angles. Just as non-conforming as the rest of him.

He reached over and moved a chair out for her. "Want something to drink?"

"I'll take a Coke."

When the young woman waiting on them had taken their orders and left, Terri jumped in. "So how mad is Joe?"

"You should worry more about Tee than Joe. She'll cut you in half without giving it a second thought, whereas Joe actually has a conscience."

Terri nibbled on her lip, then stopped. She'd signed on with this bunch so that she could find the snake who had screwed her. BAD didn't operate like any other agency she'd ever run across, sidestepping politics and red tape with equal skill. One of the many things that had held great appeal for her after trudging through layers of bureaucracy in the DEA.

But she had to keep in mind that the BAD agents she'd met generally lived up to the acronym. Having no criminal history put her in the minority.

"I can do this job, Carlos."

He tapped his fingers in a rhythmic wave to some silent melody or thought, then sighed. "That's what Joe and Tee think is your biggest flaw as an operative."

She managed not to cringe over the criticism. "What?"

"Trying so hard to convince everyone that you're capable

of doing the job." Carlos sat forward. Warm brown eyes took in more than she wanted to share. "If they hadn't thought you were capable, you'd have never gotten an offer or been brought inside this program. Stop wasting your energy and brainpower on something you don't have to prove. They believe in you and I believe in you, but the next time I say you need backup, don't buck me on using a partner."

Terri accepted the mixed blessing and reprimand. Nice to know Carlos, Joe, and Tee had faith in her, but she still hesitated to put another agent in danger by working with her.

Carlos watched her with an assessing gaze, clearly waiting for an acceptable reply.

"I hear you. It's hard not to second-guess myself, considering my history with a partner, but I admit I could have used one last night." There. That hadn't been too difficult.

He nodded, studying her for a couple extra seconds. Would he believe what she said or recognized it as an attempt to pacify him?

"Made any contacts yet?" He leaned back again.

Nervous hairs danced along Terri's arms at a question she'd been dreading worse than a pop quiz back in high school. Her position in the field depended on her ability to network and build underworld relationships. She hadn't found one person willing to talk to her, not after her last contact turned up with his throat cut the day after Conroy died. But neither Carlos nor Joe wanted excuses and both expected results, so she used the only thing she had in hand.

"Yes, I have."

Carlos blinked, surprised.

Her lips curved with a smile a second too soon.

"Really? Who's your new contact?"

Good question. One she couldn't answer. Terri worried the inside of her cheek with her tongue. How would Carlos answer that? She sat up straight, then leaned in. "I swore to him I'd keep his name secret. I'm sure you understand I trust you completely"—yeah, right—"but I really don't want to risk even breathing his name."

He became very still, staring silently, then his fingers tapped again. "Let's say I understand . . . for now."

She'd take a reprieve, even if it was temporary.

"What have you got so far?" His sharp gaze flicked right and left, scanning, but she knew he wouldn't miss a word.

"Possibly something, but I don't know if or where it fits with our investigation. There was a guy who got to the container ahead of me, but didn't get to the drugs. He'd opened several bundles and wooden crates. Shouldn't he have known the cocaine was packed inside the metal frame around the generator?"

Carlos narrowed his eyes in thought. His thick-lashed gaze slid to hers. "Could you tell what he *did* take?"

"From everything I could see, nothing. I think I must have walked up the minute he'd gotten inside. He'd scattered some items, ornate carpenter tools."

"You said that last night. Do you remember anything else?"

"Not really."

Carlos nodded. "So tell me again exactly how you managed to get away?"

The semester she'd spent in psychology class had taught

her body language said more than words in a covert situation. She took a breath and lowered her shoulders, her tone a professional recounting. "An unidentified man showed up and pulled me back a hair before the guy inside the container took a shot at my head."

"Who is this guy? What does he want?"

"I don't know who he is, but he knows our *target*." She used "target" rather than Marseaux's name in a public venue and hesitated to say more about her new contact. Not until she could figure what this mystery guy was up to and how he was tied to the Drake body stolen from the morgue.

That corpse had vanished so fast no one had even fingerprinted it. All they had in terms of an ID was the visual.

And she'd never forget that handsome face on the corpse.

Carlos folded his arms over his chest. He had an Armani face and a backstreet attitude. A prime example of the strange breed of men she'd met at BAD.

"Why did he help you?"

Thankfully, the waitress showed up just as Carlos asked that question so he'd hopefully attribute Terri's jump of surprise to the interruption. She took her time sipping the cola, searching for the right answer. There wasn't one.

Terri pushed the glass aside and faced him. "I don't have an answer for you on that, but he's my new informant. He showed up at the right minute and saved my butt. I don't think he's working against us, but I'm not sure who he's involved with." That was the best she could do to help BAD and not jeopardize her phantom.

Her phantom. *Wrong mind-set, Mitchell.*

"We need to get inside the Drake house."

"I already have," she admitted.

"Without a backup?"

She curled her fist, which was out of view in her lap. *Don't sound defensive.* "Yes, but nothing happened. Someone had been through the house opening drawers."

"Probably DEA."

"Possibly," was all she'd say rather than completely lie to Carlos. She didn't even know why she felt the need to protect the guy she'd met there, but guessed it had to do with him helping her grandmother last night. That and the mixed-up feelings she had for a man who had saved her from getting killed and stolen a kiss in the dark. "I didn't see anything that would help us. Just a house full of memories."

Sad ones.

"Keep your ears tuned at the precinct. Someone is helping our target." Carlos crossed his arms, his face a mask of contemplation. Jazz music spilling from overhead speakers did little to ease his tense posture. "No one wants to find out it's a man, or woman, in blue on the target's payroll, but we can't ignore an obvious place to look."

She nodded. "I know, and I've been studying the officers to see if anyone fits the pattern, but nothing so far."

"Someone is stalking the target's men and contacts. We need to find this guy they think is Drake. Whoever he is, he's running a scam for some reason and might know something we don't."

Terri held her tongue. She couldn't share anything yet. Not until she had a solid ID on her contact and had gotten a few answers of her own. "I'm on it."

"We're shorthanded down here with most of the BAD agents in India."

"What are they doing there?"

"You heard about the rural town that virus wiped out?"

"Who hasn't? It's all over the news."

Carlos moved his head closer and kept his voice low. "This is the third similar incident in a little over two years. All identical in how the villages were wiped out with no trail of how the virus got there. Joe thinks someone is testing a biological weapon."

"Those poor people." The idea that someone would kill peaceful men, women, and children in so hideous a way was nauseating. The photos and reports had been more than she could take. Terri had stopped watching several days ago. She couldn't look at another child's body covered in patches of mangy skin, split like an overripe melon, cracked and bleeding. Expert reports indicated the victims had first suffocated as their throats swelled, then the virus literally ate its way out of the bodies, then disappeared when exposed to heat from the high temperatures created by fever.

"If Joe is right, I don't understand what the terrorists are doing," Carlos said. "Why do they continue to test it when the results are identical?"

"Maybe they're changing the technique of introducing the virus and keep looking for the most efficient method."

"Maybe."

A possibility bounced into Terri's thoughts. "Does Joe think our *target* here is connected somehow?"

Carlos stared at her, his gaze flattening into an unreadable one. "Two different cases. You focus on your mission. Put this bastard and anyone connected to the investigation behind bars."

Terri felt, more than knew, that he'd just confirmed her guess, which sent chills up her body. Could money mean that much to the drug dealer to risk biological warfare?

"I'm all for nailing him," she said, indicating Marseaux. "But we still have no link even between him and this drug shipment." Her mystery man had better not be connected to Marseaux or her position with him would shift quickly.

"What is the DEA up to?" he asked, jostling her thoughts.

"All they've done is harass me and everyone at NOPD about the missing body. I don't get what's so important about finding that body or how it fits into all of this."

"We know Nathan Drake was working for Marseaux, but not who killed him. Marseaux may have sent someone to retrieve the body to get rid of any evidence, which would explain why the DEA is all jacked up. We just need them to stay out of our way."

That made as much sense as her theory, she supposed. "Good news is that politics within the DEA might work in our favor. Josie Silversteen is trying to locate the body before Brady does to earn her brownie points, so those two aren't talking. The backstabbing witch has a hard-on for me she's extending to Conroy and made it clear she'd come after me with all she had if I help Brady. My bet is Josie never got over being one of the few women Brady didn't share a bed with and plans to make him pay for his friendship with me."

"Is she the only one Brady didn't share a bed with at the agency?" Carlos speared her with a level gaze that said not to try to dodge him.

"No. I stayed out of that bed, too. We never quite connected all the dots to make that work, for which I am now very thankful."

"Smart. Get us the report on what they found in the container," Carlos said, changing the subject with an abruptness that was disconcerting. He stood and tossed some bills on the table. "Don't run yourself into the ground. These things take time so nothing is going to happen quickly."

"I understand." She stood and started to walk away.

He placed a gentle hand on her arm. "Give your body a chance to fully heal."

She hoped the embarrassment that hit her didn't show on her face when she forced a smile. "My leg is fine."

Carlos moved closer to her. "Be careful who you connect those dots with when it comes to any man in this business."

"Including you?"

"Ah, *chica*, especially me." He grinned and winked.

"Thanks for the warning, but I'm not interested in connecting the dots with anyone right now."

Carlos squeezed her arm gently, letting her know he believed her.

She answered with a smile, glad he'd bought her bold-face lie.

CHAPTER EIGHT

erri had just reached her desk when Captain
Philborn walked up, a frown in place. Late one
night while poring through files, she'd overheard
two officers chuckling about "Constipation Philborn." Sad,
but the name fit. She hadn't seen a different expression since
entering this precinct three weeks ago.

Wonder if his downturned mouth was permanent, like
the Riddler's from the *Batman* movies?

"What can I do for you, Captain?" She bent her neck back
to look up at his honey-brown face. The top of his buzz-cut
hairstyle was six feet and seven inches from the floor.

"We've dusted and removed all the drugs. I got the
DEA and the city climbing up my ass about releasing that
container."

"Why would the city care about turning loose a container that's part of an investigation?"

Lines creased his forehead. The change had an unpleasant effect on his face.

"Mayor is close friends with the import-export group that owns most of the legal property inside."

"Did you get any hit on prints yet?"

"No. All we're coming up with at this point are prints of workers. And we didn't lose any of the coke."

Something was off on this drug bust. She toyed with the pen in her hand. "Are you thinking about turning the container loose?"

"No. I'm not too worried about the mayor. I mainly need a reasonable excuse to buy time to keep it out of the DEA's hands." His eyes crinkled, as if he were trying to smile. Scary.

"Good, because I still need to review everything to make sure the coke was the only content the intruder was after."

"What else would he have wanted?"

"I don't know, but as your techs no doubt noticed, there was a box opened. It doesn't make sense, because if Marseaux sent the intruder to get the shipment he should have known where to look, wouldn't he?"

"Unless the perp was trying to snatch Marseaux's shipment or throw us off."

Well, duh. She had a whole new respect for Philborn. "Good point."

"Get me a report in soon." A quiet order, but one Terri understood to mean he expected something tangible from her quickly.

"Gotcha. I'm headed there as soon as I finish several

things here. By the way, has anything turned up on the Drake body?"

"No. Tired of hearing about that from the DEA, too. She acts like they did us a favor with the container and wants me to put people on finding the damn body. Like I have that much resource available."

"Who are you talking about?"

"Josie Silversteen. She came by looking for you. Asking questions, all nice and cheeky."

The bane of Terri's life could use a prescription of Prozac. "Thanks, I'll get in touch with her." Just not during this lifetime.

"You're welcome." He lumbered back to his office.

Her cell phone chimed. She answered it, but the call rolled to voicemail. Before she could check for the message her desk phone rang. She immediately looked across the room and lifted the receiver to her ear.

"Now, I know you weren't ignoring me." Sammy sent her a high five.

"When did you think I was ignoring you?"

"I called you twice earlier on your cell phone but it went to voicemail."

Terri glanced at her battered cell phone. Maybe if she got a leather case the phone would survive another month around her. She'd always been hell on anything electronic. "No, my phone's acting up. Whatcha got?"

"A little more info on that ghost."

"It's not a ghost, Sammy."

"Hey, I'm just sharing the facts as I get them. FinMan just turned up dead. Throat cut."

Terri waded through a mash of emotions, from disappointment to disbelief to horror. "Where did you hear that?"

"My buddy at the morgue, but this time the DEA has a guard in place until their techs arrive to transport it."

A bad feeling seized Terri. Was she attracted to a killer? Had her phantom murdered a man?

No, he wouldn't do something like that.

Based on what hard evidence? None. Hormones were not a dependable barometer of innocence.

She hung up and dialed her grandmother's cell, but Grandma couldn't talk right then because they were busy at baggage claim in O'Hare. Terri called Brady and got his voicemail, but didn't leave a message.

Time was ticking away. She had to get back inside that container. Terri packed up, waved at Sammy, who was walking toward her desk with a couple files, then drove to the yard. This time, she locked her car and made sure to carry both her weapon and cell phone in her bag, but an hour later her frustration had doubled. Nothing new revealed itself.

She packed up and drove home, not looking forward to an empty house. Like her grandmother, she'd always liked the nighttime, but was tired of spending so much of it alone lately.

Except for unexpected visits from her phantom.

She parked her Mini Cooper, hoisted her tote bag onto her shoulder, shut the door, and beeped the locks shut with her remote key. At the house, she unlocked the dead bolt and entered slowly, weapon drawn, and stood quietly inside, listening for any movement.

Like she'd hear a phantom that moved like a whisper?

She'd locked all the windows that morning and dead bolted both doors. Enough with the paranoia. Besides, he'd only entered *after* she was in the house . . . so far.

A note on the fridge from Grandma directed her to the aluminum foil-covered dish of food and a chilled bottle of wine with instructions to enjoy. She'd lock up and let the food warm while she soaked in a hot bath.

Terri stood very still, listening. The sensation of not being alone crawled up her spine. The longer a person spent in law enforcement, the more attuned they became to the unknown threat.

Closing the refrigerator door and lowering her purse to the table, she raised her weapon, gripping it with both hands. At the door to her bedroom, she glanced inside.

The room was black as a tar pit.

Not a sound. Maybe it was Grandma being gone and no television that had her jumping. She stepped inside and reached for the lamp next to her bed when a voice said, "Don't touch the light."

She really was getting tired of this.

❧

N athan leaned against the wrought-iron gate where a tree blocked the view of him from Terri's house. He'd barely gotten here ahead of her pulling into the driveway. She'd gathered up her bag, then hobbled into the house.

She sometimes limped when no one else was around. What was wrong with her right leg?

He could ask her if she'd talk to him again. The whole point in his standing out here like a stalker.

Walk across the street . . . or not?

Nathan dug a rut in the rich soil with the heel of his boot, procrastinating.

She wouldn't be happy to see him again, but he was quickly losing his objectivity because of her. He had to convince her to share what she knew, then back away from this before she ended up dead and not just limping. Spending another half hour of debating would just waste what was left of the night.

Time to make a move or get off the pot.

He heaved a deep breath, admitting silently he wanted to see her again. Stupid, stupid, stupid to even think about her.

Screeching guitar music blared from a car loaded with teens that whizzed past, disturbing leaves and debris along the narrow street. And drawing his gaze back to her bedroom, which remained dark. She hadn't even turned on the light.

With any luck she'd still be in the kitchen, dressed, so this time he might be able to concentrate on talking to her. Instead of paying more attention to all that creamy skin he'd like a second shot at.

As if she'd let him near her again.

Nathan checked the area. A few people half a mile away and some dog digging in a yard nearby. Nothing for real concern. He started across the street. Terri should be alone.

Her grandmother had left with some friends and a suitcase early this morning. Later, Terri had rushed out to the car like she was late for a lunch date.

He paused. A *date*. That soured his already low frame of mind. Scowling, he moved on, reaching the rear of the house. Daydream later, when she was long gone from sight. He'd never been this distracted on a mission and had better buckle down if he hoped to survive.

Out of habit, he tested the lock on the back door. Unlocked. Hadn't Terri learned anything from the last few days?

Turning the handle carefully, he slowly opened the door and eased inside. The vent light above the stove cast a yellow hue on the worn oak table and white Corian counters.

A quick check confirmed no one in the kitchen or the living room. He hesitated, debating his next move. When had he ever second-guessed himself? Never, but he wasn't sure he could take another night of seeing her in a towel, or sans towel, and walk away.

There was only so much any man could take.

A soft murmur reached his ears.

The skin along his neck tightened in warning.

Nathan slipped closer to the long hallway. Terri's room was at the very end.

A voice spoke too low for him to catch the words, but he had no question on the gender. Male.

Not alone. Nathan clenched his fingers and stretched them, buying a minute to think. Hadn't figured on her having company, which didn't sit well at all, and he didn't really care to figure out why. He had to get out of here right now if there was any hope of not embarrassing her and sparing himself vivid details of what was going on back there.

This royally sucked.

Terri had sure acted like an available woman. She'd responded to his kiss as if she enjoyed it and wanted more. *Screw this. Get the hell out.*

Nathan couldn't make his feet move any more than he could ignore the green haze of jealousy he suffered at the thought of her in there with someone else. When had she gotten to him?

He shoved his black mood about-face and started to leave when Terri's voice clearly snarled, "I don't give a damn what anyone told you, I don't know who this Drake guy is—"

A hard slap of flesh against flesh cracked the air.

Terri cried out in pain and sounded as though her body had hit the floor.

Nathan wheeled around and moved with the speed and stealth of a cougar on attack. At the door, he inched close, taking in everything within a second. Terri was sprawled on the floor, wiping blood from her mouth. The window shade hung half torn down from where she'd grabbed at it, allowing a smear of light into the room.

"Get up, bitch. I'm not through with you." Hatchet, one of FinMan's goons Nathan had been hunting, stood over her, waving a gun. He was the only bodyguard not accounted for yesterday when the other ones were sent for a long vacation in the hospital.

Nathan shot into the room, not trying to hide his entrance.

Hatchet spun around to his right. His left hand followed with the weapon, bringing the handgun up to shoot.

Nathan caught Hatchet's left hand, shoved it up, and slammed a hard chop to break the goon's arm at his elbow. Hatchet dropped the gun, yelled, and swung his meaty right paw in a power slam, bouncing it off Nathan's head.

Ears ringing, Nathan reached for the gun. Hatchet was lithe for all his bulk. He kicked, trying to boot Nathan under his jaw, but missed. Adrenaline flowed through Nathan like nitrous for a racing engine. He spun and landed on all fours, then shoved to his feet.

Terri struggled to stand, splitting Nathan's attention. He yelled, "Stay back."

The distraction gave Hatchet an opening to produce a switchblade. He slashed at Nathan's neck, barely missing, spinning off balance. Hatchet fell against a dresser, yowling in misery. The sharp edges of his broken forearm bone stuck out of the skin, blood running freely.

Everything slowed as it always did when Nathan sensed the approach of an inevitable outcome, knew the next moves as if he and his opponent had been given a script. When the choice came down to kill or be killed.

Hatchet would catch his balance, jump back to face Nathan, and attack. Nathan would block with one arm and use the other to ram his fist into Hatchet's neck, crushing his windpipe.

Terri would have a front-row seat to the gruesome death.

Hatchet caught his balance and jumped back around, pain gouging deep lines into his face, sweat running, but he was a moose and not going down easy. He clenched his teeth and growled, on attack.

Nathan snatched up a standing floor lamp, swinging it horizontally, connecting with Hatchet's knife hand. The knife and lampshade went flying. Nathan immediately reversed direction with the metal pole, cracking it hard against Hatchet's head, knocking him across a chair. He landed upside down on his head and stopped moving.

Nathan heaved one breath, then another before moving over to nudge Hatchet's bad arm. Not a sound.

He checked for a pulse—alive—then pulled a couple of wire ties from his pocket. He bound Hatchet to the chair in a way the goon couldn't maneuver even if his arm didn't have a compound fracture, then placed one wire tie above the break as a tourniquet to stem the blood flow.

When he swung around, Terri struggled to get up on her feet. She grunted something unladylike.

"You okay?" Nathan straightened his hood back into place to shield his face, not sure how much she'd seen in the dark room. He moved toward her slowly, not wanting to frighten her after what she'd just witnessed.

"I'm fine." Terri leaned up on her left leg, obviously babying her right one as if she had an injury. She was almost completely upright when her right leg folded. She cursed, arms flying out for any support.

He caught her before she went down and pulled her to his chest. She clutched at his forearms, fingers digging in for dear life. He didn't mind the pain. He could feel the steady beat of her heart in time with his thundering heartbeat. That's all he cared about right now.

She could have died. His fault.

FinMan's goon had come here searching for *him*.

She shuddered. Her body trembled, the aftermath of shock taking over no matter how tough she wanted to be.

Nathan turned his attention to comforting her. He drew her close, holding her securely with one arm and rubbing his other hand up and down her back, whispering that she would be all right.

And she would. No one was going to hurt her again.

Not and live to tell about it.

The acrid smell of fresh blood stained the air. He lifted her into his arms.

"Put me down." She snarled like a wounded bobcat. "I told you I was fine."

"You're a bad liar to be in the business you're in." He carried her into the living room. The couch backed up to a glass window covered by a dainty sheer. Streetlights pierced the thin material, casting a dusky hue over the room. The room smelled faintly of cinnamon and apples from the potpourri in a glass bowl. Everything about the decorations shouted feminine, from the white lace curtains to the pink crocheted doilies. Tidy, inviting, and warm.

Except for Terri's room right now, but Hatchet could wait. He wasn't going anywhere and he wouldn't bleed to death.

She huffed an exhausted sigh. "Don't worry. I'm not going to wig out on you."

Nathan lifted an eyebrow over her bravado and settled both of them on the couch, careful with her leg. "Well, *I* might wig out, so let me sit here a minute and catch my breath."

She made a sound in her throat that he translated as disbelief. "I had a shot and should have taken it."

"Why didn't you?"

"I thought he was you."

His heart dropped at that. Worse than putting her in danger, he'd caused her to hesitate. He'd recognized her training the first time she fought him. Terri could handle herself, but he'd skewed her instincts.

"I'm sorry." When was the last time he'd said that to anyone? He leaned back, drawing her close, and something surprising happened.

She stopped grousing and held tight to him.

He waited for her to come to her senses and shove him away, but she didn't. She drew a long breath and exhaled, a deliberate effort to calm herself.

An antique mantel clock ticked away in the silence. He sat holding her, content to stay this way for as long as she'd allow it.

He'd meant only to soothe her, but she'd flipped the tables on him. Having a woman turn to him for comfort thawed a layer of the frozen shield around his heart.

Her hair tickled his throat and smelled of strawberries. He loved strawberries. Nathan dropped his chin and inhaled deeply, then kissed the top of her head.

Terri stirred. He eased his hold to allow her to move as she pleased.

She lifted away from his chest and stared at him.

He tensed. The room was dark and the light from outside the picture window behind his head would keep him silhouetted.

She lifted her hand toward his hood.

He considered catching her hand, stopping her from unmasking him, but a part of him wanted Terri to see his face.

To know *him*.

Not some phantom she'd heard about.

She didn't touch the hood. Her fingers slipped inside the cloth and cupped his chin in her palm.

His breath caught at the unexpected touch.

Her eyelids fluttered shut. She smoothed her hand over his cheeks, caressing his face, then sliding her fingers over his eyelids, as a blind person would do to memorize the shape. He closed his eyes to allow her complete access. Her fingers glided light as a feather, feeling each hard edge, his nose and farther down to his mouth.

Her gentle exploration fed a savage part of his soul that had been starved too long for human contact.

With one finger, she traced the curve of his lips.

Nathan released the breath he'd been holding and kissed her finger.

She stilled.

Had he broken the spell? Tell him he hadn't. He couldn't recall being touched so gently. As if she tried to soothe the beast inside him.

She moved her finger away to her lips, kissed it, and returned the soft pad to his.

His heart stomped a beat of desire so hard he could hardly breathe. When she leaned her face closer to him he was sure the organ had hooves.

He lost all ability to care about the consequences and

leaned forward, cupping her cheeks and touching his lips to hers. Unlike the quick stolen kiss, this one reached deep into his soul and unlocked feelings he'd buried long ago. She kissed him back, her mouth a turbulent mix of passion and virtue.

In that moment, he longed so much for the life he'd once thought would be his, but never would, that disappointment twisted sharp as a knife blade to his gut. Any opportunity for a life he'd want was as dead as his mother and brother.

So what was he doing kissing a woman he'd never see again once he disappeared? Ending the kiss was almost as painful as accepting his destiny.

Terri must have sensed the change within him. She eased back without complaint when she had every right to question his actions. "Why did you come here tonight?"

"To talk to you."

She shook her head. "You didn't knock again."

"Sorry, bad habits are hard to break," he joked.

"Lucky for me this time," she murmured and smiled, then winced. Street light from the window caught her face. Her cheek was swelling.

How could any man raise a fist to a woman? "Let's get some ice on that."

"I've got to call the police . . . soon." She pushed up out of his lap.

Yep, the spell was definitely broken.

"No rush. Hatchet might lose some blood, but his pulse was steady." Nathan stood and wrapped his arm around her waist, concerned her leg injury might cause her to fall.

"I need to get him out before he makes a bigger mess," she grumbled.

She didn't pull away, so Nathan walked her into the kitchen and gently lowered her into a chair. The hood fell forward, keeping his face hidden. "Want to tell me about your leg?"

"Not really."

He had to appreciate her honesty. "Got any Ziploc bags?"

"Third drawer, left of the sink." The swelling affected her speech, garbling some words. That jaw would hurt like the devil tomorrow.

He found the box and withdrew a bag, filling it with ice. Glancing around, he snagged a frilly towel hanging on a drawer handle and wrapped the bag in the towel before handing it to her.

"Thanks." She cupped the makeshift ice pack to her face and winced.

Hatchet deserved the compound fracture.

"You want some tea or something?" Nathan's mother used to like tea when she was upset.

"No, but thanks for offering. I'm good right now, really."

"What did Hatchet want?"

"Is that his name? Fits him."

"He's one of FinMan's bodyguards."

She adjusted the bag slightly on her face. "Hatchet must have missed the party when you put the others in the hospital."

Nathan flinched. That removed any doubt he had

about whether she knew if he was responsible for Hatchet attacking her or not. "What did he say?"

"Said he came looking for you."

"Why?"

Terri scooted around until she could prop her elbow on the table and support the ice pack with her hand. "Marseaux's hunting FinMan . . . thinks he ratted out the drug shipment . . . because you scared him. Marseaux wants his product. FinMan figured he could make peace if he delivered the shipment." Her gaze wandered around the kitchen before she added, "Going to be a trick for anyone to get their hands on that shipment now."

Nathan caught her meaning. The drugs had been removed from the container and were likely in NOPD lockup.

"Since Marseaux is hunting FinMan, I'll have to assume he didn't kill him," she added. "Did you?"

"FinMan's dead? When?" He watched her eyes to see if she believed him. No judgment, but no decision, either.

"Last night. And if you didn't kill him, any idea who did?"

He shook his head. "The list of suspects is virtually endless."

"Where were you last night?"

"Alone, Terri. I have no bullshit alibi at all and I'm not going to pretend I do. You can either believe me or not. Your choice. But you've seen me enough that I think you'd know what the truth is."

The brief pause that followed flooded the room with tension. He waited for her to condemn him like everyone else, then enjoyed a rush of relief when she nodded her acceptance.

"In that case, you need to hide out." Her earnest gaze implored him to heed her words. "Everyone is after you."

"What do you mean by everyone?" He knew who wanted his head, but wondered if she knew all the players.

"DEA wants you 'cause they think you're the missing Drake body or connected to the missing body. Marseaux wants you because he thinks FinMan spilled his guts to you. Hooknose Rodaine and Johnny Boy want you for kicking their asses. NOPD wants anyone connected to the missing body, the drug shipment, and Marseaux, plus they think you killed FinMan. That pretty much sums it up." She hiked a sardonic eyebrow.

"What about your agency? Are they after me, as well?"

Her gaze fell away to study the worn oak tabletop. "Not yet."

She hadn't told her people. Nathan tried to figure out why she'd shielded someone who had caused her so many headaches.

What an unusual woman. Special.

That longing for a woman surfaced again, but his body only wanted one woman. Her. He could do without his mind tormenting him with the impossible. She was the kind of woman who wanted—no, deserved—a man with a future and he had none.

"Who are you?" she asked so softly he could have ignored the question, but wouldn't. "I've just given you a little trust, something that doesn't come easy for me. Will you trust me enough to show me your face? Tell me who you are?"

She'd earned his trust, but he hadn't stayed alive this long by giving it so easily. Nathan wanted to tell her, he really did. But the more she knew about him the worse it would complicate her life.

Compromise her life.

And she'd likely withdraw from him in disgust if she knew he was an ex-con.

"Are you willing to trust me without question?" he asked.

Terri paused, questions racing across her gaze. "No. I trusted the wrong person once." She worked her jaw back and forth, wincing before she continued. "That mistake cost my partner his life and gave me . . . an injury I doubt I'll ever stop feeling. At this point, unconditional trust is something reserved for someone I care deeply about, like my grandmother."

"Good." He smiled at her look of surprise. "That's how it should be."

"I'm glad you understand. Given our situation, I think we both need to be honest."

"Agreed. Now, about this case. I want you out of it. What's it going to take you to see reason?"

Terri sighed. "Look, I understand. But it's not like this is a new revelation for me. I spent two years in the field with the DEA. I'm well aware of the risks connected to investigating drug runners."

"Something tells me there's more going on with your

case than drug running." He moved to stare through the doorway to the living room, then back to the kitchen windows, studying everything outside.

Terri carefully watched for another chance to catch a look at his face. She'd seen quick snippets when he fought in her bedroom, glimpses that had shook her, but not enough for her to determine if he was truly related to the Drakes.

Maybe if she saw him in daylight she'd believe he was real. His face had felt real. Not a latex mask as she'd speculated.

She wished now she'd pulled his hood off if for no other reason than to have seen his eyes.

And for one fleeting moment, she'd had the intense feeling he would have let her unmask him.

"What do you think is going on besides drug running?" she asked.

"I have no idea . . . yet," he muttered, then turned to her, strategically standing as far away as he could when he faced her. "That's the problem with this kind of work, lack of information until it's too late sometimes."

This kind of work. Terri lifted her head away from the ice and set the bag on the table, thinking on his words. "That sounds like you've either been in this field before or are now. Which is it?"

He leaned against the refrigerator, arms crossed. "I have some experience in a past life."

"When, where . . . what did you do?" She tried to imagine all the possible answers. Her heartbeat quickened. Sure, she was being foolish, but she wanted him to be in law enforcement, maybe working as a contractor like she was. Then he wouldn't be a criminal.

"Trust me, you don't want to know and I don't want to talk about it."

Her excitement deflated. "Are you a criminal?" No point in avoiding that question any longer.

"Depends on your definition of a criminal."

She shook her head. "That's not an encouraging reply."

"I don't want to encourage you."

That hurt, but she'd told him to be honest.

"You should pack up your grandmother and get out of here until this blows over," he said.

"My grandmother is away for a few days. I'll send her out to see her sister in Texas when she comes home. Much as I appreciate your concern, I can't turn my back on this case. There *is* a lot more at stake than just drug running, but that's all I'm willing to share until I know more about you."

He didn't move from where he leaned with arms crossed. She could tell by how tight his fingers gripped his forearms that he didn't care for her reticence to abandon the case.

"In spite of what happened tonight," she continued, "I can take care of myself."

"Why don't you have a partner? Backup?"

"My business."

"Who do you work for?"

"Think I'll follow your lead and plead the fifth, as well."

He let out a frustrated breath. "Someone got that container yanked out from underneath the DEA and I doubt you have that kind of pull on your own."

She slapped the ice pack down on the place mat next to her arm. "You have no idea what kind of pull I have."

"I heard you left the DEA under questionable circumstances. If that's the case, I can't see how they'd fold under pressure from you."

He might not have meant to embarrass her, but he'd done a good job of it. "What I do and how I do it is none of your business."

"It is now."

"How do you see that?"

"Marseaux is targeting you because of what I've been doing. If you aren't going to get a partner, then I'm your backup."

"Having a partner or not is my business. Stay out of my way." Terri's reputation had a long way to go before being completely mended, if ever. All she'd need would be for someone to catch her being friendly with a guy who probably had a rap sheet as long as her arm. She should have a gun on him.

But he'd saved her life tonight or, at the very least, from a severe beating.

"I appreciate your help." She stood, needing to feel on equal footing with him even if he did tower over her. If he thought she was a pushover just because she'd indulged his alpha display when he'd carried her to the living room, she'd straighten him out on that real quick. She didn't need a man to coddle her.

Especially one on the wrong side of law enforcement.

"I've got to call the police, get this guy booked and make a report," she said. "Unless you want to explain your part in this, I suggest you leave now."

He lifted away from the refrigerator and moved forward, radiating danger with every calculated move. When he reached her, his body blocked out what ambient light filtered into the kitchen from the windows.

She held her place, waiting to see what he'd do. He cupped her face with his hand, gently rubbing his thumb across her cheek. Terri couldn't have moved, even if she'd wanted to. She stared at the dark shadows of his face.

Two dark eyes peered intensely at her.

"Thanks." He'd whispered as if afraid someone might hear him.

"For what?"

He brushed a lock of hair from her forehead, then dropped his hand away. "For letting me hold you tonight." Then he moved and was gone before she could recover.

For letting me hold you tonight. Her heart thumped. With six words he'd scrambled her emotions all over again.

Who could he be? What was he after? Answering those two questions would solve this case faster. Or force her to choose between allowing him freedom to move and issuing an APB to have him picked up.

Terri wobbled her way to the phone and dialed the precinct. Once she identified herself, explained the situation, and assured the officer on duty she was okay, she hung up and waited for the furor to erupt once they showed up.

She leaned against the sink cabinet and moved her swollen jaw around. When her gaze landed on the ice pack creating a puddle of water on the place mat, she froze, then moved her hand to the third drawer on her right. She opened it and stared at the box of Ziploc bags as if she'd found a buried treasure.

In a way, she had.

She didn't trust this Drake impersonator beyond certain limits, but they had forged a fragile alliance born of intersecting paths. And much as she wanted to deny it, she liked this man. There was something honest and sincere, even if he wouldn't share his identity. If she knew who he was, would it change the way she thought of him right now?

Terri wiggled a clear plastic bag out of the box, then used her fingernails to lift the whole box and dropped it into the bag. She pinched the top and slid the plastic through her fingers, sealing his identity inside.

Decisions, decisions.

Sergeant Taggart got up from his folding chair for the third time and stretched his legs. Clouds covered what was left of a full moon. If he wasn't so close to retirement, he'd pitch a fuss over babysitting a container full of crap. A retirement cut to the bone by those highfalutin politicians. Twice the vote had come up for higher wages and increased retirement benefits in the past five years.

Twice. They'd voted "no" both times. Those thieves had it good, slept in fine homes, and had a meaty retirement socked away. And what did they do for a living?

Sure as hell didn't protect the citizens like he did.

Hell, he needed protection from the politicians. What

did he have to show for all these years? Not much but worn-out shoes. At least he'd been inside, nice and warm, until tonight.

He eyed the shipping container with disgust. Who was going to steal a generator that weighed as much as his car? The drugs were locked up. The rest of the contents sounded like the garbage his wife, Erma, used to drag home from yard sales. God rest her soul.

He opened his faded white and red Igloo cooler to root around for a cold soda. The radio played one of his buddy Frank's favorite country tunes, reminding Taggart they were supposed to go fishing this weekend.

Unless he got stuck guarding this stupid container again. The captain had raised sand after that consultant woman let someone break into it.

Taggart fingered his keys, which included the one to unlock the container, which he'd made those boys at the gate hand over in case it rained tonight. The sky had been overcast all day. He reached down into his duffel and fished out his flashlight.

Captain had reamed the guys working the gate after the night the container had been broken into.

What was the big deal anyhow? Taggart unlocked the lock, pulled it off, opened the door a few inches, and hooked the lock back in place. He eased the door farther open, watching the gate, but those boys had been talking about the ball game when he came in. Even if they were paying attention, you couldn't see a blasted thing that far away. Once he was inside the container, he thumbed on his flashlight and ran the beam over the contents. Fingerprint dust was everywhere. The first four boxes were piled with Erma trinkets. But his eyes lit up at the fifth one.

Carpenter tools. Nice ones made of teak. Damn crime tech's fingerprint dust covered the fine wood pieces.

Taggart lifted a high-quality hand plane, an L square, and a narrow saw. This is what Erma should have put on the mantel. He snooped further and found a couple more tools. The place was a mess. Bet the importer would dump all this stuff and claim it on his insurance. Wouldn't waste his time cleaning the powder off these beauts.

How would anyone know who took these teak pieces since the container had been broken into once? Just be a bunch of finger pointing. He glanced around behind him, then back at the tools. Make a nice bonus, better way of saying thanks for all the years than a damn watch. If he asked, he'd just hear "no."

Then all this would end up as firewood for some home-less party.

Taggart carried his handful to the door and stuck his head outside. Coast was clear. He shoved them in his duffel and reached for the lock, then paused. Frank liked tinker-ing with wood projects as much as Taggart did.

He lifted his flashlight and squeezed back inside. Next shift was two hours. Nobody would be the wiser.

CHAPTER NINE

Nathan shifted in the narrow area where he stood between the Dumpster at the rear of the NOPD parking lot, which, lucky for him, backed up to a brick three-story building. The space stunk from vagrants—and probably a few officers—using it as a urinal.

Tight fit for someone his size, but this spot gave him a clear view of the rear exit of the precinct where Terri consulted. Officers and detectives had trickled in and out during the past hour he'd stood there watching squad cars, dark sedans, and one blue Mini Cooper parked in the lot. Terri had parked two spaces over from the Dumpster ten minutes ago.

Twilight encroached on the small lot, waking a few critters in the Dumpster who were now digging around. A yawn caught Nathan by surprise. Been a while since he'd run forty-plus hours without sleep. He had another stop tonight he'd planned to make once Terri arrived at work, and stayed put for a while. He'd left the Black Death parked a block over. Close enough to reach quickly so he could follow Terri, but too far to keep an eye on her outside the building.

The door to the precinct opened and two male officers came out discussing something. They climbed in on each side of a cruiser and drove away. Another couple cars pulled up, belching out more officers of both genders.

A midnight blue Crown Victoria swung into the lot and crept along as if the driver were searching for a premium parking space. Might as well have marked the tag "Federal employee." The car stopped behind Terri's, then swung into the next row over in a spot that faced the rear door of the precinct.

Nathan might have left sooner, but the driver stayed in the car for twenty minutes ... until Terri emerged from the building.

A stocky guy with unkempt brown hair climbed out of the blue Ford. His suit needed pressing, but he was FBI, DEA, or the equivalent. Nathan squeezed closer to the end of the Dumpster near where Terri had parked.

She hurried through the paved lot toward her car and the Dumpster. She wore jeans, a windbreaker, and sneakers. Clothes that worried Nathan. She was up to something.

The Fed climbed out of his sedan and yelled, "Yo, Mitchell, hold up."

When Terri paused next to her car, the frown she quickly hid said she hadn't wanted to be caught. "Brady. What are you doing here?"

Nathan couldn't really afford the time to follow her around all night and still make his next stop. He was weighing his choices when Brady said, "We need to talk about Drake."

⤐

Not now, Brady. Terri leaned against her car, hiding how she put her weight on her stronger leg.

"I have to get rolling. NOPD doesn't pay me to dally."

"You're your own boss, right?" His question had been more test than rhetorical. "Not like you clock in and out."

"True, but giving the customer what he pays for is expected. What do you want?" She had some snooping to do, thanks to more data from Sammy. Brady was holding her up.

"Okay, I'll get to the point. Lot of rumors circulating around the DEA on that Drake corpse. My boss and a few others higher up think you're withholding information and either know where the body is or that you know someone who does."

"What!" Who would run with that baseless rumor? Terri tapped her fingers on the car hood, thinking. She stopped tapping. Josie, that wart, was doing this to her.

"Hey, I'm doing all I can to help you, Terri. I've tried to tell my SAC you wouldn't do that, withhold evidence . . . or protect someone."

"'Protect someone'? Like who?" But she had a feeling about exactly where this was going. Brady expected sympathy from her for problems with the special agent in charge of his division? Wasting his time.

"An informant." His reply hit the air heavy as an albatross and landed between them.

"I am not protecting a criminal, if that's what you're insinuating." Terri shoved away from the car and leaned forward. "I do not know where the Drake body is. I'm not the enemy, dammit." She hit the car body with the flat of her hand. The only informant she could get to talk to her was the man everyone thought was Drake, but she wasn't sharing that.

"Whoa, hold it." Brady lifted his hands in surrender. "I didn't say you were protecting a criminal. I'm on your side. I've been catching hell from my SAC over the body and not getting the tip first on Marseaux's drug haul at the docks."

"I can't help you with the body and don't think you can blame me for not getting the tip first." He could blame her for getting the container snatched out from under the DEA, but she doubted he could find out about Joe's favor.

"Look, Terri. I stood up for you when Conroy was killed, told everyone you were both ambushed."

"I appreciate that, and . . . I haven't forgotten what you did that night." Terri suffered a wave of remorse. He *had* shot the guy knifing her.

"I'm not trying to make you feel bad or like you owe me for anything, I just, well, I don't want anything to happen to you, especially after all you've been through. You still mean a lot to me." He shoved his hands in his pockets, looked down, and scuffed his shoe over the gravel as if thinking. When he stopped fidgeting and looked up, the sincerity in Brady's gaze made her feel petty for having avoided him.

"Look, Terri, if you'll work with me and share some information, I'll share what I can, too. That's the only way I can help prevent you taking the rap for the missing body."

She studied the toe of her sneaker this time. If she made a wrong move or trusted the wrong person, again, Josie would destroy what credibility Terri had regained with law enforcement. On the other hand, if she didn't work with Brady, Josie might not have to break a sweat to destroy Terri if the body didn't surface soon.

"What are you going to do about Josie? She's on a witch hunt to get me or Conroy. Can you believe that? If she doesn't prove I was helping Marseaux with shipments, then she's going to hang Conroy with being dirty. And she thinks the Drake body is tied into all of this, even threatened me if I helped you."

Brady cursed and tossed in something derogatory about how he had nothing for women raised with silver spoons in their mouths. "Her only investment in *any* case is if it will get her promoted. And she wouldn't have the chance she has now if you were still with the DEA. She can't hold a candle to your marksmanship or investigative skills. But she'll be out of your hair for a day or two." He grinned. "She just got a hot tip about the Drake body being held in a Baton Rouge funeral home."

Terri held her smile over the "hot tip" that Brady must have orchestrated. She appreciated the plug about her skills, but Josie was no slouch. "So we've got a day or so before she figures out someone sent her on a wild-goose chase?"

"Right."

"Okay, what do you want from me?"

"I need to know what was in that container." He gave her a pointed look. "The DEA should have gotten it first."

"Please, don't expect any sympathy from me over the DEA losing that pissing contest."

Brady held up his hand in a sign of truce. "Let's agree to disagree. I need something to appease them over the missing body so my boss believes I'm still on top of this case."

"You haven't told me what case yet," she pointed out.

He stared hard, an intimidating gaze if she didn't know him so well. "We're still after Marseaux, but unlike when you were on the case, now it's about more than just drugs. We think he's supplying arms to a terrorist group or funding them in exchange for better international connections. I'm coordinating efforts with the ATF."

She nodded and made understanding noises to let him think this was new information for her. So the DEA was after the same thing as BAD.

"Okay, your turn," he said. "I don't see any harm in letting me know what the NOPD finds out in the container, or anything else related, since I'll eventually see it in a report. But having it before the report to discuss only with my SAC would be a huge help for me."

Terri tapped a finger against her car's shiny paint job, thinking. What would be the problem in sharing nonclassified information with him if it meant getting a few snippets from the DEA? None she could see. One thing BAD had taught her was that rules had to be bent occasionally for the greater good.

"Okay," Terri agreed. "The coke shipment was sealed inside a frame of steel tubing welded together, which formed a crate for a generator. The night I went to inspect the contents before the crime lab showed up to dust, someone had broken in ahead of me arriving. I surprised him."

"You didn't get hurt, did you?"

"No." She squirmed under his concern. The only way she could work with Brady at this point was if they kept it strictly professional. "I don't think he got anything." She paused. That was enough to share for now.

"When will the container be released to the DEA?"

Not until she gave the NOPD the go-ahead. "I don't know, but I'll check on that for you."

"Good enough." Brady glanced over his shoulder when a squad car rolled in and parked near the building, then he turned back to her. "Want to grab a bite?"

"Sorry, I need to get moving and do a few things at home." Terri cringed inwardly at the brief flash of hurt in Brady's face, but he masked it just as quickly and kissed her on the cheek.

"Just as well, since I need to get back. We'll talk more later." He walked to his car.

Terri waited for Brady to leave before heading to her next destination, one she wasn't sharing with anyone. Just as she pulled out to leave, Sammy came through the back door of the building, muttering something to himself or maybe the ground since his head was down.

She chuckled. What could have made Mr. Sunshine cranky? Terri stopped her car in his path.

Sammy's head jerked up and the angry eyes of a man ready to use his outdoor language met hers until recognition took over. He came around to her open window.

"What's got you riled up?" she asked, smiling.

"Sorry about that face." He shook his head, then leaned an arm against the roof of her car and groused, "I've got the midnight-to-seven graveyard shift tonight guarding that damn container. And tomorrow night and this weekend at night."

"I thought Taggart was on the night shift."

"He was, but that old fool must have took a liking to something. The captain had some dude come by from the shipping office to verify the contents and the guy went ballistic when he found stuff missing that our techs had inventoried."

"Like what?" She considered going ballistic, too, but not on Sammy. She wanted Taggart's head for tampering with the contents. "What is Taggart saying?"

"I don't know what he got. Taggart swears he hasn't touched a thing. Reminded the captain that container had already been broken into so anyone could have taken some of the contents, yada, yada, yada. Don't say anything. Captain swore me to secrecy. He's pissed, but he doesn't want Taggart to get fired and lose his pension. Captain said he thinks Taggart will send the damn junk back anonymously by mail in a few days."

She sympathized with Sammy, but the captain was right to put someone capable on guard. "This interfere with a hot date?"

"Not unless you're going out with me." Sammy grinned and waggled his eyebrows.

He was a cutie and charming, but teasing her. "I'm flattered, but old enough to be your . . . big sister."

Sammy grinned. "I do have a honey. Been dating her about six months. Thinking about poppin' the question next week on her birthday."

"Good for you. She's a lucky girl and you better make sure I get an invitation." Terri suffered a flash of longing for what those two had. She'd never felt that strong attraction to any man.

Until she'd met a phantom in the night.

That was wrong with a capital *W*.

"You will. See you tomorrow." He strolled away toward a cruiser.

Terri wheeled out of the lot and worked her way to Interstate 10, then picked up Interstate 610 and headed west. Twenty minutes later she exited just past the airport and followed her GPS directions to the address on her sheet in an industrial area. She found a place to park in the lot of an equipment rental business closed for the night.

A thin sheet of light hovered. She backed her car into a concealed spot beside a flatbed truck and locked up, then stretched her legs before skirting carefully along to the next block. Cars and pickups streamed by in short bursts. When she reached the corner of a lot speckled with a few oak and scrub pines, Terri picked her way through weeds until she paused at a tree next to a chain-link fence surrounding the property of a shipping company. One with ties to Marseaux, if the information Sammy's detective friend had shared was correct.

She considered all the possible ways someone would be alerted to her presence and concluded the worst danger would be hidden trip wires to a silent alarm.

Pulling a navy blue knit cap from her purse, she put it on her head, stuffing her blonde curls inside. Terri scanned the terrain one more time before she scooted from the tree and squatted down at the base of the ten-foot-high security fence.

The front office area was dark, the empty parking lot closed for the day. But lights shined in the yard behind the building. Working through knee-high weeds, she finally made her way to a row of overgrown bushes she could hide behind. She grunted over the discomfort and inched forward until she could see the activity inside the secured shipping yard.

Men moved around on a dock. Two seemed to be loading a wooden crate.

Her only problem was the distance from the dock did not allow her to hear anything, but this had been spur of the moment. After tonight, she'd have a list of equipment to bring back for surveillance. To reach a better spot she'd have to cross a section of land with no bushes to shield her from view.

What were the odds of making that sixty-foot span and not being seen? Not bad if she could crawl low enough to be hidden by the weeds. She leaned forward on her knees, preparing to crawl. *Please don't let there be snakes in this grass.*

"Don't," whispered in a low male voice so close she almost came out of her skin.

Terri froze, panting. Her heart beat fast as a drumroll. She swung around slowly to find a hooded male hunched close to her. His face was covered by a black stocking mask, which should have rattled her even further . . . if she hadn't realized who he was.

"What are you doing here?" she hissed.

"I'll tell you if you tell me why you're here," he answered.

"No. Leave." What was with the men in her life?

"No. *You* leave."

"What are we? Four? I don't have time for this."

"Yes, you do. Even if you reach the far side of the fence where you can hear better, then what?"

How did he know what she was doing? "I'm not sharing my plan with you."

"Because you don't have one."

"Do not make light of my abilities."

"I'm not, but I am questioning your common sense by coming here without backup."

He had her there, but she'd be damned if she was going to admit it to a man she couldn't call by name.

Someone on the dock shouted.

Terri turned to see and was hauled backwards against a hard chest before she could look.

"Want to get your head blown off?"

So now he's *angry?* "Not particularly." She started to say more, but felt his heart thundering behind her, his muscles tense beneath the T-shirt fitted to his wide chest.

He curled his body, drawing her closer to him until his warm breath whooshed over the skin at her throat. He quietly said, "One of the men on the dock has a scope on his rifle. If you'd moved another fraction past the bush, he might have seen you."

"A damn eagle couldn't have seen my head with a cap on it in this little light."

"I wasn't willing to take the risk of being right."

He'd been afraid for her?

That was . . . nice. Her insides turned gooey. His arms held her close, safe. Terri tried to recall when she'd last felt safe in anyone's arms. She'd been wary as a wild dog when Grandma took her in, afraid to trust anyone. Her mother had been gunned down in the middle of the night—wrong place, wrong time—while in the arms of a man she'd cared for.

The vigilante shooter thought he was killing a man who had murdered his boyfriend. During interrogation, the shooter claimed he had no idea the bullets he'd pumped into a man in bed had killed the woman—Terri's mother—sleeping beneath the sheets. Or that the man had been an undercover cop trying to find the real murderer.

Much as Terri would like to indulge in a decadent feeling of being held safely within this man's arms, if only for a short while, she had a job to do. Wrong place. Wrong time.

He relaxed his hold, but not to the point of releasing her. "If you go, I'll share what I find out tonight. Promise."

Why did *she* have to go? "We are not negotiating."

His sigh was loaded with frustration. He muttered, "You're making me crazy."

She smiled over the what-am-I-going-to-do-with-you tone. Fair enough, since he was making *her* crazy. "What if I don't go?"

"Then you'll be an accessory to the fact and, no, I'm not

going to tell you what you would be an accessory to. What did you hope to get out of this tonight?"

"Just observing."

"Then do as I ask and I'll give you more information than you would have gotten from outside the fence and without getting hurt. But you don't want to be here tonight."

"Why can't you tell me what you're going to do?" She twisted to face him. The night had snuck up so there was little to see, even with the overflow of light from the security halogens that had blinked on in the yard.

He shook his head. "That would be almost as wrong as taking you inside with me."

"You're going inside?"

Another sigh filled with impatience. "See? Now you know what I'm going to do."

She shivered over the idea of him going inside and possibly getting hurt. Or worse.

He rubbed her arms.

Damn, damn, damn. She wanted to drag him away from here, protect him from himself. "Do you have a death wish?"

"Not anymore."

What was that supposed to mean? Terri ran through several possible scenarios, but she was not going inside there and did not want to be an accessory to a crime, regardless that the crime was against a drug-dealing scumbag.

"Okay, I'll go," she finally agreed. "But I wish you would, too."

"Then we'd never see the end of this and the sooner this

mess is done, the sooner I can get around to something I want to do. Let's go. Crawl on all fours. It's easier on your leg than squatting." He didn't give her a chance for another word when he took her hand and pulled her along.

Terri kept up with him as he wove her back to the road a different way. How well did he know this place? When they stood up, he caught her around the waist with his hand and guided her across the street . . . to her car.

So he'd followed her? Where was his car?

Several paces before her car, she noticed the black stocking mask dangling from his waistband. When had he taken it off? They were walking under a light next to the building she'd parked on the side of. If she tricked him into turning her way, she might get a look at his face.

"What is it you want to get around to doing?" she asked.

The squeal of tires turning into the parking lot raked her nerves. Before she could say, "Hide," she was plastered against the wall and her lips covered by a mouth so incredibly hot she thought her lips would melt. He kissed her without abandon. She kissed him right back, hungry for what he offered. A hand cupped her bottom and lifted her up against him.

Scratch that. Lifted her against his erection.

He drove his fingers into her hair, holding her close, deepening the kiss.

Don't stop, please don't stop.

Her hands roamed his chest and shoulders, then cupped his head. She wanted to pull off the hood, feel his hair and face, but not enough to chance ending the kiss.

The fingers driving through her hair smoothed along her neck and down between them to cover her breast.

She tensed with the zing of heat that pulsed from her nipples to her groin and shuddered every time his fingers moved.

"Get a room," someone yelled from a passing car. Loud music blared. What sounded like a beer can hit the wall ten feet away, then loud laughter as the car cruised through the lot.

That should have brought her back to earth, but she couldn't break loose mentally or physically. She clutched his shoulder, and arched up, groaning at the feel of him.

She wanted that, wanted him.

He stopped. Stopped!

"They're gone. Let's go," he croaked, sounding winded. Had kissing her been that tiring?

A lightbulb of understanding blinked on in her mind. He'd only kissed her to hide their faces. Obviously he'd missed the connection she'd felt.

Next thing she knew, he was dragging her along in the dark again. She stifled the urge to scream.

Yeah, everything about that kiss was stupid, because he could be dangerous. But if he was going to hurt her he'd had plenty of opportunity.

They were almost to her car when a sharp cramp in her thigh caught her out of step. She tripped and he swung around, catching her before she went down. The man had lightning reflexes.

"Sorry. I should have been more careful." He stood still, breathing hard. She didn't think it had anything to do with physical exertion, so maybe he *had* been just as affected by the kiss. Talk about a heady feeling.

"I'm okay," she told him.

"Test your leg."

No one else paid any attention to her leg. How did he know her so well? Terri shifted her weight and gritted her teeth over the ache, but said, "It's fine."

He slowly removed his support until she was standing again. She used her remote to open the locks. When she reached the driver's door, he opened it for her, but kept his face turned away.

"You asked what I wanted to do?" he said.

"Yes."

He turned slightly, but still didn't face her. "Kiss you."

As if her heart wasn't still thumping, it took another leap at that. She slid onto the leather seat and, without looking up, said, "Who are you?" But this time she asked softly, with yearning he had to hear.

"I can't tell you until if and when it will not put you at further risk or jeopardy, particularly with your agency."

"I never actually said I was with an agency."

"You didn't have to. Where are you going from here?"

"Back to the precinct."

"Do me a favor and stay there for another hour at least." He closed the door and turned to start walking away.

She shoved the key in, turned the ignition, and hit the window button to lower it. She pulled alongside him. "If you aren't with law enforcement or a government agency, what is so important that you're willing to go inside that property knowing you may die?"

He paused. "The same reason I can't run you off from this case . . . justice." At that, he continued walking.

She tried to swallow the lump in her throat as he disappeared into the night.

A phantom? Possibly.

A turn-on? Definitely.

But what else?

She pressed the accelerator and turned her car back toward the main highway. He'd be watching for sure.

Terri tapped a finger on the steering wheel. Something was going down inside that warehouse. Brady might share his leads if she included him now.

But where would that leave her mystery man?

"Terri Mitchell is definitely with some agency, because the paperwork is buried in so many layers nobody can figure out who authorized her consulting contract," Duff said quietly into his Bluetooth headset. Fra Bacchus had texted him a message to call immediately, but there had been no real emergency. The wine sometimes gave the Fra an urge to be more talkative than other times. Duff eyed a pair of girls sashaying past Café Du Monde where he'd just met with a contact. The redhead with the sleek boots was a looker, but the blonde . . . now she was prime.

"I don't like it," Fra Bacchus answered. "What about the product?"

"I've got the container under twenty-four-hour surveillance. They switched to one guard last night. If that holds true tonight, we should have no problem."

CHAPTER TEN

Nathan waited until the taillights of Terri's Mini Cooper shrunk to two glowing red dots.

After that kiss, he'd never get any sleep tonight. Or tomorrow night.

He'd never ached for a woman, but he did now. Not just to make love to her, although that was central to every thought that skated through his mind. She had an energy and freshness all her own. Everything about her drew him, even when she was snapping at him. Sometimes, especially, when she was crabby.

Like now, but at least she'd be safe while he finished here, then Nathan would follow her home.

He waited for two cars to pass by, then moved across the front of the property, sucking deep into the shadows. Nathan couldn't believe Terri had been heading straight for a trip wire that would have set off alarms. His lips curled at her lack of training, but then she'd never been trained for Special Ops.

She definitely kept him on his toes. Being around her thrilled and frustrated him at the same time. He wanted what she clearly offered, wanted what she made him feel again.

But he had as much chance of ending up with a woman like her as having a normal future to enjoy with a partner.

Besides, sooner or later she'd learn his true identity.

Or at least one of them.

He was either Nathan Drake, who she believed was dead and involved with a drug lord—oh, and don't forget army deserter—or he was Jamie Drake, ex-con with a two-year prison sentence for drug dealing on his record.

Great choice. On one hand, a felon, and on the other, a felon. Take your pick, identical twins.

Identical losers.

Then again, he'd never been identical to Jamie. His brother had been born with brains. Nathan's IQ was no slouch, but he was destined to do the dirty work. And he wouldn't have minded if his brother had lived to do something worthwhile in this world.

Nathan stopped when he reached the side entrance to the warehouse. Why had Jamie come to work at this shipping company? Jamie had to have known something wasn't straight with the job or he wouldn't have left the cryptic message on the refrigerator. Marseaux's group here must have been paying his brother in cash or the Feds would have traced a connection back to this place by now.

Taking a deep breath, Nathan used the small B&E tools

Jamie had caught him employing once to open their back door when Nathan had come home unexpectedly on leave. He didn't explain them and Jamie hadn't asked. Nathan had more back at base, so he left this set in his and Jamie's red toolbox, taped to the inside and accessible only when the drawer was removed.

Thankfully, some things hadn't changed.

Just inside the door of the warehouse was a walkway that ran left and right with rows of tall shelving adjacent to the walkway. Deep male voices talked back and forth near the loading dock.

Nathan moved silently across the slick concrete floor toward the voices, but far enough back to be out of sight. When he reached the end of the shelving, he had to wait for the right moment to move to one of four head-high stacks of wooden crates. He'd made it to the last one next to the corner of the building when the door he'd entered opened.

Nathan dove around the side of the crate that protected his position. If no one walked over to the wall.

Hooknose Rodaine was marched in, hands tied behind his back, blood dripping from the corner of his mouth. Right eye was swollen. His head was still bandaged from Nathan's discussion with Hooknose, but he was obviously out of observation for a concussion.

Hooknose shouldn't have pulled a gun on Nathan, which turned out to be a favor, since the snitch had carried the first decent weapon smaller than a rifle. His .357 Magnum was now tucked inside the waistband of Nathan's jeans at the small of his back.

Showing no regard for having his hands tied, Hooknose swore at everyone, but serious gutter cursing erupted at one person in particular. Zink, Marseaux's first lieutenant.

Nathan squinted. The bony guy on the dock wearing a business shirt, pressed slacks, and slicked-back blond hair didn't resemble the burly Zink Nathan remembered from back during the trial. This version looked sickly. Dabble too much in the snort and that stuff will kill you.

If Nathan didn't get his hands on Zink first.

Two years ago, Jamie had gone to Marseaux for a loan, nothing more. One of Marseaux's men had tricked Jamie. Zink used him to get one of his men free after a bust.

Nathan had been the one to take care of his brother when Jamie had hugged the toilet for sixteen hours, returning too much alcohol ingestion back to nature. After that, the hardest thing Jamie would touch was the occasional beer . . . only with Nathan.

Zink was as much at fault for setting up Jamie the first time as Marseaux.

They all owed Nathan for two years of his life and more.

"What's the deal, Zink?" Hooknose yelled at him. "I've known Marseaux for eight years. Eight years. Most people aren't smart enough to stay clean in this business. I do and I keep my ear to the ground, telling him anytime I got news, so what's this bullshit?"

Zink finally turned away from where he was overseeing the packing of some gaudy-looking glass statues. Nathan couldn't tell if the shipment was camouflaging illegal products, but why would they be here at this time of night for what looked like two crates being loaded into a truck. Going for overtime pay?

"Shouldn't have told anyone about the shipping company." Zink pointed a finger at Hooknose for emphasis.

"I didn't. I swear it."

"I know differently. Got proof. Whatta you got?"

Hooknose stared silently, then started shaking his head. "Not true. Drake isn't dead. He knew things, got it from others, not me. The bastard jumped me from behind and cracked my head."

From behind? Nathan shouldn't have been so easy on the sniveling liar.

"I-I didn't say nothing, not really," Hooknose continued. "The guy ain't dead. Nahwlin's PD must have put out a false story. I bet Drake is working with them. He was asking questions about this place, as if he hadn't been here for a couple weeks. Spooky. I didn't say nothing he didn't already know. What'd you expect me to do?"

"I got a skanky dog with more brains than you and bigger balls." Zink stopped to approve something on the crate packing, then turned back to Hooknose. "Eight years in this business should have taught you what happens to people who can't keep their mouths closed."

Nathan shouldn't feel any responsibility here since Hooknose was another layer of skin on the underbelly of New Orleans illegal activities. But neither did he want to watch someone killed in cold blood because Nathan had questioned him. He was only playing judge and jury with the ones behind pulling Jamie into this and getting him killed.

Criminals that would never have to walk into a court and be tried by twelve jurors, because they were made of Teflon.

Nathan sized up the opposition. Two men were rolling the second wooden box on a dolly to the end of the dock. One jumped down as the crate was lowered on the hydraulic platform.

That left Hooknose, Zink, and Zink's backup, a redheaded guy with a matching beard that belonged back in the sixties. Plus Red Beard had an automatic weapon hanging from his shoulder.

"No, no, no. This ain't right. Drake is shaking down everyone. Ask FinMan. I heard Drake busted up his bodyguards."

Zink grinned at Hooknose. "I've already heard FinMan's lame story, as well. He won't be ratting again ... ever. Tie his feet."

Red Beard produced a length of wire and wrapped it around the snitch's ankles, twisting the ends securely.

Hooknose's face squeezed with anxiety.

Nathan had no remorse for FinMan. The slimeball had boasted over how he had both the cops and Marseaux in his pocket. Had threatened Nathan with cutting him to pieces while alive and letting him bleed slowly to death.

Of course, that was when FinMan thought his muscle was only the press of a button away. When he'd slipped his hand under his desk to press a silent alarm, his face had lost color when no one came busting through his door, guns blazing, to save his worthless ass. Changed his tune then and started dealing immediately.

"No, Zink," Hooknose pleaded. "Don't do this. I got the inside line on where they put the coke. We can get it for Marseaux."

Red Beard shoved Hooknose down on his knees. Serious begging rolled into action.

Zink stood over Hooknose. "Marseaux's got bigger concerns than the snort from that shipment. I'll tell you the same thing I told FinMan. Drake is dead. If you were stupid enough to believe some guy scamming you, you deserve to die. Like the old saying, dead men tell no tales."

Nathan sighed, pulled back the hood hiding his face, and stepped out from his cover. "This one does."

The three looked up. Hooknose's mouth dropped open. Red Beard squinted as if he needed glasses to see that far.

Zink muttered, "No fucking way."

Nathan shrugged and crossed his arms, for about half a second. Zink whipped his hand behind his back and he pulled a small canon into view.

The two men loading the truck dove into the cab from opposite sides. The engine fired into action and tires squealed as they fled from the lot. Not sticking around for the fun, eh?

"Who the fuck are you?" Zink cocked the gun. Red Beard had swung the automatic from his shoulder.

Nathan dove behind his barricade of crates. He hoped there was more in these boxes than glass doodads.

Shots pinged off the top of the wood, ricocheting against the wall. Splintered pine hit Nathan on the head and shoulders.

"Don't hit the fucking boxes, moron." Was Zink going for manager of the year?

Nathan peered between two crates.

Zink and Red Beard had split apart, moving toward him and cutting off his exit passage in two directions. Nathan stayed hunched and shuffled quietly around stacks of crates, drifting deeper into the warehouse.

He reached around and slipped out his weapon, then started moving quietly. He found a spot where he could stand at the end of an aisle out of view and see anyone approaching from the loading dock area.

Red Beard stepped cautiously around the far end and eased down the walkway, passing row after row of shelves on his left. Thick silence tightened the air. Each time he paused, he'd glance to the right first, check the separation in the rows, then to his left and move on. Sweat trickled along the side of his face and droplets clung to his beard.

When he reached Nathan's row, Red Beard glanced right.

Nathan moved forward, cupped his mouth, and snapped his neck in one move. He lowered him to the floor, dragged the body a few feet out of view, and removed his rifle.

An M-16 with a scope—nice. Loaded—even better. Nathan shoved the .357 inside the front of his jeans to keep handy.

Moving carefully around to a new spot, Nathan paused at the sound of struggling. He bent his head low and found an opening to peek through.

Hooknose was wiggling spasmodically toward the door. He wouldn't get far with his legs tethered.

Zink popped into the space between Nathan and Hooknose, raising his handgun to aim at Hooknose.

Nathan stepped out. "Miss me?"

Zink yanked around, weapon arm following as smoothly as a dancer's move. But Red Beard had shared his toys. Nathan swung the M-16 like a bat, ramming Zink's head.

Just when things looked promising, the rear door slammed open. He sighed. That meant at least one more to deal with. The guys hauling the shipment must have called in reinforcement.

Nathan angled for cover. Zink was still out cold, but in plain view. That wouldn't be so bad if he hadn't fallen on his weapon. No way to get it from him without drawing attention. Nathan lifted his hood back in place and blended into the shadows.

Until he knew who had entered, he wasn't showing his face any more than he had to.

He expected to see bullets fly any minute, but all he heard were footsteps and a high-pitched curse. Female.

"Might as well come out, Drake," a male voice called out from between him and the door. "I'm tired of you shaking down my people. I paid you too well to turn on me this way. Good thing I was already headed here when I got a call from my men or I might have missed you . . . and this little gem."

Nathan had heard that voice once before. Back during . . .

Anton Marseaux stepped into view.

With Terri.

The bottom fell out of Nathan's stomach. Marseaux had her with his arm around her throat and a hand cupping her mouth. His other hand pointed a Walther PPK at her head. The color had washed out of Terri's face and it wasn't because of the massive overhead lights.

"Drop the purse." Marseaux had paused next to a crate. Terri unclipped the strap of her shoulder bag and tossed it on the wooden box.

Marseaux moved three steps away until his back was to a wall. "Come out, Drake. Or I'll kill her."

Nathan stood. "She's not involved in this."

"Really? Could have fooled me by the way she'd reached this building. Don't blow smoke up my ass and tell me the woods are on fire. She wouldn't have made it past two of my cameras undetected without being trained. I'm figuring she's the DEA bitch you've been spilling your guts to."

"What do you want?"

"Your weapons, for starters."

Nathan walked past Zink's prone body and laid the M-16 upon a crate on his left, then placed his handgun beside it.

"Move forward."

Nathan took several steps.

Marseaux said, "That's enough."

More than enough to see Terri's eyes, which should have been rounded in fear, but God love her, the woman was spittin' mad.

Of course, after hearing that comment about working for Marseaux, she might be just as mad at both of them. "Let her go."

"Why should I?"

"You want me. Let's trade."

Terri's eyes widened, then changed from anger to fear. For him? Nathan didn't deserve her concern. He'd gotten her deeper into this than she should have been.

"Way I see it, I get you both," Marseaux quipped.

"Let her go and I'll tell you who ratted out your shipment."

That got Marseaux's full attention. "Tell me now unless you want to watch her brains sprayed across the floor."

Nathan shook his head. "Let her go first." He held his hands up, showing he had no weapon.

A gun cocked behind Nathan. Ah, hell, Zink was back up on his feet and had the .357.

"I got your back, boss," Zink called.

"Okay, I'll trade." Marseaux flashed a smile of victory and released his hold on Terri.

Nathan moved forward, within twenty feet of Marseaux, who pushed Terri to move.

She stumbled.

Nathan had to clench his fists to keep from reaching for her or they'd both wind up full of holes. She took another step and started to speak, but rapid shots blew out the overhead lights.

Nathan dove forward to grab her and came up empty. Praying she'd found cover, he rolled to his right as more bullets snapped all around them.

A third shooter had entered the fray, but that didn't mean he was a friendly. Could be NOPD or an enemy of Marseaux's.

The place was stark black, except for where the outside lights shined in past the open loading dock.

What Nathan wouldn't give for his night-vision monocular right now. He silently worked his way back to where he'd left the M-16.

More scuffling noises reached his ears from two spots, but not a third. Marseaux and Zink most likely. Neither had shown any covert ability.

Where was Hooknose? Ambient light dusted over a blob near the rear exit door that had stopped moving. Nathan doubted Hooknose had been hit. More likely he was waiting to see the winner of this.

Nathan inched his hand up to where he could hook the rifle with a finger and start slowly moving it to the edge above his head.

Something clicked and six security lights beamed on.

He yanked the weapon down into his arms.

Someone shot the two overhead lights closest to the entrance door. The new shooter.

Two more explosive shots rang out close, which sounded like the SIG Nathan had seen in Terri's purse. He had her position.

Zink jumped up and pumped a round down the aisle toward the door. The unknown shooter nailed Zink with one shot between his eyes. Nathan estimated the unidentified shooter's position at a new spot seventy feet away from his last location.

Trained marksman.

Three quick steps pounded toward the rear exit door next to the loading dock. Nathan turned in time to see the back of Marseaux as he leaped over Hooknose's body and fled out the door that slammed shut with deafening finality.

His pulse thumped hard. One shooter left.

Terri was between the two of them, but she was trained and armed.

He was stuck in a bad spot that would be hard to defend. Not enough boxes to hide behind and he couldn't risk moving to another position. The long pathway on each side of where he huddled ran straight toward the shooter's last position.

He hoped for law enforcement. Wouldn't be good for him, but at least Terri would walk out of here safe.

It was going to come down to who had more firepower and Nathan was sure he'd lose that match.

"Don't shoot," called out from down the aisle, closer this time.

Huh? Nathan cocked his head, confused. Like he would hold his fire because the enemy said so? "Give me one reason not to," he yelled back.

The shooter pitched something small that skated along the slick concrete floor down the aisle.

Nathan prepared to dive toward Terri to shield her if the object had been a hand grenade, but the piece of metal was too small to be that. When it stopped sliding, he stared down at an Army Ranger challenge coin . . . with a dent.

Nathan looked up to see Stoner walking between two rows of shelves toward him.

"What the hell?" Nathan stepped from his cover.

Stoner cleared the end of the shelves. He flipped up his

monocular and grinned, extending a hand to shake with Nathan.

"Freeze or I'll shoot."

Nathan swung his head to find Terri in a three-point stance, her 9 mm pointed at Stoner, who hadn't moved a muscle upon her command.

"He's not the enemy, Terri," Nathan told her calmly.

"I don't know that."

"I do." Nathan checked Stoner, whose gaze was still locked on her weapon, then he glanced back at Terri. "Listen—"

"Sorry, but there's only so far I'll take this alliance we've developed. I don't even know who *you* are, but Marseaux does. You didn't deny working for him."

Nathan couldn't fault her. "I'll explain, just don't shoot. Put your gun down and let's talk."

Her eyes rounded, then narrowed. "I don't trust you not to trick me."

"Smart woman," Stoner murmured.

Nathan growled at him. "You're not helping."

Stoner shrugged nonchalantly. "Thought you were glad to see me."

Terri huffed impatiently. "Cut it out, you two."

Nathan took a gamble and laid down his weapon, then moved toward Terri. Her SIG swung a couple inches horizontally to point directly at him. He kept moving.

"Don't." She uttered the warning. Her trigger finger moved a fraction.

"I'm not going to trick you."

Terri wasn't sure she could believe this mystery man so

easily anymore. She gripped her weapon tightly, prepared to use it if he didn't stop moving forward. "*Freeze!*" Her heart beat so hard she couldn't take a breath. *Didn't he believe her?*

When he ceased moving, she shifted her weight onto her stronger leg, preparing for an attack. She'd been such a fool to worry about him when he was one of Marseaux's people. Granted, he had not harmed her, but she didn't trust anyone not to trick her. Not after a felon had sent her into an ambush.

The tall black guy wore a single night-vision headpiece and hadn't budged since seeing her weapon. Tall? How about as big as a bear and an expert with that wicked-looking rifle hanging from the front of his vest.

"Terri?"

Her gaze bounced to the man inside the hooded jacket, but she kept the black guy in her peripheral vision since the men were only about six feet apart and obviously familiar with each other. "What?"

"I have never hurt you and I have no intention of starting. You believe that, don't you?" he asked in a patient tone. She'd used the same let's-be-calm technique many times in dealing with a threat.

But she couldn't lie since they both knew he'd saved her butt more than once and had never harmed her. "Yes."

"Then trust me not to trick you."

Trust him. Was he serious? She'd already given him more trust than he deserved. If anyone with BAD, the NOPD, or the DEA found out how much time she'd spent with a man who was clearly avoiding the law and involved in this investigation she'd be toasted on a skewer.

He took another step, carefully holding his arms at his side. She could tell he weighed each move before making one.

Her palms dampened. She didn't want to shoot him, but if he gave her no choice she would. Rule of the streets—he who hesitates loses. The night Conroy died, a movement behind Terri had caught his eye right before she was struck, but he'd hesitated. Why? Had he known the attacker?

The stranger in the hooded jacket moved forward.

She swallowed and tightened her finger against the trigger.

Then he reached for his hood and lifted.

No other motion could have held her mesmerized the way that simple gesture did.

His face slowly emerged as he moved another step. Gray-blue eyes held her gaze, refusing to let go. The soft material slid back, inch by inch. A familiar straight nose and slash of cheeks came into view.

Terri's lips parted. Her throat dried.

When the hood dropped to his shoulders, his face was completely exposed, right down to chiseled lips that could have been shaped by a master sculptor.

Nathan Drake, in the flesh.

CHAPTER ELEVEN

"You're Nathan Drake." Terri stared at the face that should have had a bullet hole in the middle of its smooth forehead.

"Yes. Don't shoot me." He gave her a smile meant to lower her defenses. Worked pretty good.

What would be the point in shooting him if a bullet in the head hadn't killed him?

That thought was almost laughable.

Terri lowered her gun. "How can you be alive?" There had to be an explanation. She'd only jokingly thought of him as a phantom.

"It's a complicated story. I can think of better places to discuss it than here."

She looked around, coming to her senses.

Grunting in the corner drew her attention. Nathan stepped around, putting himself between her and the sound.

"What are you going to do about him?"

Terri jumped at the deep voice that boomed behind her. She scooted next to Nathan, then realized what she'd done and backed away from both men.

Nathan turned around, scowling. "You scared her."

"No, he didn't," Terri lied, embarrassed. "Who is he?"

"Terri Mitchell, meet Vic Stoner." Nathan added, "A good friend."

"Your only friend," Stoner muttered, then offered his hand to Terri. "Nice to meet you, ma'am."

Terri stared at the huge hand while this Stoner patiently waited on her to decide if he was friend or foe. She finally placed her hand in his. He could have crushed every bone, but he was careful when he gave her a firm shake.

A banging noise had Nathan scowling again. "I've got to do something with Hooknose." He paced off toward the exit door. Terri followed several steps behind until she saw the body trussed up on the floor squirming in place.

Dropping into a squat, Nathan said something in a low terse voice. Hooknose nodded vigorously. Nathan produced a switchblade and cut through the guy's bindings in two slashes. Hooknose was up and out the door with the speed of a roach being chased with a pesticide.

Nathan strolled back to her, eyes searching in every direction, alert.

"What did you tell Hooknose?" Terri retrieved her purse and tucked her weapon inside, then latched the strap in place.

"That if I were him I'd find a hole to hide in for a long time. And if I heard he said a word about tonight to anyone, I'd find him in his sleep and . . . well, he understands it wouldn't be pleasant." Nathan cut a questioning gaze at Stoner. "What are you doing here?"

Stoner's eyes shifted, taking in everything around him. "Like you said, bro, better places than this to talk."

"True." Nathan gave the warehouse a last glance, then used hand movements to communicate with Stoner, who nodded as if they'd discussed an exit plan.

Everything about these two indicated covert training.

She'd save her questions for later. Nathan put his hand out for her. Terri ignored the gesture and nodded toward the entrance—a silent order to lead and she'd follow.

His eyes grim, he dropped his hand and strode down the aisle. She took a breath, glad to have survived, and kept pace in spite of her aching leg, which diving for cover hadn't helped. Outside, the men moved in tandem, Nathan taking the lead and Stoner following as they covered ground.

In fact, the men moved as a unit.

These two had worked together this way before, but where and when?

"I had no problem getting into the container, but there were only eight vials. Should have been a total of ten." Duff placed the foam-lined case that had slots for ten vials on the polished mahogany desk. His hand trembled when he pulled his fingers back.

Fra Bacchus used a bony finger to press a button on his desk phone. "Linette, please come in."

The door opened and the Fra's knockout assistant came

in as silent as a prayer. Legs a mile long and a body Duff had imagined naked many a night aboard his boat. If only she'd been born a blonde.

"Take this to the infirmary." Fra Bacchus handed her the case.

When she turned to leave, Duff noted how the Fra's wrinkled gaze followed the sway of Linette's hips. Was the old bastard doing her? Duff could do without that visual. The sad slant of her eyes hid secrets and pain he didn't want to know about, either. Get used to it. Everyone had a cross to bear.

Linette shut the door quietly, just like everything else she did.

"I can't hide my disappointment, Duff," Fra Bacchus began. His arms were crossed, wrapped inside the long sleeves of his robe. The Fra liked that monk-looking garb in private, but outside these walls he wore custom suits made by Italian tailors. Clothes better suited to his public persona of an international investor and rare wine connoisseur.

Duff had thought long and hard on this before coming in. He knew better than to show up short two vials with no plan for retrieving them. "Someone got into the container and took the other two, but if they knew what they had, why not take all ten? I think whoever stole the teak tools has no idea what they got. If we could get our hands on the list of everyone who's been in that container, I could find those vials in no time."

"True, but acquiring that list may take too long and interrogating everyone would draw unnecessary attention."

Thanks for no help. Duff clenched his clammy hands. He worked to keep calm, not to give away his nervousness. "I still have a day to get the other two vials. I'll have them."

"How?" Fra Bacchus uttered that one word with the force of a sharp cleaver slicing a head. No question whose head the Fra wanted to sever right now.

"I have resources I can tap to find out who's been inside the container." Not exactly the truth, but Duff wanted to appease the Fra until he located the other two vials or he'd end up with a dirt nap. "Don't worry, I'll be discreet."

"You're to deliver the first pair of vials today," Fra Bacchus snapped. "That doesn't leave much time to search for the missing ones."

Duff glanced at his watch. Just after midnight. "I thought you planned to test the virus first. Make sure the product works as quickly as we've been told. Who do you plan to use for the test?"

"Our guests."

The prisoners Duff had been ordered to bring in rather than take lives. No unnecessary deaths. The Fra sure liked that word "unnecessary." Guess one unlucky bastard just became a necessary guinea pig.

"The test should be ready. You can observe." The Fra pressed a button on the phone again. "I'm ready for you to serve our guest." He released the button and stared hard at Duff. "I want you to understand how potent this virus is and the danger of it falling into the wrong hands."

Duff opened his mouth to argue that he fully understood those elements.

"Don't. Speak." The Fra raised a remote and pointed it at the wall behind Duff, who turned to watch.

The wall separated to reveal a flat-screen plasma monitor that flashed to life, transmitting the image of a room with one small table next to the door and a single bed. A man wearing only boxer shorts lay prone on the bed, his shoulder bandaged. The other arm was draped across his face. His chest rose and fell with slow breaths. The sheets and his briefs were soaked with sweat that ran off his body in streams.

A second man was tied to a chair with ropes. He was slumped forward in the same state—clothed in boxer shorts only and perspiring profusely. His head had dropped until his chin hit his chest.

Duff couldn't see the face of the patient on the bed at this camera angle, but the bandage had him guessing. He'd shot a cop last night before he'd brought him to the Fra's lab.

A panel in the wall of the room on the television screen moved up for a tray to be shoved inside onto the table, then the panel slid down. The plate on the tray was filled with a decent-looking steak, potato, and broccoli, plus a bottle of water.

The clink of the sliding door closing drew the attention of the guy lying down. He lunged for the water, ripped the cap off, and guzzled it straight down, water pouring out of his mouth. He coughed and choked, then fell to his knees.

The man in the chair came alive and opened his mouth to yell, but only croaked out, "Water, water, please, water."

His pleas were too late or too low. His roommate had

emptied the bottle in one long slug as if delirious with thirst.

The Fra motioned a hand toward the screen. "The room is kept at a hundred and five degrees to keep them thirsty. We gave him a mild sedative so we can see if having drugs in his body will make a difference. I doubt he even knows the other subject is in the room with him."

Duff nodded, unable to break his gaze from the screen, anxious and curious. He'd heard about this virus and had seen the results, but not the actual process of dying.

"It won't be long now," Fra Bacchus said.

Nothing seemed to happen for about ten minutes other than the guy having a shortness of breath, then scratching.

Duff was just about to turn away at fifteen minutes when an agonizing groan came through the speakers. The guy on his knees doubled over, then twisted in a sickening shape. He yelled, "Help me. Help me, I'm sick. I need—" After that, he sounded more like a tortured animal than a human.

His buddy in the chair cried out in raw terror, "Help! Get in here. He's sick!"

The victim's skin began to swell. He clawed at his neck and face, drawing blood that ran freely. His skin changed, darkening in some spots and hardening. The swelling continued. He beat the floor and slapped his face, crying out and writhing around. His body jerked spasmodically from a fetal position to arching backwards of its own control. He grabbed at his crotch and fisted his hand around himself, screaming in pain.

Duff cringed and closed his legs in a reflexive move to protect his genitals.

The man in the chair called out for help. He wrenched back and forth, trying to get out of his bindings, but the chair legs appeared anchored to the floor.

Duff gripped the tops of his legs so tightly his nails dug in. He'd seen a lot of deaths, plenty at his own hands, but nothing like this. His stomach roiled when the victim's skin cracked and blood oozed down his side. Oh, hell, the guy's head split in the back. Fluid ran out.

Duff turned away, wanting to block out the screams and crying.

"Do not turn your head!" Fra Bacchus roared.

When Duff straightened to watch the rest of this hideous movie, the victim flopped around, foam pouring from his mouth all over his face. His eyelids had split, no longer capable of shielding golf ball-size eyes.

He was unidentifiable.

Not even human.

The second guy in the chair was hysterical, sobbing and praying.

Duff panted, trying to catch his breath. He squirmed in his seat, unable to hide his reaction and fear. "We're sure this isn't airborne, right?"

"Relatively sure, which is why this was a vital experiment to assure we received quality merchandise. That only took one eyedropper of the virus in a glass of water. The second prisoner in the room will be tested for infection prior to releasing this virus in our next trial location."

The screen blinked off. Duff swung around as the door opened and Linette entered. His heart still pounded so loudly she should have been able to hear the thuds. He needed a drink . . . definitely one with a tamper-proof cap.

She placed two fat writing pens on the Fra's desk, then left.

The Fra lifted the silver pen for Duff. "This contains the vial of the active viral agent."

Like he wanted to touch that shit after what he'd just seen? Duff stared at the pen with the respect of a man facing a poisonous snake about to strike.

"The virus is perfectly safe within this vial and the pen," the Fra explained. "Even if you drop the pen, the vial will not break, so you are safe."

Still skittish, Duff forced himself to take the pen, but he stuck the serum inside his leather jacket, anywhere but in his pants pocket. He grimaced again at the thought of how that poor bastard had grabbed himself.

"Take this one to Parker." The Fra handed him a second pen the same size and shape, but dark blue. "This is the antidote."

"What about the other vials?" Duff asked. "Don't you want them delivered, too?"

"They will be safely stored in our vault until you have completed the first leg of this assignment."

Duff bit back his anger. The Fra was treating him like a kid who couldn't handle too many things at one time.

Fra Bacchus settled back in his chair, arms hidden once again within the robe. "Remind Parker that the minute the first outbreak hits the news, he is to wire the final funds or the other two events planned will not happen on schedule."

"Yes . . . Fra." Duff shivered and struggled to speak. "As you wish." He stood and licked his dry lips. "Can you vaccinate me?"

"No, the antidote only works on an infected patient."

Patient, or victim?

"You'll be fine, Duff. I wouldn't risk this getting out except at the proper stage. Make sure you deliver the active serum to our contact in Chicago by ten a.m. this morning, but get right back here and find those other two vials."

Nathan led Terri and Stoner to a narrow strip behind a building half a block from Marseaux's warehouse. Terri stopped a few feet short of where he'd parked his Black Death.

"That the one you restored?" Stoner ran a hand over the Javelin's polished hood.

"Yep." Nathan opened the door. Glow from the interior light reached Terri, where she stood silently observing him.

Nathan still couldn't believe Stoner was here. He had a thousand questions and bet Stoner had just as many. "We need to talk. Soon."

"Tomorrow. You got a cell phone?"

"No."

"I brought one just in case." Stoner handed him a small black Razr phone. "I'm in there as S. Call me in the morning." His eyes slid over to Terri, then back to Nathan. "Don't have to make it early." He turned to Terri and said, "Nice meeting you. Thanks for not shooting me," then grinned and strode away.

Nathan tried to force his shoulders to relax but he was tight as a knot. Terri could have died. Again. And now Marseaux would have his men searching for her.

He raked a loose strand of hair off his forehead that had broken away from the ponytail when he'd dropped the hood, then he wheeled on Terri. She'd been so quiet for the past fifteen minutes he couldn't decide if she was angry, confused, or still upset from being grabbed by Marseaux. Nathan told himself he had to be calm, but dammit, she shouldn't be here right now.

"Why didn't you go home when I told you to?" He immediately regretted the edge in his voice and opened his mouth to smooth it over before he upset her when her gaze hit him full force.

"When did you get the idea that I had to follow your suggestions?" she tossed right back at him. All bite and no tears.

"It *wasn't* a suggestion."

She shoved her hands to her hips and leaned in. "I was giving you the benefit of the doubt when I said 'suggestion.' I don't take orders from anyone, especially someone I don't even know." Her voice raised on the last words.

Nathan crossed his arms and stepped forward. "You know me."

She scoffed. "Tonight's the first time I've even seen your face."

"What I look like doesn't mean anything."

"It means you might be a criminal."

Crickets chirped. The wind ruffled debris along the ground. Nathan waited for her to condemn him as a drug dealer, because a file full of papers said so. Couldn't she trust her own instincts about someone to tell the difference between a suspected criminal and a real one?

"So what's the verdict?" Nathan asked, unable to take her silence any longer. He braced himself for her condemnation, hating how much her disgust was going to suck.

"I don't have one. I don't know what to think."

Not a condemnation, but no rousing vote of support, either.

He had his back to the light from the car. "Forget seeing my face tonight. You can't see it right now. Tell me . . . the truth. What do you believe about me?"

Her hands dropped from her hips to her front pockets. The blonde curls swept to the right when she tilted her head. She tapped a pink fingernail against her cheek in thought, her gaze transmitting how judiciously she chose her words.

"I believe you were trained professionally to do covert work, probably in the military. I believe you are not working for Marseaux now, but can't speak for prior to meeting you. I believe you are not a phantom, but can't explain the body in the morgue." She paused, grinding loose gravel against the pavement beneath her heel. "And . . . I believe you're hiding something, but I don't know if it's a crime."

She had every reason to question him and his record, but had judged him more fairly than he'd have thought. His anger dissipated as quickly as it had come. "Thanks."

"I'll keep your identity hidden for as long as I can. So here's the question: Why can't you share some trust back and tell me the truth about why you're here?"

"It's not a matter of trust on that. It's more a matter of not wanting to get you any more involved than you already are."

"My life and career have been threatened how many times now? I am involved, like it or not. The only way out is to get to the bottom of all this."

His hand moved on its own to her hair, fingers lifting her curls. "I know that, but it doesn't change that I've brought trouble to your door and now have to find a way to get you out of this before it gets worse."

"Then tell me what we're up against."

We. *Had she really said "we"?* Nathan was so surprised he stopped talking. What could he say to that? He hadn't thought in terms of "we" since being in the army or with his brother.

This woman fought to stand alongside him.

Since he was stuck for a response, Nathan changed the subject. "Let's get out of here first. Where's your car?"

"A couple blocks down the road toward the main highway. I found a turnoff close enough to hike through the woods to the shipping company."

He bit hard to keep from yelling at her. She had skills to be an investigator, but not a covert agent, dammit. Yet she'd come back to that warehouse, clearly planning to come inside. "Get in and I'll drop you off."

She crossed her arms, a sure sign she was digging in her heels to talk.

"We aren't out of trouble yet," he reminded her.

She cast him a malevolent grimace before she moved away.

Once they were both in the car, he fired up the engine and motored slowly out to the road where he hung a left. He glanced over at Terri and tried to recall the last time he'd had a woman in the car. Never. The last female he'd had in here before he went into the army had been a girl, not a woman.

He followed her directions to where he had to admit she'd hidden her car well. That didn't curb the flash of body-clenching anger at the idea of her hiking alone through these woods, even with a weapon in hand. He was clearly not meant to be involved with a woman in law enforcement. No matter how skilled she was, he would never be able to come to grips with her in danger.

He parked the car and told her, "Wait until I come around."

"I can—"

"Don't even start on me." He got out, checking the area as he moved around the car, and opened her door. On closer inspection, she'd picked a better spot than he had, but that didn't change what she'd done. On a compromised leg.

When he closed the door behind her, she sidestepped between him and the car, then slapped the palm of her hand against his chest. "Let's get something straight. I am not a helpless little female. I'm a trained professional."

He shifted his gaze to her upturned face. Her hand might as well be a branding iron sparking heat where she touched. Nathan covered her hand. "I don't think you're helpless."

"But you don't think I can handle this job."

"That's not true."

"Okay, what *do* you think?"

"That you're capable of anything you want to do, you're amazingly gutsy, and—" *Don't say it. Stop while you're ahead.*

His heartbeat ramped up. Her fingers relaxed and moved over to his left side, above his heart.

"What?" she'd asked in a husky voice that shoved him past any ability to think straight.

"So . . . damn . . ." Nathan lowered his head. ". . . hot." And kissed her. She tasted sweet and sassy, his favorite flavor. When she raised up on her toes, he wrapped an arm around her, lifting. His fingers slid around her neck up into that mane of wild curls.

CHAPTER TWELVE

*S*he tasted as succulent as a forbidden fruit. Key word being "forbidden." Nathan knew all the reasons for not kissing Terri, which would be easier to accept if she weren't crawling up his front side.

Man, she was hot.

Terri panted, breasts rising and falling against his chest, turning his mind to mush.

Nathan swept his tongue along her lips, which parted instantly. She kissed without abandon. The hand on his chest fisted a swatch of his T-shirt, twisting and using the grip for traction to draw him closer.

He backed her up to the car. Couldn't get much closer together, unless he removed some clothes that were in the way. Her hips undulated one time, rubbing his erection. He sucked in a breath and put a hand on her hip to keep her from moving or she'd find out how very long it had been since he'd felt anything so provocative. He caressed his way up her abdomen, enjoying the feel of a woman with soft curves.

She hooked her hand around his neck, holding their lips together, down for the count.

Don't stop before one hundred.

He cupped her breast and she shuddered. When he brushed his thumb across the straining tip she gasped, arched.

He teetered on the brink, holding his resistance so tightly his body thrummed with surging energy.

Sirens screeched from the main highway hardly a mile away, getting louder. Heading toward them.

That dumped a cold wash over him. "Baby, we've got to go." He started peeling her off him. *But, hold that thought.* Right. By the time she got in the car and down the road, she'd come to her senses.

"Where are your keys?" His voice had turned rusty dry.

"Uhm, uhm." She was all elbows and arms, untangling and reaching into her shoulder bag.

Nathan snatched the keys from her hands as soon as he saw them, opened the car, and got her belted in. He didn't want her driving off half alert.

"I got this!" she griped at him.

He grinned. She was hitting on all cylinders again and would be fine on her own. "Drive within the speed limit and don't make any sudden moves."

She slammed the door and cranked the engine, then rolled the window down. "Need I remind you that I'm *with* law enforcement?"

Good point. "I'll be right behind you." Nathan climbed into the Javelin and fired up the engine. He backed around, avoiding trees, then followed her Mini Cooper out of the woods.

They hadn't gone far down the two-lane road before a police cruiser and ambulance passed by. In his rearview mirror, Nathan could see both vehicles slowing to turn in at the shipping company. Who would have called the police to Marseaux's place? Not the drug dealer.

Nathan played everything that had happened in the warehouse back through his mind. He finally recalled what Zink had said that bugged him.

Marseaux's concerned about more than the coke from that shipment.

What else had Zink been alluding to that was Marseaux's problem? The boxes the intruder had been searching through?

And what the hell did they contain?

⊷

Terri parked her car and climbed out. She stared at the empty driveway, waiting. Why hadn't Nathan pulled in right behind her? That car sounded like the engine had enough power to keep up with her and then some.

What was she going to do when he got here? Invite him in for coffee? Ask him if he'd like to chat over dinner? Maybe catch a movie in between being shot at?

Or better yet, how could he be walking around alive, which begged the question, Who the hell *was* that body in the morgue? He had plenty of explaining to do. She didn't care if it took all night, she wanted answers.

On second thought, she had bigger problems if it took all night. She couldn't drum up an ounce of good sense when he was in the same room with her.

You're so damn hot.

Men had flirted with her over the past couple years, but nothing she'd taken seriously. No offers she'd been willing to act upon.

Nathan hadn't flirted. He'd barely spoken at times, but he'd left no doubt that he was interested in more than stolen kisses. At least he did when he wasn't growling at her.

The guy had to work on his charm.

Instead of polite chitchat, maybe she should just be direct and tell Nathan what had been on her mind for days. Him.

And Brady thought she didn't know what she wanted? Ha. She wanted a man she knew nothing about, only learning his identity an hour ago. See? She knew.

Pathetic.

Still no black Javelin pulling in. Why had she agreed to wait until he got here to go inside? She was armed, tired, and ready for a bath. If he wasn't going to show up right behind her, she wasn't going to wait.

Terri jerked up her shoulder bag, pulled out her SIG, and used her hip to shut the car door. She dug for her keys on the way to the kitchen door. After climbing the two back porch steps and fumbling with the keys twice, she found the right one and stuck it in the lock, then paused.

The sound she'd caught hadn't been loud, but she was tuned for it this time. She swung around, weapon up. "Freeze."

"Don't shoot, it's me."

"Who taught you to walk like a damn ghost?" She blew out a harsh breath.

"I told you to wait." Nathan emerged from the night. He didn't stop until he'd lifted her off the steps.

"Where's your car?"

"Out of sight. Getting a little cranky, are we?"

"I'm getting a little tired of your nonanswers."

Nathan opened the door slowly. When she stepped up to go inside first, he stopped her with his hand. "Stay behind me."

"No problem," she muttered. "You'll give me a better target that way."

The tired sigh he expelled spawned a twinge of guilt over snapping at him. He was an operative of some type with elite training. Common sense said to let him go in first, but her pride was tired of being trounced lately.

"Don't fight me on this, Terri." His whisper sounded exhausted. How many days had he been on the run all this time? Where had he been sleeping? At the Drake house? Not a safe place for him to hang around.

She caved. "Go ahead."

When Nathan entered, she followed and tried to match his stealth, which was not as simple as she'd thought. Within a few minutes, he led her back to the kitchen and let her turn on the vent light over the stove.

Terri dropped her purse on the counter and noticed a small black gym bag on the floor by the door. She ignored it for the moment and turned to him.

Nathan pulled a chair out and sat down, propping his elbow on the table to support his head.

Now that she could see him better, he did look whipped, probably from stress as much as lack of sleep. But she needed to know more about him. She'd let her emotions get tangled up and couldn't keep walking this tightrope.

He was either a criminal or not.

She was either going to trust him or not.

"Go ahead. Ask whatever you've got on your mind," he said.

"I need to know if you're a criminal."

"It depends."

She wanted to scream. "Stop giving me cryptic answers. I'm standing here talking to a man who was on a slab in a morgue a week ago. I've been meeting you more than half-way. You've got to give me at least that much, too."

He scrubbed his hand over the shadow of a beard on his jaw, then raked his fingers through his hair and sat up, crossing his arms. "You saw my *brother's* body. Jamie."

Terri scrunched her eyebrows together. "How can that be? He's still in prison."

"I told you it was complicated. The more I tell you, the more complicated it gets because then you'll have to decide who to believe, me or . . . everyone else."

She leaned back against the countertop, taking in what he was offering. He made it her choice to become more involved with him than she already was. If she asked for the rest of what he held back, she might have to choose which side of an invisible line to stand on at some point—his or the law's.

He'd stepped into harm's way to protect her. Had been willing to give himself up to Marseaux in exchange for her.

She'd played by the rules for a long time and been burned. Maybe it was time to gamble on her instincts again. She'd let him talk, then decide what to do with what he told her.

"I want to hear everything," she said.

He nodded. "Jamie and I are identical twins."

She had a bone to pick with Brady. He'd failed to share that little detail. In fact, that should have shown up on Sammy's computer search on the family. Why hadn't that been in the records? "Go on."

"I was in the military two years ago when Marseaux screwed Jamie over."

"So your brother was running drugs for Marseaux?"

"No." Nathan's point-blank tone allowed no argument. "Jamie didn't so much as take aspirin and only drank an occasional beer. He was a straight arrow and smart as a whip, brilliant, in fact."

The admiration in his voice plunked her heartstrings. "So how did he get involved with Marseaux?"

"Dad died when we were eight, so it was just the three of us. I went into the military as soon as I was old enough, thinking I'd put away enough money for Jamie to go to college and I'd get in on the GI bill. He had the grades, but he couldn't find anywhere that would offer a full ride. While I was gone, the city condemned the area where he and my mom were living. The house wasn't much, but she owned it. They needed more money to get another place."

"I know how hard it has been since Katrina. I'm lucky Grandma has been here for so long. What did your mother do about a house?"

"I was on a mission, out of touch, or I would have come up with a plan. Jamie went to one of Marseaux's supposedly legit businesses, an investment group, to get a loan. The manager said the loan was questionable, but if Jamie worked for one of the companies they owned stock in, he'd have a better chance with his limited credit. Jamie was brilliant, but naïve. The classic genius who needed help tying his own shoes." Nathan smiled, his eyes staring at nothing in particular as a warm memory flitted past his gaze.

Terri waited for him to continue, but was starting to get a bad feeling about where this was going.

"Anyhow, Jamie found out too late he'd stumbled into a snake pit and was expected to mule drugs. He walked away, something no one does to Marseaux, because he assumes you're going to rat on him. So next thing I know, Jamie is calling to tell me he's a week from being convicted and sent to prison. Plus, we'd just found out that Mom had ovarian cancer."

Damn, she couldn't imagine having all that dumped into her lap at once. "I'm sorry," she whispered, not sure if he even heard her.

"I left the military to . . . take his place."

She stilled at his words. "You mean you came home to take care of your mother?"

"No." Nathan leaned forward and propped his forearms on his knees and dropped his head. "I took Jamie's place the last week of the trial."

She couldn't fathom what he was saying at first, then the whole picture hit her. "You did his time? Two years in prison?"

Terri had stepped forward, struggling to understand why any person would willingly go to prison. "Why?"

His head shot up. He stood, towering over her. Imposing and hurting. "*Why?* Jamie would never have survived. He'd have been dead in a week, if that long. Our mother needed someone here and I . . ." His Adam's apple moved with a hard swallow. The pain swimming in his eyes broke her in half. "Unlike him, I knew how to survive. I had to protect them."

But who'd protected Nathan?

He'd gone to prison to keep his brother alive. Most people could only dream of that kind of love and devotion. She could imagine the anguish over finding out, after all, that Jamie had been killed.

How had Nathan held on to his sanity?

Terri moved forward and he stepped away, wary as a caged animal. "Everyone is not your enemy, Nathan. Someone might be willing to help you if you'd step out from behind those walls."

"You can't help me. I don't want you involved with what I'm doing."

How could she reach a man who believed that? How long had he fought the world alone? Terri wrapped her arms around her chest, stifling the urge to just hug him.

"If that's the case, why did you kiss me?"

"I shouldn't have."

"That's not what I asked. Why did you kiss me?"

"The same reason I had to smell you that first time. I want you." He stared at her, searching her face, then added, "But I won't act on that. You have my word."

His blunt honesty touched her. He could have come up with a list of excuses, but chose the hard truth. And she bet it was difficult for him to admit he wanted anything for himself.

That he wanted her took her breath away. She definitely wanted him.

Nathan shook his head. "I shouldn't have kissed you. I'm going to protect you while we figure out what Marseaux is after. I need you to do as I ask and not take risks. I don't want you hurt."

But he was willing to bleed for everyone he cared about. Emotions closed her throat. Her common sense and law-enforcement training did nothing to sway her from moving forward to wrap her arms around him.

"No." He stood rigid as a statue.

"Yes." She rubbed her hand up and down his back, hugging herself to him with her other arm.

He didn't move for another few seconds, then the tension in him snapped. He hugged her to him with a desperation she doubted he'd ever exposed before.

Terri continued to soothe him, hoping to ease the deep misery. He'd thanked her for letting him hold her the other night. How long had it been since anyone had held him?

Two years of surviving in prison only to walk out into a bitter world where he'd lost everyone he'd ever cared about.

Terri flinched at the brutality. At the pain he must carry with him every step of the way. Just like her.

She'd never known her father. He fled as soon as he found out her mother was pregnant and had never come back. Her first year in the DEA, she'd looked into him only to find out he'd died years ago from a drug overdose.

Terri had been a teen when she lost her mother and had thought she'd never get past the heartache, but she'd learned to live with it because of Grandma, who had held her and loved her.

Nathan had nobody.

He lifted a hand to her hair, smoothing her curls over and over again. He kissed the top of her head. She leaned her head back and stared up into his gray-blue eyes.

"Now you know why I didn't want to tell you," he said. "You asked if I'm a criminal? I went AWOL, defrauded the government, and am technically an ex-con with a record, too. That's why I said the answer depends on your point of view."

Brady had said Nathan was MIA, but she couldn't share that without divulging a confidence with a DEA agent.

"Did Stoner know you when you went AWOL?"

He nodded. "We were on a four-man mission that we'd just completed and were to be picked up the next day, which meant going to debrief. Would have tied me up for a minimum of ten days. Then it would have taken even longer to get approved for leave to go home to Jamie and Mom. I left Stoner a sign that I was gone and wouldn't be back."

"But he covered your back tonight." She wanted the significance of that to sink in.

"Yes. He's the only person I've ever trusted, besides my brother."

"What about me? Don't you trust me?"

He captured each side of her face with his hands and

stared at her with those stormy eyes. "Given what all I've shared tonight, you should know that answer."

Terri smiled. She wasn't sure how this would play out, but she couldn't label him a criminal by her definition.

"I have to stay out of sight around you or you'll be in a worse situation trying to explain me."

He was right about that. "You need to stay out of sight until we figure out who killed your brother and who wants you dead." She felt his loss deeply, and the last thing she wanted was for him to be hurt any more. "I'm so sorry about Jamie."

He nodded. His eyes were shiny. "Me, too."

"Do you know where his, um, body is?"

His eyes went dead. "Yes. I took his body to someone who buried him properly in a crypt, a friend whose dad had known ours. I wasn't letting anyone cut up my brother in an autopsy. Add that to my crimes."

And Nathan was back to a hard tone, but she was starting to realize how much easier it was for him to expect condemnation than understanding. "Do you know who killed him?"

"Not yet, but I will." The cold determination in his voice sent a shiver down her spine.

"Do you know what Jamie was doing with Marseaux?" Terri had to be careful not to share anything she'd heard from Brady. She might not be on good terms with the DEA, but she wouldn't screw over Brady.

"Not much. I visited a couple of Marseaux's associates, who said Jamie was working in the shipping office, but nothing unusual. I just don't know why he would go to work for one of Marseaux's fronts."

Because the DEA cut a deal with him to go undercover, because they thought Jamie was you and that he could help you get out of a sentence he got you into. Damn, that sucked. How on earth would Nathan deal with that joyous news?

It would kill him.

She knew she should tell him, but she couldn't bring herself to hurt him any more. God knows he'd been hurt enough. All she wanted to do now was protect him and get him out of this mess alive.

And to keep him out of jail.

She rubbed her cheek against his shoulder. "So you don't think Jamie knew anything about Marseaux being involved?"

"I think he did by the time he died, but I don't know if he did when he went to work at the shipping company. If he had, I don't understand why he would have taken a job there. Not after what we'd done to keep him out of prison."

She squeezed her eyes shut. *He was trying to get you out of prison.* Sharing that would leave Nathan more raw than he was now. Nathan had offered more about Marseaux's operation than she'd gotten from anyone else, but he wasn't finished. Where would he turn that anger when he learned all the truth?

"Nathan?" She carefully hid her concern. "Did he leave you any clues as to why someone targeted him?"

"Not really. I have the note you saw on the fridge that makes me believe he had an idea he might be in danger. There was an insignia on the back of it."

"What type of insignia?"

He fished the note out of his back pocket, unfolded the yellow paper, and flipped it over.

Terri stared at the line drawing of a design she'd only seen one other time. Conroy had shown her the same logo in gold on the corner of expensive linen paper she hadn't been able to track.

At Nathan's silence, she raised her eyes to his expectant gaze, obviously waiting for her to be more forthcoming. Her partner had died right after discovering the paper and sharing his intel with her. Too many things were coming at her. She'd hit the limit of what she could comfortably reveal, but had a bona fide reason for not turning Nathan in or telling BAD more than she deemed necessary. He was her new trusted informant.

"What do you know about Jamie's death?" he asked.

"I saw your brother's body in the morgue for about fifteen minutes. I heard speculation he was working for Marseaux and that he may have tried to cross up a drug deal."

Wrong thing to suggest.

Nathan's steel-gray gaze turned stormy black. "Jamie would never work for—"

"Hey, I said I heard *speculation*, not that I thought he was a drug runner. I never even met your brother."

Nathan leaned back hard. A sigh escaped. "Sorry, I'm just sure whatever involvement he had with Marseaux was innocent."

"Did he leave any more notes?"

"I believe he would have, but I haven't found them."

"That's why the drawers were open in your mother's house."

"Yes, but Jamie wouldn't leave notes in places so easy to find. We always had a joint hiding place for valuables in other houses. I never lived in this one. I don't know where he put anything he wanted to keep safe, but I know he would have left me information . . . somewhere."

Terri took in the worry and exhaustion lines around Nathan's beautiful eyes. He needed rest. She wouldn't press him further right now. Angling her head toward the door, she asked, "Is that your bag over there?"

"I'm staying here tonight. I can bunk on the floor."

"What if I say no?"

"I'll just break in after you go to sleep and still bunk on the floor."

She stifled a smile at the irritation those words evoked. She didn't doubt his words for a minute. Brady would warn her she was asking for trouble she could ill afford, but she'd taken bigger risks as a teen than letting a stranger sleep on her floor for one night. Especially a man who had saved her butt more than once and might be the key to unlocking this investigation.

"Why don't you get a shower, then I'll take one?" Terri suggested.

"I have a better idea. Join me."

CHAPTER THIRTEEN

*J*oin me? As in join me to take a shower?

Terri blinked, at an immediate loss for how to respond to Nathan's bold request. "No" was the correct answer if she could get her brain and her body to agree. She should be laying down some basic guidelines for cohabitating, not considering how much she'd like to see that body in full commando.

The conscience she'd developed since coming to live with her grandmother had to be the only reason her next words were, "I don't think so."

He almost smiled. Almost. "I didn't mean *technically* in the shower, but in the bathroom so you'll be close enough for me to hear."

Yeah, of course. In what universe would this gorgeous guy ever be interested in seeing *her* naked? He acted as though he'd wanted her in the dark, but in the light of day? Maybe not.

She struggled to find a cute comeback to hide the embarrassment heating her face. He saved her the trouble when his gaze drifted up and down her with an undisguised intimacy. "You can turn your back when I step out . . . or not."

More than her face was hot now. *Don't even think about sitting that close to all that male, unclothed with steamy water running down every cut of his hard body. Take a breath and set him straight—yet again—on how this is going to work.* "I appreciate your concern, but I'm pretty sure the worst thing that will happen to me without you is a paper cut. We need to respect each other's space if you're going to stay here tonight."

There was that tiny hint of a smile on his face again. He still doubted her skills.

She should have shot him when she had the chance. "Towels are in the bathroom closet."

"I'll be right back." He walked away and disappeared into the living room, then returned just as quickly and locked the kitchen door. "Both doors are secure. Are there any unlocked windows?"

"No." She stuck a hand on her hip. "Want to set up a perimeter monitoring system while we're at it? I know where an after-hours electronics store is."

"Good idea. Then I can construct an RFID chip to inject you with so that I can monitor your whereabouts twenty-four/seven."

She rolled her eyes at him. He was relentless. "Whatever. Take your shower so I can." She grabbed her purse on the way out of the room and deposited it inside the doorway to her bedroom, then headed down the hallway.

She retrieved a towel and washcloth from the linen closet on the way, then stepped into the narrow bathroom.

Grandma had upgraded a few things over the years with the exception of this one room. Her eighty-year-old house hadn't changed much, which meant there was barely enough room in the small space for one person.

Just another reason why Terri had no intentions of sitting in this room while Nathan showered. Naked. Wet. Gorgeous.

Her clothes were too warm and confining all of a sudden, especially in this tiny space. Terri dropped his linens on the sink counter and swung around to leave that erotic image in her dust. She plowed into Nathan, whose body was as solid as the walls of the house.

He gripped her shoulders, steadying her. "Whoa. What's wrong?"

Every imposing inch of him filled the doorway. The spark of heat that lit his gaze quickened her pulse and deepened her embarrassment, which brought out her worst attribute. A flash-point temper.

"Don't sneak up on me, dammit." She sounded like a shrew, but every time she got close to attractive men she turned into a bumbling idiot.

"You told me to come in here."

"Don't be obtuse. Move out of my way."

His eyes twinkled in amusement. "No." He slowly shook his head. "I don't want you too far away while I shower. Don't make me tie you to the toilet."

She couldn't get far enough away at the moment. "Look, bud. I'm trained. Ticked off. And I have a loaded weapon.

You should take particular note of the loaded weapon part when annoying me."

"Why are you annoyed?"

She'd talked herself into yet another corner, but refused to lose this battle. "Oh, I don't know. Maybe because I've got a man in my house everyone in the NOPD and DEA thinks is dead—whose body they're all looking for. And if they find him in my house, what little career I have managed to hang on to will be over. Got any idea if McDonald's is hiring? I might need a contact there." She crossed her arms, ignoring the voice in her head snickering at her for conveniently side-stepping the part about how she hated to not feel in control.

Just standing this close to this man swung her world sideways.

Nathan stared into lush forest-green eyes. Intelligent eyes that judged him with every blink. And she should. Irritation mixed with curiosity rolled off her in waves. He'd like to think the curious part was feminine interest, but wouldn't set himself up for that letdown. This woman was law enforcement.

Keep that foremost in mind for any hope of remaining free to hunt down Jamie's killer.

If he had any sense of self-preservation he wouldn't be spending the night in the same house as the voluptuous Terri Mitchell, but leaving her alone after tonight was out of the question.

Not to mention, Marseaux would come gunning for both of them and Terri would be the easiest to locate.

"Move." She cocked her head and gave him an exagger-ated sigh of impatience.

He wasn't used to being countermanded by anyone and had no way to keep her locked in here. "Make a deal with me."

"I'm listening."

"Turn on your hallway light. Get your gun and sit in a dark corner in the bedroom until I come out. It's the best defensive spot right now. I know you're a well-trained agent, but I also know that you've seen what kind of monsters these people are and what they do to people every bit as capable as you. So, please, for my sanity, humor me in this."

He could see the debate in her face. This woman took her word seriously or she'd have agreed just to get him to move. His respect for her climbed several notches for that alone.

"Okay. Only so I can get a shower at some point before daylight, but don't get it in your head that you're calling the shots in my house or with my investigation."

"Never crossed my mind." He should give her the truth—that he fully intended to call the shots to keep her alive—but given her current frame of mind, her pride might overrule her good sense.

Nathan backed out. When she stepped past and strode down the hall, he waited until she entered the bedroom with her weapon before he showered and shaved in record time. Outside the bathroom, he stepped into the bright hallway and listened for any disturbance. In two strides, he stuck his head around the doorway slowly and whispered, "Terri?"

"*What?*"

He smothered a grin at her put-upon tone. "Your turn." His eyes adjusted to the dark as she emerged from the far corner next to the window. Smart choice.

She opened a drawer, dug around, closed the drawer, then pulled a fluffy pink robe from her closet. Nathan moved to the side of the doorway when she headed toward him. The minute she stepped into the light he saw what she'd taken from the drawer—cherry-red lacy underwear meant to make a man beg.

His mouth dried out so quickly, he couldn't have spoken if his next words would save his life.

She caught the direction of his gaze and stopped moving.

Tension compressed the air between them, breaking Nathan's attention from the wisp of material to fix on Terri's face. Her eyes took in everything he'd exposed in that brief moment.

He knew without a doubt she'd read the bold desire in his face. In his face? Hell, she'd seen more than that. He was hard as the barrel of the SIG she clutched in her other hand and it was tough to hide in this pair of jeans.

Nathan cleared his throat, as uncomfortable as he'd been on his first date.

She smiled, damn her. "So glad to see a hot shower didn't zap all your strength." Her eyes dropped to his crotch, then she breezed past him.

The little demon.

"Terri."

She paused and swung around. "What?"

"One warning, that's all."

Her confident mask flickered, but she reined in her momentary insecurity. "Meaning?"

"Don't tease a lion that's roamed the jungle alone for two years."

⟨✦⟩

Terri rolled onto her back, for the fourth time in the past twenty minutes. How could Nathan be comfortable in the living room? On a couch that was a foot shorter than him?

He wouldn't even discuss comfort, stating the best place for him to be was where he would hear someone trying to enter one of the two doors.

She kicked the covers off and climbed out of bed. The hardwood floor was chilly, a welcome change from baking in the sheets. She hadn't planned on wearing more than her underwear to bed, but she couldn't run around the house undressed, so she'd pulled on a white undershirt that stopped short of her red panties.

Terri walked to the window, lifted the black-out shade, and parted the sheers with her fingers, gazing out at the empty street through the slat of her shutters. She turned away and navigated the room with her night-light. Maybe she'd use her booklight to read for a while. Just as she reached her to-be-read stack of novels, a loud boom sounded outside.

Nathan appeared out of nowhere, lunged into the room, grabbing her on his way down as they hit the bed as one. He rolled her beneath him.

"What's wrong?" She struggled to move, but he had her pinned tight.

"Shh."

The boom she'd heard? "That was a backfire, not a gun."

He didn't answer her. That alone silenced her.

She squirmed until she could see his face, then wished she hadn't.

Above her was the rigid jaw, sharp cheeks, and dark eyes of a dangerous predator, anticipating a threat and ready to attack. He stared at the window, but she could tell he listened for any change or sound.

Her heart raced.

This was a man who had been in Special Forces.

And had survived two years in prison.

But he would never harm her. She knew this with a certainty Terri hadn't been willing to entertain, much less believe in for a while. Her mind conjured up warnings she beat back into submission, ready to trust her instincts again.

She'd been intimate with a couple men she'd thought were special, but realized now neither of those would have put themselves on the line for her.

Nathan had, more than once.

Even now, he shielded her with a body built for power. Defined muscles covered his upper torso. He flexed an arm, the cut of his bicep deep, no doubt sculpted from relentless exercise. His wide chest hovered over her, protectively, but he used his solid forearms to hold his weight off her.

Except from the waist down, where they touched intimately.

She felt his gaze before she lifted hers. The thin material left no question over his state of arousal. All she had to do was lift her hips to feel every inch of that.

Don't tease a lion that's roamed the jungle alone for two years.

He'd given her fair warning. She'd have to take responsibility for anything that happened after this point.

Her mind turned into a chaotic debate. *Don't let this chance pass. He's interested. Don't be stupid. He's on the run.* She closed her eyes. If only she could quiet her thoughts so easily.

Use the excuse of the boom outside to dissipate the heat simmering between. Or to suggest he let her up to make coffee since they were both awake.

She opened her eyes. He studied her with a gaze that swirled darker by the second, until those eyes reminded her of an ominous gray storm cloud waiting to explode with lightning. His chest rose and fell with one deep breath after another.

The longer she stared up into his smoldering gaze, the less she cared about backfires, coffee, or moving one inch from this spot.

Terri licked her lips, lost in the tempest building between them. She lifted a hand up between them and smoothed the pads of her fingers lightly over his face.

He closed his eyes. A shudder ran through him.

To know she could stir him so was exhilarating. She'd never thought of herself as a babe or sex kitten, but watching this incredible man react to her touch was intoxicating.

And seductive. She wanted more.

Terri rubbed her palm across his cheek, then glided a fingertip over his lips. He kissed the finger, then drew it into his mouth, nipping lightly, teasing with his tongue. He kissed her palm. His fingers toyed with her hair.

She lifted another hand to his chest, feeling the steady beat of his heart quicken.

His lips met hers, kissing, gently urging her with his touch for more. His hand moved from her hair to her neck, smoothing his fingers across her skin, tantalizing her with his light touch.

Her eyelids fluttered closed, intensifying her other senses. She breathed in his male scent, engaging parts of her mind and body that had been dormant too long.

The gentle fingers brushed along her shoulder to her chest. She held her breath, anticipating his touch, waiting, waiting until . . . his finger glanced over one hard nipple straining against her thin undershirt. He held the tight bud between his fingers, then moved his thumb slowly back and forth, gently torturing her.

Sensations shot down to where her thighs clenched.

Between her thighs felt damp and hot, needy as hell. She moved her hips against him and he groaned, then stilled, breathing as if he'd just outrun a bullet.

"Terri . . . I'm a losing bet."

"I don't think so."

He stared past her head, swallowed, then lowered a gaze so full of longing that her heart bled for him. "I can't st—"

She covered his lips, not wanting to hear, because she knew with a certainty he'd tell her the brutal truth. Of course, he figured on running, but she wanted a chance at preventing that. If she told him so, he'd be out of her arms in a flash, always ready to protect everyone else first.

Well, not this time. She'd never known another man the way she knew Nathan. She could live with however this turned out.

Terri moved her fingers to cup his smooth cheek, freshly shaved. "Stop treating me like I can't make my own decisions. I'm clear on what we're up against, who you are, and my role in all of this. That doesn't change the fact that I want you to make love to me, touch me, kiss me."

His breathing quivered, debate wheeling through his gaze, but he held himself in check. Out of emotional reach.

She'd fought for everything she'd ever wanted in life and wouldn't quit now. "I want to feel you deep inside—"

He covered her mouth, the kiss savage with need. She ran her fingers around the thick sides of his chest to his back. His long hair fanned across her cheek, the fine ends touching her fingers, which raced along the muscles rippling his back.

His lips demanded more, but tenderly now as his tongue played slowly with hers. He softened the kiss as if he finally realized not only had she not run, but she was dragging him closer. Holding him was like embracing a magnificent jaguar. Powerful, dangerous, and unpredictable.

She'd risk tempting the wild side of this man tonight, trust her instincts that she was right about him.

His mouth tore away from hers to her neck, his lips languid and urgent at the same time. She lifted her hips and rubbed that impressive erection.

His entire body clenched. He sucked in a breath and lifted dark eyes so filled with lust to meet hers she should be backing away and probably would have from any other man.

"I'm not a china doll you have to be careful with, Nathan, and I'm not afraid of you."

He let out a pent-up breath. "Damn, you're something." The kiss he gave her this time was one of surrender.

Warmth blossomed in her heart.

He latched two long fingers under the lacy edge of her undershirt, then slowly lifted the covering, forcing her hands above her head and unwrapping her from the waist up. When she started to pull her hands back down, he whispered, "Grab the bars in the headboard."

She wasn't sure if the shiver ran through her body from anticipation or the promise his voice held that she'd need the anchor.

When he lowered his mouth and hands to her breasts, she realized it had to be the latter. His tongue brushed one hard nipple and she clenched against the bolt of exquisite ache. His thumb brushed the other nipple, once, twice, again. She cried out, begging, her toes curling.

He kissed the hard bead, drawing it into his mouth to spin his tongue across the tip as he suckled, the dual motion driving her insane. His thumb continued to brush over and around her other nipple so slowly the contrasting frictions brought tears to her eyes.

Her body trembled, shuddering under the onslaught of sensations she could barely stand. The turbulence built, higher, closer to that peak, drawing her tight from end to end.

"Not yet." His mouth abandoned her breasts and she caught her breath before he kissed her with thundering passion. His hand massaged her breasts, fingers barely grazing her swollen nipples, but the brief touch shook her. Then his fingers smoothed along her abdomen, farther down, until he slipped a finger inside her panties, between her legs.

She knew he kissed her but her mind and body had focused on that one nerve center. His finger moved within her damp folds and she whimpered, releasing his lips to torture her nipples again. He grazed his teeth across the bud and pulsed a finger inside her at the same moment.

Her body bowed. Her skin burned with need.

His finger pumped once, again, then pulled out, drawing a wet stroke across the spot begging to be touched.

As if hearing the silent plea, he zeroed in and stroked her softly, then more earnestly. She didn't know when her hands had gone to his back, but she clutched his hard shoulders and arched, moving toward that blinding light he led her to and pulled her back from over and over.

"Please . . . now . . ." She panted each word desperately.

One lick of his tongue across her nipple and she let go, her insides splintering in a thousand directions. She cried her release and tumbled through a liquid blast of pleasure.

Time zoned out, expanded, and collapsed into a limp fog before the world slowly refocused.

She opened her eyes to his feral smile. Perspiration dotted his forehead. "That was unbelievable." She lifted her hands to unbutton his shirt.

"I don't have—"

"Nightstand on my left. You didn't think I'd let this go anywhere without condoms, did you?" She couldn't believe the extent of his control. Two years. The man had a steel will.

"You're a goddess for sure."

She liked the sound of that.

He lifted off the bed and first shed his shirt, exposing a honed chest ripped with muscle, then stepped out of his jeans. Reminding her of an earlier wish to see him fully commando.

Done. The hard planes of his cut body were almost as impressive as his surging erection, but that was going to be hard to top.

Nathan sheathed himself so fast it practically hurt to touch his swollen cock. He dropped a knee down alongside her, then removed the whisper of red material she still wore, sliding the panties along her legs. He moved to where he could follow the path with his lips, kissing and teasing sensitive spots.

Nathan tossed the red panties aside and stared at her soft body, lush with curves and ripe with passion. "You're so beautiful, soft curves and so hot. Holding back is close to killing me."

"Then don't wait any longer."

He didn't deserve this gift, but he'd be damned if he was going to walk away. Couldn't walk right now if the house was on fire.

His groin was so full he felt true pain, but as fiercely

as he wanted to drive into her at this moment he wanted to make love to her more. He ran his hands up her legs, noting the scar on her right leg. Running fingers inside her thighs, he gently parted her legs and knelt between them.

She reached out to him. He took her hands and pulled her up on his thighs, then cupped her bottom and lifted, his eyes lost to everything but her searing green ones. She hooked her hands around his neck and kissed him. Lovingly. Her fingers stroked the side of his face.

Nathan lifted her higher, then lowered her until the tip of his cock inched inside her. Sweat trickled down his chest at how tightly she gloved him.

She pulled her lips from his. "I won't break. I want you, want this. Now."

He drove up into her and gasped for air, losing all thought when she lifted almost off and slid right back down his length. Nathan bit hard to keep from coming that instant. The shaky control he'd been clinging to stripped free of his hold. He drove up hard, another stroke to the hilt, then again. She wrapped her arms around him, hanging on, urging him on.

His release clawed through his center, breaking free and screaming with independence, sparing no part of his body as he plunged over and over until milked dry. While the last tremors sizzled along his skin, he held her close, hugging her to him, possessive.

He'd never wanted to possess anyone, but he wanted this woman in a way he knew would hurt like a bastard when he walked away. He laid her boneless body down on the sheet. She murmured some order about lying down now and they'd shower in a few minutes.

Always wanting to be in charge. He smiled until his conscience poked a finger of guilt at him for taking advantage of her offer, knowing he had to walk away.

What the hell was wrong with him?

How had running back here to protect her gotten so out of hand?

Because he'd forgotten his initial plan the minute his tongue tangled with hers.

She'd stood on the opposite side of a gun from him once already. Twice, actually. If she knew his intentions for his brother's killer, Terri would look at him through the hard eyes of a cop instead of the soft eyes of a woman.

Besides, he couldn't make love to her, then just walk away. She wasn't that kind of woman.

Her delicate fingers caught his hand and tugged him down beside her. He drew her into his embrace, her back to his chest, wrapping his arms and legs over her and rubbing his chin along her hair.

Maybe he could stay when this was all done.

Nathan rolled his eyes. Oh, sure. Then he'd have an address for the president to send a full pardon to if he didn't want to remain dead since he'd defrauded the government in a court case and had gone AWOL.

When was he going to learn to stop wanting the impossible?

Obviously, no time soon, since he wanted Terri Mitchell.

❧

Terri poured herself a cup of coffee, wondering what she was going to have to do to convince Nathan he had more options than he thought. He was already withdrawing from her this morning, becoming more remote. She knew why he'd backed away—because he either believed he was going on the run or going to die—but he could damn well give her a chance to help him.

"What's your schedule today?" he asked.

"Good morning to you, too." She turned around slowly and leaned against the counter. Nathan wore jeans and a faded green T-shirt, unremarkable clothing if not for how the material clung to him like a second skin. *Stop paying attention to his body and start figuring out what he's up to.*

"Good morning," he said. "Now, what about your schedule?"

"It changes throughout the day. Why do you ask?"

"It would help me if you were around the precinct for a while today so I could do a few things."

She laughed, but not with any humor. "What is it going to take for you to understand that I don't need a bodyguard?"

"Remember the backfire last night?"

"I remember every detail of last night. Do you?"

"Terri, last night was . . . amazing, but—"

"If you say it was a mistake, I swear I'll shoot you where you stand."

"A night spent loving you would never be a mistake."

Damn, but he had a way of turning her heart into Jell-O.

"However, that doesn't change the fact that I shouldn't have and . . . won't again."

He also had a knack for turning her temper valve wide open to steaming. "Don't I have a say in this?"

He hesitated as if he wanted to say something else, then sighed and shook his head. "If you won't accept that it's not a good idea given my situation, then at least understand that I can't watch over you if I'm involved."

"And I've told you I don't need you to guard me." She gripped the mug of coffee with both hands to keep from flinging it across the room.

"That was no backfire last night. There's a chunk of wood missing from the frame of your window."

"No way." Her skin felt clammy. Stars sprinkled her vision.

"You okay?"

No. Terri forced herself to straighten and fight through the light-headed moment. "Yes, just a little surprised. We haven't had any drive-by shootings here."

"This wasn't a drive-by. The slug looks to be from a high-powered rifle. The angle indicates the shot was from a roof."

Her knees weakened over that. Grandma could have been here.

"Sit down."

"Don't tell me what to do." Yeah, she sounded like a be-yotch, but treating her like some simpering female ticked her off.

"Have you always been this hardheaded, or is it just me that brings out your worst side?"

That shot her blood pressure back up to peak level. She sat the coffee cup down with a solid *thunk* and stepped away from the sink. "Oh, this isn't my bad side, baby. Trust me, it gets much worse."

Terri grabbed her purse off the table. "Guess I'll just let you lock up since you haven't needed a key yet." She made it to the door when a hand on her shoulder stopped her.

"Please."

She sighed. He could say more with one word than any human she'd ever met. Terri stepped around, breaking loose from his touch. Her cell phone buzzed, but she ignored it.

"About last night—" Nathan started.

"I'm through talking about it."

"I don't want to hurt you."

"I'm a big girl, capable of making big-girl decisions. You make it sound like I expect some sort of commitment, but I'll ease your conscience. I'm not the marrying kind, so don't break out in a sweat because things got hot." Some of that was true.

"You don't do one-night stands."

No, she didn't, but that didn't mean she wouldn't consider a full-fledged affair, anything to buy time until she could figure out how to keep him out of jail. "You don't know."

"Yes, I do. But it doesn't matter. I can't treat you like a casual roll in the sack."

"Why not?"

"Because you don't feel like that to me." He cupped her cheek. "You're special. Wish we'd met in a different life when I might have a chance with a woman like you."

How did he always manage to leave her speechless?

Her cell phone buzzed again. He moved his hand from her face. She glanced down. Carlos Delgado. She couldn't ignore this one, but couldn't take it right now, either.

"Get going, but stay around the precinct until five p.m., okay?"

"I'll think about it, but only because I have paperwork," she grumbled.

He touched two fingers under her chin. She should ignore him and answer the phone that still buzzed loudly as an angry hornet. Instead, she lifted her eyes to his.

Nathan lowered his head and kissed her sweetly, then lifted his lips from hers. "Thanks."

"For what this time?"

"For a night with you."

That did it. She wanted to climb his bones again right here in the kitchen. If she didn't get out of the house right now, he would be thanking her for so much more.

Her cell phone buzzed insistently. "I've got to get this."

"Go. I'll be right behind until you get inside the building."

Oddly enough, she was starting to think of his over-protective nature as sweet. Terri rushed out the door and climbed into her car. She was backing out of the drive when her phone kicked up a fuss once more. Had to be Carlos again. Probably madder than all get out. But when she flipped it open, the caller was Captain Philborn.

"Mitchell here."

"Come straight to my office when you get here." He was not happy about something.

"Sure. Is something going on?"

"Yes. We'll talk."

Terri frowned. Why the secrecy? "I'll be there in fifteen minutes. What are we meeting about?"

"Fingerprints on a plastic bag."

Oh, no, no, no. She forgot about the bag she dropped at the lab yesterday . . . before Nathan identified himself last night. "The lab got the prints matched? Great." Perky might cover her panic. She knew who the prints belonged to now. *Act like it's no big deal.* "Were they Nathan Drake's?"

"One set was. The other is yours. Josie Silversteen is here with me and neither of us is happy right now. You'd better show up with answers."

And here she'd used the NOPD lab to avoid the headache of using BAD's, thinking Carlos would figure out who Terri was using as a contact. She hadn't planned on Josie banging one of the lab techs, but she bet that was how the DEA knew anything about the fingerprints.

That would be the least of Terri's problems if she didn't come up with a reason for her prints to be on the same bag as Nathan's.

CHAPTER FOURTEEN

Traffic was light along Basin Street, but Nathan checked every car he passed or that passed him while he cruised the area near the St. Louis Cemetery. Nothing odd or suspicious going on. He parked between a van and a suburban sport utility, then slipped away, strolling along the sidewalk until he reached the wrought-iron entrance to the cemetery and walked in.

Marble mausoleums taller than him crowded the space not taken up by sculptures. He could never get Jamie to come here as a teen. His brother couldn't even look at a cemetery in passing after burying their dad.

And now . . .

A movement on his left—alley cat after a mouse—whipped Nathan's mind off what he couldn't change to why he was here.

He located the left turn he'd been watching for, then strode seventy feet and hung a right, where he found

Stoner leaning against a massive mausoleum in the shade. This way, they could talk quietly face-to-face and watch each other's back. The cemetery offered a better exit plan than a restaurant. They could leave together, then split up if they picked up a tail.

Nathan pulled up two feet from Stoner. "Thanks again for last night. How did you know I was there?"

"You're welcome." Stoner's gaze touched on Nathan, then swept past continually as he spoke. "I got back here about ten days ago. Took a while to find Jamie. While I was hunting him, I ran across a lot of useful information on Marseaux and figured out Jamie had gotten involved with that bunch."

"Why did you look for him?"

"Didn't take much for me to figure out why you walked away from the army."

Nathan crossed his arms and stared at the ground. "About how I left you in Bolivia—"

"I understood. I won't condemn you for doing what you think you had to for your family."

How could his friend forgive him when Nathan couldn't forgive himself? He faced Stoner. "You should. I walked away from my team."

"You think the three of us couldn't get out of there without you?"

"No, but—"

"The tricky part was how to report you missing."

"I was AWOL."

Stoner's smile was as sly as a fox. "All we knew when we returned to camp was that you were gone and so was your pack. Best we could figure, an unfriendly took you prisoner. We stayed another two weeks, then reported you MIA. By the time the army got around to notifying your family, they'd moved with no forwarding address."

Nathan unfolded his arms, shocked that he was considered MIA and not a deserter. Stoner and his team had gone out on a limb to protect him. Terri's words came to him: *Everyone is not your enemy, Nathan. Someone might be willing to help you if you'd step out from behind those walls.*

Stoner's eyes sharpened at something beyond where they stood, then relaxed when he glanced back at Nathan. "I got on the Net the minute I was back at base, scanning for any news in New Orleans about you or your brother. Thought something might have happened to your mom. That's when I found a news brief on how Marseaux had slipped through the DEA's fingers again, but several people were being prosecuted. Jamie was listed as one. He was convicted, sent to prison . . . but he didn't go, did he?"

Nathan shook his head. "No. He wouldn't have survived."

Stoner nodded. "That's why I came back to New Orleans when I got out. I figured him and your momma could use some help until you were released. By the time I'd gotten here, your momma had passed away. Sorry about that."

"Thanks." Nathan silently cursed himself. *Thanks?* That was all he could say to a man who had covered his ass more than once in the army and came here to help his brother? He struggled for words that equaled Stoner's, but finally just gave up and asked, "How'd you find Jamie? He and Mom moved into another house right before she . . . died."

"I went to the cemetery and waited each day, thinking he'd show up again and he did. Put some flowers there. I followed him home and couldn't figure out what to say that wouldn't freak him out since he didn't know me. If I said I knew you from the army, he'd think I was here about you going AWOL. If I said I knew he was Jamie, he'd have panicked. So I just watched and followed."

"Did you see where he went the day he died?" Nathan's heart flipped over with hope of some solid intel.

Stoner nodded. "He was working at that shipping company and had been meeting someone on the sly in hotels. I couldn't figure out who, but the last night he went to meet someone he left his car at home and climbed into a black panel van. I ran the numbers with a cousin at the DMV. Stolen tag. I followed the van until we got into Fat Tuesday traffic. Jamie climbed out of the van and vanished in the crowd before I could pull the car to the curb and follow him."

Nathan hit the side of his fist against the marble wall. "What could he have been doing?"

"Don't know. Marseaux's probably the only one who can answer that."

"Jamie would have left me a note. He always left notes about what he was doing or secrets he only shared with me. I just haven't figured out where he hid them."

"You're sure he hid them in the house?"

"I found a cryptic note on the refrigerator that he left because he didn't think he'd make it to the prison to pick me up. He knew he was going to die. I'm positive he'd leave more than that to help me understand."

"But I'm saying, are you sure he'd hide those in the *house*?"

"Where else would he—" Nathan stopped himself the minute it hit him. The notes wouldn't have been in the house. "Let's go." He spun around and headed for the Javelin with Stoner close behind.

At the car, Nathan slid into the driver's seat and Stoner dropped into the passenger seat.

"I haven't even thought about the hidden panel beneath the dash where we used to stash condoms." Nathan felt underneath the dash with his hand until his finger hit a latch. He popped the latch and the panel fell open. A roll of money bounced on the floorboard. Not what Nathan had hoped to find.

"Don't jump to conclusions, Nate."

"I'm not." He lifted the roll of hundred-dollar bills and shoved it into the console. "But what was he doing with that kind of cash?"

"Don't have an answer for you, but Jamie will as soon as we find the notes." Stoner flipped the visor on his side down and up, then opened the glove compartment and rooted around.

"He was too sharp to pick a hiding spot just anyone could locate."

"You told me you two always picked the same places. Since the money was in that place in the dash, where else would *you* hide something in this car?"

Nathan leaned back, thinking. He'd been so busy trying to figure where Jamie would put the notes in the house that he'd missed the obvious. Closing his eyes, Nathan mentally studied the car, searching for a place.

Suddenly, the simplest thing hit him. Jamie wouldn't have hidden papers that would take a lot of space or be hard to print and keep up with.

His genius brother would have used something faster and easier to transport.

"Jamie would have put any information on a USB memory stick," Nathan said. "I just know it. Now, where would he put it?" His gaze skipped from the steering wheel to the rearview mirror to the buttons on the tape player. He smiled, recalling how Jamie had gotten on his ass when Nathan wanted to remove the eight-track player and install newer electronics.

Nathan stopped smiling and unlocked the console where one tape was stored. A tape player head cleaner. He yanked it out.

Stoner produced a pocketknife Nathan used to pry open the case, where he found a USB memory stick inside.

"My brother's got a laptop at home," Stoner suggested. "But it's on the other side of Lake Pontchartrain."

"I don't want to be that far away from Terri. Have to go see what she's up to soon, but I made her agree to stay at the office until five p.m. to give me some time."

"And you think she'll stick to that?"

"Not really, but she said she had a couple hours of work. I'll hit a cyber café and read this thing." Nathan reached under the dash to close his trapdoor.

Stoner gave him a probing stare. "Found yourself a nice girl there."

"She's not mine."

"From what I saw, she's interested."

Nathan sat up and ground his teeth. "Doesn't matter. I'm on borrowed time. Once I find out who killed Jamie, I won't be able to see her anymore and she won't want to see me."

Stoner shifted his bulk, leaning an elbow against the window. "You can keep Jamie's ID and go to the parole meetings—you don't have to run."

"I don't have time to make a parole meeting, and even if I did the minute the NOPD gets wind of me being in town, they'll figure out who's been jacking up Marseaux's people. They think Jamie was a drug mule, so the first thing they'd nail me on would be breaking my parole rules. Won't take long before they aim the same weapons at me they point at Marseaux."

"Has to be a way out of this mess."

"This is a no-win situation. I appreciate your help, but you'd be wise to stay away from me."

Stoner smiled. "What? And miss all this fun? Besides, they shot at me, too. Where I come from, that's war. How about cranking this beast and take me back to my ride."

Nathan drove over to Stoner's burgundy Ford Excursion.

"Hold on a minute." Stoner got out and opened the door on his ride, leaned in for a few seconds, then turned around, eyeing the landscape.

He returned to the car and handed Nathan a 9 mm H&K. "As long as you're going to blow your parole anyhow, this is better than that crap you had last night. We're going to need more equipment. I've got some people to see. Call me as soon as you get anything off that memory stick." He climbed into his sport utility and sped off.

Nathan drove away and called the precinct. He finally got someone who knew Terri, since it appeared not everyone did.

"She's in a meeting."

He really hated vague phrases like that. "I'll call back."

~⊷~

Terri had rushed up the steps to the second-floor precinct offices. Not that she'd been in a hurry to explain the fingerprints, but she had a feeling something else was going on.

Had the DEA gotten their hands on the container?

When she reached the door to Captain Philborn's office, Terri took a deep breath and tapped.

"Come in."

Josie sat next to Philborn's desk with her chair turned so that she could swing the shapely leg she had crossed. How did that woman work in tall strapless heels? She wore a trim aqua-blue linen skirt suit with a low-cut black shell top and crisscross patterns on her dark stockings.

But her most unnerving asset was the victorious smile she hardly tried to smother.

"Have a seat, Mitchell."

"What's up?" Terri sat down, feeling a little frumpy in her khaki pants, tweed jacket, and basic white button-down blouse.

"Lab reports came back on this bag." He lifted the Ziploc that now had dust residue on it. "DEA went through the Drake house and dusted everything that had been used or could have been handled. Where did you get this and what are your prints doing on it if this is a piece of evidence?"

The DEA must have gone in after Terri broke in.

Josie's grin widened.

She really hated that woman, but Terri would never come to a fight unprepared. "My grandmother happens to live a couple streets over from the Drakes. Grandma is blind and likes to walk all over the place. That's how she met Lydia Drake, who would bring her ice tea her son made when Grandma came by."

"Nice home and hearth story." Josie flicked her hair when she turned her head. "I don't have all day. Explain the bag. There are reports all over town about Nathan Drake. Are those his fingerprints?"

"Why are you asking me? I thought the lab already confirmed they were his prints."

"Don't be coy." The true Josie surfaced, with claws showing. "Since we don't have a body to confirm identity, we believe Nathan Drake is alive and threatening people, which means he faked his own death."

Terri couldn't resist mocking her. "And maybe fat flying fairies ate the rest of your blouse, which explains why so much of it's missing. Did it not occur to you that Brady might have been wrong about the body ID?"

"He wouldn't have made that mistake."

Josie supporting Brady worried Terri. Or was it just a matter of how a family fights among themselves until one of theirs is attacked, then they close ranks?

"I heard this Drake guy or the phantom, depending on what you believe, was threatening criminals," Terri defended.

"The law doesn't condone vigilantes, regardless of who they kill," Philborn interjected. "Back to the bag."

"I don't condone vigilantes, either," Terri clarified quickly, annoyed anyone would think she did. "As I was telling you, my grandmother walked over to see Lydia before she died, said she was very frail. While there, Grandma missed a step and bumped her head against the doorjamb. Lydia's son brought her an ice pack, which she carried home. I tossed it in the freezer in case we needed it again and forgot all about it until this week. I just thought I'd see if his fingerprints were on the bag so that we'd have a good set of prints for identifying the body once we found it." Had to be one of the worst stories she'd ever made up, but that's all she had on short notice.

"Why weren't your grandmother's prints on the bag?"

"She was walking right after Christmas. Grandma wears gloves all through the winter."

"Next time, inform me when you think you have evidence on a case," Philborn said with his standard tone of dismissal.

"Yes, sir. Sorry for any inconvenience I might have caused *you*." Terri popped up, not minding the pain of moving so quickly this time. She headed for the door.

"Wait a minute," Josie stammered. "She's hiding something."

Philborn stood up, his next sign of dismissal. "Thought you said you were busy. We wouldn't want to waste any more of your valuable time."

Josie's eyes narrowed to slits. "When do we get the container? The DEA wants to see the contents before everything is distributed among your officers."

Terri started to speak, then caught the mean glint in Philborn's droopy eyes. "Our business here is finished. The DEA will get access to the container when I say so. Right now, it's a crime scene in our jurisdiction."

"I've got some paperwork to do, but let me know if you need anything, Captain." Terri gave him her best good-girl voice.

"That's fine." Philborn was already sitting back down.

The venomous stare Josie sent her way should have poisoned the air. She caught up to Terri at the door. "I don't know what kind of crap you're pulling, Mitchell, but you won't have much longer to play these games. Just let me find out you've been helping Brady and you're cooked. I'm close to finishing this investigation and plan to wrap it up in the next few days. I can't wait for you to see my thorough report."

Terri stared a hole through her. Josie wasn't bluffing, which meant someone had concocted hard evidence against Terri that would hold up in court unless she got to the bottom of this first. "I have two words for you."

"Oh, yeah?" Josie smiled, a toothpaste ad for the devil.

"What-ever—"

"That's one word."

"—bitch."

Josie snatched up her purse and stalked from the room.

Philborn chuckled, a deep rumbling noise that shook the room. "I like that. Wish I'd thought of it."

Terri smiled. "Is that all you need from me?"

All the fun rushed out of his face. "No, close the door."

Her heart slid south. She shut the door, then sat down to face him. "What's wrong?"

"Sammy's missing."

She frowned at his dire tone. "What do you mean, missing? Late for work?"

"No. He went to guard the container last night. When the next shift showed up this morning, he wasn't there. They found some drops of blood on the ground."

Terri clutched her throat as fear gripped her. "Not Sammy."

"It's worse. I can't turn that container loose anytime soon. We lost some of the contents last night. I think whoever came after something in that container did Sammy serious harm. I just don't know why they would take him with them. We found a casing, so we think he was shot. If they wanted to kill him, why not leave the body there?" Philborn shook his head and stared at nothing in particular. "I don't know, maybe he's alive."

Being tortured probably. What other reason would someone have to keep him breathing? Terri's heart wrenched at the thought of sweet Sammy hurt. "Do we know what's missing?"

"My men couldn't tell for sure, but I do know some of those teak tools are gone." Philborn watched her for a minute. "You don't look surprised, so I'm guessing Sammy told you about Taggart lifting some parts. I can't say much to Taggart now that the rest of it has been ransacked, but that old codge shouldn't have touched a thing there. I put a call in to him, but haven't heard back yet. Why would a thief want those?"

"I've got to see the container again. Maybe I'll be able to

tell if anything else is missing and what the thief was after."
Terri stood up.

"We got a team of three guarding it, but you be careful.
I'm starting to think this thing is hexed."

"I will be. I've got to make a couple calls first, then I'm
heading over. Please let me know as soon as you hear anything about Sammy."

She couldn't believe she'd just been talking to Sammy
last night and he might be . . .

Think positive. He was alive and they'd get him out.

Terri checked her watch. She'd told Nathan she'd stay
here another three hours, but she hadn't really sworn she
would. It wouldn't take her that long to go to the yard
where the container was stored and return. Besides, she
didn't have Nathan's cell phone. If he wanted to share, he
could start with sharing his damn cell phone number.

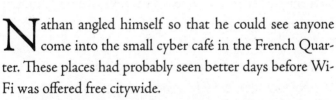

Nathan angled himself so that he could see anyone
come into the small cyber café in the French Quarter. These places had probably seen better days before Wi-
Fi was offered free citywide.

At the moment he shared the cyber bar with three
whispering teenage boys hunched around one computer
and a woman dressed in scrubs next to them. The only
other person in here was the young woman working
behind the counter, who'd accepted a hefty tip to stick an
OUT OF ORDER sign on the two monitors closest to Nathan
to make sure no one sat down beside him.

He shoved the key into the USB slot and opened documents in order of dates in each name. The first several were scanned shipping forms, then the next was a Word document with pasted e-mails between Marseaux and someone listed only as V.

Jamie had been a wizard on the computer before now, but to hack his way into Marseaux's personal e-mail? That was talent.

Lost talent that could have done so many great things.

The sick ball of pain in his gut rolled around. Nathan shoved his misery to the side and kept looking. Didn't take long to figure out that Jamie had known the shipping company where he worked belonged to Marseaux. The next questions were why had he gone there and what had he stumbled upon?

Nathan scrolled through the list until he found "Hi Nate."

He paused, realizing this would be a letter from Jamie, then clicked on the document. Pain slashed through him over the surreal moment, to read a letter written to him by someone who was gone.

> *Nate—Guess you figured out where I hid the memory stick, huh? I couldn't risk leaving it in the house since I figured someone would eventually go through the place, but they might not think of going through the car. I had to sit in the driver's seat of Big Black for a while until it hit me to use the 8-track tape case.*

Nathan stopped reading when his vision blurred. Reading this was tough, like having his brother sitting next to him

talking, but not being able to say anything back. Nathan
wiped the corner of his eye and continued.

*First, I have to tell you. I am NOT involved with
Marseaux. I wouldn't have gone near him if I'd
had a choice. The DEA said they had an offer I
couldn't match anywhere else. Well, it was more
of an ultimatum I couldn't refuse. Those guys got
their negotiation training at Semantics U. Anyhow,
this agent approached me when Mom was getting
worse, three weeks before she passed. I was tore
up and trying to find a hospice that would take her.
She fought hard, but the cancer beat her down.*

*This DEA guy who came for me said he wanted me
to go undercover at Marseaux's shipping company
and see what I could find out. He said it was a
matter of national security. Had a list of things for me
to look for. He thought I was you, with your Special
Force skills (boy, did he pick the wrong one, huh?).*

Nathan smiled at Jamie's macabre humor, but he'd like
to get his hands on that DEA agent. How had the DEA
found his brother?

*I have to tell you the truth, bro. I told him no, even
though you would have done it for your country. I
made it clear I wanted nothing to do with Marseaux.
That my brother was doing time because Marseaux
set him up. He told me that wouldn't happen and*

*he'd assure my safety. He said if I did this for the
DEA he'd get Mom into a hospice right away, get
you out early to see her . . . and . . .*

Wait for it . . .

*Clear your record. Hot damn. I was excited, except
for one thing—I didn't have your Special Force skills
and let's be real honest. I'm not brave like you.
Wish I was, but I'm not. I got a few more brain cells
than most, but no real guts in the deal, so you can
imagine how terrified I was of going undercover
even with him guaranteeing my safety. But if he
really could get you out soon so you could see
Mom, I was ready to do anything. He didn't give me
an option of saying yes or no. The last part of this
special offer was the poison pill. If I didn't do what
they wanted, he would make sure you spent another
5 years in prison.*

Nathan clutched the monitor and fought the urge to pitch
it across the room. Who the hell had done this to Jamie?
The bastard had better be wearing his knees out in prayer
that Nathan didn't discover his name.

His heart slammed his chest with each painful beat,
feeling his brother's fear in his words. Whoever was responsible for his death would pay and the devil in him would
demand double the interest.

*Like I said, I'm not a brave guy or a hero like you,
Nate, but I'm trying to pull this off. Of course, if*

you're reading this you'll know I didn't make it. I've thought about that a lot in these last few weeks and I'm sort of okay with it. Doesn't mean I'm not scared of dying. You know how I hate cemeteries, but I can't live with you and Mom both gone. You always said you'd rather be lucky than good. I hope I'm lucky, but considering my past history I'm not betting on myself.

I wish you would walk away from all of this when you get out so you can have the life you deserve, but I know you too well. You always did what you felt had to be done, always stood up to do the right thing. That's why I've tried to get you as much information as I can. I gave the DEA guy some, but I could tell the last time we met something was wrong. He didn't think I noticed, but I did. I found out there's more going on than drug shipments, but I'm not sure what. With your background, you'll figure it out. I left you the logo on the note in the kitchen in case you didn't find this. (Yeah, what was I thinking, huh?)

That image matches the logo on one of the scanned letters. I think the design is really an F and S, but I couldn't find anything that fit. One of Marseaux's e-mails to this V person said he wanted to be protected before "the" day. V sent back a note getting on Marseaux's butt for saying anything specific in e-mails and there was no such thing as protection, only a neutralizer (I can just see these two doing a secret handshake when they meet in person). This all sounds like a terrorist attack to me, but I searched everywhere for that date and there's no big event or anything I can pinpoint. My guess is some kind of chemical release or biological warfare. I listed all the international groups we shipped with on another file you'll find. Maybe with your army intelligence training you'll recognize something that jumps out at you.

Now here's the kicker. I hacked into the shipping company's accounting department and pulled up cell phone bills. I found one that had a similar number sequence to the one I'd been calling—the DEA dickhead aka JB. I didn't like JB, in case you haven't noticed. <grin> That's when I started holding back information. All JB knows is that I found the link to this F-S group, but no address. I didn't tell him about the DEA cell number. I called it from a pay phone (I felt like a regular 007 that day), but it was routed to a no-name voicemail. I bullet listed everything I found at the end of this, whether it made any sense to me at all.

That's all I have, big brother. I miss you more than you'll ever know. I sit behind the steering wheel in Black Death sometimes just to feel you with me. Momma missed you/me bad. She never believed any of those lies in the paper. I told her what had happened as if you had told me. I think she might have figured out that I was pretending to be you, but she didn't press me for the truth. She prayed for you to come home every day and made me swear I'd

*tell you how much she loved you and that our daddy
would have been proud of you.*

*Like I said, I'm scared, but I'm going to do my
damndest to make you proud. I lost a piece of my
soul every day that you sat in a prison cell doing my
time. If I die, I won't go whimpering like me. I'll go
with honor like you, since Nathan Drake would meet
death as a man.*

No one will ever call Nathan Drake a coward. Ever.

*It would make me happy and feel like this was all
worthwhile if I knew you were safe from whatever
is going to happen and could have a real life finally.
You've covered my butt my whole life. This one time
I wanted to step up and cover yours. Wish I could
see you one more time.*

I love you, bro,

    Jamie

Nathan couldn't see the bottom notes. Tears ran down
his face. He leaned his elbows on the desk and buried his
face in his hands. The pain was brutal. After all he'd been
through to protect his family in the end, Jamie had been
sacrificed for him.

Grief clawed his insides, shredding his heart. How
could he live knowing what Jamie had done?

The three boys howled at something and slapped high
fives all around.

Nathan sat up, jerked his mind back to the present, sniffled, and closed the files. He removed the memory stick, then went into the bathroom to wash his face. His hands shook with fury. JB. He had to find the DEA son of a bitch who walked his brother into a snake pit at gunpoint.

Outside the café, he climbed into his car and glanced at his watch. Terri should be at the precinct for another hour, but it wouldn't hurt to check on her. Besides, he'd like to hear her voice.

Needed to know she was safe.

He waited while the phone was transferred from one wrong desk to the right desk. Someone finally picked up. When he asked for Terri Mitchell, the woman said, "She just left. I don't know when she'll be back."

CHAPTER FIFTEEN

Nathan rammed the car into gear and sped away from the café. He dug for Terri's card in his pocket and punched in her cell phone, then narrowly missed clipping a car.

Three rings and it rolled over to voicemail.

He called Stoner next.

"What'd you find out?"

"Too much to share now." Nathan doubted this was a secure line. Dark clouds hovered over the city in a canopy of gloom.

"Got it." And he knew Stoner did.

"Where are you?"

"I-610, near the airport. Where do you want to meet?"

With no other place to start, Nathan gave Stoner the address of the container and hoped like hell Terri had gone there to dig around some more. "Do me a favor and stop by the precinct to see her. Say that she asked you to stop by. See if you can find out where she went."

"Got it. I'll be in touch."

Nathan tried her cell phone again. Voicemail. He gunned the accelerator.

⧉

Whitecaps frosted the choppy waves in the channel. Duff idled his twenty-three-foot Pro-Line out, glancing over his shoulder like a good boatman to check behind. Bloated clouds hovered over the New Orleans skyline. The squall building would follow him.

Perfect weather for this boat trip.

The salt air fingered his hair and filled his nose. He loved living so close to the Gulf of Mexico. New Orleans was the perfect place to live.

He liked storms, found comfort in the powerful lightning and thunder. That's why he'd joined the *fratelli* at nineteen when a general for Fra Bacchus had approached him. He hadn't realized until then how much he wanted to be a part of a dominant group. To share in creating a world run by brilliant men with a vision for the future and the resources to assure the success of that vision.

Once Duff reached the last two deep-channel markers, he trimmed up the props on his twin outboards and guided the boat into shallower water just beyond the channel. He set the anchor, since the storm was fizzling as it moved offshore, sparing him from having to keep the boat turned into the wind. After cutting the engines, he cast two lines out on surf rods he inserted into holders at the stern of the boat.

No bait dangled from either hook.

Lightning crackled overhead. Water pellets tapped the deck and his face. He checked the anchor line once more, which was tight, and hurried down into the cabin where his treat waited.

She was beautiful. Creamy skin, rosy lips, and a true blonde. He'd been disappointed once when the curtains hadn't matched the carpet, as his high school buddies used to joke.

He ripped his T-shirt off and stepped out of his shorts, naked as the day he'd entered this world.

Her eyes blinked open, then her gaze moved back and forth, frantically taking in her surroundings. She yanked against the ropes binding her wrists above her head. The nylon lengths were tied to a bracket he'd screwed and fiberglassed to the most forward point of the bulkhead.

When her head lifted a few inches, she spied him. Her eyes rounded. "Let me go!"

Never. Bullshit rules were for average men. He was a Fratelli de il Sovrano general, above bullshit rules. Besides, the Fra had all but given him autonomy to make his own decisions for now. That was the way Duff intended to interpret the Fra's instructions.

He stepped closer to the custom bed he'd spent hours building so that almost the entire cabin was one big playground. He hated to bump his head in tight quarters.

"Let me go, *please*." She tried to kick and jerk her legs, but those elegant limbs were splayed wide, ankles secured with ropes, as well.

"Did you really think 'let me go' would work?" He laughed.

"Please don't do this." She was panting now, breasts heaving beautifully with each strained inhale and exhale.

Exciting. But that wouldn't get him hard.

Duff retrieved a fillet knife from its holder on the wall and tapped it against one leg. Thunder rumbled outside, drowning out her scream.

"You don't remember meeting me, do you?"

"Don't do this," she begged, eyes glazed with fear.

If begging had worked in the past, he'd have been happy to find a woman who wanted to be dominated. Then he could have settled down with a wife and planned a family. That was some other lucky bastard's life.

"What do you want?" She yanked against the bindings that cut her skin until she fell back, sobbing between babbled pleas.

"I fully intend to tell you what I want, but let's not rush this, shall we? I've waited too long for my chance at you."

≈

"Was she there?" Nathan asked Stoner. He held the cell phone in one hand while he swung the Javelin onto the road that led to the police lot with the container. Rain splattered the windshield the wipers slashed away.

"No. Took me a little work chatting around the precinct, but I found out Terri left for the container an hour ago."

Just what Nathan had been afraid of. "She should have been there by now. I'm almost to the lot." He sped down the road, then slowed when he approached the entrance, where squad cars were parked, praying he'd see her little Mini Cooper parked in the gravel lot.

No car.

Why did he think his luck would change now?

"I've been trying her cell phone constantly, but all I get is her voicemail. Maybe she didn't go there first." Nathan zoomed past the entrance to the lot and found a place to turn around in the drive of a closed business. He let the car idle, thinking.

Can't just drive around in circles.

"I did hear something else at the station while they made me wait until someone could talk to me," Stoner interjected. "I managed to place two short-distance transmitters in strategic places while asking around for Terri so I could scan conversation through my cell phone. A cop named Sammy who guarded the container last night is missing. And the container was breached, too."

"That means we shouldn't have to worry about that guy coming back to the container, but Marseaux is still out there gunning for Terri."

"He's gunning for you, too."

"I hope so. I want that bastard."

"I know. I'll drive to her house to look for her car."

"Okay. There are lights and uniforms moving around the container. I'm going inside this lot to see if I can determine if she's been here. If I don't find out anything in ten minutes, I'll head from here to her house on the same route she drove the other day." He didn't have to tell Stoner he would be searching for her abandoned car.

The possibility of finding her empty car along the road

wrenched his gut. Nathan slammed that mental door shut and focused on getting her back. He would not lose her.

"If I don't hear from you by the time I reach her house, I'll be headed your way," Stoner finished.

"I'll call you as soon as I get out of there." Nathan hung up and parked his car out of sight, then hiked to the police yard. The rain covered any noise he made. He located the fence opening he'd wired back and hidden the repair with a laced vine. Once he was inside, Nathan moved silently across the lot from point to point of cover until he was within earshot of the container.

Water soaked through the hood of his sweatshirt jacket and ran down the sides of his face. He ignored the weather, intent on activity around the container.

One officer walked around rubbing his hands, then used his flashlight to check his watch. His forehead creased with impatience. He took his glasses off and wiped them with a handkerchief, then stuck his head inside the open doorway to the container and said, "I'm going down to the guard shack for coffee. You want some?"

A muffled "no" came back.

"Be gone about ten minutes."

"Go."

The officer strolled down the incline in no real rush. So that probably meant he'd left another armed officer inside.

Nathan had ten minutes to get a look at that container and find out if the cop inside knew if Terri had been there or not. The cop would think he was the guy who had broken in before. That alone might create enough fear Nathan wouldn't have to hurt him to get an answer.

Battery-operated lights had been set up outside the container. Not the best scenario to stay covert, but he didn't have time to wait for a better situation. Terri's life could be at stake. He had to find someone who knew where she was or how to reach her.

He took a circuitous route to reach the front without crossing the lighted area. One glance at the guard shack confirmed the second officer was in no rush to get back out here in the cold rain.

Nathan eased around to the front of the container. The open door blocked the view of his body from the guard shack, which was bad planning on their part but a benefit for him. The light spilling out from the glow inside the container clicked off.

Damn. Nathan had to catch the cop before he walked out of the box. He peeked inside the now dark container. Where was the cop? All Nathan could see was a flashlight someone had turned on and placed on the floor. A shoe-scuffing sound came from behind the stack of boxes next to the flashlight.

Three long steps and Nathan reached the spot as the person stood up, pointing a weapon at him

"What in the hell are you doing *here?*" Terri hissed.

"Shh! Don't make any noise," he ordered.

"Noise? The only noise you're going to hear is my gun going off if you don't stop sneaking up on me." She glared at him.

What was she ticked about? What about what she'd put him through for the past hour? Nathan bit his tongue to keep from replying since the uniformed officer could be back any minute.

"Hey, Terri?" The cop was back.

Her eyes flashed from angry to worried in two seconds.

For him? Damn, that worked.

"Yes, Ed?" She looked all around her, then pointed a finger down at the spot between her and the two crates.

Nathan crouched just as heavy footsteps crunched outside the container.

"How's it coming in here?"

"Great. I'll be through soon," she answered.

She was through *now*. Nathan cupped a hand around her leg and squeezed.

When she shot him a quelling look, he smiled and mouthed the words, "Leave now."

"The next shift is coming in any minute. Your car isn't ready. The mechanic said he can get his hands on the part first thing in the morning. Lucky for you it didn't start in the parking lot or you'd have been stuck on the highway. I can take you back to the precinct or give you a ride home. Your choice."

Nathan squeezed her leg again to get her moving.

She kicked his shin.

He clenched his teeth against a curse, then decided on a quicker tactic to get her attention. He ran a hand up the inside of her leg to her left thigh and massaged the firm muscle.

Her mouth fell open. She licked her lips and finally blurted out, "I'm ready . . . now."

So was he after that comment.

"Uh, how about warming up the car?" Terri told the officer.

"Sure. I'll be right back to get you." His footsteps moved around.

Nathan slid his fingers a little higher and she squeaked.

The footsteps paused. The cop asked, "What, Terri?"

She bared her teeth at Nathan. "I said, don't, uh, bother coming back. I'll lock up and be right down."

"You've got one minute tops. Philborn called while I was down at the guard shack and reamed my ass over leaving you alone so long."

He should. Nathan wouldn't have been so kind if she'd been harmed.

"Okay," she said, breathless. But the second the footsteps faded, Terri slapped Nathan's hand away. "What do you think you're doing?" she seethed.

"Getting you the hell out of here, now. Have him drop you at home. Pick up your car tomorrow."

"Where are you going?"

"To your house, too."

"Good, because we've got a few things to discuss." She snatched up her tote and flashlight, then stopped at the door.

Nathan was right behind her and leaned down to whisper, "I'll stay close until you're in the car."

"You may want to keep your distance with the mood I'm in."

He'd thought she was just caught off guard by him showing up here, but she sounded as though something else was going on.

"I hear Ed coming back," she warned, still angry.

Nathan melted away, keeping an eye on her while she

locked the container and Ed escorted her back to his squad car.

Once Nathan reached the Javelin, he called Stoner to let him know he'd found Terri. They agreed to touch base in the morning so Nathan could share what he'd learned from Jamie's USB stick. Terri was probably angry because Nathan had disrupted whatever she'd been doing, but he didn't care.

Worrying about her had turned him inside out. All he could think of was her at the mercy of Marseaux, a man incapable of giving any mercy.

Nathan clutched the steering wheel so tight with one hand his knuckles were white. She was safe in the car ahead.

No matter what he told himself, he couldn't relax until he had her within reach.

Starting now, Terri was staying by his side. He wouldn't listen to any argument.

She was dancing to his music until this was over.

Terri thanked Ed and strode up her driveway. She had a few choice words for Nathan, who came very close to having his family jewels reset tonight. If Ed had seen them together she'd have never been able to explain Nathan. Philborn would hit the ceiling and BAD would . . . what?

Kill her?

Terri shook her head. *Don't think about Tee's temper.* She couldn't be that bad, could she? Terri had dodged Carlos twice today, promising information by tomorrow. He was probably expending a lot more energy on the India event since she hadn't come up with a solid lead in the Marseaux case yet, but she couldn't dodge him much longer without causing suspicion.

At her back door, Nathan appeared.

She jumped. "Dammit, would you stop doing that?"

"Sure. If you agree not to scare me out of a year's growth again."

An edge cut across his words. Terri unlocked the door and eyed Nathan. What was *he* upset about? As if he had any reason to be. *She* had an investigation that had jumped track, missing container contents, a missing cop, and a possible attack of some sort happening by Monday if Conroy's guess was on the mark.

If she knew who was planning the attack, what kind of attack to expect, and the location or persons targeted, she could alert the proper agencies. But as it was, she couldn't even clue in BAD, because Conroy had convinced her the people behind this secret attack had infiltrated law enforcement at many levels. DEA, FBI, local police . . . who was to say they weren't in BAD?

Until she found the source or firm information on the attack, she couldn't risk sharing with the wrong person in a law-enforcement group who would kill her.

Terri made two steps inside the kitchen, where the vent light burned, dropped her purse on the table, and swung around to give Nathan a piece of her mind.

He slapped the door shut and walked toward her.

"You put me on the spot tonight." She wanted her gripe on the table first.

"You scared the hell out of me tonight." He didn't slow down until he pulled her into his arms and kissed her.

And, boy, did he kiss her.

Terri was lost from the second his fingers touched her. She forgot her anger, forgot the floor beneath her feet since she seemed to be floating on her tiptoes. His lips roamed over hers, urgent, desperate. She had no idea why he'd changed his mind, but she wasn't arguing.

Her heart pounding, she rubbed up against him, daring him to back away. Nathan's sharp intake of breath only encouraged her to do it again.

Terri ran a hand down to his chest until she felt his heart slamming against her palm. She pulled away. "What's wrong?"

"I couldn't find you tonight. You didn't answer your phone. Thought Marseaux had you." The savage fury in his eyes should have scared her, but she knew it wasn't directed at her. He'd been scared she was hurt, or worse.

He cared for her. He'd lost so much she could see how he wouldn't want to feel anything for another person again, which had to be fueling his anger.

"I'm sorry, my phone died on me. I got mad and pitched it into the passenger floorboard. Then the car wouldn't crank and I was in a rush to get to the container, so I forgot my phone in the car." She kissed his face, neck, lips.

He hesitated. She sensed the war that went on inside him to do the honorable thing and back away. Not if she had anything to say about it, and she fully intended to have her say. Terri would find a way to sort out his situation and save him from himself.

She wouldn't let him just slip away into the night. He'd lived in the dark too long and deserved the light. She grabbed a fist of sweatshirt on each side of his jacket and pulled him to her. "Touch me. Everywhere."

Nathan swallowed at her command. *Don't say that.* He clung to a sliver of flimsy control when it came to Terri. He hadn't meant to touch her at all, but the minute he'd walked into the house and faced her, all hope of staying away from this woman had been lost.

Her lips brushed his.

He could use a little help right now.

"Don't you want me?" She whispered it so closely, he felt the words slide across his skin, branding him with her desire.

She had to ask if he wanted her with a raging hard-on shoved up between them? Nathan opened his eyes and stared into the face of passion.

Back away. Back away. Now.

He'd wanted her since the first time he'd inhaled her scent and last night had only increased the level of that want. She smelled like a lifetime of gifts all wrapped in soft skin and sweetness. Nathan teetered closer to the edge, debating, searching for the strength to give her up.

She uttered, "I'm hot and wet for you."

All the blood in his body rushed to his groin to celebrate.

The fall this time came faster and harder.

He wrapped his arms tighter and lifted her up, lips meeting in a smoldering kiss that might never end. Her arms locked around his neck, drawing him closer and closer to the flame.

She wanted him now, in the dark of night, but what about later when the sun invaded their world again?

Terri moaned against his mouth, then growled demands he couldn't refuse. He'd worry about later when her lips weren't honing a razor-sharp need that ripped across his skin.

He backed her up to the wall and shoved her arms above her head. The fierce kiss spiraled out of orbit, along with his ability to reason and think. She curved her body up against his, rubbing his erection, which pulsed with each touch.

Nathan released her arms and shed her jacket, then unbuttoned her shirt, letting the material fall loose.

The sight of her body, dusted with light, this time really took his breath away.

Lush curves, supple skin, perfect breasts. She was a real woman and spectacular.

Terri reached for his shirt, lifting it up madly. He held her face in the palms of his hand and kissed her, lost in the feel of her mouth on his. His zipper ripped open and she drifted away, shoving his jeans down.

His muscles clenched at the wild race of her hands over his skin, but he sure as hell wasn't going to complain.

She slipped her fingers inside his shorts and inched them down while kissing his abdomen and teasing his belly button with her tongue. She cupped his erection, lifting gently, then brushing her finger over the wet tip.

Nathan slapped both hands on the wall above her and fought to keep from coming, then caught his breath.

She grasped his sac in her other hand and slowly rotated her fingers.

He hissed and clenched against the surge in his groin. He reached for her, sliding her up the wall until she stood again, releasing him.

"I want you, want this, but if I don't stop now and get a condom . . . it won't happen."

"There's one . . . in my nightstand," she squeezed out between breaths.

He lifted her, loving the feel of her in his arms. Her legs wrapped around his waist. He stepped out of his clothes and strode to the bedroom, where he lowered her to her feet and kissed her. His fingers reached for the nightstand, found the knob, and opened it while she tortured him all over again. If she kept it up, this would be faster than the first time he ever had sex. This time he could see in the drawer and felt a certain amount of relief that there wasn't a large boxful of condoms.

Terri whisked the condom from his hands and sent him up the wall when she sheathed him.

She raised the tawny-green eyes of a tigress to his and licked her lips. Blood roared like hot lava through his veins, damming in his erection.

He was going to explode, but not until she did.

She pushed him back until he was against the wall and ran her hands down along his hips, closer to his cock. He grabbed her wrists in one hand and raised them above her head, then swung her around to the wall.

He kissed her again. Man, she was hot and spicy all mixed together.

Slowly, he knelt, teasing his tongue along the smooth skin. He paused to lounge at her breasts, feasting until her cries threatened to destroy him. Nathan peeled her pants down until they circled her thighs and stopped.

He kissed the slip of silk panty shielding his target, then slipped a finger between her legs and gently rubbed across the taut material.

She quivered and gripped his shoulders. "Nathan!"

He ran a finger under each side of the dainty underwear and slowly worked them down along with her pants to the floor until she was free of them. He kissed the shapely, sculpted legs on the way. Smoothing a hand along the inside of one leg, he returned to the juncture and delved inside her heat, gently teasing the folds.

Her high keen rocked the room, threatening to disintegrate his waning discipline.

She spread her legs wider, allowing him access to paradise.

He lathed the delicate region. Her raspy breaths and strained cries drove him harder to please her. She tensed for what seemed a long, long minute, straining to reach that plateau, then buckled with a hard shudder. Her soft cry of victory echoed through the dark room.

Nathan supported her as he rose back to his feet, then cupped under her arms and lifted her into the air.

Passion burned in her heavy-lidded gaze. Her legs went around his waist and he had to bite down against the need to drive into her at that moment. He lifted her higher, kissing her nipples, then circling his tongue around and over. She writhed, rubbing harder against him.

"Now . . . want to feel you. Now."

Nathan ran his tongue over the sensual path between

her breasts, then up to her chin and ear and lowered her slowly, pressing the head of his erection inside her. Every muscle in his body quivered with the strain of waiting, held taut in anticipation of the moment her heat would surround him.

Terri's nails dug into his shoulders. Her body arched rigid, breasts pressed against his chest.

When Nathan pushed all the way in, she gasped. He groaned and held still a moment, trying to keep enough blood in his head to stay upright. Nothing in his past endeavors matched the honest response of the woman in his arms.

Kissing her had driven his fantasies to new levels.

Watching over her had been a pleasure-filled torture.

Making love to her was beyond his imagination. And he considered himself a pretty creative thinker.

Terri moved up and down, insistent for more.

Nathan sure as hell wasn't telling her "no" at this point, but more like "not yet."

He leaned in, pushing her back so the wall supported her. His fingers brushed over the pebbled tips of her nipples and her nails dug in for dear life. Rocking his hips forward, he drove deep and backed away, a slave to her whimpers. He toyed a thumb over one nipple, gently worrying the anxious tip, then reached between them with his other hand.

The pressure in his groin threatened to go at any minute, but he fought the urge ruthlessly. The ride would be longer this time. He shoved deeper, deeper, then faster.

"Come on, baby," he coaxed her, loving her response.

The need for his own release twisted his insides, danger-ously close to overtaking him. He fingered her curls and toyed with the wet heat he found.

Her legs clenched his back and she bowed up, snatching another ride on ecstasy. When she tumbled back to him, Nathan cupped her bottom with both hands and pushed one hard time to the hilt.

His control snapped, ricocheting spasms through his cen-ter. Muscles gave in to the wild rush. He didn't know when the shudders ended, only that one minute he lost touch with reality and the next he was holding her close to him, kissing the top of her head, both of them catching their breath.

A feral thought swept through him, freed from the dungeon of his soul before his conscience could block it.

He wanted this woman, today, tomorrow . . . forever.

Terri kissed his chest. Nathan tasted salty and mascu-line. Their lovemaking hazed the air.

She clung to him when he carried her across the room and lowered her to the bed, then watched him walk away, headed toward the bathroom. *Not an ounce of fat on that ripped body.*

The first time she'd felt him in the dark she'd figured he was a gym rat. Just hadn't guessed it was Club Fed.

He returned with a damp cloth and she let him clean her, then he climbed into bed and wrapped his arms around her. He pulled her close, wrapping his body around her protectively.

Nathan had rescued her more than once, but this time from the jaws of despair. It wasn't that she didn't know what she wanted. Or that she wasn't the marrying type.

Terri finally saw the truth. She'd never wanted to risk caring about one person the way she cared for Nathan and had never met a man she was afraid of losing. But she didn't want to think about losing him now, not when she'd just found him. An unexpected contentment settled over her heart, warming her soul.

What about Nathan? Would he be willing to fight for his freedom and stay? He believed he had no chance at life. She'd gained his trust, but could she gain his heart?

The afterglow began to cool.

Insecurity butted her contentment aside. She'd told him she wasn't looking for a commitment, to keep things simple. But something changed and now she didn't want to give him up, no matter what.

He kissed her hair. "You're only quiet when you're thinking. What's up?"

She drew a deep breath, squeezing contentment back inside to wrestle with her doubts. "You, I hope." He tweaked her butt and she grinned.

If she only had now with him, she'd make the most of it and accept his decision when the time came, if he really *was* determined to leave. But that didn't mean she couldn't try to change his mind. Nathan had given his life for his family, made every sacrifice asked of him. She cared too much about him to be one more person for whom he had to sacrifice himself.

She would not expect more from him than he could give.

If she got her heart broken now, she couldn't blame it on Nathan.

He rolled her over onto her back and kissed her. Took control of this round. He kissed with serious intent and tenderness, the way a man should kiss a woman. She ran her hands over the cut of his chest, touching a scar not long healed. Had to be from prison. Terri lifted up and kissed it. If only she could reach his other wounds so easily.

His fingers slid up her leg softly, then stopped at the ugly scar inside her right leg. "Does it hurt?"

"Not right now."

"This time will be much slower," he said, then nipped her skin.

"Like my heart can take slower."

"Your heart can take anything."

She certainly hoped so. Either way, she intended to push it, and him, to the limit.

CHAPTER SIXTEEN

"I have to show up at the office." Terri swiped a brush through her hair just enough times to feel like she'd given her locks a chance to act right.

"You're a consultant." Nathan's reflection loomed in the mirror behind her. *Nice pecs*, she mused.

"Terri?"

"What?" Her gaze shot up to his face. "We have a cop missing, contents missing, and a possible—" She halted before "terrorist attack" came out.

He angled his head and raised an eyebrow in question.

Crap. She turned around and leaned back against the sink. "I'm responsible for this investigation."

"There's more you aren't telling me." He crossed his arms.

"Yes, but I can't."

Something passed through his gaze that could be disappointment. "I'm going to help you first, then finish what

I came here for, so if you decide to trust me I can be an asset."

That gouged her conscience. She'd obviously trusted him with her body and wanted him to share what he knew, so how could she hold out? Nathan was her best informant.

Only informant.

"I guess you aren't going to tell anyone," she muttered, making her decision.

He shook his head and gave her a wry smile.

She tossed the brush onto the counter and turned around. "Let me get dressed and we'll talk."

"Good idea, or this will be a short discussion." He hooked a hand on each side of her waist, just above her panties, and slid his fingers up, piling her tank top over his wrists until his thumbs brushed across the cups of her bra, hardening her nipples.

She grabbed his upper arms. "Stop, I'm going to be late." That didn't come out too convincingly.

He kissed her, teasing with his tongue to the same rhythm as his thumbs, and her knees threatened to fold. She shuddered, trying to hear that small voice reminding her that she had to get to the office.

Nathan ended the kiss and stopped toying with her breasts, but he continued to hold her. Good thing, since she'd lost track of any muscle strength below her groin.

She blinked her eyes open. "I hate you."

The evil dog smiled at her. "No, you don't."

"Yes, I do. I want to continue. I have to leave soon. So now I'm going to be miserable all day."

"Just giving you something to look forward to later." He

released her and she sagged back to her feet. "Thought you had to get dressed."

Terri huffed and rolled her eyes. "Men." She changed to brown corduroy pants and a crème-colored turtleneck so she could wear her short boots, to be prepared for anything today.

When she walked into the kitchen, Nathan handed her a mug of coffee. Her kind of man. "I'll tell you what I know so far," she started.

"My former partner, Conroy, had gone undercover to worm his way inside a renegade bunch of drug mules trying to get on Marseaux's payroll. While trying to build inroads with Marseaux, the men got wind of an offer to sell them information from an unknown woman. They didn't want any part of it, but Conroy convinced the leader he could check out the woman and get information without spending a penny, even though he planned to pay the woman if she really did have significant intel. He finally met her after some convoluted instructions the CIA would have admired. She claimed to have been an unwilling member of a powerful organization that is manipulating everyone from Marseaux to our government."

"A conspiracy?" Nathan sounded as skeptical as she had once been.

"I know what you're thinking—wacko. My first reaction, too. Even Conroy admitted his initial impression was 'mental case.' She said she was twenty-three. He said you could tell she'd been a gorgeous blonde at one time—which meant petite with perky boobs—but looked rough for her age." Terri scoffed under her breath. "Men."

"What?"

"I get so tired of being judged in between 'not tall' and 'too full-figured to be petite.'"

"How big a guy was Conroy?"

Terri cocked her head. "He was five-ten and lean. Why?"

"Because he'd want a woman who made him feel big. I like a woman who's more than a . . . handful." Nathan gave her a wolfish grin.

She shook her head. "Yeah, well, I was never petite. I filled out early and with not much less than I have now. My first year in the DEA, I felt like every man in the department couldn't see past my cup size."

Nathan ran a finger down her cheek. "You're intelligent, sexy, gorgeous, and passionate. Any man who'd only notice your breasts—beautiful as they are—is missing the whole package and the real woman inside."

For a man of few words who was rough around the edges, Nathan could charm the pants off any woman. Terri had to find a way to keep him near until they could clear his name. She leaned in to hug him and kissed his chest, then pulled away, hoping what was in her heart didn't show in her eyes.

He studied her with a curious expression, then blinked and stepped away, crossing his arms as he leaned back against the wall. "What else did this woman tell Conroy?"

Yes, he saw that look on her face. Terri sighed and continued. "Conroy said the woman babbled, turning her head constantly to watch, as if she expected a threat. He was ready to give her a few bucks and blow it off when she told

him she knew what had happened to a DEA agent in Cali-
fornia who had been missing for two months. She gave the
missing agent's undercover name and his real name ... and
how he was killed."

"Was the body found?"

"No."

"So why did Conroy believe her?"

"Because she had a photograph of the dead agent with a
newspaper headline showing the date, which matched the
day our West Coast office lost contact with him. The photo
had been proof of the contract completed. She snuck the
photo out, thinking it would be worth enough money to
get her out of the country, but wouldn't tell Conroy where
she'd been living. She'd been raised in a wealthy Swedish
family that had told her from day one she was special and
being groomed for a great honor. At nineteen, she was sent
here to a *fra*."

"A *'fra'*? What the hell is that?" His eyebrows drew
together in a tight frown.

"It's Italian for brother. Conroy offered to put her in
touch with a friend—*me*—so I could get her to a safe house
since he couldn't blow his cover, but he said he wanted the
name of the organization first. She got agitated and said
she couldn't even speak the name for fear of putting her
family in jeopardy if anyone found out she was the one
who had told."

"Did she have any significant intel?"

"She knew about Marseaux, which confirmed some
things we knew, and she knew about a drug shipment coming in this week."

"Did she say who the buyer was?"

"No, she rambled about hidden dangers in the shipment and 'attacking innocents.' The cocaine has been tested. Premium product, nothing added." Terri had pieced together everything she could recall after the attack, but she'd missed something.

"Why did she come forward now?"

"She told Conroy she hated being forced to service this old *fra*, but had been afraid to try to escape after hearing what had happened to other women who had tried. The women in this bonded slavery were all blonde like her, except for a black-haired female assistant, who gave this blonde a break from the old man's bed on occasion. After she overheard some men talking with the *fra* about how they needed people to test a virus on, she panicked. She was terrified she'd end up as a guinea pig, because the *fra* had just called her useless for being sick and crying all the time. She was pregnant and hadn't told him. While he was in bed one night with his assistant, she snuck into his office and found photos of hideous deaths the men had brought with them. That cinched the decision to escape."

"Did she have any of those photos?"

That would have been too easy. Terri shook her head. "No, she was afraid to take something he'd just gotten in since he might notice current photos missing. She dug around until she found the DEA agent's photo with his name and alias on the back."

"How does this tie together with Marseaux's shipment?"

"I don't know. I've been through that container over

and over again. I can't find anything missing except the teak carpenter tools. I wish I'd unpacked that whole box now. If Monday is a terrorist attack, we only have a couple days."

"Have you contacted anyone in national defense?"

"Be serious. I don't have enough proof. I found out all this the night I met with Conroy. He finally convinced her to meet me. I got a text message to meet Conroy about a big break in the Marseaux case, which is what I told our SAC the day I went to meet Conroy. But when I got to Conroy, he shared everything, including that this organization of *fratelli* had their people working covertly inside every government agency . . . even the DEA. That's why he was careful about what he told me via text message. We were ambushed before he could lead me to the woman."

"That's how you were injured?"

"Yes."

Nathan's fierce gaze chilled her. "Who else knew about the meeting?"

"Everyone working on the Marseaux case. We had over twenty agents and NOPD detectives. I had a tracking chip in my phone. All I had to do was hit a stored three-digit number, then hit send, which I could do without looking at the phone, to call in backup. I never got a chance. Someone hit me over the head first."

"Any idea what happened to the woman?"

"No, but I doubt she made it." Terri had worried over her many nights, wishing she'd been able to help her. "There's been a rash of missing blonde females. Five in the past eight months fit her description. By the time I was out of recovery, I was under investigation for Conroy's death and suspected of playing for Marseaux's side. Incriminating evidence *appeared*. I haven't contacted any agency about this intel, because I don't know who I can trust. If I could find hard evidence to prove there was going to be an attack, I'd at least send it in anonymously. I've researched everything around that date and there is no major event: the president isn't traveling, the date doesn't have a meaning like 9/11 did, no dignitaries are coming here. I have nowhere to point to as a location or person to protect." She took in a deep breath and let it rush from her lungs, as if that would flush out her frustration of being no closer at this point.

"Who would go to that much effort to frame you?"

That was something Terri wished she knew. "My first thought would be Josie—a DEA agent—since she hates me, but I can't make that fit in my mind. She's been a roaring pain in my side since our first meeting, but I have to give the witch credit. She's made her share of busts and is a stickler for playing by the book. I've never trusted Brady's partner, Donnie Sinclair. But it may be more personal than anything. He gets on my nerves with crude jokes."

"What about Brady?"

She should have answered quick and decisively, but got hung up on how to explain her relationship with Brady. "No, and if you'll stop scowling I'll tell you why. We, uh, dated for a while. We never were intimate," she rushed to add. "He's still interested, but I'm not. He followed me that night, because he later told me he'd suspected Conroy for a while and was worried about me. We argued about that one when I was in the hospital, but I couldn't fault Brady.

If he hadn't shown up and shot the guy attacking me with a knife, the second stab would have split my chest."

"That doesn't mean he's trustworthy," Nathan pointed out with extra force.

She started to defend Brady, but realized Nathan was speaking as a man who had just slept with her and suspected any man.

"He's been sharing information, so I have to trust him for now."

"I don't. Let's go over everything you and I have so far. I didn't get a chance to tell you that I found Jamie's notes."

"Really?" She watched for any sign of emotion, but Nathan shared nothing with his stern expression. He kept his emotions tucked far away. She couldn't fault him in light of all he'd endured.

"Jamie found that same date in Marseaux's correspondence with a man called V. Jamie cross-referenced every date and event he could find, too, and came up empty. He was thinking biological warfare or a chemical release."

"Nothing fits. How would anything like that be transported in tools? The small handsaw and planing tool I saw had ornately carved teak handles. There was a solid wood L square. I didn't dig farther in the box, but nothing looked suspicious."

"I don't know," Nathan murmured to himself. "We're missing something significant."

She checked her watch. "I really have to go. If I don't show up today I'll draw attention neither of us needs."

"Then go."

Nathan was back to two-syllable sentences.

She asked, "What are you going to do today?"

"Watch your back."

"I'll be fine."

"I'll make sure of it." He cupped her face in his hands and kissed her so tenderly she wanted to melt. When he stopped, Nathan said, "I—" then paused.

"What?" She tried to read his eyes, but he just shook his head as if reconsidering his words.

He kissed her forehead. "Let me know if you need a cell phone. I'll get one from Stoner. Keep my number with you."

"I can't get anything done while worrying about you out on the streets with the entire world looking to hang you."

Nathan sighed and took her hand. "Trust me. I can handle this."

She didn't doubt his skills, but she did worry about what he'd do once he found his brother's killer.

Would he truly wait for justice?

~⊶~

B rady and Donnie were waiting by her desk when Terri walked in. She didn't have time for this. "I'm in a hurry, got a lot to do today," she told Brady as she walked up.

"Won't take long." He cut his eyes around, then back to Terri. "Need somewhere private to talk."

She considered arguing, but Brady said he would be quick so talking to him might be more expedient. "Follow me." When Donnie made a move, she started to halt him.

"Wait out here for me," Brady told Donnie, who curled one side of his mouth, annoyed. But the sidekick did as told.

She led Brady to a small meeting room and closed the blinds as he shut the door. Terri turned to him, but was not sitting. He'd said brief, so they could stand.

"I called the prison where Jamie Drake was serving his time. He's out and has been since Fat Tuesday. I couldn't see how Drake would be out early, but couldn't make sense of the Drake sightings. Warden said the paperwork was *lost*."

That fit with what Nathan had told Terri. Suspicion coating Brady's last comment quirked her own curiosity over the paperwork being lost, but she was glad something had worked in Nathan's favor. She held her peace, waiting for more.

"Warden wasn't too chatty until I told him we had a string of deaths related to the Drake murder since Jamie had been released. Jamie Drake is officially a suspect."

Terri froze at those words. "What murders do you think he committed?"

"Bennie Larriot, FinMan, and now Hatchet."

"Hatchet? The guy who broke into my house who we arrested?" That couldn't be right and she knew it. "We have him in custody."

Brady shook his head. "You *had* him in custody. He was shot by a long-range rifle on the way out of his arraignment hearing."

"When?"

"At 5:10 p.m. yesterday."

The shot was made right after she'd left for the container. She hadn't seen Nathan all day, not until after 6:00 p.m. That didn't mean he was guilty.

But another death while he slipped around the city didn't look good for him, either.

"What makes you think the shooter is Jamie Drake?" she asked skeptically.

Brady frowned slightly, just enough to let her know she'd sounded a bit too defensive.

"I mean, the first place I'd look would be Marseaux," she explained to cover her slip.

"Not Marseaux's style. He normally has them capped up close, then the body left in an outline. None of these were killed that way. All three claimed to have been interrogated by Nathan Drake. He and Jamie were identical twins."

She narrowed her eyes on him. "Something you failed to mention that night in the morgue."

Brady shrugged, his gaze straying enough to undermine her trust in whatever he deemed worthy of sharing. "I just found out myself when I started suspecting the Drake in prison was after Marseaux's people. The intel we had when I cut the deal with Nathan Drake failed to include that. I'm not holding out. I've shared more than I should have with you."

She couldn't argue with his last point, but she didn't want to accept that Nathan was killing people in cold-blooded murder. Terri studied Brady's face, searching for a sign that he was lying or holding back.

He met her gaze and held it, unflinching.

Pretty convincing, which meant she had to accept what he told her. Even if the victims were criminals, she couldn't abide murder and especially a vigilante. Not after a self-proclaimed vigilante had murdered her mother, an innocent bystander.

Brady cleared his throat in warning. "We have to find this guy. He's a mental case, a dangerous one. And we think he's Nathan, not Jamie."

"Why?"

"I did some digging on the Drake in prison and doubt Jamie would have lived two years in the pen. Added to what we've heard about one running around loose who's supposed to be a ghost, we think it's a better bet that Jamie was killed."

Terri schooled her expression to cool professional, but her stomach knotted over how Brady and his team were putting two and two together. She should be thankful for whatever reason had delayed the prison paperwork or Brady would have figured this out sooner.

Brady wasn't through. "If we're figuring right, then we're dealing with someone who has Special Force skills and a vendetta against anyone he considers at fault for his brother's death. Dangerous mix."

She swallowed the lump of anxiety threatening to suffocate her. The Nathan she'd gotten close to was not a vigilante. He was doing . . .

What?

Tracking down people involved in his brother's death.

Of course, she'd never clarified what Nathan was going to do once he had that evidence.

Terri felt the need to point out something, but kept her tone clinical. "You said Nathan was MIA or went AWOL, take your pick, to come home and care for his sick mother.

So now you're saying he took his brother's place in prison, did two years?"

"Sounds pretty noble out of context, but the bodies are piling up so I'm just looking at the evidence with an objective eye."

That hit home. Spending the night wrapped in Nathan's arms sort of undermined any hope of objectivity. "I suppose you have a point."

"Terri, this guy was a killing machine before he went into prison. Think that softened his personality at all? No. He's out for blood. Once he finds out I cut the deal with his brother, I'll probably be next." Brady shrugged, but sent her a quick glance. His eyes searched hers for a reaction. Sympathy?

"I think—" What? That Brady was wrong because she'd slept with Nathan and that proved his innocence? Worse. She cared for Nathan. What a mess. Brady was waiting for her to finish her sentence. "—we should consolidate efforts so we can find this guy killing people." Whoever he was.

"Me, too, but I want you to be careful. I'm worried you're not just working on a drug case, something that could get you hurt."

"Why do you say that?"

"I know about the break-in at the container and the missing NOPD officer."

Nothing leaks faster than news around a police station. "What's that got to do with this?"

"Okay, here's why I didn't let Donnie come in here with us. I'm going to square with you. Remember the virus outbreak in South America two years ago?"

She nodded.

"Those deaths match the ones in the Congo last year and India this week. I have a contact that believes those outbreaks are related and thinks it may be some sort of biological testing. I need any information that might be related, no matter how obscure."

Just what Conroy had feared, but she couldn't bring herself to tell Brady. When Brady shot the killer and went to call for an ambulance, she'd crawled over to Conroy, who had lost so much blood she couldn't see the wounds. She'd held him close, knowing he wasn't going to make it.

Conroy had whispered, "Tell . . . no one . . . not even . . . Brady."

She'd given Conroy her word, so she now said, "I wish I had something to tell you, but I don't."

"What about the container breach?"

"You're right, someone got into the container," she admitted. No point in protecting that.

"Rumor has it that some of the shipment was already missing." Brady leveled her with a don't-bullshit-me gaze.

How much had he heard about the missing materials? Did he know about the teak tools or was he fishing for more information?

She shrugged. "Philborn doesn't tell me everything. How do you think any of this is connected?"

Lines creased Brady's forehead. Not entirely satisfied with that answer. "I might know by now if this Drake guy wasn't shutting down informants. If we end up with a viral outbreak, he's at fault for holding up my investigation."

"That's a stretch." Too fast and too defensive yet again. She clamped her lips shut.

"He's going after everyone connected to Marseaux. Word on the street is to hide until he's caught or killed, so our intel is drying up faster than rain in the Sahara." Brady raised his hands in a dismissive gesture as he paced back and forth. "We may have a national threat brewing with no way of determining what it is, where it will happen, when it will happen, or who is behind it. The longer this damn vigilante is loose, the harder it's going to be to find answers."

She had to do something and everything came back to the contents in that shipping container. If Brady was right, the stolen contents might be the key to all of this. Had Taggart stolen something that would offer a clue? She had to find out, and soon. With so many innocent lives at stake, speed and efficiency counted right now, but Conroy's dire warning not to trust anyone tripped up her urge to tell Brady more.

So what had Brady come hoping to gain from this meeting? "What can I do to help?"

He swung an assessing stare her way that had caused others to squirm, but she returned his level gaze until he broke eye contact and spoke. "Let me know when you get *any* lead on Drake, regardless of which brother it's about."

"I'll dig around and see what I can find." She reached for the doorknob.

Brady nodded and walked out the door she'd opened.

Terri had to find Taggart and determine if he had some of that teak tool shipment.

But first she had to speak to Nathan. She had questions for him. What she did about him after that depended on his answers.

Putting herself on the line was one thing.

She couldn't allow a vigilante to put innocent citizens at risk.

Terri plopped down at her desk. Her car keys and cell phone sat on top of a stack of files with a note from the mechanic saying he figured she was looking for the phone and the car was ready. She flipped the phone open that—yay!—appeared to function. The voicemail was filled with one terse message after another from Nathan, then one from Grandma, who had called to say she was feeling a little under the weather and might come home early, but not to worry. She hoped Terri was doing something besides working all night.

If Grandma only knew.

That call had come through over an hour ago. She wished Grandma had called the house or the station. Grandma had both numbers. Terri tried her grandmother's cell number and got her voicemail. She shouldn't stress. Her grandmother was with friends who all had Terri's number, but that didn't stop her from worrying. She replayed Nathan's messages. He never said more than six words and left no name, but she heard his worry.

He didn't act like a killer or sound like one.

But she'd been wrong before, and this time the consequences could be deadly.

Duff couldn't ignore the buzzing phone any longer. That Fra Bacchus chose to call instead of text message meant he was upset. Duff answered, "Yes, sir."

"You didn't report in."

"I don't have anything to report yet, sir."

"What happened?" The Fra slurred his words. Lunchtime, which meant bottle number two for the day.

"The person I was trying to get an appointment with did not show." Where had the Mitchell woman gone last night? Duff had driven to her house, the container, then the precinct, where her car was parked. A mechanic showed up to tinker with the car for a bit, then left it with the hood up.

"All night?" Fra Bacchus's snarly tone raked across Duff's nerves.

"The person had car trouble and was stranded at work all night." Not exactly the truth. Duff had waited for her to leave. Mitchell must have gone home without her car, because she walked up to the precinct today. Someone had dropped her in the area. The mechanic returned this morning to finish whatever he started last night, but Duff had taken advantage of the hood being up to do a little work of his own while the car was unlocked.

"Our drop-dead time for this project nears," the Fra said.

Duff smiled at the play on words. Drop dead. How apropos. "Not a problem. I did some work personally on her car that should expedite transmission of information. I still anticipate having the product by no later than tomorrow morning, as the client has been informed." He'd inserted a voice-activated transmitter that would pick up any conversation in the car.

"You're sure you were clocked in all night."

"All night," Duff answered with conviction. The Fra wouldn't understand. He couldn't fault Duff. If all the vials had been in the container yesterday, Duff would have been done with this task by now. The Fra had women at his fingertips. A man that old and pickled on wine had no idea the strain Duff had been under for the past two weeks.

If Duff had picked up Mitchell first, he would have committed a worse transgression than a sin of the flesh; he'd have ended up having to explain an unnecessary death. As it was, he was calm after enjoying the little cherry playmate he'd met along Canal Street. His favorite hunting grounds.

"Starting now, check in every four hours until this assignment is completed."

Duff lifted a fist and shook it. *Don't treat me like a child, dammit.* He opened his fist and rubbed his head. "Yes, sir. Anything else, sir?"

"Yes. The appointment you're trying to make has become necessary."

Duff felt a surge of excitement. Necessary, as in a necessary death? "Yes, sir. I'll execute the contract," he answered in code.

"Exactly," the Fra confirmed and hung up.

Duff closed his eyes and leaned back, smiling. Bonus time. He pictured the young wholesome blonde from last night who had slid into the passenger seat of his rented Jaguar.

Almost as easily as her nude body had slid over the transom of his boat four hours later, weighted with anchors tied to her neck and ankles. Crabs would clean the carcass in no time.

Duff drummed his fingers on the steering wheel. The Mitchell woman had to know where the other two vials were. If she didn't know or refused to comply, Duff had an effective way of withdrawing information he felt sure would lead him to the vials.

Then he'd leave her tucked away for a midnight morsel.

CHAPTER SEVENTEEN

Nathan cranked the Javelin as soon as Terri stepped out of the precinct. He pulled into traffic, slowly following her until she was a block from the building, then moved up beside her at a cross street. Once she was settled in, he needed to ask her about the DEA agent "JB" referenced in Jamie's letter. He should have asked last night and would have if he'd been able to keep any blood in his brain around her. But the minute he'd put his hands on her, his mind had turned to mush.

She walked in front of his hood, then swung around to the passenger side and climbed in. Her gait was stiff, but he didn't think her leg was to blame.

"You okay?" he asked, then moved into the flow of traffic.

"Fine."

"Anything happen at work?"

"Not really."

Nathan checked the traffic behind him and gave her

a minute to talk, but she wasn't saying a word. "What's wrong?"

"Nothing."

Did this have to do with last night? He'd never been smooth when it came to the day-after discussions, which was why he should have avoided the night before. Like there was any chance he would have walked away from her last night.

She turned to him, eyes worried over something. Hell, what had happened since she'd left him this morning?

"Have you murdered anyone?" she asked.

That was a tricky one. "What's your definition of 'murder'?"

She glared at him. "Don't play twenty questions with me right now. Yes or no."

"I was in the army, Terri. Special Ops, sent into the most godforsaken places you can imagine, where I did unspeakable things. We weren't exactly sent in to teach our enemies to knit. Of course I've killed people."

She wrapped her arms around her stomach and looked away as if asking these questions bothered her as much as him. "Let me rephrase that. Have you killed anyone that was not under orders?"

He could say no, but didn't want to lie to her. They'd agreed to be honest. "Yes, but they deserved to die."

"That doesn't make killing okay."

"You can't say that. You weren't there." Nathan took the ramp to Interstate 10 East.

When she swung back around, fire danced in those green eyes. "Yes, I can say it's wrong. You can't decide who lives and who dies, even if they're criminals."

He'd been judge and jury more times than he wanted to remember, like when he'd killed the two slimes raping that girl in South America. He didn't talk about those times and tried hard not to think about them, but he wouldn't apologize for doing what he'd believed was right. "Some criminals can't be brought to trial."

"You said you were after the same thing as me. Justice. So I want to know, what are you going to do when you find the man who killed your brother? Because I have no doubt that you *will* find him."

"I'll make that decision when I'm faced with it."

"That's not good enough."

"That's going to have to be good enough for now!" He glared at her for pushing him to think past his grief and anger to answer the question that had plagued him since walking out of prison.

Someone had to be punished for killing Jamie.

Marseaux was untouchable or so it seemed, since law enforcement and the courts hadn't found a way to capture him yet. If he wasn't stopped, how many more would die? How many more families would be left bereft?

Someone had to keep the monsters at bay.

"Nathan, you've got to turn yourself in."

What the hell? He scowled at her. Had she been smoking some of the DEA's impounds?

Tears pooled in the corners of her eyes. "Brady found out you were released and suspects you of trading places with Jamie. An APB was being issued on both of you as I was leaving the precinct." She sniffled and stared out the windshield. "I'll help you. Come back with me."

"No."

"Don't you understand?" she breathed, turning back to him and fisting her hands. "They listed you as armed and dangerous and you're to be brought in at all costs. You're suspected of killing three men."

Fury and disbelief tangled inside him. "Who the hell is dead now?"

"Bennie, FinMan, and Hatchet."

He scoffed at the mere thought of wasting his time and skills on their worthlessness. If he was going to bear a murder rap, it would be for someone worth the rest of his life. "I didn't kill *them.*"

He checked the traffic following them closer. No tails. No blue lights. Nathan glanced at Terri, who stared at him with sad eyes that questioned his statement. "I did *not* kill those men, Terri. Hell, you know I could have killed Hatchet that night in your bedroom—" And wanted to for hurting her. "But I didn't. And you saw me turn Hooknose loose. I didn't have to do that, either."

"Then give yourself up."

"No. Given what I've been through, I'm not real trusting of the court system. I'm going to find my *brother's* murderer and I'm not going back into a cell. Been there, done that, and I won't look out through bars ever again."

"A vigilante is a criminal. I won't help a criminal."

Then get out. It was all he could do not to lash out.

No words had cut him quite like hearing her denounce him as a worthless criminal, no better than Marseaux. "You'd think differently if it was your family."

"No, I wouldn't." She held his glare for long bold seconds, then broke the staring contest. "My mother was killed by a vigilante who thought he was shooting a man alone in bed. He didn't realize she was beneath the sheets sleeping when he pumped bullets into the bed of a man he thought had killed his gay lover. Sure, I wanted to hurt someone when I heard how my mother died. I went pretty wild for a while, but I was a teenager with no family." Terri propped her head against a fisted hand, her elbow supported by the door handle. "But as an adult, I've channeled all that pain into working with law enforcement to protect innocent people."

"This is different—" Nathan started.

"The vigilante killed an undercover cop who was trying to find someone murdering gays. My mother had been seeing the cop. Wrong time, wrong place, but that doesn't change that they are dead because someone let pain blind them to following the laws."

"Terri, I'm trained—"

She held up a hand to stop him. "I don't care how trained you are, it's not right. I understand your pain, believe me, but I can't condone unlawful retribution. And I can't keep sharing details of my investigation with someone bent on serving his own needs. If you aren't going to turn yourself in, take me back. I have work to do."

And he'd thought his life had sucked? His admiration for Terri kept taking giant leaps, but nothing was going to deter him from his path. His brother was dead and someone had to pay.

Nathan shook his head. "We still have to figure out what's going to happen in the next few days." He took the first exit off the interstate and headed back toward the precinct.

"We probably won't find out anything in time, because you're interfering with the investigation."

"How do you figure that?" Anger flashed through his words.

"Marseaux's contacts have started going to ground. They're afraid of the Drake ghost. We can't get anything from anyone."

Nathan tapped his thumb against the steering wheel. If he didn't find Marseaux soon, he'd lose any chance of moving freely around this city. Wasn't going to take long for every cop in town to be watching for his face.

This license plate would be released with the APB and a '72 black Javelin stood out in today's traffic, especially since there'd only been twelve of them ever built.

And his was probably the only one still on the road.

But he couldn't let Terri down, either. His plan of attack had been so much simpler before she broke into his mother's house. "I'm not walking back into a jail cell while the person who killed Jamie goes free. Don't ask me for the impossible."

"Then at least leave Marseaux's people alone until we find out if there's going to be a terrorist attack. Can you do that?"

He wanted to say yes, but what if he came face-to-face with Jamie's killer? She couldn't expect him to let that bastard go. "I'll do my best."

"'Do your *best*'? We're only talking about saving lives here," she snapped.

"No one saved Jamie's!" he roared. "Hell, it was *the law* that put him there and cut him loose to die! I told you I was an ex-con and that I'm looking for Jamie's killer. None of this is new. What's really eating at you?"

"Oh, let me see." She lifted her hand, then started counting off fingers. "One—you're on parole and hunting down Marseaux to maybe or maybe not kill him. Two—there's an APB out on you with a shoot-to-kill order. Three—a terrorist group might be targeting an American city with a biological agent that could kill untold numbers. Are you hearing a pattern here, Nathan? The word 'kill' getting through? People are going to die. You could be one of them."

She was hurting and he was the reason.

Nathan reached over to cover her hand. She tried to pull away, but he wouldn't let her.

She covered her eyes with her free hand. A tear ran down her cheek.

How could one drop of water do so much damage to his heart?

Nathan pulled over into the emergency lane and clicked on his flashers. When Terri looked up, he used his thumb to gently wipe the damp streak along her cheek and leaned over to kiss her. "I knew better than to drag you into my problems."

"You didn't drag me. I came willingly. I don't want you killed in a shoot-out or by Marseaux. I was there, Nathan. I watched Conroy die before my eyes when there was nothing I could do. *Nothing*. Even with all my training and a gun in my hand, I was helpless, and it's a bitter feeling of worthlessness I have to deal with every single day for the rest of my life. I don't ever want to relive that again and definitely not when it concerns someone I care about."

Nathan winced at the pain in her voice. He leaned over and kissed her cheek. "I'm sorry."

She cupped his neck, kissing him back ... a gift he didn't deserve but desperately wanted. He'd lived inside a hollow cavern he'd called a body for so long he considered it home. But she'd brought life back into his jaded world, had jump-started his heart and now the organ bled for her.

When he ended the kiss, Nathan held her face between his palms, wishing he had the right words to fix everything. Not his strong suit. "I'll do whatever it takes to help *you*, but no one else."

Terri nibbled on her lower lip, contemplating something. She leaned back, out of his grasp, swiped a hand across her eyes, then took a breath as if her next words required strength.

"It's not that simple. I can't walk a tightwire between you and the law. I know you're a good and decent man. I went to work this morning thinking I could find a way to give you a chance at staying free and having a life. But you don't want that. You want revenge more than you want anything—or anyone—right now."

Revenge was all he'd been living for, but when he looked at Terri he wanted so much more that his burn for vengeance simmered. Didn't matter. He was a hunted man. Staying with Terri any longer only drew her into a danger his presence had created for her. He couldn't live with himself if she was killed.

"I'm clearly on one side of the fence," she said. "The question is, which side are you on?"

The right side.

But this wasn't the time for pretty words and promises. He'd always taken the hardest path and he wouldn't take her down this road with him. "My own side."

Disappointment darkened her gaze. "What would Jamie want you to do?"

Nathan leaned back against his seat, flipped off the emergency blinkers, and pulled back out into traffic. He tried to ignore her question as they rode in silence. That would be about as easy as ignoring the scent of her, which he'd never get out of his car or his mind. Making Jamie's killer pay was the last thing he could do for his family.

How could he live knowing Jamie's killer enjoyed life while his brother decomposed in a tomb?

Goddamn them all.

But then maybe he was the one truly damned.

Nathan wouldn't shirk his duty. "Jamie wouldn't want me to put myself in danger—"

"Then don't."

"—but he'd understand that I have to do this. I can't live knowing his murderer walks the streets free. I. Can't. The only reason he was in danger was to help me. I owe him justice. If not for me, he'd be alive."

"If not for you, he'd be in jail."

He didn't want to hear that. "Yeah. I sacrificed two years of my life in hell so that he could be shot in the head and his body dumped naked on some docks. Forgive me if I'm just a little pissed off about that."

Nathan watched the traffic ahead, the cars surrounding them and behind, anywhere but her face. He needed to find out who JB was in the DEA, but she'd be duty-bound to alert the agent if she did know him, so asking her for more information only pulled her deeper into this mess. He could find his own answers and never planned on working with law enforcement. No one had ever fought his battles.

He wouldn't let Terri take the heat for helping him.

Jamie's death was on Nathan's head. He wouldn't add hers.

"Stop here," she told him over a block from the precinct. He hated to drop her so far away, but pulling closer to the building with this car was not wise.

When the car stopped moving, Terri opened her door, then paused. "I don't want to see *your* body on a slab in the morgue."

"I know." He struggled to end this on a good note, but there was no right way when everything in his world had gone wrong. "Let me know when you're ready to drive home. I'll follow you and . . . stay near." He couldn't walk into that house and not make love to her, so he'd just patrol the outside on foot tonight.

She nodded, stepped out, and closed the door.

Nathan watched her until she disappeared inside the swinging door. His chest tightened at the finality of watching that door close.

During Nathan's tour in the army, Jamie used to tell everyone his big brother was saving the world.

What would Jamie want him to do?

Save the world.

Out of habit, Nathan glanced around, checking people walking, cars moving past on his side, then his gaze moved to the rearview mirror.

An NOPD squad car was slowing down and angling to pull in behind him . . . and parked.

Nathan moved his hand to the gearshift.

Terri walked into more than the normal zoo on the second floor of the temporary precinct building. Sharp words and grim faces painted the room with a palpable tenseness. One pocket of officers and a couple civilians murmured, shoulders hunched in a cringe.

"You aren't getting that damn container," Philborn shouted at Donnie Sinclair, who stood with three other DEA agents looking just as hostile.

"People are dying and you want to play who's got the biggest dick? I'll show you as soon as the court order gets here. Your ass is fried if you don't open that gate to us." Donnie wheeled around and stormed out. The other agents followed suit while trying to maintain a regal Fed air.

Terri trotted over to her desk, glad not to have been a part of that war. Several officers she passed at desks seemed to be moving fast with a purpose, talking excitedly and speed typing.

Or did she just feel sluggish after her draining ride?

An NOPD detective sat hunched over his desk, elbows propped with one hand holding the phone and the other holding his head. ". . . just because she fits the description of the other blondes, it doesn't mean your girlfriend has disappeared. I understand, but I still have to send you to Missing Persons to start there and they won't issue a bulletin until she's been gone for forty-eight hours. I know you're worried, but call more people and see if anyone saw her on Canal Street or has heard . . ."

Terri got to her desk and checked her messages. Taggart hadn't returned her call, but she wasn't surprised.

Was he not at home or just ignoring the phone when it rang?

Out of habit, she turned to where Sammy normally smiled at her from his desk. Her heart squeezed over the empty chair. He'd have Taggart's home address.

Where was Sammy?

If he'd been kidnapped, they should have heard something by now. Her stomach twisted at the reality of not hearing a word in the first twenty-four hours—probably dead. The callous agent inside her knew the chance of survival, but the woman who cared for the young man with big plans had a harder time accepting cold statistics.

Who was the young woman Sammy had planned to marry? Why hadn't Terri asked her name?

And, dammit, why wasn't Sammy here for her to ask that?

Terri hit her fist against the desk. If Marseaux killed Sammy, she was going to . . .

What? She understood the urge to personally go after scumbags like Marseaux, but she would not cross the line into vigilante territory. Her job was to bring criminals to justice, not play judge, jury, and executioner.

"We'll have to turn over the container to the DEA."
Philborn had silently walked up to her. The usual hum of
noise across the room had cranked up another notch since
she'd walked in the door.

"I heard Donnie yelling about that. He was just here
this morning with Brady, so what pushed his button now?"
She glanced around. "Or have you gotten word on Sammy.
Is that what everyone is so tense about?"

"You haven't heard?"

"Heard what?" Now that she paid closer attention, the
atmosphere was more than agitated. The room was filled
with matching bleak expressions.

"About the viral outbreak. Killed sixteen so far. Looks
like the same thing as the one in India."

"Here, in this country?" She stood up. "Oh my God.
Where?"

"Chicago."

Terri's ears rang. She couldn't speak. Blood rushed
from her head, spinning the walls of the room. She heard
Philborn from a distance saying, "Sit down."

Next thing she knew her head was between her legs.
She had to call Grandma and get her home. Terri shoved
her head, swallowing against the nausea. "I'm okay, really."

Philborn looked worried. "You need a doctor?"

"No, it's just . . . my grandmother is in Chicago."

"Oh, shit."

"I have to call her. Go do whatever you have to. I'm
fine."

"Okay, but don't stand up quick again." He lumbered
back to his office.

Terri hit speed dial and prayed her cell phone would work. After three rings, voicemail picked up on Grandma's phone. "Dammit." She pounded the desk. Then her cell phone dinged with a voicemail from an hour ago. Why hadn't the damn phone rung?

She punched send to dial her message box.

Terri, this is Grandma. I'm fine, just feeling like I'm getting a cold and don't want to fly with my head stopped up tomorrow. We all . . . to come . . . They let us fly standby . . . flight's not full so I'll . . . coming in on . . . flight . . .

Terri's heart thumped over the distress she heard in her grandmother's voice, but thank God she'd already gotten a flight before the airport was shut down. She grabbed a pen to jot down the flight information, but the message broke up before she could hear all of it.

She lifted the damn phone to smash it against the desk, but stopped before hitting the hard surface. This haywire electronic nuisance was the best chance of Grandma contacting her until she got home. Grandma must have made it out or she'd be calling Terri at work, home, and everywhere if she'd heard about the virus. So, logically, her grandmother was en route to New Orleans. That was a plus. She tried once more to reach her grandmother and got voicemail.

God, please let Grandma be on the way home. Safe . . .

Terri went cold as another thought occurred to her.

What if that virus had come from their seized container? Had the virus been transported in those teak tools?

The dates didn't fit, but maybe they had to move up the attack.

If the viral outbreak and this container shipment were connected, her grandmother was just as vulnerable here, and maybe more at risk, until Terri solved this case. Grandma knew nothing about BAD. She thought Terri really was freelancing as a consultant. Call Carlos to help?

Terri started weighing the pluses and minuses, a major one being that she still didn't know who to trust in any agency with her life. Trusting her grandmother's with BAD or anyone else in law enforcement was out of the question.

Grandma knew Nathan, or at least that he was a Drake.

Bad as it sounded, Terri's best hope lay with trusting an ex-con.

She might not care for Nathan's tactics, but she did trust him to find a way to protect her grandmother. The plus would be sending him out of sight until she figured some way to clear Nathan of the charges. She used the desk phone to call him, grateful that she finally had a number for him.

"What's up?" Nathan answered sharply as if he was in a hurry.

"Have you heard about the viral outbreak in Chicago?"

"Yes. Got a lead yet?"

"Not yet. I called because Grandma is in Chicago."

He cursed low, but she heard every word. His anger on her behalf softened her insides. She believed him when he said he hadn't killed the three men, but Nathan hid secrets and couldn't see past his need for revenge. They had nowhere to go from here that wouldn't end up with him on the wrong side of a police-issued weapon.

"The good news is that she's on her way home," Terri continued. "The bad news is her message on my cell phone broke up so I didn't get all her flight information."

"What do you need me to do?"

Was he driving? Sounded like the car motor in the background.

"Can you find somewhere safe for her until we get a handle on this? I won't be able to go home and keep an eye on her and I don't want someone coming into the house to get me only to find my blind grandmother."

"I'll handle it."

That was the man who had stolen her heart. Nothing was too much to ask of him . . . except to abandon hunting for his brother's killer.

Then again, maybe she did ask too much of him.

"She'll call me as soon as she lands," Terri explained. "Her friends will take her home. If you could pick her up from home, I'll call you as soon as I hear from her."

"Stoner will—" He paused. Definitely street sounds in the background. "—take her somewhere safe. Too dangerous to be with me."

The APB. Open season on Nathan Drake. "If you'd come in—"

"Write this down," Nathan said, cutting her off. Then he

rattled off a phone number Terri scribbled on a sticky note before continuing. "Call Stoner with details. For security, tell your grandmother when she meets him, to ask Stoner where he last worked with me. South America. He has family close to New Orleans in Metairie. She'll be safe."

"I'll call you as soon as I hear from her." Terri stopped talking and listened closer. A car engine—the Javelin?—revved high and tires squealed. "What are you doing?"

"Driving. Anything else?"

Sirens squeezed through the phone line.

Terri hunched close to the phone and whispered, "Are you being chased?"

"Yes. Little busy right now. We through?"

Was he serious? How could he sound so calm? "No. You better not get caught, dammit."

"Don't plan to." The squeal of rubber on pavement stretched for two seconds, then louder sirens filled the lines before a *click*. He'd hung up.

She clutched the phone. What if they caught him? Would he give up or get shot? The nausea was back. Grandma wouldn't like being picked up by a stranger, but if Terri told her Vic Stoner was a friend of hers and the Drake boy, as Grandma called Nathan, she would probably understand and go with Stoner.

Terri's cell phone buzzed. She answered it without looking at the ID in case Nathan had called back with some last words to give her before he got shot or died. Melodramatic? Probably, but she was involved with a lunatic. "Mitchell here."

"Terri, you okay? You sound sick," Carlos said.

"Allergies."

He seemed to accept that. "I've been trying to reach you between coordinating with the teams in India."

"My phone has been acting up."

"I'll get you a new one, but you should be checking in more often."

She accepted the criticism, glad he sounded too tired to chew on her worse. "I didn't have anything . . . until now."

"Really? Have any idea who released that virus or what it is?"

"Not yet, but I might soon. Where are you now? Do you have computer access?"

"Yes, I'm at our satellite office in Baton Rouge, but I'm leaving soon. Retter and his team are held up getting out of India, so I may have to put a team together for Chicago."

"I have a lead, well, more of a hypothesis, but I need to get out of here to talk." If Terri couldn't get Grandma home any faster or save Nathan from the police, the least she could do was find the damn missing tools and see if there was anything there that could help them. "I need someone's home address."

"Whose?"

"Fred Taggart." She gave Carlos everything she had on Fred, starting with his badge number.

Carlos had the address in one minute. "Need a partner?"

"No. He's a friendly. Let me get down to my car and I'll catch you up." She walked out to the parking lot with two officers, who climbed into separate squad cars. Nathan wouldn't be here to watch over her if she ran into trouble. She hurried to reach the exit ahead of both cars, then waited on them.

When she pulled out, they were right behind her. Her car purred while she waited on an opening on the main thoroughfare. She scooted out ahead of a string of traffic, leaving the two squad cars stuck.

And anyone who might have been right behind them hoping to follow her.

What was Nathan doing? Had they caught him? Instead of the GPS she should have had a police scanner installed. Terri tried Nathan first—voicemail—then called Carlos back.

Carlos answered on one ring. "What are you going to do at Taggart's?"

Shake that fool until his teeth fall out if he doesn't hand over what he stole. "Nothing that requires two people. Just going to ask him for contents the captain believes he took from the container to determine if he has anything that will help with the investigation. I'll offer to keep him out of trouble if he comes clean."

"So what's your hypothesis?" Carlos prompted.

"I think the drug shipment was a Trojan horse to get something more important out of customs quicker. With New Orleans so shorthanded on law enforcement, they probably figured getting to it in the police yard would be less trouble. The dead body threw a kink into getting the container released, so the NOPD gets a tip on drugs inside and, *bam*, the container is released into their custody. If the person who broke into the container had gotten what they wanted the first time, it wouldn't have looked odd, but they broke in twice so it was clearly not for the drugs. The steel frame had been opened the first time and the drugs were removed."

"What do you think he was looking for both times?"

She whipped her car around a bus that had stopped in her lane. "I'm thinking a virus was transported somewhere in that box of teak pieces. Nothing else makes sense. I only unwrapped a couple of tools when I first searched the container, since those didn't appear to be anything but merchandise. I don't know if the duty cop from that night has something significant or not, but if he does I'm going to get it."

"Joe's short on people for Chicago. I may be on the way there next. He's got two teams arriving in Nashville this afternoon from India. Call me as soon as you determine if Taggart has anything we want. If he doesn't hand it over willingly, I'll send Retter to retrieve it." Retter was part of their clean-up and extraction unit. When things got messy, he was one of the agents who got dirty.

"I will," she said and hung up. She should have finished that sentence, which was, "I will ... not leave without everything Taggart stole." She didn't need BAD's top muscle.

Her phone rang again.

Grandma. Thank goodness.

CHAPTER EIGHTEEN

Terri read house numbers as she cruised down Taggart's street. His neighborhood was west of the city, far enough away not to have been flooded from the looks of the houses in good repair. Her cell phone rang. "Mitchell here."

"We think we found Sammy." Philborn sounded more glum than his usual flat personality.

Think? She licked her suddenly dry lips. "What do you mean? Is he alive?"

"No, and we can't visually identify him. Running DNA tests and checking for dental records."

"Oh, dear God. Was he burned?"

"That probably would have been better. Looks like some kind of virus. We're thinking the same thing that hit Chicago. Our ME quarantined the body and called the CDC. It's pretty disgusting."

Her stomach lurched. "Where did you find him?"

"In a plastic bag next to the Dumpster in our parking lot. We don't know who dropped it, but they wanted to leave a message. Doesn't fit Marseaux's standard MO, except for the arrogance. Where are you?"

"Running down a lead on the contents." There was Taggart's brick home. "I've got to go, but I'll fill you in as soon as I get back." She'd have to at this point. But the minute she was out of here, she would personally put her grandmother on an airplane to visit Grandma's sister in Houston.

New Orleans might not be safe now.

Bile climbed her throat at the quick image of Sammy killed like those poor people in India and Chicago. And if her theories were right, this proved someone had control of a deadly virus and was carefully choosing targets.

How dare they play God?

Terri hung up and pulled into the drive behind Taggart's late-model pickup truck parked inside a carport.

She rushed over to the front door and pounded. A television played inside.

Loud grouching carried above the television announcer, then the door opened and Fred squinted at her. Dressed in a white undershirt and faded jeans, he was the epitome of a man trying to enjoy his time off. "What do you want?"

"The tools you stole from the container."

He curled his lip. "Don't come here with that crap. Plenty of people have been in that container." He tried to close the door.

Terri slapped a palm against the door and shoved her booted foot against the kick plate. She locked evil gazes, but hers brimmed with months of frustration and boiling anger over the news of Sammy's death.

"I'll keep this simple, Fred. No one knows I'm here, for now. Sammy's disfigured body just showed up at head-quarters. He was killed by the virus unleashed in Chicago today."

Fred's wrinkled face paled.

Been watching the gruesome news, huh? Timing is every-thing.

Terri didn't miss a breath. "Philborn is close to figur-ing out the tools you palmed from the container match the rest of the contents stolen when Sammy disappeared . . . working *your* damn shift, I might add. Those tools could be the key to figuring out who is behind this outbreak. If Philborn comes for those contents, you'll lose your pen-sion and go to jail. But that's a much better scenario than if you don't give them to me this minute and you accidentally come into contact with that virus."

Fred's eyes watered. His hands shook, then he mum-bled to follow him. The house reeked of fried fish. Fred led her through his wood-paneled living room, where a stuffed bass was hung on the wall. The television had come from a different decade, but the grotesque pictures streaming past of victims in Chicago came through as clear as the national news anchor's voiceover.

Fred opened a door to what should be a bedroom, but the space had been turned into a workshop with a table saw and lathe. Terri waited as he pulled out a drawer on a tall metal chest, then stepped aside quickly, staring at the drawer with sweaty horror. "This is all of it."

She scanned the drawer containing three pairs of beautifully carved tools. Two L squares and two small narrow saws with teak handles, plus two carpenter levels with sealed glass tubes of liquid mounted with tiny gold screws within a cutout section of wood. The bubble inside the tubes indicated when the two-foot piece of teak was perfectly level.

The tubes could just as easily contain a lethal virus.

Terri picked up the carpenter level to examine closer.

"What if you break that?"

"I doubt anyone would ship something this deadly in a glass container that would shatter easily." She hoped not, but that didn't stop her heart from pounding with a healthy amount of trepidation. Upon close inspection, she could see a small ring at the top that slid clockwise when she put a fingernail against it.

She laid the tool back down, slid the ring halfway around, exposing the top of the vial. Using two fingers, she gently lifted the vial from the bracket.

The second vial released just as easily. Both were sealed with a rubber coating on one end, but one had an *X* etched in the tube and the other did not.

Terry picked up a soft cloth and wrapped the vials carefully, then turned to leave.

"Look, I'm sorry about—" Fred started to say.

"Save it for Sammy's family. I've got to go." Terri raced out of the house to her car.

❧

"Make it fast. I'm waiting on another call," Duff told Parker. Not exactly a cell phone call, but a message. Duff had sent a text message confirmation to Fra Bacchus that he'd located the last two vials ten minutes ago. The transmitter in Terri Mitchell's car relayed enough of her conversation for him to know she had them, but not where she'd gone.

What was taking the Fra so long? He normally answered quickly when it was a matter of interest to him.

"Just wanted to let you know everything is falling into place here." Parker's enthusiasm poured across the lines.

Duff's mouth curved up mildly, his eyes sliding to the laptop on the passenger seat of his car. He'd just closed the monitor from covertly observing Parker's meeting with Senator Hutchinson of Illinois, whose next stop was a press conference for the viral outbreak. The senator's face had split with a campaign smile when he learned Parker could make him a hero on tonight's news once he announced the possibility of an antidote. Parker's price—votes for Zolono Pharmaceuticals—had dampened his excitement.

After the meeting, Duff had tuned in on a call between Parker and the scientist at Zolono who had agreed to be the one to "create" an antidote in exchange for the money to get his daughter into Harvard. The Fra would be pleased when Duff shared that nugget, though Duff couldn't figure out why the scientist mattered.

Everyone had a price.

Duff stretched his neck, ready to move all this along. "That all you have to tell me?" .

"No." Parker snapped the word, clearly put out with Duff's no-nonsense tone. "I've made the transfer."

"Good." Duff's phone dinged with a new message. "I'll be in touch." He ended the call, then read the text on his screen.

> *D—Good work. I will be out of pocket for today so I've asked Consul Vestavia to direct you until I return. He will be in touch shortly, but keep an eye on the bird for me, as well.*
>
> *FB*

"The bird" would be code for Brady. But Duff frowned as he went over the message again. He didn't even know this Vestavia guy. How could the Fra hand him off to a consul in the middle of this project? The Fra should have had Duff meet the consul in person first.

Was the old guy getting too pickled to do his job?

Duff's phone dinged again. A message from CV—Consul Vestavia. A consul outranked a general, so Duff opened the message and started reading his next instructions.

❧

Nathan wrenched the wheel hard to the right, sliding the Javelin around a corner. Felt like two wheels had lifted. He couldn't afford to lose the traction. He backed off. The rubber grabbed so he shot forward down a one-way street.

The wrong way.

A Volkswagen pulled out to turn.

He slammed the horn. The Bug drove up on the sidewalk.

Sirens chewed up the air, closing in.

Nathan dug out the USB memory stick and shoved it into his jacket pocket. He spun hard to the left and made two more turns until he saw an overhead door hanging half open on a warehouse with broken windows and missing sheet metal.

He drove in, bouncing across wood, and rolled down the windows. Sirens blared coming close, closer . . . loud . . . then the sirens passed by and faded away.

This car was too easily recognizable. With seven hundred horses under the hood, Black Death could outrun just about anything, especially an anemic police cruiser.

Radios would be a little tougher to beat.

He cut the engine and sat there a minute. *Welcome to my new life.* Might as well get used to it.

Nathan shoved his cell phone in a pocket and locked the car. Moldy air snuck all around him, dank and depressing. He walked around, running his hand over the top. Just let this baby be here when he got back . . .

Pulling the hood over his head, he walked to the street, turned left, and started strolling slowly along. Once he reached the Square, he dialed Terri. Voicemail.

Was she not answering or was that damn phone not working?

He hit speed dial on his phone. When Stoner answered, Nathan said, "I'm on foot."

"Where's the Jav—"

"Parked." Probably for the last time. But he was willing to kiss it good-bye to keep Terri safe.

Nathan turned to face a store window when a police cruiser passed by. "Where are you?"

"Waiting outside Terri's house for her grandma."

Nathan turned in that direction. "I'm heading your way. When is her grandma supposed to be there?"

"Twenty minutes ago. When Terri called, she said by the time her grandmother called to say she was back in town she was already close to home. I have a bad feeling about this."

So did Nathan. "Sit tight. I'll be there in less than ten."

Terri jumped in her car, took one look at Taggart standing in the doorway, and ignored the pasty fear on his face. Her cell phone rang as she was backing out. "Grandma" popped up on the caller ID.

"Are you with Stoner?" Terri answered, checking around her as she headed back to the station.

"Your granny's with me," an unfamiliar male voice informed her.

She hit the brakes. "Who is this?"

"You don't have a lot of time for questions if you want to get your granny back."

Her vision swam in tears. "Don't you dare hurt her. You can have me."

"I don't want you. I want those two vials. I'm betting you know where they are."

She wanted blood.

If she turned those vials over to him, people would die. Many people. Nathan's warning that she would feel differently if her family were threatened or harmed hit her. The urge to kill this man was so strong she couldn't deny it.

"If you don't, I'll just be done with Granny."

"No, I do know. I'll bring them to you."

"Perfect. By now, you surely realize I'm well aware of who you are in contact with and that I have people inside law enforcement. So believe me when I tell you Granny will die if you call anyone on any phone. Come to this address."

Her heart racing from fear and anger, Terri scribbled down the address. By the time she got there, she'd have a plan on how to get her grandmother to safety before she handed over the vials. She would have to. Because once she handed them over, Terri understood her grandmother and innocents would die . . . and she would, too.

"Maybe her grandma tried to reach Terri, but got her voicemail like I've been getting, and left a message on their home phone," Nathan suggested as Stoner followed him into the courtyard behind Terri's home.

"I hope so, but I wouldn't put money on it."

Neither would Nathan. He opened the back door to Terri's house and listened, then ceased all verbal communication until he and Stoner had secured the house. Nathan went to the home phone system. A light blinked with messages.

The first one was her grandmother at the airport in Chicago, telling Terri her flight info. The next one was her grandmother in New Orleans stopped in traffic a mile from the house. Nothing else.

"I think the traffic jam is suspect," Stoner said.

"Me, too."

The house phone rang. Nathan let it go to voicemail so he could listen to the caller before picking up. A hang-up.

Stoner walked in from the living room. "Someone just checked out my SUV. Male. Operative."

Nathan nodded and moved into the dark hallway. Stoner took up another position inside the living room.

The door to the kitchen opened slowly a few minutes later, followed by the barrel of a weapon. Once inside, the man started forward, checking the house the same way Nathan had. When he reached the hallway, Nathan made his move.

He hit the guy hard, knocking him back into the kitchen. The intruder caught his balance and swung the weapon up, but Nathan was on him in a nanosecond. He shoved the weapon arm up and back against the doorjamb, knocking the gun loose. This guy was big and lean with muscle, but fury blasted through Nathan on an adrenaline wave nothing would have stopped. He caught him around the throat with his forearm.

A *flick* sounded and the tip of a blade pierced Nathan's shirt, breaking the skin.

"Back away, fucker, or it goes all the way in," the guy warned.

Stoner stepped into view and put the barrel of his 9 mm H&K against the man's forehead. "Drop it. They can patch a knife wound, but I doubt we'll find all the pieces to put your brains back together."

The operative actually pressed on the knife. If Nathan didn't need to find out what this guy knew about Terri, he'd have grunted with the pain, but Stoner would kill the bastard at that.

A slew of cursing spit out of this bastard's mouth before the knife clanged against the hardwood floor.

"Who are you?" Nathan demanded. When he didn't get an answer, he said, "If you've hurt Terri or her grandmother, I promise to make your death slow and agonizing."

"I don't have Terri," the guy answered.

"Then who are you?"

The man didn't answer.

"NOPD?" Nathan asked.

"Do I look like a fucking pig?"

Not really. Nathan scrunched his forehead in thought, then it dawned on him. Of course. "You're with the agency she works for."

The man's features went blank. "What agency, gringo? I don't know what you're talking about."

Yeah, right. "What's your name and why are you here?"

"Why *you* here, gringo? You here to hurt women or you just want to steal something?"

Nathan tightened his grip while Stoner searched him for a wallet.

The man banged his head back into Nathan's face, slamming him in the nose. Damn, it hurt, but not enough to make him loosen his hold. He'd been trained in the army to stay tough even while being beaten with the stock end of a rifle. And that was nothing compared to what prison trained him for. A little slap on the nose wouldn't do anything except piss him off.

"Carlos Delgado," Stoner said.

"What agency is he with?"

"There's no badge. Only his license."

Nathan tightened his hold again. "So what are you doing here, Carlos?"

"Pissing you off."

Stoner held his gun up to Carlos's forehead. "Let's just off the bastard and then work on saving Terri and her grandmother."

Before Nathan could move, Carlos lifted his feet and kicked Stoner back. The sudden shift in weight was enough to bring Nathan down, too. Carlos spun before he swept his feet out from under him.

A shot rang out.

Nathan and Carlos froze as Stoner stood up with the weapon trained fully on Carlos. "Enough with the dancing. The next bullet is between your eyes."

"All right," Carlos said, moving into a stance they all knew meant he was waiting for an opening to disarm Stoner.

Stoner lowered the gun to Carlos's crotch. "Should we continue splitting hairs?"

"Not down there, amigo. Take the eyes, please."

Nathan pushed himself back to his feet and exchanged a look with Stoner. "He's obviously well trained. I say Fed."

"He has the look, but he fights like someone from the streets, not one of them Ivy-trained overachievers. And he doesn't reek of military."

Stoner had a point.

"Fuck it, shoot him."

Carlos didn't even flinch as Stoner squeezed the trigger. He didn't plead, beg, or even blink.

"Damn," Stoner said as he fired the bullet so close to Carlos's face it would have killed him had the man even breathed. "I thought I was stone cold. You make me look scared."

A muscle worked in Carlos's jaw. "You gonna shoot me or just play games?"

Nathan stepped forward. But before he could speak, his phone rang. Seeing the caller ID as Terri, he snatched it up and answered.

"Nathan, I need you to come get my grandmother." Terri carefully enunciated each word.

Every alarm in his body rang. This wasn't like her and the underlying tone of her voice said she was scared. "Where are you?"

"I'll tell you in a minute. You have to come alone." Her voice quivered and his gut tightened.

"Tell *them* I understand."

"Good." She gave him an address in the St. Bernard Parrish.

Nathan gripped the phone so tightly that he was surprised it didn't shatter. "I'm coming to get you."

"I know," she whispered. "I'm sorry."

"No, they'll be sorry."

The line went dead.

"Was that Terri?" Carlos asked.

The concern in his voice was too real to be feigned. "Yes. I have to go."

"Where is she?"

"In trouble, as usual."

Carlos cursed in Spanish before he sneered at Stoner. "Put the damn gun away. We're obviously on the same team. I came here to check on Terri and make sure she was okay."

Nathan shook his head. "Then you'll understand why we don't trust you."

Carlos took it in stride. "I don't trust me most days. However, I'm an expert at . . . difficult extractions. Give me the address so I can get her back and give her a piece of my mind."

"Like hell," Nathan growled. "You let them take her. He's the only one going with me." He pointed at Stoner.

Carlos sent a dismissive glance at Stoner, then raked Nathan with black eyes. "I didn't let anyone take shit, boy. And I can level the same thing back at you. How did *you* let her get taken?"

Nathan hated the fact that he had a point.

"What I thought," Carlos said. "She don't listen to me *or* you. Now we got to go get her." He looked at Stoner. "You got any experience?"

Stoner smirked at Carlos with bored patience. "I'm former army intelligence, Special Forces, on contract to the U.S. government now for national security. That good enough for you, *amigo?*"

Carlos returned the stare with one that said he was less than impressed. "It'll do."

Nathan shoved his phone in his pants pocket. "I'll take your number and call if we need you, but"—he stepped close to Carlos—"if you show up where you aren't invited and put her at further risk, I'll kill you before they get a shot at you."

"Trust me. You're a rookie." Carlos gave them his cell number. "You can't fight these people alone."

"I lost rookie status long before you were born. I don't

intend to fight them," Nathan replied. "Marseaux wants me. I'm going to trade places with Terri. You got a helicopter close by?"

"I can get one."

"Then get it if you want to help. If we need the cavalry, you won't reach us fast enough without one."

"At least give me an airport or location close to where you're going."

"Lakefront Airport." Nathan looked at Stoner. "Let's go."

❧

"He's coming," Terri told the man who identified himself as Duff, which she doubted was his real name. She used her free hand to close the cell phone and placed it on a small desk.

"Make yourself comfortable and have a seat." Duff stood at the front of the ravaged classroom, pointing his gun at her sweet grandmother like a demented teacher picking on a helpless student.

Broken windows did little to dissipate the smell of mildew crowding the air in the abandoned school, another casualty of Katrina.

Terri lifted the two vials lying on the desk into her left hand, careful to keep her 9 mm aimed at the deadly capsules.

Her bluff had worked, almost. But not as she'd planned.

Spiked blond hair, tall and slender, the man who had identified himself as Duff was attractive for someone insane. He clearly enjoyed this.

He'd broken out in laughter at her offer that she'd hand over the vials as soon as her grandmother was delivered to the closest police department where someone could call to confirm she was safe.

Duff suggested what he considered was a better idea. Call Drake and Terri could walk out with her grandmother or he'd kill both of them right now. That's when she'd found out there had been ten vials originally and Duff's people only needed six, right now. Losing this pair carrying the virus and the antidote would be inconvenient, but wouldn't delay their schedule.

However, if he delivered the two she held at gunpoint he'd be handsomely rewarded. So he'd deal if she would.

Terri had to choose. Her grandmother's life for Nathan's.

Noooo. Bile lurched up her throat every time she thought about what she was drawing Nathan into. His voice echoed in her mind: *Trust me. I can handle this.*

Trusting a criminal had almost gotten her killed last time, but there was no one she trusted more at the moment. BAD would come in with a team. That might work or Duff might be alerted and kill her grandmother.

Nathan was highly trained and as stealthy as a ghost. He would find a way in without putting her or her grandmother in danger. She just wished she knew he would have a way out. Terri wasn't leaving without him.

"Don't want to sit down?" Duff taunted. "Then hand me the vials so you can both leave as soon as he gets here." He grinned, toying with her like a cat played with a mouse.

She scoffed at him. "Contrary to many obnoxious jokes, blondes aren't stupid."

Terri split her vision between the vials and her normally robust grandmother, who now huddled next to Duff looking frail and old. Grandma's intermittent silence mixed with low murmurs scared Terri. She needed her grandmother lucid enough to escape when she gave her directions.

"If not for your being a nuisance and Drake's interference, this wouldn't have happened." An arrogant smile tilted his lips.

Now Terri understood what drove Nathan to hunt down his brother's killer. If anything happened to Grandma and Terri survived, she would hunt this man to the end of the earth.

Even though she'd met plenty of snakes like this, she still didn't understand them. "Why are you killing people? Are you part of a terrorist group?"

Duff laughed, his gun bobbing carelessly around her grandmother. "Terrorists? Be real. Don't compare me with those bottom-feeders. Their vision is too narrow and self-serving. Like *they* deserve to inherit this world? They're no more capable of ruling than the rest of you ignorant fools."

Weird and mental guy, but Duff was hinting at his leaders. Terri asked, "So who *does* deserve to rule?"

"The most enlightened geniuses of our generation."

Geniuses. Could this be some wacko cult? If so, this would be the first one sophisticated enough to bring in a deadly virus. No, this was too international feeling. And, if this group was truly made up of geniuses and possessed any serious level of organization, the world could be facing something far worse than a cult.

Terri narrowed her gaze at him. "So these killings aren't about some terrorist demand?"

"A terrorist demand is trite compared to what we fight for."

Keep him talking. The more she learned, the more she could use to find these bastards and stop them. If she lived. "So what *are* you fighting for?"

"No harm in telling you since *you*, unfortunately, will not be here to see the results of our labor." Duff's shoulders tipped back, full of self-importance. His eyes glowed with the chance to brag. "We're committed to protecting the world from itself. There is no one nation with the intellectual capacity and true power necessary to rule all nations, but there is a governing body of geniuses that will one day emerge when the world is ready for their leadership."

Lunatic. Zealot. Moron. Take your pick, any of those would fit this man. Terri sorted through all he said, but came up blank. No terrorist group. No particular nation. What did these people want?

The door behind her opened.

She froze.

"Don't shoot her, Teto," Duff called out. "She's got a gun on the vials."

A sob from her grandmother reached Terri's ears. Tears threatened at how afraid her grandmother had to be. God forgive her, but Terri wanted these men to die.

Footsteps tapped coming up from behind her, then passed on her left and walked toward Duff. A Hispanic man wearing a camo T-shirt and jeans walked up to whisper something to Duff, who smiled and said, "You have everything ready?"

"Yes."

Duff turned to Terri. "Our company has arrived."

∼

Nathan stopped just inside the tree line and studied the expanse of weed-ravaged playground between him and the school through his night-vision monocular. The sun had dropped out of sight, leaving the world tinted with twilight. Stoner peered through a pair of night-vision binoculars, sweeping them slowly across the terrain.

"They know I'm here." Nathan recognized a trap.

"Yep. You set?"

Nathan reached in his pocket and pulled out the Army Ranger coin and offered it to Stoner. "Keep it this time."

Stoner lowered the glasses, looked at the coin, and shook his head. "Not yet. I think it's got one more life in there for you. I'll call Carlos as soon as I have Terri and her grandmother."

Nathan shoved the coin back into his pants pocket. "I hope you're right about the coin, but either way, get them out of here."

Waiting any longer wasn't going to lower his chances of being shot on the way to the school. Nathan pointed to the right and Stoner disappeared into the woods. If Nathan didn't take a slug going straight in, he'd meet Stoner next to the entrance door, which stood wide open.

He kept low to the ground, zigzagging across the field until he reached the door. A minute later, Stoner arrived with his monocular in place. Nathan led the way into the dark building. Light shined from one doorway. When he neared it, he peeked around the corner and took in the scene.

Terri stood with her back to him in the middle of the room.

Two men at the head of the classroom faced her, with Grandma between them.

Nathan raised his monocular and stepped into view. "I'm here. Let the women go."

Everyone in the room tensed except for Grandma, whose lips quivered.

"In due time." The one holding Terri's grandmother had spoken. "Put your weapon down."

Nathan tossed his gun onto the closest desk. "Who are you?"

"Me? I'm Duff." He grinned. "And this is my partner, Teto. Want to introduce your partner?"

"What do you want?" Nathan kept his eyes on Terri, who hadn't moved a muscle.

"Terri knows what I want, don't you?" Duff said.

She nodded.

"Bring the vials up here and we'll trade, as agreed."

When she moved, Terri lifted two small vials off the desk in front of her and carried her SIG in her other hand.

Nathan realized she'd been holding them at bay by threatening to shoot the vials. His heart hammered at each step she took forward, but he couldn't move and risk getting her shot.

When Terri reached the front, she held up the two vials with the weapon pointed at her hand. "I'll blow my hand off if you try to trick me. Turn my grandmother loose first."

"Terri, don't, they'll—"

"I know, Nathan. Please take my grandmother out of here."

"As you wish." Duff led her grandmother by the arm to the center aisle, then instructed her to walk straight forward.

When her grandmother reached Nathan, he took her arm and whispered, "My friend Stoner will take care of you. I'm not leaving without Terri."

Tears streamed down her wrinkled face. She trembled violently. He eased her out the door and passed her off to Stoner, who had been close enough to hear everything. Then Nathan turned back to Duff. He realized then that Terri intended to give her life to free him and her grandmother.

"Marseaux wants me, not Terri. I'll come willingly if you'll let her go."

"No, Nathan!" she cried out. "They released the virus in Chicago—"

Duff raised his .357 Magnum to shoulder level, pointed at Nathan. "Hand Teto the vials or he dies now."

She handed the vials to his partner.

Duff whipped an arm around her throat and choked her into silence. Once she was quiet, he shoved the nozzle of his weapon under Terri's throat. "Marseaux isn't part of this. He's just a puppet we use when necessary. You give him too much credit." He kept his gaze on Nathan, but spoke over his shoulder to his partner. "Check the vials to make sure they are marked correctly and she didn't switch them with two phony ones, then prepare to leave."

Teto nodded and turned away to a box on a table to the side of where they stood.

"Handing you over to Marseaux isn't near enough payback for causing me to look bad with the order," Duff told Nathan. "Much as I'd like to exact revenge on you, I can't do so without permission. Everyone within the Order, including me, must follow rules, or there is chaos."

"What order?"

"Fratelli de il Sovrano, of course."

The *F* and *S* from Jamie's note. Nathan didn't know what kind of bullshit he was spouting and frankly, he didn't care. All that mattered was getting between that gun and Terri. "So what do you want?"

"You have the vials, let him go," Terri pleaded with Duff.

Nathan shook his head. "If you want revenge, trade me for her."

Duff cackled. "You think this is a negotiation? No, no, no. I have you exactly where I want you—in the middle of nowhere."

And sharing more than expected, which told Nathan these two planned to kill him, Terri . . . and her grandmother, which would include Stoner. He pressed for more.

"Why are you releasing the virus? What do you hope to gain?" Nathan shifted his weight, but was actually moving forward with each slight adjustment in his stance.

"You wouldn't understand." Duff glanced out the broken windows as if he expected someone.

"Why wouldn't I understand?" Nathan wanted to hold Duff's attention.

"You don't have the IQ, not like your brother's. He could have comprehended the significance of our work."

"Jamie?" Nathan fisted his hands. "What do you know about him?"

"That he was never meant for this world. He was too soft and naïve. Actually, he was too stupid to live. That's when I realized he couldn't be the brother with military background."

The walls closed in. Jamie had been used as a pawn in some freaked-out plan. And Nathan knew without a doubt that he was facing Jamie's killer. He wanted to find out more, then kill this animal, but not with Terri's life at stake. He'd lost everyone he'd ever loved.

What a hell of a time to realize he loved Terri and couldn't lose her.

Why was this Duff talking so much? The skin along Nathan's neck tightened as it always did when something wasn't right. "What are you waiting for?"

"My next orders, of course." Duff removed his arm from around Terri's neck, then said, "Make a move and Teto will shoot your boyfriend."

Nathan picked up the distinctive sound of a helicopter approaching. Carlos was quicker than he'd have thought possible, and closer than he would have expected them to come.

To buy some time and help cover the sound, Nathan asked, "Why did you kill my brother?"

"I needed a body. He was handy. But after all the trouble I went through to steal Brady's gun to shoot your brother, your girlfriend let the body disappear before hanging Brady with the murder. My life would have been much simpler for the past two weeks if she'd just done her job."

This bastard had to die. Nathan's hardest decision would be choosing which way to kill this animal so as to cause the most pain.

The chopper whomped louder.

Nathan couldn't believe the agency Terri worked for had just landed outside the building without one of them out there waving the team in.

"There's my ride," Duff crooned. He shoved his weapon into his belt and reached over to the desk for something, then turned to Terri. "Don't go looking for your buddy Stoner. You didn't really think I'd let him walk away with your grandmother."

"You bastard!" Terri shouted, jerking hard against Duff's grip, but he held her firm.

"Every good general has a sweeper to clean up behind. He'll assure that neither you nor Drake will leave here. Besides, you'll be busy once I execute my last order for the two of you."

Terri twisted her head to face him. "Doing what?"

Duff grabbed her arm, yanked her to him, and stabbed a hypodermic needle in her back. "Fighting for your life."

"Oh, God, the virus!" Terri screamed, grabbing at her shoulder and backing away.

"No!" Nathan charged forward.

Teto's gun exploded.

A bullet hit Nathan high in the abdomen, spinning him around. His chest hurt like hell. He fell over a desk and landed on the floor, but shoved himself upright and turned back to Terri.

She stumbled toward him.

Duff and his partner raced from the room.

Nathan reached Terri. He snatched the needle out and held her to him. "BAD's sending a helicopter. Just hold on."

The chopper outside lifted off.

Terri trembled, then shook harder. "Stop . . . Duff." She started panting, fighting for air.

"Don't talk." He lifted her into his arms and turned for the door. "Stoner called—" Please, God, tell him Stoner made the call. Nathan had to take a breath. The slug hadn't gone through his bulletproof vest, but it might have broken a rib. "He's on the way to a safe place with your grandmother. He called Carlos. Your agency is on the way." They'd better be, but he needed her to believe her grandmother was safe.

"They can't save me."

"Don't say that."

"Nathan." She struggled for every breath. "Please, listen. I-I . . ." Terri gripped his shirt, eyes wild with fear and fighting to speak.

"Baby, save your energy." He carried her outside and stood in the empty schoolyard, dividing his attention between watching her and listening for any sound of a chopper. The bleak exterior of the building looked as desolate as he felt.

Where was that damn chopper?

"No, listen. I'm sorry I told you to turn yourself in." She swallowed. Her face twisted with pain. "You were right about Jamie." She wheezed. "I understand now."

Staring into the face of the woman he loved, he saw what blind revenge had cost him. He should have seen where this was all going to end up. "No, I was wrong. I should have tried harder to protect you." All he cared about right now was keeping her alive.

His ears perked at the sweet sound of a chopper heading their way. "You're going to be okay."

"It's impossible." Her breathing evened out, giving Nathan renewed hope. Terri lifted a hand to his cheek. "I love you."

"Nothing's impossible. I'm not losing another person I love." Nathan smiled and started to kiss her when she convulsed violently and screamed in agony. He struggled to hold her in his arms.

The helicopter landed. Armed men poured out, weapons pointing at him.

"Put her down, Drake. You're under arrest," Carlos ordered.

"I'm unarmed and I'll turn myself in," he yelled over the roar of the jet helicopter blades. "She was injected with a virus. Help her," he begged, tears in his eyes.

❧

D uff climbed the stairs rather than take the elevator, as directed by Consul Vestavia in his last text message. Fra Bacchus had said to follow Vestavia's instructions to the letter. The Fra would not be disappointed. Duff had carried out his orders precisely as Vestavia had instructed him to handle the Mitchell woman and Drake.

He didn't always understand the purpose of a task, but Duff had proven he was one of the *fratelli's* best generals.

Duff exited the elevator on the fourth floor of an office building along Canal Street. The Fratelli de il Sovrano probably owned the building. Hell, he didn't meet a soul on the way in and none of the doors he walked past had any business identification. At the last office on the left, he entered a room with one window, but it was on an interior wall, not one that showed outside.

Blinds on the other side of the window shielded any view.

What hit him as particularly odd was the utilitarian feel of four blank white walls, a table, and a chair in the middle of the room. They usually went in for a snazzier style than this.

A black box the size of a gift box for a writing pen sat in the center of a basic gray metal table.

"Please have a seat, Duff." The tinny voice came from a speaker he now saw above the window.

The door lock clicked.

Duff stared at the doorknob, then at the window. "What's going on?"

"I'm Consul Vestavia. Do you have the vial?"

"Yes."

"You injected the woman with the other one?"

"Of course," Duff said, wary now. "I did exactly as instructed."

"Good, but I'm sorry to tell you there's a problem."

"What kind of problem?"

"We've encountered one case of airborne infection. Took a while for it to show up."

"What!" Duff's eyes bulged. His mouth dried out.

"Yes, but don't panic. That's the reason we're in two different rooms, just as a precaution. And that's why I sent for you right away."

Sweat trickled along Duff's neck.

"You deserve the contents of that vial you're carrying. There's a syringe on the table. You have my permission to inject yourself."

The antidote. His knees weak, Duff scrambled to fish the vial from his pocket. He sat down at the table and reached a shaking hand to open the black box. The syringe inside was more precious than gold at that moment.

He jabbed the needle at the rubber-sealed end of the vial and missed, cursed, then jabbed again and drew the liquid into the syringe. He stretched out his arm, relieved to find a plump vein standing up. Duff stuck the needle in and injected the fluid, clenching his teeth over the burn.

The loud panting he heard was his own. He was hyperventilating.

"Take it easy. You'll experience some discomfort due to receiving a stronger dosage through injecting rather than a diluted amount in water."

"Y-yes, sir." Duff thought about Teto. Must not rank high enough to be saved. Too bad for Teto.

"You have served the Order well on this project."

Duff tried to calm down and let the medicine work.

"Not quite finished, but I'll be fine. Don't worry. I'll deliver the other two vials to the cities once you tell me where. Be there in time for the vote." His skin itched and his mouth tasted awful.

"That's not necessary. We've always had everything in place to assure the anticipated outcome of the pharmaceutical company vote in the Senate."

"But the Fra said—"

"Fra Bacchus is no longer in charge of this operation."

Duff shivered. "Are you now a *fra?*"

"I am much more powerful than a brother. You address me as Father."

Duff drew back in shock. He scratched at his skin. His stomach churned. "No one in the Fratelli de il Sovrano is more powerful than a *fra*. This is blasphemous."

On the other side of the window, Consul Vestavia, a direct descendant of geniuses all the way back for twelve hundred years, pressed a button. He waited as the window became transparent from both sides.

Duff stared, openmouthed. "Impossible."

Vestavia leaned back in his chair, enjoying the expression on Duff's face. "Surprised to see me? Nothing is impossible for us. True blasphemy is you and Fra Bacchus running your own little operation, putting this Order in jeopardy. Did you think no one would notice your special projects?"

"I did as instructed. I—"

"Yes, you did follow instructions. But you killed Jamie Drake even when you figured out which brother he was. I gave Jamie my word he'd be safe, that he was under my protection. You killed a brilliant mind we—the *angeli*—never got a chance to tap. The Fratelli di Sovranoi has survived for seven hundred years only because of the *angeli*, the truly enlightened. The *fratelli* are mere servants. They just don't realize that all of you will eventually serve us."

Duff's face crumpled. "I don't understand. What about"—he coughed—"the Renaissance?"

"It is well under way. The *fratelli* are executing each step toward the Renaissance they believe is within their power, for now. As one of the ten *angeli*, I make sure the *fratelli* on this continent follow the steps precisely. The viral attacks in remote areas have been tests to see the level of response from different nations. This attack on U.S. soil is merely one more test. We are methodical and patient. It takes time to slowly collapse the walls of an enemy. Citizens will lose faith in ruling governments when we build fear with biological warfare and undermine financial institutions. With twenty-one hundred strong across the world in prominent positions, the *fratelli* are undefeatable. And in the end, the *angeli* will emerge from secrecy to take their place as the rulers."

"I-I didn't know about you, but I can serve you now." Duff coughed harder and shook. Sweat covered his face and arms.

"You have broken too many rules, but two in particular. The sin of the flesh and unnecessary deaths. You didn't know the reason I put Jamie undercover at the shipping company was to search for any ties between Marseaux and the Fratelli de il Sovrano that could be traced, but that's why we have rules about no unnecessary deaths. Killing him put the Order at greater risk . . . and did you think no one would find out about the women you took out on your boat who never came back?"

Duff grabbed his head with both hands. "The serum is making me sick."

"As it should. You see, I figured out what you and Fra Bacchus were trying to do to me. The virus is not airborne. You just injected yourself with the virus. You will now become the supreme sacrifice as a message to any who fail to follow the rules."

Duff twisted out of the chair in pain, hitting the floor and convulsing. "No! Give me the antidote. Pleaseeee." He screamed and jerked. His body curved at unnatural angles. His wailing cries filled the speaker.

Vestavia smiled and removed the DEA badge from his suit that identified him as Special Agent Brady and placed it on the table at his right. The door to the hallway opened.

"Hello, sweetheart. Figured you'd be ready to celebrate."

Vestavia turned to Josie, who carried two martinis. She handed him one and sat down on the arm of his overstuffed chair. "Brilliant plan to spike Fra Bacchus's wine, then send Duff the text message. Nothing nicer than predictable servants."

"Thank you, my dear. Duff really thought I didn't know he'd stolen my weapon to kill Jamie. I consider this act a matter of weeding out the gene pool." He studied Josie's flawless features. He had to give the *fratelli* credit. They were unmatched when it came to choosing women who would serve the Order. But he was the master who had

seen potential in this woman to be more than a mere servant to the old *fratelli.*

Duff writhed in pain, screaming and clawing at his
skin.

Josie wrinkled her nose in disgust. "How long will it
take, Brady?"

"Father," he corrected.

She grabbed her throat. "I'm sorry, Father. I meant no
disrespect."

He pulled her onto his lap and cupped her breast.
"That's all right. You'll have all night to pay penance while
the rest of the plan falls into place."

"As always, I am a loyal *angeli* servant." She smiled
seductively.

"Your family trained you well and their loyalty will be
rewarded."

"The reward of serving you is ample." She eyed his
crotch.

"More than that, you're about to get a promotion."

"Really? I'm honored, Father. When will this happen?"

"At the same minute I receive my promotion and you're
given orders to hunt me down."

❧

Nathan paced his room. If they were going to hand
him over to the Louisiana penal system, what were
they waiting for?

A sick feeling hit him. Could they be waiting to see if
Terri died? It had been almost twenty-four hours. Please,

God, tell him she'd lived. She survived the short flight to Kenner, but he'd been taken away in handcuffs the minute they landed. Nobody had said a word. Strangely enough, he'd been given clothes and toiletries, then put in a room with a bathroom and shower. This three-story building was close enough to the New Orleans airport to hear the jet traffic landing and taking off.

The door opened, admitting Carlos.

Must be time to go, but Nathan wasn't leaving until someone told him Terri's status. "How is she?"

"See for yourself." Carlos walked out.

Nathan caught the door before it shut and followed close behind. Carlos led him down a hallway with doors and up a set of stairs that opened onto the equivalent of a small hospital ward.

He paused at a glass window. Terri lay on the other side. She was alive. Only one tube ran from her arm to a drip. He noticed Carlos waiting next to an open door and moved forward.

When Nathan passed in front of him to enter, Carlos said, "Don't think this means you're going to be free to go and don't try to make a run."

"I said I'd give myself up and I will. No fighting."

Carlos's forehead creased with mild curiosity. "Interesting."

Nathan walked over to Terri and took her hand, which felt small and cold. He brushed his palm over her hair and leaned down to kiss her, not giving a damn who watched from outside.

The door whooshed open. A brawny guy in a white coat entered and checked her vitals. "Looking better this morning."

Nathan turned a worried face to him. "Will she be okay?"

"I think she's going to be fine."

"How did she survive when the others didn't?" Nathan asked.

"Yeah, how come?" Terri asked, groggy.

He glanced down to see her smile at him. Nothing could have brought his heart all the way back to life but that.

The doctor jotted notes. "Best that I can tell, she was injected with antibodies, not the virus. If she hadn't been hit with such a large dosage, she wouldn't have gotten so sick."

Carlos came in. "She going to be okay, Mako?"

"My doctor is named 'Mako,' as in a shark?" Terri asked.

"She's going to be fine," Mako told Carlos, then turned to Terri. "That's my agency name and don't believe anything they tell you about me."

"You got an hour, then back to your quarters," Carlos told Nathan.

"'Quarters'? You mean *cell*," Nathan countered.

"Call it whatever you want, but I'll be back in an hour."

Stoner passed Carlos on his way in. He smiled at Terri and shook Nathan's hand. "You're looking much better than yesterday."

"Thanks, Stoner. How's Grandma? Is she upset?"

"Just calm down. Your grandma is doing real fine. She

was pretty scared until I told her you were safe, then I took her to my maw-maw's house. Maw-Maw lives alone and normally don't cotton to strangers, but she really likes your grandma. They were talking up a storm this morning when I checked on her. Of course, she wants to know how you ended up in that schoolhouse with a crazy man."

"Oh, I know. I've got a lot of explaining to do," Terri said. "But at least she'll be around for me to explain to."

Stoner shook his head. "I don't understand why Duff injected Terri with the antidote."

Nathan snorted. "I don't think he realized it was. The crazy bastard must have mixed up the vials and thought he gave you the virus."

Stoner picked up the remote and pointed at the television in the corner. "By the way, you need to see what's on TV."

The image lightened to show a sterile newscaster. "Zolono Pharmaceutical Corporation came out miraculously, within thirty hours of the viral outbreak in Chicago, with an antidote. The CDC received an anonymous tip, which they passed on to the DEA, resulting in a scandalous report that Zolono had created the viral outbreak as part of an elaborate plan to gain the support needed for the upcoming Senate vote."

The scene flashed to an arrest in progress.

Terri jerked. "Turn that up."

". . . CEO of Zolono was arrested today by DEA agent Josephine Silversteen, daughter of the prestigious Silversteen Banking firm, along with Zolono's top scientist after a tip that the attack in Chicago was linked to the next

Senate vote on a potential takeover. The DEA acted on what they called indisputable evidence delivered to their office in New Orleans, which led to the discovery of a vial of the virus at the Zolono laboratory. Concurrently, in D.C., lobbyist Parker Jones was arrested for orchestrating this 'white-collar' terrorist attack with 1.5 million dollars transferred to him from Zolono to secure the vote. Upper management denies any knowledge of this heinous crime. In another top story, international investor and rare wine collector Victor Bacchanalia was found dead in his New Orleans hotel room last night, of an apparent heart attack . . ."

Stoner lowered the volume.

Terri was stunned. "I've never liked Josie, but I've always given her credit for being good at her job." She looked at Nathan. "Wonder if she snaked Brady on this?"

He shrugged. "I've been kept in the dark since I got here."

Stoner gave Nathan a head shake and shrug, indicating he couldn't see Nathan until now. "Carlos told me the DEA has been informed, but that's all I could get out of him. He said Joe and Tee would fill you in."

"Okay." Terri squeezed Nathan's hand.

He smiled down at her.

"Yeah, I know," Stoner said, turning to the blinds that he closed. "I told Carlos to do himself a favor and let you two talk. He said he'd give you an hour, so I'm going to cut out before it's up." He pointed the remote, flicked off the TV, then put his hand on the door handle.

"Stoner?"

He stopped. "What?"

Nathan walked across the room and extended his hand. "Thanks for everything. I wouldn't be here and Terri wouldn't be alive without you. Hope to see you again in ten years."

Stoner smiled. "We'll see about that." He walked out.

"Ten years. What do you mean?" Terri pushed up on her elbows.

"Lie down and take it easy," Nathan groused.

"I'm fine. I feel a little like I'm ready for real food." She shifted over when he got to the bed.

He sat down next to her and put his arm around her shoulders, hugging Terri to him. "That's good to hear. You need to get better."

"What was that crack about ten years?"

Didn't think she'd let that go. "I turned myself in."

"No!"

"Yes. I told them I'd go willingly so they'd get you medical help."

"But Nathan, you didn't do anything wrong."

"The NOPD thinks I killed people. I didn't so they won't find any evidence, but I've still broken parole big-time."

"What about Duff? He admitted killing Jamie."

"I watched you die in front of my eyes and swore I'd stop searching for revenge if you lived. You asked me once what Jamie would want me to do. He said in his last letter to me that he hoped I would eventually find peace and be happy. I thought he meant I'd find peace once I made his killer pay, but I knew in that minute Jamie would want me to let it go and do something good for the world. That was his way. I'll just have to wait until I'm out of prison again for a chance at living his way."

"Oh, Nathan, what are we going to do?" She reached up and kissed him before he could answer. He wrapped her up tighter, feeling as though his world made sense if only for the few minutes he had now.

He kissed her, savoring this one for all those he'd miss.

When he peeled his lips from hers, he stared into eyes that cared so much, his heart ached at the thought of leaving her. Just once, he'd like to get it right. He kissed her and held her close for a long time, wishing for the impossible again.

Just wasn't in his cards to have a life of his own.

"You can't spend the next ten years of life waiting on me," he finally told her.

"Oh, I won't spend them being quiet. They aren't putting you in a prison until I've exhausted every means to keep you out. I love you."

He brushed his thumb over her cheek. "I love you, too. So much that I won't let you wait. I've already told Carlos I'll go willingly and not fight my sentence. I gave my word."

∽

The twelve ruling Fratelli de il Sovrano elders in the United States met around a black onyx marble table in a Phoenix hotel owned by one member.

Fra Diablo called the room to order. "I'd like to welcome our newest elder approved unanimously. Fra Vestavia was successful in finding the traitor within our Order. Every international Order has been informed of the penance paid. Though he was once a revered general for us, Duff was sacrificed as an example to all who would deceive the Order. He committed the sin of defiance, the sin of flesh, and of unnecessary deaths. Our success depends on discipline, from all. For that reason and the recent unexpected seat left open by Fra Bacchus, Fra Vestavia will now join the table as an elder."

Fra Vestavia had been standing near the door and now took the vacant seat. "Thank you all, brethren. I'm honored for this promotion. We all grieve for Fra Bacchus, who succumbed to heart failure during his sleep. May he rest in peace. Anton Marseaux failed to contain his people so we can no longer support his position in New Orleans. We'll have someone to take his place shortly."

Murmurs echoed his last comment before Fra Diablo said, "Please share what you learned while exposing the traitor."

Pulling papers from his briefcase, Fra Vestavia passed a set for each around the table. "The first round of viral tests has been successful. Once we have completed the study of national defense response, we can move to step two. In the meantime, I have found an exciting opportunity that we should explore—now—with six months left until the U.S. presidential elections and the dollar on decline with Canada. We can make surgical strikes that will reverberate around the world and turn allies into enemies."

EPILOGUE

Terri tapped her fingers on the chair arm, tired of waiting on Joe and Tee to start this meeting. Joe had said to be in the Nashville, Tennessee, headquarters at 1330 hours and by her watch it was 1335. They'd kept her in the infirmary for two more days, then sent her home for another four . . . without seeing Nathan.

You need the rest, Terri. She'd heard that one time too many. She was fine, more than fine, and ready to set a few people straight. Terri pushed forward on the chair to get up when the door opened.

Carlos held it open. Nathan stepped inside the room, damp hair pulled back into a ponytail. He looked tired.

She'd spent every minute traveling to Nashville planning to give all of them a piece of her mind—including Nathan—for keeping her in the dark. Now all she wanted to do was hug Nathan and convince him to fight the system once more.

Joe walked in from the connecting office that belonged to Tee, who followed right behind him. Like Nathan, Joe had long dark hair in a ponytail. His eyes were a steel blue that took in every detail the instant he looked at something. He was dressed in a white button-down shirt, with a red tie and navy blue slacks, and he was all business.

Tee was so tiny, most would dismiss her as powerless. But she had an aura of danger about her only matched by Joe's quiet threat. Her white suit and light blue blouse set off her Vietnamese coloring to perfection. She was a beautiful woman, with shoulder-length black hair.

Joe narrowed a menacing grimace to Carlos. "I wasn't ready for Nathan. I haven't had a chance to talk to Terri first, so Nathan, would you wait outside?"

Terri fisted her hands but held her composure. "If it's all right, I'd like for him to hear everything said."

Nathan didn't even look at her. He stood with his hands in his pockets waiting for a final verdict.

Joe debated for a few seconds before he nodded. "Have a seat, Nathan." Then he introduced himself and Tee.

Tee cocked her head at Terri. "Patience is a virtue."

Joe snorted. "Excuse me, pot, could you not pick on the kettle?"

Tee passed him a look that promised Joe would regret that comment later.

He disregarded the life-threatening stare. Joe's eyes bored into Terri. "I thought you'd like to know the DEA has determined you were in no way at fault for Conroy's death."

Terri wasn't quite ready to be relieved. "Are you sure?"

Joe walked over to his desk and leaned a hip against it. "Positive. Looks like Brady set you both up." Joe dropped a folder in front of her. "When I spoke to an associate in the DEA about Brady's deal with Jamie—who Brady believed was Nathan—the DEA was unaware of the arrangement. One of the reasons I waited to meet with you was to give him time to get back to me. The DEA now believes Brady was the leak to Marseaux and tipped them to the ambush. After a deeper look into his background, they found out his ancestors changed the family name when they migrated to this country. His great-great-grandfather's name was Vestavio Braido, an Italian family suspected of harboring and training assassins for a couple decades."

"I'd like to kill that bastard," Terri muttered with a death-threat edge.

Nathan had been sitting quiet as a statue, but turned to her and lifted an eyebrow at that.

She shot a look of "what of it?" right back at him. Shouting that instead might get a rise. She hated the blank mask of acceptance he wore. *Fight to stay free, dammit.*

Joe ignored the silent interaction and continued. "They have to find him first. Brady's disappeared and he's listed as a top ten fugitive. Marseaux's body was found riddled with bullet holes at the south end of the docks, outlined with spray paint. That means he's gone, but we don't know who is taking his place."

"What about Duff?" She could envision a painful death for him, too.

"Duff was found dead five days ago. He'd been given the virus. Not a pretty sight."

That topped her worst plan. Terri glanced at Nathan. "Are you angry you didn't get a chance to deal with Duff yourself?"

He shook his head and swallowed, but wouldn't look at her when he answered. "No. I'm done with going after revenge. I've had plenty of time to think about it and based on what I've just heard, Jamie's death has been avenged. All I want to do now is get to prison so I can start doing my time. I want it over and done with."

She fisted her hands, wanting to scream at him. He'd already written off any future for the two of them.

As if he heard her thoughts, Nathan turned his face to her with a sad smile. "Shit happens, Terri. And I'm really sorry it happened to us." He stopped, his mouth set in a grim line.

Joe cleared his throat. "You stepped outside BAD parameters while on this case, Terri," he said, pulling her attention. "Learn anything?"

He meant her working without a partner, but she was in no mood to be agreeable. She thought on his question a minute before answering.

"Yes, I did. I learned that the bad guys are not always bad, the good guys are not always good, and to quote the pirate Captain Barbossa, the parameters are like rules, mostly guidelines. And that it takes a little bit of bad boy to fight the evil in the world."

Tee inclined her head respectfully. "They can be taught. Who knew?"

"I also figured out that I no longer want to do field work," Terri added.

Nathan sat up. "Really? You'd leave field work?"

"Really." She smiled at him. "You and Grandma need me. Neither one of you can stay out of trouble without me."

He shook his head, the excitement disappearing from his eyes. "Going to be a while before I'll have any chance to get into trouble. I plan to ask Warden McLaughlin to put in a word for me, but I meant what I said about moving on with your life."

Terri reached for his hand. She knew how hard it was for Nathan to consider asking anyone for help. Now if she could just get him to realize she was not giving up on him.

She was not leaving him like everyone else had.

Joe scratched his chin. "By the way, that little prison issue of yours . . . gone."

Nathan swung his gaze to Joe. "What are you talking about?"

Joe shrugged. "Your brother made a deal with what was at the time a bona fide representative of the DEA. He kept his part. DEA owed you a clean record. One thing in life I hate is a lying asshole, so I made sure they did what they were supposed to. Including an honorable discharge from the military."

Tee gave Nathan an almost warm half smile. "You're a free man, Drake, regardless of which identity you choose. And while you're at it, how about another one. We've looked over your files and with your training and courage—"

"—we'd like to have you join BAD," Joe said, finishing her sentence.

Terri took Nathan's hand in hers. He gazed into her eyes and said, "Let me think about it and get back to you."

"Yeah, like maybe in two weeks, since I'm still technically on medical leave," Terri added.

Tee tapped her nails against the table. "You got twenty-four hours to decide and you really want to say yes. We don't want civilians walking around who know about us. Got it?"

Nathan gave her a cocky grin. "Wow, you're like a ferocious bunny, aren't you?"

Joe laughed. "Worse. A bunny can be fluffy sometimes. Tee always goes for the throat. Trust me. I'm her partner and she's shot me three times now."

Tee rolled her eyes. "You're such a crybaby."

"Let me almost shoot off one of your testicles and see how you cope."

"You shouldn't have moved, Joe. It was your fault."

"Yeah, everything's my fault."

Tee winked at him. "Good, then we agree."

Joe rubbed his forehead, then pushed a hard stare at Nathan.

Nathan inclined his head a short nod Joe must have taken as a firm answer. One warrior giving his silent word to another. "Good. See you in two weeks."

"Thanks, Joe and Tee. Since this is the only vacation we'll get for a while, let's go." Terri grabbed Nathan's hand and hurried out.

Stoner was waiting in the hallway. He shook Nathan's hand. "I signed on with this bunch as a contractor. If they didn't talk you into staying, I'll need that voodoo coin of yours."

"I'm keeping it for now," Nathan said.

Carlos came up behind Terri and hugged her. "Glad you're better."

Nathan hooked Terri's arm and snatched her away, then tucked her next to him.

Carlos lifted his hands. "Dude, relax." He sauntered off.

Nathan muttered something Terri barely caught about how they might have to talk about her working here.

She laughed as she led him outside to Commerce Street. The local Nashville traffic was humming as tourists drifted along the shops and restaurants soaking in the home of country music.

Terri looked up at Nathan. "What do you want to do?"

"Something I thought would never happen again," he said, taking her hand and leading her toward the small garden to the side of the building. He wrapped her in his arms and kissed her.

She stopped and stared into his eyes. "You thought you'd never get to kiss me again?"

"That, and I thought I'd never get to ask you to marry me. You deserve more than a man with my history, but I found you and I want to keep you forever."

"Okay, deal." Her soul beamed with happiness. "I want you forever, too. You're going to have to find me a ring soon."

"I plan to have one on that finger today."

"Good, because I already have your engagement gift."

His eyebrows lifted at that. "Does it involve a soft bed, cool sheets, and all night long?"

"Well, that will be part of the benefit plan." She winked. He kissed her and she wondered how long it would take to find the soft bed and cool sheets so they could start on all night long. The sooner the better.

She broke the kiss and took his hand. "Come with me." Terri led him to the street and raised her hand as if flagging a cab. In thirty seconds, a shining black car that screamed speed and looked nothing like a taxi pulled alongside the curb.

A long-legged brunette with a short, no-nonsense haircut, boots, jeans, and red sweater hugging her slender curves got out of the car. "Sweet ride. Here's the keys, luv." She tossed them to Nathan, who snagged the key ring.

"Thanks, Rae," Terri said. "I'll be back in two weeks."

"Rockin' news." Rae gave Nathan an admiring once-over, then looked at Terri. "Bloody nice bloke you've got there. Try not to hurt yourself with two weeks off." She strode away.

"How did—" Nathan just stared at the Javelin, then he looked at Terri with wonder pooling in his eyes.

"I called the NOPD as soon as Stoner told me about losing Black Death. Philborn appreciated what I did to help them break this case and asked what he could do. I told him where the car had been left so he retrieved it. No one had touched the car."

"Thanks." He swallowed, staring his future in the face. "I'm going to spend the rest of my life finding ways to show you how much you mean to me."

"If you'll fire this baby up and head for a hotel, I'm up for your first effort."